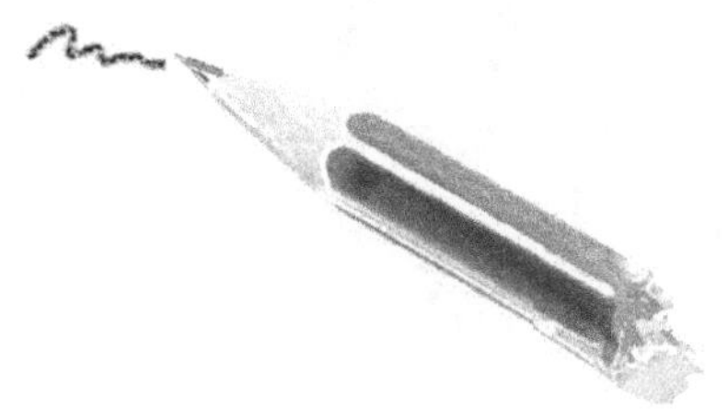

This book is dedicated to my super-talented sister, Pauline, who, when we were kids, spent endless hours with me, drawing at the kitchen table.
Girl, maybe I never told you, but you're a tough act to follow.

And to my mom, who never stopped drawing and painting. I'm quite certain she is the only person ever to mingle the smells of oil paints with bread baking to make a best-ever childhood memory.

Sketchy Characters

SHEILA McGRAW

2022 Fables•Press

Copyright © 2022 by Sheila McGraw
Cover by Sheila McGraw

Published in the United States
by Fables•Press
Fables•Press is the imprint of McGraw Studios LLC, Texas

ISBN 978-1-63363-560-9
eBook ISBN 978-1-63363-561-6
Library of Congress Control Number: 2021953523

PRINTED IN THE UNITED STATES OF AMERICA

Sketchy
Characters

FABLES•PRESS

Fables•Press is the imprint of McGraw Studios LLC, Texas

PART ONE:
The Beginning

Sheila McGraw

Chapter One:

The Rain

Marilyn woke to her breast vibrating and pulled her phone from her bra. The caller ID read *Fran*. At the ungodly hour of 3:15 a.m., her head was too woolly to answer. Disoriented, she blinked at the realization she'd couch crashed. She ran her tongue over scummy teeth, flexed stiff joints, and straightened twisted clothes that smelled of stale party cigarette and weed smoke. Her phone stopped vibrating then started again. No doubt it was a pocket-call since Fran was cramming for the bar exam and studied late. Marilyn let the call go to voicemail and returned the device to its holster. If it wasn't a butt call, Fran would leave a message.

The atmosphere was peculiar, the air nearly viscous, like syrup she could scoop up in her hands, and the dark was too dense. She could be at the far reaches of a mine shaft the way her eyes wouldn't adjust. She recalled watching the TV news, but now the screen was black and the constant, tiny, bright lights on her electronics were out. The sounds were wrong. Driving rain was pummeling the courtyard and the upstairs apartments' balconies, but the usual rattle of a dozen air conditioners and hum of her ancient, round-shouldered fridge were missing. She lay in the opaque dark and listened to the battering downpour.

As manager of the two-story, forty-unit, dilapidated development, *The Moderne*, Marilyn's one-bed, one-bath apartment was supposedly a perk. However, through some employer-double-speak, its value was magically skimmed from her pay, which dropped her salary below minimum wage. She didn't argue. She'd needed the job and the accommodation.

The Moderne was built in the mid-sixties when Houston was obsessed with all things space travel and mushroom-clouds. The trend spawned massive construction of atomic-ranch bungalows, outfitted with modern art and Jetson-inspired furniture. For the owner, *The Moderne's* mid-century-modern, architecturally-authentic pedigree was both a point of pride and an excuse to avoid updating the structure or grounds, lest its heritage be compromised.

She considered that the power failure may be the sixty-year-old breaker box finally giving up the ghost. On the other hand, the storm or the infamously deregulated and unreliable Texas electricity grid may be the cause. In any case, it was her duty to report the outage to her boss and the power company.

Marilyn stretched, closed her eyes, and was drifting off again when Aunt Zabi's voice whispered, *C'mon kiddo, better get on it before the tenants wake up.*

True, Zabi. They'll start their bitching around five.

Marilyn's Aunt Elizabeth—shortened to Zabi—adopted Marilyn when she was orphaned at eight. While Zabi had died of cancer five years before, she lived on as Marilyn's alter ego who often subbed for her conscience and weighed in on thorny issues. Marilyn swung her legs off the couch, but before her feet met the floor's surface of tile and rug, they were plunged into tepid water to mid-calf.

"Holy fuck!"

Alert now, she fumbled with her phone, and turned on its flashlight. The beam swept the room, revealing an eerie aquarium with ghostly forms of half-sunken furniture. Her throw rug's fringe slowly wafted like tentacles in the murky water.

She sloshed to the front door and opened it. Floodwater outside was the same depth as indoors. The courtyard was now a lake. Two battery-operated LED spotlights cast a feeble glimmer through sheets of rain.

Generally, people tend to think of floodwater as rainwater, and relatively clean, but having experienced several floods, Marilyn knew better. She was standing in a cesspool contaminated with who-knew-what effluvia—dirt, road grease, oil, dog and cat shit, rodent droppings, rotting garbage, insecticide, and more. And soon, when the sewers became overwhelmed, there would be human waste.

She texted Fran: *I can't believe I was at your place just a few hours ago. When did the party next door end?*

Fran: *Not sure. I left around midnight.*

Marilyn: *I'm flooded and about to head upstairs. RU ok?*

Fran: *Yes I'm ok, but what's with all this freaking rain?*

Marilyn: *Dunno. At least ur apartment is on the fourth floor. Stay dry! Later gator...take care.*

Marilyn stepped outside and slogged alongside the building, hammering on doors and windows, shouting, "Flood, flood!" There were muffled shrieks from residents waking to find themselves in a nightmare. Doors opened and disoriented occupants emerged, some in pajamas and robes, others hastily dressed in clothes already drenched. Marilyn shouted orders. "Just bring your most important personal papers, your phones, and chargers. Stay close to the building, away from the pool. Go upstairs to the walkway."

Back inside her apartment, items liberated from low shelves were floating. There was a bamboo bowl of receipts, a wooden sewing-notions box, and a dream-catcher from a childhood trip to New Mexico. A pair of red wooden lobsters from Maine were seemingly resurrected, bobbing in the eerie calm against the steady background of the rain's endless drumroll. Should she grab anything? Maybe the snow globe of Niagara Falls? None of her possessions were of value, all plucked from a bargain basement's floor, a yard sale's folding table, or a rummage sale's bin. Nothing would be salvaged. She must leave and never return to yesterday's life.

The close, acrid atmosphere smelled of wet dog with chemical and mildew undertones. The flood continued slithering in without a sound, a stalking presence, its silence disturbingly at odds with the looming catastrophe. With the water now knee high she turned her thoughts to survival. Paradoxically, rain boots had tipped on their sides and sunk, while platform-soled sandals were drifting like mini-pontoons. She made her way to the bedroom where a pot of ivy trailed like seaweed across the surface while floating veils of floor-length curtains were being tugged under. The box spring, mattress, and pillows were now giant sponges.

Rolling luggage was impossible, and she pulled her big hiking backpack from its high shelf. The bottom dresser drawers were waterlogged and she shoved in clothes from the top two, T-shirts and jeans, underwear, documents, a toiletry kit, phone and charger, and laptop. Then she added her fridge's sparse contents that didn't need cooking—cheese, three hard boiled eggs, bread, crackers, peanut butter, bottled drinks.

Time to go. Marilyn waded through the now mid-thigh-high floodwater to the living room where more objects—a wooden bowl of pistachios, the remote controls for her electronics, and a wine glass—wobbled over and circled her legs. She grabbed a Diet Coke that had risen from the depths.

Marilyn put on a short, plastic poncho and slipped her feet into submerged Crocs. At the door, she looked back and shone her phone's flashlight on her hard-won possessions bobbing at angles in her wake, and in that instant, she realized the flood had probably tripped the main breaker, causing the power outage. Otherwise, the water could have been electrified.

She was lucky to be alive.

Marilyn called the apartment complex's owner, and left voicemail informing him of the flooding. One of the tenants, Jon, emerged from his apartment wearing hip-waders and a backpack. Jon was about Marilyn's age. The guy was a chronic flirt, and nice enough, but a bit too much *everything* for Marilyn's taste, too tanning-bed tanned, too gym-rat muscular, a bit too baby-faced, and given to wearing too much aftershave. Single, Jon was a chronic flirt who spent a good deal of time hovering hopefully around Marilyn's office.

Jon frequented The Art Guild where Marilyn regularly posed as an artist's model. While he didn't "turn her crank" romantically, she greatly admired his artistic skill and the realism of Jon's artwork.

Jon greeted her, "Welcome to Houston in mid-June."

"It's barely hurricane season, and we already have this storm. Houston has only two seasons. Summer and fall are hurricane season, and winter and spring are no-AC-season." She smiled.

Jon nodded. "Ha. We should start calling them Hurricane and No-AC. It could become a thing."

Marilyn said, "Check you out in your waders. Aren't you a good Boy Scout."

"My mom would be proud." He walked stiff-legged and slow against the water's pressure, arms held bent and wide above his waist.

Marilyn laughed. "You're doing the zombie lurch."

"No wonder. This has to be the zombie apocalypse we've been warned about."

"The zombie apocalypse starts later when the water recedes, and the drowned people wake up."

"I just checked the news." He moved closer. "In the few areas that aren't flooding, there's already looters."

She shook her head. "Assholes." With the flashlight on high, she continued knocking on doors and windows. The rain was falling with force, dimpling the water's surface, more like volleys of cascading gravel than rain.

Apartment by apartment they checked that everyone was out, then climbed to the second-floor outdoor hallway. During the night the temperature had dropped dramatically from the day's heat, and the soaked group were shivering, stunned, and confused, whipped by the wind and the stinging torrent.

Jon glanced around. "I don't think you have a job anymore." He spread his arms indicating the devastation.

"Yep. I've been here a year, but I guess all good things come to an end."

He smirked. "You've been underemployed and underpaid too long."

"Hmm…no shit. Maybe it's a kick in the pants to do something else." With her bank account empty and her one credit card nearly maxed out, she wasn't sure how she was going to kickstart another career or afford an apartment.

The upstairs tenants, bleary and sleep-wrinkled, opened doors as they woke to Marilyn's persistent knocking. Most were openly generous, letting their neighbors in, and then there was Marge Walters. Marge's appearance never varied, with her steel-gray hair in a mannish cut, her large braless breasts wobbling under a threadbare faded house dress, and her expression of a surly Persian cat.

"No one's coming into my place. Fuck the lot of you." She slammed the door.

Marilyn shrugged, and she and Jon laughed.

Soon, everyone was inside their neighbors' dark apartments, curled on sofas or perched on breakfast barstools, to sleep and wake in fits and starts, to hear the rain lashing in sheets against the windows, to monitor the rising waterline through the night. Jon motioned Marilyn to a window and quietly indicated for her to look at the water level, which was now lapping inches below the second floor.

Guided by her phone's flashlight, she made her way through the darkness to the bathroom where she shook out her waterproof poncho over the bathtub and hung it on the shower-curtain rod, then she wrung out her long dark hair in the sink and dried her face as she considered her status—carless, jobless, homeless, and broke.

Marilyn found Jon sitting on a barstool, eating cookies. She sat beside him.

He whispered, "A friend of mine called around noon yesterday and said he was stocking up on food. I was like, why? It's not going to affect us. We weren't even in *the cone of probability*. Or is it *the cone of uncertainty*?"

"The cone of *shit's about to get real*." They chuckled and a sleeping form on the sofa stirred. She dropped her voice, "It made landfall in Corpus Christi. We didn't get any storm surge. Hard to believe this much rain is an outer band." She shifted her posture and took out her phone. "Where are you going to go?"

"At first, I thought I'd get out of the city, go to my pop's place near Dallas, but no one can leave with the highways flooded."

"Yes," she whispered, checking her phone for updates. "They're saying the gas stations' tanks are empty, and the trucks can't get into the city to fill them."

She remembered riding out Hurricane Ike and was pierced by a pang of sorrow for the people in Corpus. This storm had snuck up on them. "If we were downstairs right now, it would be two feet over our heads. If we didn't have a second floor, where would we have gone? To the roof, I guess. What in God's name is this? There's some wind, but this isn't hurricane wind. During Ike, the main thing wasn't the rain, it was the wind, ripping off roofs, uprooting trees, pulverizing stuff, and so noisy. I remember lying there in the dark, listening. The noise was like ice in a blender—for hours—with all sorts of crashing and banging of stuff being ripped apart and thrown against the roof and the walls."

Jon shook his head and shrugged. "Are you scared?"

"Yes. No. Not exactly. But my point is that this isn't a regular hurricane. The water better stop rising soon, or we'll be on the roof…and then what?"

"Whatever this is, it's fucking biblical." Jon moved closer and whispered, "Do you think it's some kind of terrorist attack?"

She smirked. "You're nuts."

"What about my nuts?" He grinned and winked.

She noticed Jon had a black plastic canister sticking out of his backpack. "Did you bring your drawings?"

"Yup. They're worth real money, you know. Or at least they will be when I'm famous."

"They'll be worth even more if you don't survive this hurricane." She smirked and reached for the cylinder, but he chased her hand away with a flurry of faux slaps.

"We better die to make our drawings valuable."

"No thanks." She smiled and ran her fingers through her wet hair. "I have no idea how we're going to escape. It better stop raining soon, or we'll be in trouble."

Chapter Two:

Escape

Near dawn, the profound dark edged into an anemic, flat daylight, and the floodwater, which had breached the second-floor outdoor hallway, was slinking in under the apartments' doors. The residents shared whatever was in their pantries: chips, cereal, bread, crackers, milk, cheese, and packaged meats that were still cold in the silent refrigerators.

Marilyn opened curtains. "I'm happy for the daylight and to see my surroundings." She poured granola into a bowl and added milk. The apartment where Marilyn and Jon were holed up was littered with three other refugees from the downstairs units. One, who had fallen asleep on the floor had been rudely awakened by creeping water, the others in a recliner chair and on the sofa, were still snoring.

Marilyn took a stool at the breakfast bar and dialed Fran, "Hey, Fran, thanks for calling earlier. If we'd waited even a few more minutes to leave it would have been difficult. All the main floor units are flooded to their ceilings. There's no way this place will be salvaged. So, it looks like I'm homeless, although obviously, I'm not alone in that state of affairs."

"Shit!"

"How are you doing?" Marilyn asked.

"Neither my building nor the parking lot flooded. I'm looking out my window, and starting a couple of streets over, it's drowned. I guess this area is higher than most. If you can get here, you can stay at my place as long as you like."

Marilyn said, "Thanks. I'll find a way to get there. I don't know how I'll repay you, but I will."

"Oh, come on. I'm happy to have you here."

"It's hard to believe that just last evening I was at your place, partying."

In the background, there was a knock at Fran's door, and she called out, "Hang on, I'll be ready in a sec."

"You have a visitor?" Marilyn asked.

"It's the Lads. I'm going with them to see if we can help people in the immediate vicinity. If you get here before I get back, you know where the key is, and help yourself to food, clothes, whatever you need."

"The Lads are going out…*to help people*? They must have been struck by lightning, or something."

Fran laughed. "Maybe they need a real purpose instead of their *Transcendalia* bullshit."

"No offense, Fran, but your optimism is epic."

The Lads, as they were called, were Declan and Shawn, a pair of British drug-dealing surfers who lived next door to Fran and pretended to be new-age gurus. They wore East-Indian dhoti pants with the wide low-slung crotch, Jesus-boots-style sandals, hipster-bun hair, and trendy facial mulch, all of it liberally doused with patchouli oil. They earned additional cash by running a scam they called Transcendalia, which touted holistic treatments involving massage, copious weed, and injections of ambiguous supplements. Their apartment, albeit odorous of sandalwood incense, was at odds with their Hari Krishna pretensions, resembling a frat house more than a spiritual retreat.

Outside were excited voices, and Marilyn moved to the window, the floodwater now over her ankles. "Holy crap. Looks like Louisiana sent some angels our way. The Cajun Navy is here. I gotta go. Be careful out there with the Lads. They're jerks!"

"I will." She laughed and hung up.

The Cajun Navy, volunteer boat owners who assist in search and rescue efforts, had sent a flat-bottomed swamp boat, the type with a huge fan on the back. Marilyn and Jon helped the more infirm residents first.

Jon said, "This is a nightmare. So much for The Moderne." Jon shook his head. "It's toast." The boat made three more trips before Marilyn and Jon finally hitched a ride. As they wound through submerged suburban streets, Jon said, "Hey, I didn't see Marge get in the boat."

Marilyn inhaled a small gasp. "Oh my god, you're right. I didn't see her either."

"Oh well. That old battle-ax is tougher than Chuck Norris. She'll be okay."

Marilyn shook her head. "I hope so."

In the relentless, chilly rain they traveled several miles to higher ground and hiked a freeway overpass to another boat ride. The trip ended at the library, which had been built on a ten-foot-high mound of landfill and had a massive generator that powered heat and air conditioning, lights, and a TV. Uninterrupted coverage of the storm was showing the city's cavernous convention center teeming with urban refugees sitting and lying on cots. They had made it out alive, displaced in a storm of thousand-year likelihood. The makeshift beds were fully occupied.

"Glad we're here, not in those lines of camp-cots with all sorts of soggy strangers and their kids and dogs." Jon peeled off his waders. "There's only about fifty others here."

"Amen to that. And we've got all the reading material you could hope for."

They made sandwiches from Marilyn's food. She said, "I can't believe that twenty-four hours ago we were at the Art Guild." She swallowed a bite of her sandwich.

"Yep." Jon exhaled a dreamy sigh. "Yesterday I was drawing your fine nekkid body."

She laughed and shoved his shoulder. Yesterday. This flood would forever be a demarcation point. Yesterday was already *before* and now was already *after*. Yesterday, *before,* she had gotten ready for her life-drawing gig. She'd showered and struck a few poses in the mirror to observe the artists' view—creases or no creases, crotch or no crotch, saggy or firm. She checked for cellulite, wrinkles, dimples, pimples, and bumps. She was tattoo-free, with the type of olive complexion that tans easily, her hair thick, dark, and long. Yesterday, as always, the Art Guild had smelled of oil paints, turpentine, and chalk, mingled with coffee from the adjoining café. She had entered the large, white-painted, high-ceilinged room with the models' stand. And after modeling, when it was still *before*, she had gone to the Lads' party next door to Fran's apartment.

"I'm going to bunk down and catch a nap, if possible," she said, and arranged her backpack and clothes as makeshift bedding on the library's industrial carpet. She lay down and draped a folded T-shirt over her eyes.

Jon said, "This is nice, lying beside you. We should do more of it."

Marilyn lifted the T-shirt, gave him an eye-roll, and replaced the T-shirt. She breathed deeply, yawned, and hoped for a brief respite from the destruction.

Marilyn woke to Jon shaking her shoulder.

"Hey, lady, wakey-wakey. There are some people

going in the direction of Fran's place. You should go with them."

Marilyn rubbed her eyes and looked around, disoriented, until everything came rushing back, and lying on the library's floor made sense. "Right. Strength in numbers. Thanks for waking me."

"No problem. You only slept for twenty minutes or so."

Jon had called a friend who would let him couch surf. He was traveling in the opposite direction, and they hugged and parted ways.

Chapter Three:

The Trek

Marilyn headed out with three couples. They hitched a boat ride until they ran aground a couple of miles from Fran's building, then hiked in waist-deep water. The day was heating up and the going was slower than expected with uneven ground and obstacles hidden by the water's mucky opacity, its depth judged against traffic signs, lamp posts, and mailboxes. Curbs, planters, and garden ornaments were trip hazards. Gardens turned to mud sucked on her crocs.

In turns, the rain died then suddenly recharged. The water's resistance was like pulling a heavy weight or climbing a never-ending hill. Marilyn's strength was giving out. She was sweating and took a swig from her water bottle, emptying it.

Zabi's presence whispered, "Water, water everywhere, but not a drop to drink. You'll be okay. Just keep putting one foot in front of the other."

As they moved along, others appeared and silently joined them. At one point, Marilyn put their group at twenty.

A man shouted, "Watch out! Fire ants ahead!"

Marilyn looked up from peering through the murk, trying to anticipate the next deathtrap, and saw a crusty, brown floating mass the size of a dining table. She'd read about the ants; how they hooked together to form a floating platform to keep the queen and the rest of the nest safe, then the dry ones switched out with the ones underneath.

Zabi whispered, *And we think we're so smart, yet ants are more civilized and cooperative for the common good than most of the people I've ever met.*

No shit, Zabi, although this storm will be a good test for humanity.

Fire ants—their venom is the same as bees, and enough stings can do serious, even life-threatening damage. A current was carrying the mass on a collision course with the group, and as they moved aside, one of the women was suddenly plunged in water to her ears. She thrashed, groping for higher ground, and others lent her a hand and steadied her footing back onto the pavement. Through a plume of disturbed silt, Marilyn saw an orange shape, a traffic cone, part of a roadwork excavation.

They kept moving through the persistent rain, and the same man who gave the ant warning yelled, "Watch out for snakes. The water will drive them from their nests."

Someone said, "Shut the fuck up," and laughed.

Marilyn shielded her eyes from the rain and gazed along the road. The destruction of mile upon mile of structures and vehicles was daunting. Apart from the unyielding downpour and someone softly crying, there was no sound: no sirens, no traffic, no birds. Occasionally there was the cry of a bedraggled cat, perched on a railing, a branch, a stairway.

Over and over, the group gravitated to higher ground off the road and walked through developments that had been built on raised lots, where the water was only inches or a foot deep, and through parking lots, where cement curbs and shrubs were the main obstacles. The side streets with older homes were impassable, with only roofs visible.

The group dwindled as others left for their destinations on secondary roads. Finally, a familiar food market appeared. Marilyn waved to the remaining group and turned onto Fran's street. Lights shone in some windows of the five-story apartment building. Through some strange twist of fate, the building and several surrounding suburban blocks hadn't lost power, and neither the parking lot nor the building had flooded.

Water had been tracked into the muddy and musty lobby and the elevator. The fourth-floor linoleum-tiled hallway smelled pungently of marijuana and cabbagey cooking smells, but right now, this place was heaven. Trembling from cold and exhaustion, her muscles shaking with exertion, she knocked on Fran's door. No answer. Marilyn was surprised that Fran and the Lads were still out on their rescue mission.

She located the key in its hiding place on top of the fire hydrant cabinet, let herself into the apartment, called hello, but got no answer. Fran's books were piled on her table with her laptop shut down and closed. In the bathroom, a hairbrush and mascara were on the vanity. There were pajamas draped on her unmade bed. Marilyn stripped off her wet clothes, dropped them in the sink, and showered, the water heating her chilled scalp, pounding her shoulders, and running over her goose-bumpy skin. The pulverizing effect brought on delayed shock and sadness at the incalculable loss for so many, and she wept, sobbing into the spray.

Toweled off, her hair blow-dried, she dumped out her backpack on the sofa, which would soon double as her bed, and dressed in one of her few clean, dry outfits. She then busied herself, putting food away, rinsing and draping her flood-wading clothes on the shower rail, plugging in her phone. She turned on the TV to nonstop footage of the storm. The female news reporter was in front of videos of people being helicoptered off rooftops.

The TV newscaster said, "Inland flooding that leads to drowning usually occurs during flash-flood conditions." The images changed to photos of highway exits under floodwater. "Nearly half of all flash-flood fatalities are vehicle-related. Don't drive into water if you can't see the bottom. As they say at the weather service, 'Turn around, don't drown.'"

Marilyn went to the balcony and opened the door. Her fingertips strayed to her cheek, then her lips, at the spectacle of endless water. The street and part of the parking lot had become immersed since she had arrived. Fran. Where did she go? Fear gripped her. Please be safe. The clouds were a noncommittal gray that had descended onto the city like a pelt. The news reporter interrupted Marilyn's thoughts.

"Never underestimate the power of fast-moving water. It can roll boulders, uproot trees, destroy buildings and bridges, carry away vehicles, and create deep, new channels in the earth."

The words *Turn Around, Don't Drown* rolled across the chyron. The fridge reflected Fran's unintentional foresight. She'd stocked up to hunker down and study for her bar exam, with sandwich fixings, coffee, bottled water, ready-made microwaveable packages of entrees, vegetables, salad, and dressing. There was what Fran called her "plonk"—an inexpensive, albeit decent white wine—and more food options in the freezer, altogether enough for three, even four people, for a week or longer.

Muffled conversation and footsteps, then steady thumping bass intruded from the adjacent apartment. The building was notorious for its lack of sound insulation. Thank God. Fran and the Lads were back from their humanitarian mission.

Chapter Four:

The Lads

Marilyn rushed next door and attempted to walk in, but the door was locked, which was unusual. She knocked. Declan cracked the door a few inches. She directed her gaze along the hall, then turned back, making only direct eye contact. In the past, Fran had warned Marilyn that Declan-the-narcissist assumed any woman who looked at any part of his body other than his eyes wanted sex.

There was a noise behind him and Declan looked over his shoulder into the apartment, which gave her a moment to size him up. While the Lads promoted new age sensibilities, his shirtless upper body was more likely fashioned by CrossFit and weightlifting. His torso was strap-like, with symmetrical swellings of muscle and ropelike tendons, his skin undulating with each flex or gesture. Declan turned back to stare at her. Oddly, his face seemed as if it belonged to a fat person. It was round, puffy, and lacking definition with lips that were straight across and squared off at the sides, suggesting a mail-slot.

"Hey, Declan…" She took a step, expecting entry, but he held his ground. She tried to peer around him, and he shifted to block her view. "Fran said she was going with you and Shawn to help rescue people. Is she here?"

"No. Erm…" The lads had British accents, which she believed they exaggerated in the belief it added to their Boho image. He had the lag-time of a stoner, finally registering her question. "We decided," pronounced *desoyded*, "not to go, so Fran went on 'er own, love. Or she might've gone wiff someone else."

"What? What the fuck? No. Come on. She wouldn't go on her own. It's too dangerous. And it'll be dark soon. Did she say she was going with someone?" Declan shrugged and picked at some loose paint on the door frame. She reached out and touched his wrist. "Please, Declan, think hard. Did you see her with anyone?"

There were marks, scratches, across the peace-symbol tattoo on his forearm. He noticed her glance, pulled his arm in behind the door, and put on his best I'm-not-such-an-asshole smile. "Lookit, mate. Fran's a big girlie, in't she? She wan'ed to 'elp people, so I reckon she went to 'elp people." He started to close the door.

Marilyn placed her palm on the door and demanded, "Where did she go? What area?"

He shrugged again. "No eye-deer, love." He leaned on the door harder. "No need to get yer knickers in a twist."

There was low conversation behind him, and Marilyn pushed the door, bold now. "Who's here?"

"No one's 'ere love. It's the TV. We're watchin' the weather bird reportin' on the storm."

"Can I come in and watch with you? I'm worried about Fran."

"Nope, I have a client. Gotta go."

"Seriously? A client in the middle of this weather? How did they even get here?"

"Fuck you, Mar'lyn," he said with a flat chuckle, "I gotta go to the loo. When ya gotta go, ya gotta go. So toodle-oo, I'm off to the loo." He shoved the door forcefully. She jumped back as it slammed, and she heard the deadbolt slide home.

In Fran's apartment, the newscaster was still doing voice-over dialogue while photos showed more footage of helicopters and boats. The announcer intoned, "Flash floods with rapidly rising water can reach heights of thirty feet or more. They can also cause catastrophic mudslides."

Marilyn called and texted Fran every fifteen minutes, but her calls went to voicemail. On Fran's balcony, sheltered from the pelting rain by the balcony above, she stared into the void. The drops that hit the railing splashed, reaching her, and her reflection in the window showed frizzy hair. As dark descended, the rain kept coming. The power failure and low cloud cover rendered the normally festively-lit downtown dark, while weak lights shone in some homes equipped with generators and in random groups of houses that had power.

Was Fran's disappearance an emergency yet? All the first responders were rescuing people. While Fran's lack of response to Marilyn's texts was unusual, her phone might have been dunked, or maybe the battery had died, or Fran was so caught up in her rescue mission that she was ignoring calls.

Marilyn called Earl and Rigby, both life-drawing attendees who had been at yesterday's session and who had attended the Lads' party, after. Earl's went to voicemail, but Rigby picked up on the first ring. "Hey, Marilyn, what's up?"

Rigby was in her mid-sixties and rail thin, her name most likely appropriated from the Beatles song, "Eleanor Rigby." She chain-smoked Marlboros and dressed in thrift shop finds. Yesterday's outfit was a men's red and white houndstooth shirt over a vintage Janis Joplin T-shirt, and leggings. Her silver hair was streaked magenta and green.

"Hi, Rigby. Have you seen Fran today? She and the Lads were supposedly going out to help people, but the Lads are here and Fran's not."

"I must be hallucinating. Did you just say the Lads were going to *help* people? Helping people isn't in their DNA." There was the sound of Rigby inhaling a cigarette. "There's a rumor that Fran has a sugar daddy. Maybe she went with him."

A shard of anger pierced Marilyn. "A rumor, huh? I don't believe that for an instant. Fran told me that while she was getting her law degree her father was paying her bills. Fran would never prostitute herself."

"Calling it prostitution seems a bit harsh," Rigby said. "Just sayin' maybe she went with him."

"Not harsh. It all comes down to money for sex. Even if the sugar daddy enjoys his sugar baby's companionship—"

"I call them sugar cookies."

Marilyn sensed Rigby's grin. "That's cute. But as I was saying, if sugar daddy likes his sugar, um, cookie," she smiled, "enjoys their dinners—even romantic dinners—and so forth, it still boils down to the sugar baby being available for sex when her sugar daddy is horny. Kind of like an affair but the monetary angle makes it prostitution. Plus, the sugar daddy can dump her any time he wants."

"Yeah. I guess," Rigby conceded. Her lighter snicked and she inhaled. "Kind of like an escort, but with just one customer. But I also heard that a rich-guy-car picks her up on the regular."

"That doesn't mean anything. Who told you that?"

"People saw her get into a limo."

"Fran told me she was interning part-time at one of the top law firms, which might explain the limo. Rigby, I really hope you haven't been spreading the sugar daddy rumor about Fran." Marilyn had witnessed Rigby run her mouth before and was aware she thrived on gossip, but this was too personal. Her concern about Fran's safety made her protective and more prickly than usual.

Miffed, Rigby said, "Oh for fuck sake. Don't go getting all up in arms, now."

She wanted Rigby's help to find Fran, didn't want to alienate her, and changed the subject. "Also, maybe I have another lead. The last time I chatted with Fran, she said she was dating a geologist, last name of Rockwell. Did you ever meet him?"

"Nope. Never met him. Great name for a geologist."

Marilyn looked at the rain slashing at the window and beyond it the endless void of night. "I think if she went off with someone, she would have texted me or left a note. It's just so out of character for her to vanish."

"Yup. It's weird," Rigby said. "This flooding is nuts. I guess life-drawing will be cancelled for a while."

"No kidding. I hope the Art Guild didn't flood. My apartment is flooded to the ceiling."

"Sorry to hear that. Sounds like you're homeless *again*. That last time, you had a trifecta of bad luck. First, your live-in boyfriend brought home his pregnant eighteen-year-old baby-momma. Then you got downsized from your job, and also realized too late that you'd put your savings into a Ponzi scheme."

Marilyn's ire returned and a stinging sensation spread through her. "Wow. You certainly summed that up." She heard the anger in her voice. "Did Fran tell you all this stuff? Anything else you want to hit me with?"

"Darlin' don't be mad. You were living at Fran's place, going to the Lads' parties, and modeling at the Art League. How could anyone *not know*? In fact, one time I overheard you talking about the Ponzi scheme. You were being brave and presenting it as a humorous anecdote, but of course it hurt you. Besides, no one thought less of you. That crap happened to you, not because of anything you'd done wrong. It's okay. It was a reminder how fast that shit can happen."

"Okay, okay. It's been a long crazy day and I'm

exhausted and worried," Marilyn said, stopping short of apologizing. "You know, for months before the hurricane everyone was talking about the women showing up at that homeless camp under the freeway bridge."

"Yeah, they were naked, beaten, and overdosed. The cops had assumed they were junkie-hookers, until a few parents raised hell." Rigby sighed.

"They finally started investigating, but now I think of Fran being out there somewhere. If there's a serial killer on the loose…well, I'm scared shitless."

"Let's keep the faith. Get some sleep."

"I'll try." They said goodbye and hung up. Marilyn tried 911 again, but there was nothing but dial-tone. Dial-tone! She hadn't heard that in ten years at least. It probably meant that the overburdened cell systems had crashed.

The mayor appeared on TV. As if he had read her mind, he apologized to the population of Houston for their emergency services' lack of response. He appealed to their common sense and patience explaining that all first responders were busy rescuing people from life-or-death flood situations. He instructed those who had fled into their attics, chopped a hole, and were awaiting rescue from their roof to hang a towel or rag so the helicopter pilots could spot them.

What if his message was going into the ether? People could have dying batteries in their phones and no electricity, texts and calls that wouldn't be delivered on the overwhelmed cell-systems, trapped in their attic, desperately kicking at their roof to create an opening to climb higher and higher until they ran out of higher. Or what if they weren't strong enough to kick through the plywood and shingles? And where was that towel the mayor spoke of? Probably submerged in the main floor bathroom. What a nightmare. If she ever bought a house she'd keep an axe, hammer, and saw in the attic…and towels.

She watched another news cycle, then after midnight

the exertion of her escape caught up to her, and she bedded down on Fran's sofa for a few hours of fitful sleep.

Marilyn woke at five, went to Fran's bedroom door, and peered in, hoping she had arrived during the night, but her bed was empty. She showered and dressed, poured muesli into a bowl, and plopped some yogurt on top. The news was running some new flood footage and she watched a few minutes. "Okay. Screw this," Marilyn said aloud. "Time to act, not sit passively by, waiting." She dialed Andy, the life-drawing group's organizer.

"Hey, Marilyn, everything okay? Are you safe?"

"I am, but I can't find Fran. She's been missing since midday yesterday, so she was gone all night. The Lads…" Marilyn recounted the harrowing hours spent hoping for Fran's return. "Anyway, she's gone, and I can't find her. I've been calling 911 but can't get through. I'll keep trying."

"Fuck," Andy said softly.

"Can you please call all the other drawing group members to see if anyone has heard from her? And please call the Lads. They're acting kind of strange."

"Of course. No problem."

"I'll call Rigby, Jon, and Earl. Hope to see you soon," she added, and they said goodbye and hung up.

She called Earl again, expecting voicemail, but he picked up and said he'd heard nothing from Fran.

She said, "By the way, the hurricane left me homeless. I want to stay at Fran's until she comes home but after that…if you hear of an apartment or even a room that's available, let me know, okay? I want to move ASAP. Oh, and a job. I need a job."

"I've got a friend crashing at my place already," Earl said. "Otherwise, I'd move you in. But, yeah, I'll ask around about the rental and who's hiring."

"Thanks, Earl." They signed off, and she called

emergency again. This time it didn't go to dial tone. It rang twenty times then cut out. Finally, when she'd lost count of her attempts, she got voicemail, and left a message about Fran being missing with as many particulars as possible. Under the circumstances, while Fran's disappearance might turn out to be harmless and innocent, and while having a 911 call go to voicemail was reasonable, she was pulsating with worry and frustration.

Out on Fran's balcony, she leaned over the railing into the rain and made out a small portion of Fran's red Civic parked at the side of the building. In the drawer of a small stand near the front door, she found the spare Honda key and an umbrella and ran down the stairs. She removed her sandals, popped the umbrella, and waded through ankle-deep floodwater to Fran's vehicle. Whether Fran left on foot or with someone, they could have only gone a few blocks unless a boat was flagged down or commandeered.

Zabi whispered, *This gets weirder and weirder.*

A spike of trepidation rushed down Marilyn's spine. *My thoughts exactly.*

She opened Fran's car doors one by one and examined the interior. In true Fran style, other than a grocery bag hooked on the gearshift for what Fran referred to as "carbage"—which contained a Kleenex and an empty Starbucks cup—the vehicle was empty and clean, and neither Fran's purse nor her phone were in the car, which Marilyn took as a good sign. She took a deep breath and steadied herself before turning the key to open the trunk. The lid popped up, and looking into empty space, she exhaled in relief.

The rain had eased but judging by the two-foot-deep water in the road, she would be trapped for the foreseeable future. Back in Fran's unit, she dialed 911 again, left another message that Fran's car was at her building, the address, and the car's license number.

Next door, at noon, the Lads' heavy metal rock began thumping. She called Jon. He picked up and said, "Where are you?"

"I'm at Fran's place."

"I should have known. I can hear the Lads' bass in the background."

"Yep. Listen, Fran's missing."

He inhaled sharply. "What do you mean, *missing*?"

"She's not here and I can't find her."

"Yoiks," he said, "I haven't heard from her."

Despair crowded in. "I'm a bit freaked out. Where did you end up, Jon?"

"I'm at a friend's house. They're letting me stay for a few more days. Then I'll have to get lost."

"Glad you're high and dry. The storm was so weird, the way it was all rain with no wind to speak of."

He said, "Yep. They're saying it kept picking up water and circling back to dump it on us. Unusual not to have hundred-fifty-mile-per-hour winds."

"Stay safe. Let me know when you are resettled."

"You too. Keep safe," Jon said quietly.

His usual jokiness seemed to have been crushed by the hurricane. Marilyn tried to think of where Fran may have gone, her favorite places. Instead, memories of their friendship came tumbling in. Marilyn and Fran had met when both had arrived at Luna's Mexican Restaurant for an online date with the same man. As they approached his table his error dawned on him and he went pale. Fran and Marilyn stood on either side looming over him, and he scrambled out of his seat and dashed from the restaurant. Marilyn asked, "You hungry?"

"Hell yeah," Fran said, laughing.

They had traded online-dating war stories over margaritas and fajitas—the drunks, the married liars, the momma's boys, the know-it-alls, the highly religious, and many more. Finally, in unison they said, "I give up!"

They were different but truly clicked. Fran had waitressed and finally tackled her dream of studying law, while Marilyn had bounced from situation to situation, what she referred to as her "whiplash life." Both women had remained loyal, helpful, protective, supportive, and everpresent. Fran's souvenirs and knickknacks echoed fond memories. A carved bear reminded her of their failed camping trip. Dire warnings of bears and snakes had inspired them to check into the nearest Hyatt. And there was her collection of Mardi Gras beads, mugs, and glasses acquired from multiple watering holes during a boisterous drunken New Orleans tour.

She rubbed her eyes. There must be something she could do to find Fran.

Chapter Five:

The search

Marilyn accessed social media site by site, leaving messages on boards for Fran's law school and the Art Guild, on Instagram and Facebook, she tweeted and instant-messaged and shared. She paced the apartment, opened the balcony door, and closed it again against the rain. A wave of helplessness washed over her. Did being utterly dependent on electronics put the lie to those so-called advancements?

Was there a better way to draw attention to Fran's disappearance? She called the local TV station's newsroom and left a message. Then the television showed the newsroom three feet deep in water, the staff nowhere to be seen. *Shit!*

Maybe Fran had gone to a relative's, or her parents' house. She rifled through Fran's drawers in the hope of finding a book of contact numbers but came up empty. The building's super should have emergency contact numbers for Fran. She dashed down the stairs to the rental office on the main floor where there was a hand-scrawled sign, *No rentals until the flood is over.* When she dialed the posted phone number, she heard the faint ringing of the landline in the deserted office. Crap.

Marilyn stood a moment, considering what to do next. At the Lads' most recent party—hard to believe it was just the night before last—Rigby had said she was *heading upstairs* to her apartment, which meant she lived on the top floor. She dialed Rigby. "Can I come see you?"

"Sure," Rigby said. "Look for the red door with yellow and purple lightning bolts."

Marilyn knocked, and the door swung open to Rigby smoking a cigarette and wearing pajamas printed all over with garden-gnomes. "Welcome to my life, what I call my *Game of Crones.*"

Marilyn stepped into Rigby's studio apartment, which was, unsurprisingly, eccentrically decorated and infused with an overpowering odor of cat-piss-ammonia and tobacco smoke. The place was quite dark with only a few low-wattage mood lights glowing, but Marilyn's job after her last homeless stint and before she landed her job as manager of The Moderne was working for The Verminator, a pest control company, which had honed Marilyn's bug detection skills, and she caught the movement of several Texas-sized inch-long roaches in the kitchen area.

The ceiling was painted as a night sky, and each wall was a sponged-on primary color. Rigby's large, lurid life-drawings covered some walls, hung salon-style to the ceiling. Running the full length of one wall was a built-in seat upholstered in fuchsia that doubled as her bed. It was topped with a truckload of pillows that appeared to be sewn from recycled saris.

Zabi whispered, *I hope she doesn't turn on the lights.*

Marilyn wandered to the window. Fran's view was of

downtown, but this was in the opposite direction, toward suburbs. "Jesus, I wish the rain would stop."

"Amen. Got an ark? They say it'll let up by tomorrow."

Marilyn braved the sofa and sat warily at the front edge. A Himalayan cat hopped up, parked on her lap, and began vibrating. Marilyn scratched the cat's head, and it purred louder. She told Rigby of her measures to find Fran, and her fear. Rigby poured two glasses of iced green tea and reached over and took Marilyn's hand, an unexpected gesture of reassurance, that started tears. Marilyn said, "I'm so scared and worried."

"Me too," Rigby said. "It's going to be pretty hard to get attention with every cop and first responder hunting for Fairfield's daughter."

Marilyn stared at Rigby. "Wait. What? Fairfield, the oil baron's…daughter?"

"It was just on the news. Fairfield's thirty-year-old daughter, Darby, who is an only child, has been missing since a couple of days before the hurricane. She lived in a cottage." She crooked her fingers around the word *cottage* and smirked. "I'm sure they mean a mansion, on Fairfield's estate in River Oaks. She has a kid, a seven-year-old son, the old goat's only grandchild. Nobody's seen her for four or five days. But her housekeeper-nanny—in other words, a surrogate mother for the kid—said Darby regularly takes off for days at a time. The difference this time is that she never texted or called. Fairfield has offered two-hundred-K for info."

"Cheapskate. The guy's a billionaire." Marilyn thought a minute. "Okay, if there are a bazillion cops and citizens trying to find her, to either get the glory or the reward money, can the search somehow help find Fran, too?"

Rigby was nodding. "I think they're connected."

"Doubtful." Marilyn shook her head. "They sound so different. Fran is super responsible, while this other one, this Darby Fairfield, sounds like a flake."

Rigby turned on the TV, paused the image, and said, "Look." On the screen was a willowy woman dressed hippie style in nearly sheer cotton harem pants, a flowery peasant blouse, gladiator sandals, and strings of beads. Her waist-length fine blonde hair was gathered into a clip adorned with daisies. She looked fresh, no makeup, her pose relaxed, her smile genuine.

"Holy shit," Marilyn said. "I know her from somewhere."

"Yeah. You know her—Darby is one of the Lads' *birds*. She came to lots of their parties. Slumming. And she used to come to figure drawing sometimes. She was also one of the Lads' new age clients." She pronounced 'new age' to rhyme with sewage and smirked again. "She went for all their bullshit—got their vitamin shots, massages, and that green stuff they drink."

"Now that I think of it, Rigby, I did see her at the Art Guild, but she didn't stay, just dropped in for a minute and left. So, Fran and Darby both knew the Lads." Marilyn and Rigby stared at each other. "What does this mean?"

"Maybe nothing. It might be a coincidence."

"Or?"

"Or maybe there's no such thing as coincidence, but we have no clue if the Lads have done something with this particular little chickadee, or Fran," Rigby said.

"Yesterday when I got here, I heard noises at the Lads' next door. I figured they'd come home from their rescue mission, and I went to find Fran. The door was locked."

"That's unusual," Rigby said.

"My thoughts too. Declan answered the door and when I asked him who I could hear in the background, he said they were watching the *weather-bird*. Then he said he had a client. Then he said he had to go to the loo. Plus, he had some scratches on his arm."

Wide-eyed, Rigby said, "My god. I don't like the

sound of this. Could the Lads have kidnapped Darby or Fran?"

"Or both of them?" Marilyn rubbed behind the cat's ears. "If so, where would they have taken them? Fran and Darby need to show up soon so we can find out what happened. I'm getting more worried by the minute."

Rigby looked absentmindedly at the TV. "I sure never thought Darby was a rich bitch. Look, tattoos."

"Daisies and kittens." Marilyn sighed. "Not exactly badass. She seems nice, sweet."

"Yeah," Rigby said, stubbing out her cigarette.

"Something else just occurred to me. Another woman who came to figure drawing also disappeared. There was one a couple of years ago—I only spoke with her a few times at life-drawing—then I recognized her picture on the news."

"Right, her name was Patty," Rigby said, nodding.

"Yes. Patty. She was always so quiet, so invisible. Did you know she was a children's book illustrator? Her publisher reported her missing because she hadn't delivered some drawings, and she'd never missed a deadline before. One time, I was talking to her about her work, and she said, 'Illustrations are to a children's story what music is to a song's lyrics.'"

Rigby smiled. "I love that."

"Me too." The cat stood and stretched and plopped down between Marilyn and Rigby. Marilyn stroked the cat's back and said, "Patty was never found, dead or alive, as far as I know."

"I don't think she was connected to the Lads and their scams or parties. She isn't the type. Not that it lets the Lads off the hook."

"Now that I think of it, Rigby, a few women just stopped coming to the group since Patty vanished. It makes me wonder if anyone thought to follow up, email them or phone them. Some people are really alone, no family, no close friends, and they might not be missed."

"Are you saying there's a murderer hunting artists?" Rigby asked.

"I don't know. I hope not." The cat rolled onto its back and Marilyn rubbed its stomach. "I'm scared but also weirdly confident Fran will show up unharmed. Because…Fran. Reliable, smart Fran. But I have no clue about Darby Fairfield."

"I'll google Patty, see if she ever turned up."

Rigby tapped another cigarette out of her pack. Marilyn watched her, wondering if she was going to light it using the last one, but she set it on the ashtray's edge.

"I feel for old man Fairfield," Marilyn said. "No matter how wealthy you are, if this is a tragedy…well, rich folks bleed when you cut them, too. It's sad." Marilyn stood to leave. "I think we should stay on social media and keep on posting. I've posted on every site I have access to. Since her car is still here, maybe someone saw her get into another vehicle. Whatever happened, she couldn't have gone far with the flooding." Marilyn frowned a moment. "Actually, it's been bugging me that she couldn't have gone far. What if she's still in the building?"

Rigby gasped. "Holy fuck! I didn't think of that, but it fits. You mean someone has her in their apartment?"

"Maybe. Or she's locked up in the janitor's closet, or someplace. I'm going to search the building."

Rigby picked up her cigarette, lit it, and stood up. "I'm coming with you." Still in her pj's, she jammed her feet into flipflops, grabbed her keys and phone, and they headed out.

Chapter Six:

The Crying House

The building's layout was T-shaped, with the elevator at the intersection of the two hallways. Next to the elevator was a laundry room with two coin-operated washers and dryers, and a locked door on one wall. "This must be a custodian's closet." Marilyn rattled the handle and pressed her ear to the door. "Do you have the manager's phone number? We need keys."

Rigby dialed, explained their mission, and asked for the keys. Rigby's side of the conversation indicated the super was resistant. Rigby listened awhile, then finally said, "Hey, you can drive over here and help us—" She rolled her eyes and added, "Exactly! You can't come because of the flooding." After a pause she added, "We've tried the police. They're kinda busy."

Becoming irate, she raised her voice, "I'm not going to get any keys copied. Why would I? To steal your dirty worn-out floor mops? How will you feel when you're in the headlines because Darby Fairfield is tied up in a closet and you let her die because you wouldn't let us search."

When she hung up, she grinned, "The magic of guilt and shaming." She and Marilyn high-fived. "The office has a coded lock on the door. The combo is 7654."

They took the elevator to the main floor, entered the office, and found the keys in a desk drawer. Marilyn asked, "If you had a hostage, where would you hide her?"

"AC equipment room," Rigby said without hesitation. Back on the top floor, they climbed a stairway to the roof and searched the structure that housed the elevator mechanism and the air conditioning and heating equipment but found only cigarette butts and soda cans. Then they descended, checking floor by floor the rooms and closets that housed laundry machines, janitor's supplies, trash-chutes, and the enclosed empty spaces in each hallway intended for snack machines and ice makers which had never been installed.

Back on the main floor they returned the keys to the desk. Marilyn sat in the manager's chair and Rigby stood in the doorway, hipshot, leaning against the door jamb. "Searching is such an emotional roller coaster," Marilyn said. "You want to find her, but you're afraid of what you might find."

"No shit. Now what?"

"Isn't there a group of volunteers who search for people? They're called Texas Search, or something like that."

"I've heard of them," Rigby said, snapping her fingers. "Oh, got it! They're called Texas EquuSearch. I'll contact them."

"Great. Since we can't get into the apartments, I'll print some pictures of Fran and Darby and go door to door. Also, I've sent you a friend request. I'll do some sharing on social media. But how do we get the people hunting for Darby Fairfield to include Fran in their search?"

"I don't know." Rigby shrugged. "But I'll definitely share your posts, and ask all our friends to share, and so forth. That's the power of social media, the reach increases like a pyramid scheme or a chain letter. Remember chain letters?"

"Hell yeah. Start with two letters and end up with a zillion. Outlawed, of course. I read one time that if a virtual chain letter took hold, it could crash the whole internet." Marilyn ambled to the office door. "Do you have contact information for Fran's parents?"

Rigby shook her head. "I'll call the building manager again and get Fran's info." She sighed. "Fran, Fran, Fran…I hope you're with some dude you met while out rescuing people, and it clicked, and you guys just haven't come up for air. Hope you're fine."

Marilyn smiled. "Wouldn't that be great. I thought she maybe got stranded and hopped a Cajun Navy boat and ended up in a shelter, a church, or someplace similar. And maybe she dropped her phone overboard or hasn't been able to charge it." They smiled optimistically. "I didn't think of this before, but if you are right about her having a sugar daddy, he could be a lead. How would she have found this guy in the first place?"

"The way everyone meets these days. On a website," Rigby said, nodding.

"I'll try googling her boyfriend, Rockwell. See if I can contact him."

"By the way, where are you from originally? You don't sound entirely Texan."

"Detroit."

Rigby shuddered. "Cold up there."

"Oh yeah. Colder than a polar bear's butt on a cast iron commode…"

Rigby laughed. "How old were you when you came here?"

"My mom died when I was eight. My aunt adopted me, and we came here a year later."

"Sorry about your mom."

"Thanks, but it was a long time ago. Let's keep on top of the Fran situation."

"For sure," Rigby said, and they returned to their respective apartments.

Marilyn opened her laptop. Now what? She typed 'sex offenders' into the search bar and narrowed the search results to Fran's location. Several men lived in one residence. She clicked on the profile of each of the men, and they all seemed to have committed crimes with underage girls or boys, if that meant anything. Probably a halfway house. Apart from Fran's disappearance, was this house full of sex offenders important? Marilyn clicked on the little Google guy, picked him up with her cursor, and he swung back and forth, suspended. She lowered him onto the street and turned him to face the front of the house. Something uncomfortable was poking at her memory and she scratched at it to pry it loose.

As the printer whirred printing her "Missing" posters for Fran, she sat back, closed her eyes, and allowed her memories of one bad night to invade.

The halfway house was familiar, similar to a Victorian house in Detroit where Marilyn and her mother would shelter, a trap-house that Marilyn had named *The Crying House*. She picked up the little Google man and moved him along. The way he dangled from her cursor brought a recollection of her mother, picked up by her neck by a man Marilyn called Giant, and shaken like she was boneless.

The Crying House was originally a wedding cake of a house—Victorian, feminine and decorative, edged with gingerbread, and sporting a turret, and fish-scale-shingled gables. A hundred years on however, it was derelict with boarded windows that gave the appearance of closed eyes avoiding the view of abandoned houses, garbage-strewn weedy lots, and shifty individuals who slipped through the shadows. An attic fire in The Crying House had claimed the lives of two men, and soot dislodged by the fire hoses had dried in rivulets under The Crying House's blank eyes, as if from her mascara and tears. Marilyn had never gone up to see the fire's damage because sometimes at dusk, bats came hurtling out of the collapsed roof. Marilyn had decided that for all that had happened in that house, the house was allowed to weep. Marilyn and her mother had been homeless for more than two years. That night a cold front had crept over Detroit. She shivered remembering how it breached her flimsy clothes, and seeped into muscle and bone, scalded her bare hands, wrists, cheeks, and ankles.

They were seeking shelter in The Crying House and Marilyn's mom was meeting a client. Her mother's looks were fading at that time. Her once pleasing curves had collapsed. Her strong, even teeth were rotting, and heavy makeup couldn't hide her pocked and damaged skin. She had regular clients who paid her for sex in cash or drugs. Her client that night was Giant. He would change everything.

Marilyn sat silent awhile, then shook her memories away to concentrate on the search for Fran. She guided the little Google guy along the streets around Fran's building but saw nothing else to give her pause, such as a jail, or run-down warehouses that could be full of squatters. Next, she surfed the internet, hitting on all the sugar daddy and sugar baby sites. There were a lot, twenty-seven and counting. Viewing their sugar baby profiles would be difficult. She either had to sign up as a decoy sugar baby on all the websites and hope the right man hit on her, or pose as a sugar daddy to see if Fran actually had a profile, which would require a credit card, a man's name, and an ID. And even if she managed all that, it was likely Fran never was a sugar baby.

Did Fran really sell out in this fashion? Given her own precarious financial situation, Marilyn understood how women were attracted to the sugar-baby life.

Aunt Zabi whispered, *No, you aren't your mother.*

"True Zabi," she said aloud. "All it takes is *pay to play* one time. It's not something you can undo. Once a hooker, well..."

She sighed in frustration and went back to searching through Fran's papers and social media for any indication of where she may have gone. If only she had her phone and email passwords.

Marilyn closed her search pages and opened online forms for unemployment benefits. She knew the benefits wouldn't kick in for weeks, and hopefully she'd find work before she needed them, but finding a job after the hurricane could take a while.

Finally, in the morning's small hours, she collapsed into bed. What a fucking day. Who knew what tomorrow might bring.

Chapter Seven:

The Detectives

Marilyn woke before six to a sense of nothingness, and for a moment she had déjà vu of waking to the hurricane. This time, however, it was the absence of thrumming rain that was remarkable. Her sleep had been fitful, with dreams populated by distressed figures floating at sea and calling to her. She lay awhile and considered the timeframe of her arrival, which was the day before yesterday. Fran had been gone two days, and more daunting, two nights. She went to the bedroom door, again hoping Fran had arrived during the night, but her bed was unoccupied and untouched.

Zabi said, *Her story, when she gets back, is going to be a doozy.*

"No kidding. I can't wait to hear it." Marilyn set about reading the hundreds of comments on social media, finding them all to be hopeful best wishes, with no sightings or evidence. Damn. Like clockwork the Lads' pounding bass started near lunchtime. Sick of their imposition and her anxious worry, Marilyn opted for action and escape, and spent the afternoon going door to door in the building with her photos of Fran and Darby Fairfield, but without luck. She tacked up missing-persons posters in the lobby.

Outside the rain had slowed to a drizzle. Mother Nature's frenzied outburst had diminished to gloomily weeping, bruised clouds. She taped posters on the shop windows and bus shelters that she could walk to. Peering into windows gave her a gauge of the destruction. The flood waters were beginning to slowly recede but the tideline, like a bathtub ring, in some shops was at four feet with mold creeping over objects, a multicolored chenille blanket that spewed suffocating spores.

Back in Fran's apartment, she called 911 and left another message as she composed a snack from Fran's fridge. Then she put on Fran's noise-canceling headphones, and as she ate she googled Rockwell, Fran's geologist. The only link to a geologist with his surname was an article about warning signs of impending earthquakes in California. There were photos of earthquake damage but no author's picture.

Dark descended and Marilyn again tuned to the news, which was now concentrating on stories of annihilation, the runoff as the water retreated, looters, and rescues of people and animals. Suddenly tired of anything in peril, she watched a show about interesting vacation spots, then sauntered to the balcony where the view showed patches of light in the darkness where electricity had been restored. She lifted one earphone and noticed the Lads' music had stopped. It was after one o'clock, and she'd lost track of time. Despite feeling thoroughly awake, she stretched out on the sofa and fell asleep.

Marilyn woke to weak sunlight as the cloud cover lifted like a theater curtain, and the sky brightened like footlights coming up. In contrast to the previous days' dismal dreariness, it seemed manic. Marilyn stepped onto the balcony and her despair began to thin; however, Fran was still out there, unaccounted for, and the storm's end meant the beginning of desperate work.

On TV, the coverage concentrated on receding water and navigable roads. They warned that some streets near bayous and portions of highways were still blocked. First responders were checking houses and buildings for victims. Bodies had been found in cars, underpasses, attics, intersections. Three were suspected to be in elevators. The announcer emphasized that many elevators are programmed to return to the lowest floor to pick up the next load heading up. In a power failure, doors won't open, the elevator won't ascend, and the box fills with water, no escape. We know not to take the elevator during a fire, but in a rainstorm, how could any of us know, or even think of that?

Was that what happened to Fran, trapped in an elevator, and drowned? Then, to Marilyn's shock, a Facebook photo of Fran filled the screen. The voice-over talked about Fran's law school education, her talent as an artist. Missing—now it was real. Now, Marilyn wasn't searching on her own.

The apartment's intercom buzzed, and a male voice introduced himself as Houston Police and asked her to bring the key to Fran's vehicle. She trotted onto the balcony and saw a uniformed officer, two female techies in navy short-sleeved shirts with "HPD Forensics" in white across the back, dark pants, and their hair wound up and tied. Two plainclothes officers were shining flashlights into Fran's car.

She snatched up the car key and raced down the stairs. After the news story, elevators, especially balky ones, suddenly gave her the creeps. Outside, the temperature had risen since the storm, and evaporating floodwater made for soupy air that had clothes clinging and hair frizzing. At the car, a tech was shooting photos, and another was dusting handles and doors for prints.

The crew looked droopy. No wonder. The daunting task of finding bloated, drowned victims, the near-impossible business of getting around, while at the same time dealing with their own families' flood complications.

One of the plainclothes detectives gave her his card that read Kevin Stade, Homicide. "Oh, Homicide…" Blood left her head. "Has Fran been…"

He shook his head. "No. She's missing. We're not concerned about departments or titles at this point. We're just trying to locate people. And you are?"

"Marilyn Connor, a close friend." She said, "When I was searching for Fran, I opened the doors and trunk of her car. I hope I didn't do anything bad."

"That's okay. We'll take your prints for elimination."

She held out the car key, and as he took it, his fingertips brushed hers. Despite her worry about Fran, she noticed a strong tingle of attraction. A surprise. Given his look of sudden focus, he'd felt it too, and her face warmed. She looked away, studying the car, flustered.

He nodded and turned back to his crew. Stade wore black casual pants and an open-neck white business shirt, tucked in; its crisp collar and cuffs suggested laundering at the cleaners, and care about how he presented, possibly a bachelor lifestyle. Hiking boots were his only nod to the wet and muddy conditions.

She watched him a while. His build was solid and fit, but not overly ripped, and his good looks were indefinable, unconventionally handsome. With a faint scar on his jawline and a nose that had the hallmarks of being broken, Stade was borderline bad boy, but maybe that came with the title Homicide Detective. Exploring his features would be time well spent. She allowed herself an internal smile. Marilyn moved away, closer to the building to wait and watch awhile. The sun had brought out the whine of cicadas and birdsong.

Zabi's voice whispered, *They look like death warmed over...maybe they need some food or drinks.* Marilyn took out her phone and dialed Angel's Pizza, which surprisingly had reopened. She headed around the corner, bought two large pizzas, and a load of drinks.

Back at the parking lot, Marilyn handed over the food and the second plainclothes detective introduced himself simply as Garcia. Hispanic, he had deep brown eyes and thick black hair. Garcia was tall and large in frame and girth. His casual pants and striped Cubano shirt were disheveled, as if he'd slept in them, and perhaps he had, given the intense hours they must be working. He presented a rumpled contrast to debonair Stade.

Marilyn observed the team as they stood eating. Stade's hair was recently barbered, and he was close-shaven with a light five-o'clock shadow, a refreshing change from all the hipster scruff she'd run into lately. If Fran were present, she would have winked and declared him hot, and Marilyn would have concurred.

When they began moving away from Fran's car and talking amongst themselves, she tentatively approached Detective Stade.

He held up a slice of pizza in a salute. "Thanks. We've been running on empty."

A constant slight smile gave him a friendly demeanor, but under it was reticence. As they talked, he stood further away than normal, maybe to size up his subject's body language, and his expression had a closed-off quality. His manner was the opposite of *in your face* and had the effect of making her want to break through, to step too near, say something to crack him up or piss him off. Maybe it was a detective-tactic to take control, to provoke, get people to open up and fill any dead air with chitchat, subsequently giving up information and finally confessing. His eyes were active, missing nothing. She hid a smirk at the thought that she was detecting the detective.

Marilyn said, "My pleasure. I can't imagine how

you're coping with—uh, everything. We've been beside ourselves with worry about Fran. Any chance you can tell me what's happening? The news just said she's missing. Has there been any word at all?"

"When did you last see Fran?" he asked, making the point that he was the interrogator in this equation. Marilyn described waking to the flood, escaping from the apartment complex, dispossessed, and accepting Fran's offer of a place to stay. "When I got here, she was gone."

"Did Fran say where she was going?"

"She said she was going with the guys next door to help rescue people. The neighbors are two English guys who call themselves 'the Lads,' but when I got here, they said they'd changed their minds, and that Fran had gone out on her own."

He frowned. "Would she do that, go out into the storm by herself?"

"No. I know Fran wouldn't go by herself—she's a wicked-smart woman, studying law, about to take the bar exam." Marilyn thought a moment. "Plus, she wasn't answering her phone or texting and her voicemail was full. When night came, I got really scared for her. Being out at night when the water is black, and its depth is even harder to judge…well. And now we're at day four. Three nights she's been gone."

"We'll check her phone records."

"I called 911 and started posting on social media."

"And…?" Garcia asked.

Marilyn had been facing Stade and turned to include Garcia. "Crickets. Nothing from Fran and no sightings, just prayers for her safe return."

"We need to see inside her apartment." Garcia took a last bite of pizza, tossed the crust into the open box, and wiped his hands on a paper napkin.

"Okay. Now?"

"Yes. We're done here," Stade said. "A wrecker will come later and tow her car."

The detectives, techs, and uniformed officers entered the building. They followed Marilyn into the elevator, which shook and hesitated at each floor and stopped three inches below the threshold at the fourth floor.

Garcia said, "I read someplace that if your elevator falls, you should jump up and down. It'll give you a fifty-percent chance of being in the air when it lands." The others laughed doubtfully.

At Fran's door, the Lads' omnipresent bass was thumping, and Stade tipped his head toward the sound. "Are those the Lads?" He raised his eyebrows. "Party hearty, huh?"

"That's them." She nodded and grimaced. "Endlessly."

Stade said, "We'll need to talk to them, given what you said about their cancelled plans with Fran." The detectives stopped just inside Fran's door and surveyed the apartment, and Stade asked, "Which items are yours?"

Marilyn pointed out her belongings on and around the sofa, and the techs ambled in donning their blue plastic gloves, then carefully sifted through Fran's papers, clothes, and possessions, avoiding Marilyn's. They worked slowly and carefully, with one acting as photographer.

Marilyn sat at the dining table and feigned checking things on her phone while watching the crew in her periphery until Stade approached, and she got to her feet. He stepped closer than expected. She sensed an impending chummy conversation, and while some chat and perhaps even flirting were desirable, she needed information and edged away. "Now that you see I'm really her friend and I'm worried, I want to know what's happening. Has anyone come forward with any news—anything?"

"No. We're only getting to this case now. There's been a lot going on."

Marilyn nodded. "I understand."

The crew and Garcia left the apartment emptyhanded, leaving Stade. He said, "You have my card. If you think of anything, anything at all, no matter how unrelated it may seem, please call."

"You'll be the first to know, Detective."

"By the way, we have a pair of uniforms canvassing the building with photos of Fran and Darby Fairfield to see if anyone heard or saw anything."

"Good luck to them. I gave that a try and got nowhere."

"That's okay," Stade said. "You may have dislodged a memory and now that they're being asked again, the person might give it up. Besides, the officers will ask to look around their apartment if anything strikes them as odd."

Stade left, and Marilyn watched from the balcony as they drove away. She shook her head. "Goddammit, Fran. Where the fuck are you?"

Chapter Eight:

The Identities

Three days passed before Stade called and asked, "How are you holding up?"

"Pretty freakin' worried about Fran. Has there been any news?"

"Sorry. No, not yet."

"It's exasperating. On the news this morning there were pictures of women who are cold cases. I believe Fran is missing, not dead, but it scared me."

"Yes, we're looking into some cold cases," Stade said. "Did you know any of the women shown on the news?"

"No, but they just showed them for a minute. I couldn't get a good look at them. Are these the ones that were on the news before the hurricane? The drug overdoses? The women in the homeless camp?"

"Yes. We have the women's identities, and now we are looking for connections. Can you come to the precinct?

I'd like to show you some pictures—see if you recognize them."

"But…are the pictures gruesome? I'm not big on horror."

"No blood. They're pictures that the women's parents gave the police when they disappeared. Besides, we need to get your fingerprints for elimination."

"Okay, I'll be there within the hour. What's the address?"

She dressed in white jeans, a navy silk shirt, and sandals, thanks to Fran's closet. She googled the precinct's location close to downtown, a nine-mile trip, and used her ride-hailing app. Her driver drove slowly along side streets, dodging piles of ruined possessions stacked high alongside sodden building materials—insulation like sponges, swollen and dissolved stucco, crumbled drywall, and warped lumber—all permeated by black, green, and multicolored mold and algae. Doors and windows were propped open, and the forms of workers moved about inside, swinging hammers and wielding pry bars.

On the highway, traffic was traveling at near normal speeds. Approaching the Sims Bayou Bridge, she asked the driver to pull onto the feeder and stop on the shoulder. The normally calm, glasslike bayou was a raging and wrenching turmoil high above its banks. She watched the water's fury for a few minutes, then returned to the car.

Stade met her in the lobby, looking every bit as attractive as her first impression in a dark suit and classic white shirt, no tie. They shook hands. His palm was warm and dry, his handshake firm, and he didn't let go for an extra beat. She felt heat, her face flushed. Kissing him would be the most natural thing in the world.

Her visceral reaction to Stade collided with her agitated and anxious state. The stimulation of attraction was as irritating as it was fascinating and pleasurable. He was a distraction for her anxiety about Fran's disappearance. Was that good or bad?

He led her into a large room. Cubicles lined one wall and there were desks in the open area. Men and women, some in uniform, some dressed casually, were on the phone and typing reports. Stade ushered her into a cubicle and indicated a chair. She sat down and he circled the desk to his office chair. He opened a manila envelope, spread photos of five women on the desk, and said, "Take a look at these."

Garcia approached and hovered, observing. He was wearing khakis and a blue-and-white-striped shirt and looked fresher and more rested today. Garcia returned her smile.

To study the photos, she leaned forward, and a wave of Stade's pleasantly clean male scent reached her. She tamped down her escalating desire and focused on the photos. One was at her college graduation and a brunette in business attire was making a presentation. The other women were on vacation, their photos taken on beaches. The killer didn't have a type. They were a variety of heights, body types, hair color, and races.

"Unfortunately, most of these photos are pretty dated," Stade said. "At least we know who these women are, unlike some in our files, so we are trying to find how they were connected. They died of drug overdoses, but we don't think the overdoses were accidental. If we are correct, how did the killer know all of them?"

She scanned the pictures again, realized she'd been holding her breath, and exhaled, "I don't find any of them familiar." She paused a beat. "But you know, I didn't recognize Darby Fairfield right away. It wasn't until Rigby reminded me that she came to the Lads' parties that I identified her. Maybe they are out of context, not in the environment I know them."

"Take another look," Garcia urged.

Marilyn again examined the women's photo-faces with their wide, toothy selfie-smiles, all manner of makeup and eyeliner and rosy cheeks, their smart clothes, their youth. She shook her head and sat back in her chair and asked, "Are you familiar with a missing woman named Patty? Patty came to life-drawing. She went missing a year or two ago."

"Got a last name?"

"No. She was on the news as a missing person. Rigby said she was going to google Patty but…anyway…I guess I should research her myself."

"Who is Rigby?" Garcia asked, and Marilyn described Rigby's persona, her apartment's decor, and that she lived in Fran's building.

"That building is a real hive of activity," Garcia said with a smile. "I'll look up Patty in the system."

Marilyn said, "Rigby and I were speculating whether there's a serial killer who has a thing for female artists." She paused a moment, thinking. "You said they all died of overdoses. So, the homicide unit wasn't involved because they appeared to be accidental?" A spike of anger pierced her for the women neglected in death. "And none of the homeless saw anything?"

"Sorry, I can't let you in on what is being investigated or how it's being handled. We have rules, y'know." He smiled, revealing even, strong, white teeth.

Marilyn held back her simmering anger and the thought that these detectives were lazy, or negligent, that multiple similar deaths were somehow ignored. She picked up a photo. "Wow, she was beautiful."

Stade nodded. "Yes, she was. And to answer one of your questions, unfortunately, most of the homeless, where these bodies were found, are unreliable witnesses. They've got drug habits, mental illness, and they try to curry favor and get handouts by supposedly *helping* by giving us information, which usually turns out to be bogus. The beat cops who interview them don't understand that you gotta double-check everything they tell you. Can't just take it at face value."

"But these women look healthy and vibrant, not like

wasted, skinny junkies, so why didn't anyone look into ID'ing them before?" She was aware her tone had become peeved, if not borderline belligerent.

He shook his head. "They didn't look healthy when they were found dead. Also, deaths of homeless people are not rare in Houston. There are up to a hundred fifty a year, most from suicide and disease, but not an insignificant number from overdoses. The officers who handled the scene obviously made assumptions."

She watched him study the photos. Dark hair covered the arch of his ear, and his tanned neck contrasted with the arctic-white shirt. "I'm sorry, but I'm drawing a blank with these ladies. Anything else?"

"Yes. Fingerprints." He produced a machine and instructed Marilyn to lay her fingers inside an opening.

"Hmm, no black ink? No rolling each finger onto paper?"

"Nope. We've got all the modern conveniences." He stood. "Thanks for coming in. I'll walk you out."

Garcia had vanished.

At the lobby, Stade opened the door for her then stepped outside and stopped. "I have a question," he said.

"Shoot."

"May I buy you lunch?"

"Yes, please." She smiled. "I hope it's nearby. The storm cooled it down a bit for a few days, but this heat is pretty brutal. Typical late June weather, I suppose."

"Yes, it's nearby. Look…" He pointed to a storefront across the road and two shops down. As they walked to the restaurant. Stade said, "After talking to you, I googled the *Blokes*—or whatever those guys call themselves—on social media."

Marilyn smiled. "Ha. The blokes, I like that. They're known as the Lads."

"Tell me about them."

Marilyn explained Declan and Shawn's bullshit-guru image. She touched on their style of dress, their facial-mulch, and hipster-bun-hair, their British mannerisms and slang. She told how they met women through their Transcendalia ads, and their hardcore partying, surfing, and drug dealing.

"I don't want to accuse the Lads of something heinous that maybe they didn't do. Maybe it's just coincidence that Darby, Fran, and the Lads know each other. Also, I'm not giving up hope that Fran is alive."

"I agree with keeping hope alive, but I have to look at all scenarios. Don't worry about accusing the Lads. I'm taking everything at face value, and right now, I'm just hoping to find connections."

"Shawn and Declan are joined at the hip. Is it possible the Lads are serial killers, and the two of them work together?"

"Anything is possible. We won't know until all the puzzle pieces are together."

"The Lads killing people as a duo, and just for laughs, seems absolutely bizarre, if not downright insane."

"It is unusual," Stade said, "but it wouldn't be the first time a killer operated with a partner."

"Ugh. That adds a whole other level of sick to the scenario."

Stade said, "And it's not necessarily another guy. Sometimes the ideal partner for a serial killer is a female. A woman normalizes the killer. It's easier for a woman to gain a female victim's trust and lure her."

"Ah," she said. "Like that woman who groomed the underage girls for that rich pedophile a while back."

"Exactly. So let me get this out of the way…Did you help recruit young ladies for the Lads?"

Marilyn stopped and stared hard at him a moment, and then shook her head in disgust. "No. I did not."

"Sorry, I had to ask. While you seem completely aboveboard, I really don't know you. Insulting beautiful women is part of my job."

Marilyn gave him some side-eye and smirked. "Nice

segue, Detective."

He opened the restaurant's door to a welcome blast of cold. The décor imitated a '50s American diner with all the cutting-edge plastics of the period—black and white checkered linoleum flooring, turquoise Formica tabletops, and red-vinyl upholstery—all trimmed in chrome. A vintage jukebox played Elvis songs. The place was busy but they found a booth and studied the menu.

Marilyn inspected the interior. "Next time I'll wear my rockabilly cosplay outfit."

"What does that look like?"

"Oh, a poodle-skirt, wide patent-leather belt, bobby-socks, and saddle shoes."

"Sounds good," he said, smiling.

"At the station you said that the responding officers made some assumptions. What did they assume?" Marilyn asked.

He spoke quietly, aware of the nearby lunch crowd. "Picture how the scene would look to the officer. It's the graveyard shift. It's dark. They pull up to the homeless camp and there's a body. It's a woman. She has marks from a beating. There's a syringe still in her arm. She's naked with no ID. A homeless guy, or two, or more, has had sex with her."

"My god. How awful." She shivered.

"The homeless guys may not have realized she was dead, or they might've," Stade said softly, regretfully.

"So, the homeless said they knew the girls?"

"Sure. They'll say whatever works for them. For the police, all the markers pointed to the victim being a drug-addicted street prostitute who overdosed. Homicide showed up to these scenes, but we've come to realize that the same detective—a very inexperienced detective—attended all of these late-night calls at the homeless camp. The basics were done, fingerprints and tox-screen which confirmed the overdose. No autopsy since she OD'd. As for fingerprints, she's not in the system. With no missing person's report, she ended up being filed away."

"You're making excuses, Detective. You're saying the detective looked at clues, the location and situation, and it informed the detective enough that he—"

"She," he corrected.

"A female detective? Somehow, that's even worse, that she felt she didn't need to look any further."

"Yes. She wasn't experienced enough to realize she was looking at a cluster, a pattern. However, now that we've reopened these murders—"

"It took Darby Fairfield's disappearance to really spur the effort, right?"

"It helped. But so far Darby isn't dead. She's missing." He unfolded his napkin and placed it on his lap. "I started putting the pieces together before the hurricane. I can't tell you everything about the investigation, but I was in the morgue one day on a different matter when the attendant told me that there were five dead young women in lockers. She wanted to know what was causing a mass event like this. So, I started looking into it."

"Are there other missing women who haven't been found yet, like Darby and Fran?"

"Yes. I hate to say this, but there usually are some cold cases."

"Like Patty."

"Yes. Like Patty. Garcia is looking at the files for her."

Marilyn looked up from her menu. "I just had a memory," she said. "The blonde with the short hair…Hold on, I want to try something."

"Her name is Brittany," he said.

"Brittany." Marilyn opened her phone and looked up the Lads' Instagram. "I think I might know her by sight, but I never actually met her." Scrolling through a seemingly endless number of party photos, she finally clicked on one. She spread her fingers on the screen and in the enlarged image, the woman was in the background, blurred, not easily identifiable, dancing with a man. "Oh my god," Marilyn whispered. "Until now, Fran and Darby had a connection to the Lads, which is bad enough, but now Brittany also knew the Lads, and she's dead."

"Wow," Stade said. "Well done. Evidently, she knew the Lads, but did she also go to the life-drawing group?"

"I don't recall seeing her there, but she may have gone when someone else was modeling. Aren't your techies going through the Lads' social media? They should have caught this."

A waitress approached. They placed their orders of burgers, fries, and Cokes. "When in Rome…" Stade said.

"When in America in the fifties. You're not changing the subject away from the mistakes by the police, are you?" She raised her eyebrows and Stade smiled and shook his head. "Oh, I nearly forgot," she said. "I hate to bring this up because I don't believe it's true, and I don't want to insult Fran, but Rigby said that Fran had a sugar daddy."

"This Rigby person seems to have the inside track on everyone."

"She loves gossip." Marilyn chuckled. "I tried to see if Fran had a profile on a sugar baby website. There are tons of websites for that type of arrangement. Unfortunately, I couldn't get in without opening an account which costs money, and I would also have to supply government ID. And I don't cut it as a sugar daddy because I'm not an older, rich guy. But it crossed my mind that the police can probably circumvent all that rigmarole and see if it's true."

"Why does Rigby suspect there was a sugar daddy?"

"Rigby calls the women sugar cookies. I kind of like that." They both smiled. "She says there was gossip in the building, and Fran was being picked up at times by a limo and driver, although I think the car may have been courtesy of the law firm she was interning with part time. I'm wondering if that's who Fran left with the day of the storm. However, whenever I think something like this, I circle back to the fact that no one could go far on that day unless it was by boat."

Stade said, "Fran's disappearance is a mystery, all right, a mystery we're going to solve."

Their food arrived and between bites, Marilyn said, "I also looked on the sex abuser map and there are a cluster of offenders a couple of blocks over."

"I know the place you're referring to. It's a halfway house. Those men are on probation. I'll have a chat with the guy who runs it. Good work, Marilyn." He smiled, raising his eyebrows. "You from Houston?"

"Detroit. When my mom died, I lived with my aunt, and she'd had enough of snow and ice."

Surprise showed in his eyes. "I'm sorry."

Marilyn had found out early on that it was better to get *the story* out of the way. "It's okay. It was a long time ago."

He was watching her intently, sympathetically. "What happened?"

"Well, aren't you refreshing. Most people change the subject as fast as possible. Maybe since you deal with people dying, you're more open." She smiled and paused a moment. "It was an overdose."

He winced. "Jesus. And here I am showing you pictures of overdose victims. I'm sorry. This must be some seriously bad déjà vu."

"If it is, I don't really see it. I'm pretty objective now."

"Did you end up in foster care?"

"No, thank god. I should have, but my mother had one relative, her sister Elizabeth, who I called Zabi. My aunt took me in. I'm not overstating it when I say my aunt saved me from a life of prostitution and drugs, a life cut short. She taught me life skills, boundaries, self-respect, manners, right and wrong, and true happiness."

He said with admiration, "I'd say you're a survivor."

She paused and ate a bite of burger, then said, "Thank you. So far, so good."

"How did the overdose go down?"

"Oh, man. She was beaten up by a guy and ended up in the hospital, which got her clean. Then, when she got out of the hospital, she overdosed."

He nodded. "Quite common with addicts who get sober. When they relapse, they forget how long it had taken them to drive up their tolerance."

"Okay. Enough about me." She put her burger down and gazed at him. "Tell me about you."

"I'm a native Houstonian. One short marriage. No kids. My background included architectural college, which I abandoned for law enforcement, which helped lead to the divorce. My ex didn't want to be married to a cop. I didn't blame her. It's not always easy, but I like my job. I like solving the puzzle, although the world would be better without the victims, the pain."

They were interrupted by their server, and he paid for lunch. It wasn't lost on Marilyn that their conversation had slipped from businesslike to personal. They were talking like they were on a first date.

Leaving the restaurant, the oppressive heat was offset by the precinct's meat locker chill. He turned toward her. "I can email you the photos I showed you."

"Okay," she said, "I'll ask Rigby about the women, see if she knew any of them. It'd be great if the case could be solved, find the killer."

He smiled. "It would."

"Thank you for lunch." She took her phone from her handbag and dialed. "I'm calling for a ride."

"Take care," he said, and headed back to work.

Marilyn spent the afternoon checking social media sites for Fran sightings, but nothing was reported. She cleaned the apartment, poured a glass of wine, then sat on the balcony. The downtown high-rises changed color with the dimming light. Fran was out there somewhere.

Who else had succumbed—missing, or a victim of the killer, the faceless monster? Her own mother had become a casualty, but anyone could see the danger she courted. Fran had carefully cultivated her life, a safe and gratifying life. While no life is guaranteed to be free of peril, the odds for Fran to disappear had been so marginal. But where was she?

PART TWO:
One Month After

Chapter Nine:

Arrested

Stade phoned and said, "We'd like to come and talk with you."

Marilyn said, "Okay."

"Be there in an hour." His tone was a bit too curt for Marilyn's taste. Maybe her messed up childhood had caused him to back off. Maybe cops have too much drama to deal with on a day-to-day basis and find any baggage, someone who might be considered damaged goods, to be off-putting.

Zabi's voice said, *Or maybe he's just exhausted and busy, and it's not about you.*

Marilyn laughed and said aloud, "Ouch, Zabi. Thanks for cuffing my ears."

Marilyn called Rigby and told her the police were circling back. Rigby entered five minutes later, then Stade and Garcia arrived, and Marilyn introduced Rigby to the detectives and asked, "Has something happened?"

"We still haven't located Fran. We're here to talk to the Lads. Have you had any recollections? Anything jog your memory?" He lined up the photos she had viewed at the precinct on the breakfast bar.

Rigby tapped her finger on a photo. "This one. I met her at the Lads' parties, and she told me she had signed up for the Lads' Transcendalia workshop. She came to the Art Guild, but she took courses. She didn't come to the life-drawing,"

Marilyn looked closely at the photo and shook her head. "I don't know her."

Rigby said, "It's them two assholes next door, doing this shit." She jabbed her finger in the direction of the Lads' noise. "Them two perverts, assholes, they're the ones did it. It only makes sense."

"And you think that because…?" Stade asked in a way that sounded less than hopeful.

Rigby said, "They knew Darby, Fran, and this girl."

"And the woman, Brittany, you showed me," Marilyn said.

Stade said, "Hold on. You know all the victims too. It doesn't make you a serial killer, or even a suspect."

"Too many coincidences," Rigby said.

"As I told you, when I first got here during the hurricane and went next door, the Lads wouldn't let me into their apartment, which isn't their usual style." Marilyn took a stool at the breakfast bar beside Rigby. "Normally it's like Grand Central Station, people coming and going at will. Plus, Declan had scratches on his arm."

"Scratches?" The detectives glanced at each other, puzzled. Stade asked, "Where exactly were the scratches?"

"Oh crap. Sorry. I thought I told you about the scratches." Marilyn indicated an area on her left forearm.

Garcia said, "Could be from trying to restrain someone."

Stade slowly nodded. He closed his notebook. "We'll

have a chat with these *Lads*, get into their place. Take a look."

"With all their drugs lying around, they'll never let you in," Rigby warned.

Stade smiled. "Don't worry. We have our ways."

"Do Fran's parents know she's missing?" Rigby asked.

Stade took a long forlorn breath and nodded. "Yes. They confirmed how out of character it is for her to just disappear."

The tech waved Stade over, and he ambled along the short hall to Fran's bedroom. Garcia was opening kitchen cabinets. Marilyn stood, leaned her hip on the breakfast bar, and watched. "You guys already searched the apartment. What are you looking for?" she asked.

He looked over at her with a half-shrug. "The usual, a note naming the killer, a smoking gun. We decided to give it another look-see." He grinned at them.

"Maybe non-cops make better detectives than cops," Rigby responded. "We're open-minded."

"Really?" Garcia said dubiously.

"Yeah. Really. I think maybe cops approach a homicide case with your minds already made up. You know you're supposed to look at everything and everyone, but there's a built-in cop rule-book, and you go at it with preconceived ideas."

Garcia shook his head, perplexed. "Hope not."

Marilyn thought Rigby had a good point given how many women had met their fate before the police got suitably suspicious. Stade waved Marilyn back to the short hallway that ran past the bathroom to Fran's bedroom. Stade put his finger to his lips and gestured Marilyn near, then he pointed to the black-and-white-patterned wallpaper. At first, she didn't see what he was indicating, but suddenly she saw, in a black section of the print, a black dot about an inch in diameter with a gleam at its center. He steered her into the kitchen and said, sotto voce,

"Those guys next door drilled that hole and installed a spy-camera. It's so they could film the bathroom activity. Most people who live alone don't bother to close the bathroom door." He raised his eyebrows. "Probably there's something covering the camera on their side."

"Damn. I think there's a Hendrix poster taped to their wall," she whispered as she blushed and turned away to watch a tech take photos of the spyhole. "It's so invisible, I never would have noticed it."

Rigby nodded. "Yep, they have that Hendrix poster in their hallway."

Marilyn's face went hot, and she tried to think what images might have been captured, of her showering or worse. "Shit," she said again.

Rigby caught her expression and laughed. "It's not like you're never seen nekkid." She turned to Stade. "She models nude at the Art Guild."

Stade stared intensely at Rigby and said, "You realize there's a huge difference between voluntarily undressing and someone spying on you when you believe you are in the privacy of your home, don't you?"

It was Rigby's turn to blush. "Sure. I know that."

"This invasion of privacy is enough to arrest them. You two sit tight for now. We're going next door."

Rigby opened a bottle of white wine from Fran's fridge as they listened to the police thumping on the Lads' door. "Hey, want a fruit drink?"

Marilyn smiled. "Fruit drink, huh?"

Rigby said, "I perceive a drink made from grapes is fruity. And you know what the TV doc always says, *perception is reality.*" She poured them both a generous glass, and they sat at the breakfast bar. After a moment, there were footsteps and loud voices. And miraculously, like the end of a seemingly never-ending freight train, or barking dog, or headache, the throbbing music suddenly quit. They both sighed, then smiled.

The men's strident voices continued next door until

soon the uniformed officers emerged with the Lads in handcuffs and left with the techs following, carrying two paper bags.

Stade said, "Those guys are on their way to jail. There shouldn't be a problem nailing them with the invasion of privacy charge. The opening to set up the spy-cam on their side was big, the size of a grapefruit."

"The techs took something. Did you find some evidence?" Marilyn asked.

Stade said, "Well, the camera, of course. Plus, when things are in plain sight, we can seize them."

"What did you find?" Rigby asked. "We might be able to help if you're willing to share."

Stade shook his head. "Sorry, no can do."

"Well," Marilyn said. "You accomplished a lot just getting their music turned off."

Rigby suddenly went wide-eyed. "Hey, was it syringes you took? I saw some in their trash when I was there a few days ago. Just so you know, they gave all their ladies vitamin shots. They offered me those shots plenty of times, and I always turned them down. I wouldn't trust anything those guys put in my body, not to mention whether the syringes are sanitary."

"I was offered the vitamins, too," Marilyn said.

Stade said, "Vitamin shots."

The detectives glanced at each other and smirked, and she was suddenly certain Rigby had nailed it. The detectives left the building.

"If they didn't get the syringes, I hope they got something good," Marilyn said. "On cop shows, it has to be tied to what they're charging them with, which in this case is an invasion of privacy. Let's hope they don't mess it up."

"Talk about pressure, to find Darby Fairfield and maybe a serial killer." Rigby sipped her wine. "But, of course, tons of pressure can turn coal into diamonds."

"Yes, diamonds, or anything other than coal, gets

turned into dust." Marilyn shrugged. After another glass of wine, their conjectures, condolences, and expressions of dismay played out, Rigby headed to her apartment.

With the camera and the poster covering it on the Lads' side removed, a finger of light shone through the empty peephole. Despite the Lads being in jail, the peephole gave Marilyn the creeps and she covered it with a sticky note. And while she was relieved to have the Lads' apartment empty and quiet, obsessive thoughts of Fran and the other missing women kept her steeped in profound melancholy and frustration.

Three hours after Stade departed with Garcia and the Lads, he called Marilyn. "I'm coming back to see you."

"Oh…Okay."

She opened the door to Stade. He was alone, and his grim expression immediately revealed the purpose of his visit. "Fran?" she asked.

"Yes. I'm sorry," he said, wrapping his arms around her.

Aunt Zabi whispered, *Go ahead and feel the pain, and weep for your friend.*

And she did. Finally, cried out, she left his embrace, went to the bathroom, and pressed a cold compress to her blotchy and swollen-eyed face before returning to the living room. "I'm having trouble believing any of this is happening."

He hugged her again. "I know."

"Oh crap," she said. "I'm probably getting makeup on your suit or shirt collar." She broke away and inspected his shoulder and neck. "Phew, no makeup." She stepped away. "How did you find her?"

"We were dropping the Lads at the precinct when we got the call, and we went immediately to the scene. We found Darby Fairfield and Fran was nearby. They were on the banks of Buffalo Bayou near the Waugh Street bridge."

"That's maybe ten miles from here. How the hell did she get there?" She swiped at more tears. "It's been a fucking month. Why did it take so long to find her?"

"Even now, in some places the water is still high. We don't know a lot of things: where she died, when she died, how she got to the final location, and we don't know the cause of death yet." He sighed. "I talked to Fran's parents. They told me you two were close."

"Don't make me cry again, Detective." She took a deep breath, tamped down tears, and changed the subject. "By the way, did anyone look into the sugar daddy angle?"

"We're working on it. It will take a bit of time. We are all working twelve-to-sixteen-hour days. Which reminds me…" He looked at his watch, "I better get going." He stood and Marilyn followed him to the door, where he pulled her to him and kissed her gently.

Chapter Ten:

The After

Two days after the news of Fran's death, Marilyn woke before sunrise from restless sleep, wearily took a kitchen stool and her iced coffee to the balcony, and sat perched with her forearms on the rail, staring into the distance. The heat was oppressive, typical for mid-July. The rising sun faded into a scrim of vaporous cloud, hinting at the mugginess to come. She shielded her eyes to gaze as far as possible. Amazingly, considering the previously waterlogged landscape—and although some areas would still take time to dry—the roads were clear.

She went back to bed and, despite the caffeine, slept an hour. When she rose, she turned on TV news. While it was a relief to have the Lads gone, she desperately wanted to know if the authorities would be able to keep them in jail, and whether whatever evidence the detectives had found would tie the Lads to the deaths. Stade had made it clear he couldn't discuss internal police business, so the news was her only source of information.

Coverage had been exclusively in-depth Darby Fairfield, with Fran, Brittany, and others as also-rans. She suspected someone close to the detectives, or the detectives themselves, or perhaps Rigby, were leaking tidbits to the press. A few days ago, the reporters were salivating over the juicy morsel that the Lads had known all of the women, and suggested the Lads were guilty of multiple murders. Stade had said he was seeking how the women were connected, making their familiarity with the Lads the obvious thread stringing the murders together.

Flashing across the screen were photos of the Lads from their social media pages, including photos of Brittany at their parties. There were also ads from a spiritual website that promoted yoga studios, meditation retreats, and vegetarian cooking schools. The Transcendalia photo featured them posing with fake sprigs of marijuana.

At every commercial break, the talking-head promised a new development in the case, obvious suspense-building. Finally, the news anchor said, "We've received word this morning that autopsy results on Darby Fairfield and on Fran Dustin revealed no water in their lungs, which means they did not drown in the flood. Evidence has revealed that they died from a lethal dose of heroin."

The press had identified Darby Fairfield as a free spirit. Being a free spirit is easier when you have megabucks to do whatever your little heart desires. Darby, she of the embroidery-embellished Boho clothes, the daisy tattoos, and her long hair. Darby, who left her child with a surrogate so she could party, so she could play and chill. Did someone inject an overdose into her veins…for sport? If that was true, they did nothing to save her, didn't even make an emergency call for a hit of Narcan when she was in the drug's death throes.

Marilyn's phone rang. Caller ID read Rigby. "Hey, Rigby. How are you holding up?"

"This is total fucking shit. I keep thinking about Fran, how young she was. How much she'll miss out on. You?"

"The same. I've been paralyzed but I need to get my act together. I'll go back to my apartment at The Moderne and see what's what, but I'm sure nothing is salvageable. I'll take the bus, I guess."

"Jeebus, Marilyn. The bus, in this heat? And the stink from the stagnant water…Outdoors, it's like being in Satan's jockstrap."

"You just made me laugh. Thank you."

"At least I'm good for something." Rigby chuckled. "Well, take care."

"You, too." They hung up.

Midmorning, Marilyn boarded a bus to her flooded apartment. When she arrived, the owner was standing, shouting at a contractor for, as far as she could tell, quoting exorbitant prices. Marilyn wasn't surprised that the trades were gouging. Supply and demand, the law of the jungle. Doors of apartments had been forced open, including hers. Everyone had locked up as they left, as usual, not anticipating the total annihilation. She pulled her T-shirt up over her nose and mouth and gave her apartment door a shove. It swung open and as expected, the stink of mold and decay was stifling. There was no need to step inside, given the living, foaming, many-hued mold that crawled across the furniture and floors and climbed the walls.

So much for the complex's mid-century-modern historical pedigree. Houston is often criticized for its lack of historically significant architecture, but in some respects, given the weather and the humid climate, the city is justified. She took pictures to send to her insurance company and sauntered over to the owner.

He looked her way. "Greedy sons of bitches. They think everything's covered by insurance, but it's not."

Marilyn nodded, noncommittally. "So, guess I'm out of a job."

He shrugged. "Bulldozers are the only solution here."

"Well, you've got my number if you need a hand." She turned in a slow circle observing the complex for what would certainly be the last time and went to the parking lot to snap photos of her car. She would probably only get Blue-Book value, not enough to buy a new vehicle, and finding a used car wasn't feasible with the danger of snagging a cleaned-up flood-car, a zombie brought back from a watery grave with grit in the engine, screwed-up computers, phantom mold, and rust.

Chapter Eleven:

The Freed Ones

The next morning, Marilyn was sipping coffee as she watched TV news. The news anchor appeared with a backdrop photo of the Lads that media had scooped from social media and aired endlessly. It featured them in their dhoti pants and hipster-bun hairdos, with their surfboards, on Galveston Beach.

The reporter said, "These two men are being held on charges of invasion of privacy. There are suspicions they are also involved in other more serious crimes. Let's go live to Lance at police headquarters."

The scene switched to a reporter standing before a blocky brick building. He said seriously, "Apparently, these men are possible suspects in the murders of Darby Fairfield and Fran Dustin. They also knew at least two other women who died under suspicious circumstances."

The photo changed to a shot of Fran's building then

dissolved into another social media photo of a party in full swing inside the Lads' apartment. Despite the faces being blurred, Marilyn recognized Rigby by her costume-ish glory, along with two other artists from life-drawing. Two women's faces weren't blurred; they were Fran and Darby Fairfield. Behind them, people were dancing. On the sofa lounging or sitting on the Lads' laps were three women in skimpy club-wear, one of whom was Brittany. Declan had his hand up her skirt, and Shawn appeared to be motor boating a woman's cleavage. Someone close to the camera held a joint. On the coffee table were lines of coke and a bong, along with all manner of liquor bottles. Marilyn closed her eyes a moment and gave thanks that she wasn't present for that particular bacchanal.

The female anchor continued, "The men have been charged with invasion of privacy in connection with voyeurism of their neighbor, the same woman, Fran Dustin, whose body was found after the storm. Police have hinted at additional charges for *the Lads* as they are known, although HPD are unwilling to clarify what those charges are. Both have retained high-profile lawyers." She then abruptly altered her expression from concerned to delighted, and continued, "And on a lighter note, at the dog pound, a pregnant dog rescued from the hurricane gave birth to five puppies..."

Marilyn spent the remainder of the day making a list of her destroyed belongings and their cost, and looked up the value of her car, to submit an insurance claim. What she really needed was a steady paycheck, but who would be hiring?

Zabi's voice said, *If everyone is shooting at each other, make bullets. They already have the guns.*

"Indeed, Auntie." What services would be needed after a hurricane? Cleanup, demolition, drywall, painters, insurance adjusters. Unafraid of hard work and willing to get dirty, she sent out resumes and applications online to every cleanup company, disaster relief agency, and insurance company, until dinnertime.

Marilyn made a turkey and lettuce sandwich, but her appetite was resistant, and eating Fran's food magnified her grief. However, food, while unappealing, was mandatory, and the best place for mindless consumption was while one was distracted by the TV. She nibbled her sandwich and flipped channels hoping for a comedy, pausing when the oilman, Fairfield, flashed onto the screen. She unmuted the dialogue and caught the newscaster midsentence, "…in a stunning new development, two men arrested for invasion of privacy for spying on their female neighbor have just been released. These are the same men who were deemed persons-of-interest in the death of Darby Fairfield, and who also have connections to other murdered women."

Zabi said, *What the hell?*

"Yeah, and just, wow."

The Lads' defense attorney appeared at a media scrum talking oh-so-reasonably into a cluster of microphones. "There is no evidence the spy-cam in the wall between the two apartments was made by my clients. It could have been done by a cable installer, an electrician, any serviceman for legitimate or not-so-legitimate purposes. It could have been a previous tenant or the manager of the building. There is no smoking gun, or in this case, a drill. And as for the DNA on the syringes…"

Marilyn's jaw dropped. The detectives took the syringes after all. She tuned back in. "…DNA from both the men and the victims was on the syringes. However, drugs were not detected inside the needles."

The newscaster came back on the screen, and said, "Because the men's Transcendalia clients received vitamin injections, their lawyer argued successfully that there was no proof the contents of the syringes was toxic. At present, the men are not suspects in the women's murders. The DA has made the statement that Ms. Fairfield may well have been a victim of the nation's current opioid epidemic."

The next clip showed Fairfield looking like old-money personified. His appearance was tweedy despite the heat and his lightweight clothing. His handlebar mustache, brown brogues, and gold-topped wooden cane contributed to his horsey air.

Fairfield was rheumy-eyed with grief. His voice caught as he spoke. "My Darby. Two drug-dealing evil monsters killed my Darby and left her son an orphan." His volume strengthened. "The DA in this county is a coward, scared of his own shadow. Those lowlifes knew Darby, and other supposedly drug-overdosed women. How much more evidence do you need than the girls' blood on the syringes? They also spied on Darby's friend Fran in her most private moments. This isn't some great mystery!"

Fairfield waved his walking stick, punctuating his speech, as tears coursed along the lines and furrows of his face. "You don't have to be a Mensa candidate to join the dots. What better cover-up than to say, *oh my, the victim is an addict*, and blame it on the opioid crisis? Of course, the syringes are clean. Just wash them—all the better to laugh at the authorities. And the cops, and the DA, and the judge, all just fold and go along. And most laughable of all; they say the killers have an alibi, but their alibis are *each other*!" He laughed bitterly and began to push his way through the throng of reporters, then turned. "I'm doubling my reward to four hundred thousand for any evidence that will bring the perpetrators to justice."

The news anchor reappeared. "There you have it, fighting words from Baxter Fairfield addressing the media. This was right after the DA refused to move forward on charges and the persons of interest were released today. Now, *the Lads*, as they are nicknamed, are headed home. And as an aside, to clarify. Mr. Fairfield's reference to his grandson being left an orphan, the boy's father was killed in a car accident shortly after the child's birth."

Marilyn's phone rang with an unknown number, and she let it go to voicemail. Then she picked up the message.

A male voice said, "Hello, Marilyn. This is Mark Dustin, Fran's father, calling."

Chills ran down her arms, and tears started.

His voice continued, "We haven't met, but Fran told me so many good things about you, and I know the two of you are close…were close." He paused, then continued. "As you are no doubt aware, I've been covering Fran's expenses for law school. I've paid the rent on the apartment and the utilities until the end of the month. I should have asked you if you'd like to sublet, but I wasn't aware you were staying there until I talked again with the police this morning. Plus, I haven't been thinking too clearly the last while. The landlord has already promised the unit to someone, so the apartment must be vacated, which gives you just a week to find something else…I'm sorry."

He paused, then continued, "We're having a memorial for Fran soon. I'll post details on her Facebook page."

Zabi said, *A week of the Lads' music and their crazy friends is about all you can take. As they say, necessity is the mother of invention.*

"No problem," Marilyn whispered. "It's time to get my butt in gear." She wasn't sure where she'd go if she didn't find immediate work, maybe to a shelter. Shit.

"Anyway. Sorry…" He choked up, trailed off. "We'll be around soon to pick up her things. Thank you for being a good friend to Fran."

Hmmm…So, Fran's father was paying the bills. No sugar daddy after all.

Marilyn touched the call-back button and went straight to Mark Dustin's voicemail. She gave her sympathy, thanked him for his generosity, and said she hadn't intended to sublet. She added that he could call her anytime if she could help. *My God, how does a parent deal with the death of a child?*

She called Stade and got voicemail. "Stade, I'm sure Rigby's sugar daddy gossip is wrong. Fran's dad just called me and said he was paying her expenses, which backs up what Fran told me. Plus, she was interning at McCormick and Thorpe, part time, and it's possible that's where the car and driver, or limo, came from that Rigby said picked her up. I imagine her dad and the law firm can verify whether this is accurate. Also, a few days before the hurricane, she said she was dating a guy. I never met him. His last name is Rockwell."

Chapter Twelve:

The Session

Midmorning, the noises and laughter of sycophants followed the Lads along the hallway and into their apartment, and the pulsing of drums and bass restarted. Marilyn phoned Rigby. "The lads-holes just got back home. Their case was thrown out."

Rigby said, "I saw it on the news. Fairfield is a wreck, poor guy."

"I'd have thought by now the police would have enough evidence to say whether the Lads were the killers."

Rigby said, "It's amazing to me that those women seemed so disposable to the cops. I looked up the news reports. Because they were found naked in the homeless camp and were all overdoses, the police assumed they were homeless addicts and prostitutes. Those officers were a bunch of lazy sacks of shit, if you ask me."

"I saw a show the other day about a killer in Long

Island who dumped bodies at Gilgo Beach. The police went looking for one body and found something like ten. Stade said other Houston officers didn't think a serial killer was responsible, and of course the hurricane and the opioid crises haven't helped. But I know what you mean. It's hard to give them the benefit of the doubt. Seems like he and Garcia have been pretty much on their own investigating it."

"Yeah. I guess I've got twenty-twenty-hindsight."

"Now I'm scared of the Lads. Just because the judge sprung them doesn't mean they're innocent. I have to find a job and get the hell out of here."

"Can't say I blame you, especially considering their proximity, right next door." Rigby inhaled her cigarette. "If you want, you can sleep at my place for a few nights."

Aunt Zabi chuckled and said, *Not in my lifetime.*

Marilyn visualized the scene, the stink of cat pee and cigarettes, the cat hair, the dust, and roaches. "Thanks. That's generous of you," Marilyn said. "But I have to leave anyway. Fran's apartment will have a new tenant at the end of the month. I'll find something."

"Shit. What a clusterfuck," Rigby said despondently. "If I can help, let me know." They signed off and hung up.

Marilyn's phone rang. Stade said, "I got your message. Thanks for the heads-up. I'll follow those leads and see what's what."

"I'm sorry if you wasted your time on the sugar daddy thing."

"No problem," he said. "My detectively instinct tells me those dudes are back in their apartment, and you're being tortured by full-blast rap."

"Not to impugn your detectively instinct, but I suspect you can hear it in the background. Yes, the Lads are back since they beat the *rap*." She chuckled.

He snickered. "I saw what you did there."

"Do you think the Lads are guilty?"

"Yes, but the judge wants concrete evidence, forensics

and so forth. He doesn't have faith in my aforementioned detectively instincts."

Faking outrage, she said, "Hmph…Well, obviously, he's just a nitpicker. Any chance you'll be arresting them again soon? I'm super scared of them, especially now that they know their arrest was, in part, the result of me letting you into Fran's apartment. And with the other dead women being investigated…"

"They know it's not your fault," he said, "but of course logic might not prevail with those guys, particularly if they're looking for a scapegoat. The one with the scratches on his arm was the most pissed. Protect yourself. Don't be alone with them and move out as soon as possible. If I hear of an apartment for rent, I'll let you know."

"I have to find something quick because Fran's place has been sublet. I've got a week." Finding an apartment was one thing. Paying for it on unemployment and with only one paycheck in the bank was another.

"I'll ask around."

She said, in a flirty tone, "Well, Officer, witness protection would get me a place. You could recommend me."

He chuckled. "No witness protection for people who aren't witnesses and under threat."

"Do you need any help at the cop shop? I need a job."

"While many have said we *need help*, it was meant in a different sense. And hiring, 'fraid not." He paused a moment. "Can I take you to dinner tonight?"

"That sounds like a great idea, but are you sure it's okay to socialize considering Fran's case and the Lads, and all that?"

"If you turn me down, I might have to arrest you for resisting an officer."

Oh brother. "Would that involve handcuffs?" she asked. Her face went warm at the sexual implications.

He chuckled. "Only if you're into that sort of thing."

"I'm not, but I'll accept your dinner invitation," she said, laughing.

"I'll pick you up at seven."

They said goodbye, and no sooner had she hung up, the Art Guild called. Amazingly, the Art Guild building hadn't flooded. It was just noon so there was plenty of time before her date with Stade, and added bonus, it would get her out of the apartment and away from the Lads and their noise. The life-modeling wouldn't cover rent for an apartment. Still, adding in her upcoming settlement from the insurance company, she would hopefully be able to find shared accommodations for a while. She surfed the sparse online ads and sighed, closed her laptop, and headed for the modeling gig.

Rigby was right, the weather was a furnace. The bus shelter could have offered shade, but two scruffy men were unconscious on the benches. These guys weren't refugees from the storm, they were most likely addicts. They had the smell that was a staple of her childhood. That stink clung to the derelicts her mother hung out with. She was once again in The Crying House but shook away her thoughts as the bus arrived.

It had been more than a month since the storm, but the ride revealed a drowned city stumbling and fumbling toward recovery. Some roads and parking lots were still coated with a slurry of silt and garbage. Ironically, Houston needed a good rainfall to wash it clean. Many buildings were bisected by waterlines, at eight to ten feet. It was now apparent which houses were abandoned, awaiting the wrecking ball. Blue tarps draped roofs, covering the holes chopped for escape. There were still some mounds of debris scraped and hauled out for disposal, piled in sculpture-like monuments symbolizing both destruction and gritty human optimism and industry.

Marilyn entered the Art Guild and changed into her kimono in the ladies' room, then stared at herself a moment in the mirror as thoughts of Fran invaded—how she wouldn't be at her easel, there would be no more lovely sensitive drawings from her hand, how the world was dimmer without her spark, her energy, her smile.

She pushed away from the sink and entered the life-drawing lab. The usual artists were straggling in and setting up easels in a semicircle around the model's platform that abutted a wall. Earl arrived, and the moment they made eye contact, tears filled her eyes, and like a contagion, with no one speaking a word, Marilyn, Rigby, Earl, and two other artists were weeping.

Earl said, "I just can't believe it. How could this happen? I mean, all of it—the storm, Fran, the Lads, Darby Fairfield. There's so much awfulness. It's shocking, man." He moved close and took hold of her in an extended hug.

Earl was choir-boy handsome with lots of dark hair that flopped onto his forehead, big blue eyes fringed with dark lashes, and a good body. She had to admit, his hug felt damn good, but Stade came to mind. Nothing could compare to her chemistry with Stade. Rigby sidled up, and Earl let go of his hug, and they stood, wiping their eyes.

While Earl didn't live in Fran's building, he was a fixture at the Lads' frequent parties. Fran had discovered Earl's serious art chops and brought him to the figure drawing group years ago. Then the Lads had followed Earl to find out what the buzz was about. The Lads attended infrequently and had been expelled several times by Andy, the group organizer, for inappropriate or unruly behavior.

Rigby said, "I'm glad the Lads aren't here today. I can't fucking believe those assholes got sprung. I wish I knew what we could give the cops to help them out." She turned to Marilyn. "How you holdin' up?"

"I'm okay, I guess. I started sleeping on Fran's bed instead of the sofa. When I woke up, I felt so guilty."

"Oh, hon, don't. She'd want you to make use of her stuff." Rigby pooched out her bottom lip.

Marilyn nodded. "Okay, the group is in session. Gotta start." She stepped onto the model's stand and began a short pose.

Andy adjusted three photo lights on tripods to cast shadows and highlight Marilyn's contours. She started her timer with her toe and assumed the first short pose. The brief poses allowed her to undertake contortions impossible to hold for longer periods. She preferred dancelike poses for their fluidity, recalled from her long-ago ballet lessons. She lifted her arms and interlaced her fingers above her head, arched her back, and slid her right foot forward, her knee bent. When the timer dinged, Marilyn took the next pose, ankles crossed, bending to the right, left arm draped over her head. Jon arrived late with Pink Panther-like theatrical tiptoeing. His parody of silence elicited some chuckles. He quietly set up his art materials and easel and went to work.

After the short poses, Marilyn put on flip-flops and her robe and took a five-minute break. While she was in the bathroom stall, she heard a couple of female artists enter.

One of them complained, "This model is height-weight proportional, and she's too pretty."

The other replied, "I'll say. There's no *character.* Every sketch looks unrealistic, prosaic. Boring. Homely models are superior in that regard."

Marilyn had heard these criticisms before, and the men had agreed, discussing their art in clinical terms—composition, technique, creating a likeness, rendering, foreshortening, calculating proportion, and so on—but Marilyn knew the men's head-nodding agreement was bullshit. It was in their gaze as they carefully studied her curves and held up pencils against their thumbs measuring proportion. When Marilyn took her breaks, she walked past their drawings and saw their depictions. The female artists, without sex influencing their work, leaned toward the academic, channeling Da Vinci or Rembrandt. Meanwhile, the men created Vargas cheesecake, diaphanous Renoir renderings, or romantic impressionism.

Marilyn appreciated the women's adherence to artistic construct and boundaries; however, realistically, could men have it not be about sex when appraising a naked woman, their eyes wandering her every inch? There are porn fetish categories called NFCM—naked female, clothed male—and NMCF—naked male, clothed female. It was also possible that the dichotomy of her inaccessibility despite her nudity heightened their desire. She didn't doubt that she had hatched some masturbatory fantasies, and she quite enjoyed that thought. Did that make her a tease? Maybe. Sex—and the psychology thereof—works in mysterious ways.

Even if Marilyn knew the artists, she avoided contact with them during the session. A nude model with a group of clothed strangers, and friends, was a sensitive situation, and engaging with the artists crossed the profession's well-established boundaries. Marilyn liked the rules, and this downtown Art Guild group was sophisticated enough to tacitly observe them. For men who craved viewing a naked woman, this situation was a bargain. just a token fee and some obligatory scribbling.

For the long pose, Andy suggested she be partially draped. She slipped the kimono off her left arm, sat on the stool provided, and arranged the silk across her lap. When the session ended, Earl approached and offered Marilyn a ride.

"Thanks, but I could probably ride with Rigby," she said. "Save you going out of your way."

"Nah," Rigby interjected. "You should take him up on the ride. I like to smoke in my car, and you'll stink like an ashtray if you ride with me."

"Um…on second thought…" Marilyn said.

Earl nodded. "Your building is on my way. My place is in Seabrook, about halfway to Galveston, on the water, so I'm driving right by your place."

"I still think of it as Fran's place. Okay, I'll accept a ride, kind sir. Much appreciated."

Chapter Thirteen:

Stade

Marilyn climbed into Earl's very ordinary, older, white van that had some dents with body filler and others that needed to be hammered out. Inside, it was worn, but clean. "So, you're a nonsmoker?"

"Yes. Tried it once, but it made me sick. That was enough for me."

"Me too," Marilyn said, looking into the back compartment, which was fitted with indoor-outdoor carpet. "Do you haul art, paintings on canvas, in this?"

"No. I'm not into painting on canvas, just works on paper. I buy things at yard sales and fix 'em up, sell 'em on eBay. Stuff like that."

"You live by the water, but this van doesn't look like it flooded."

"It didn't. I crashed at a friend's place that didn't flood, overnight. The van would have flooded at my house because while my place is on stilts, I park under the house."

She recalled phoning him the day after she got to Fran's place, and he'd said he was at home. He was over-explaining. Or was he? Maybe she was overthinking. With all that had happened maybe her memory was off. Maybe she had called him later than she thought. Or maybe the flood had receded really fast where he was. "Well, as you know," she said. "I'm looking for a place to live, so please let me know if you hear of anything."

"For sure," he said.

She paused, but he didn't offer for her to stay at his house. They made small talk until he pulled into the parking lot in front of Fran's building. He put his hand on hers and said, "I'm so sorry about Fran."

"I know. Me too. It's surreal." She sighed, climbed out, and shut the door.

He rolled down the window. "Hey, would you care to go to dinner soon?"

"I'd like that a lot."

"Thursday at seven, at Empire Grill?"

"Thursday it is. Let's meet there," she said.

When Marilyn left the elevator, it was apparent from the party din that celebrations of the Lads' release were in full swing. Their door was ajar, and partiers were standing in the hall drinking and laughing. Marilyn tried to duck into Fran's apartment unnoticed. As she inserted the key, an inebriated enormous man, the type of steroid monster whose shoulders started at the top of his head, lumbered over and intercepted her.

He said, "So you're the bitch got the Lads arrested?" He blocked her entrance with a hairy tree trunk of an arm across the doorway, his hand on the doorjamb. Acrid sweat mingled with the sharp fumes of beer.

"Excuse me!" Marilyn said loudly. She turned the key, ducked under his arm and through the door. She turned and pressed the door against his bulk, but he held it open. Unable to compete against his strength she tried a different strategy and jumped away. The door flung wide, hitting the wall, and he staggered forward and fell. She stepped back quickly, pulled out her phone. "Get out of here or I'll call the cops!"

As the big guy hauled himself up, a normal-sized man entered. He asked, "What's happenin'?"

The drunk slurred, "This is the bitch that turned in the Lads."

The friend said, "Really?" He looked her up and down, also inebriated, just not as much as the goon.

Marilyn was tempted to set them straight but arguing with sozzled jerks never ends well. Instead, she retreated. "If you don't leave right now, I'm calling the police."

"We're going," the friend asserted. "C'mon buddy." He put his hand on the big guy's shoulder. "Let's leave the little lady alone."

"Fucking bitch! She's th'one tole the cops that Declan had scratches," the drunk spat. He started scrabbling with his belt and zipper. "I'll show'er what we do with bitches."

"Oh, for Christ sakes," Marilyn whispered, rolling her eyes.

"What you laughing at, bitch?"

Marilyn held up her phone. "I'm not joking. You're trespassing and just threatened to rape me. Do you think the Lads want the cops coming around today?"

The big guy hesitated.

His buddy said forcefully, "C'mon! Let's go, dude!" and they backed out the door, the friend still with a hand on the drunk's shoulder, the big jerk thrusting his pelvis in her direction.

When they cleared the doorway she lunged, slammed the door, and turned the deadbolt. Shaking, she leaned against the door, feeling the vibration of the Lads' party, and when her heart rate dropped to normal, she finally peeled herself away.

Well, that happened, Zabi said.

"Yep," Marilyn said aloud. "Looks like I have more to fear than just the Lads."

She checked the time, three hours until Stade would pick her up for their date. It had been a while since she'd been on a date. Was it a date? He was blending it with his detective work. She googled him. He had no social media presence but had been tagged by other people. The photos that included him were mainly backyard barbecues, other people's weddings, and a few of him on a boat and at sporting events. No women gushing over their sexy-cop boyfriend.

Given recent events, Marilyn decided to start getting ready to move. She took Fran's rolling suitcase from the back of her closet. She stacked her own meager belongings of clothes, undies and shoes on a dresser, then she paused a moment, assessing whether she should appropriate some of Fran's clothes. Yes, it was stealing. She gazed heavenward and said, "Sorry Fran." She sighed and shrugged, and assembled a few of Fran's outfits, along with shoes and accessories next to her clothes on the dresser. Fran's closet also yielded a date outfit, a red wrap dress and gold sandals.

At the appointed hour, Marilyn opened the door to Stade. He was wearing a dark suit and classic white business shirt, no tie, and he stood looking toward the Lads' apartment where the door was still open with partiers spilling into the hall. He turned to her, and their eyes met and held a moment too long, and something lightning-charged skipped along their sightline and invaded her veins like a shimmering thread. The jolt tempered her breathing to short, shallow breaths high behind the breastbone. Did he feel it too?

She had noticed his features when they last met, how they were generous, almost too big, but against all odds, they didn't compete and fit uncannily well. His nose and jawline were prominent, his full lips sculpted, and brown eyes wideset, his left eye with a particle of hazel that inexplicably put her in mind of a calico cat. She knew, from studying and drawing the human form, that attractiveness isn't determined by wide brushstrokes, but measured in millimeters, and beauty isn't the twin sister of pretty. Pretty is cute, a weak kitten, while beauty is a ferocious magnificent lion, often skirting the border of homeliness.

In the parking lot, Stade held the door to his SUV for her. Marilyn asked, "No police car today?"

"Disappointed?"

"Sure. I wanted to run the siren."

"Is that what the kids are calling it these days?" Closing the door cut off their laughter.

He turned into the driveway at Eddie V's Restaurant, a first-rate steak and seafood house. Shit. She'd never eaten at this restaurant, namely because she and the men she dated couldn't afford it's five-star prices. "Um, Stade…" she said hesitantly, "this establishment is out of my paygrade."

"It's on me," he asserted, and pulled up to the valet-parking stand. The lighting was romantic, the décor plush, the servers outfitted in classic black and white. They ordered drinks, hers a vodka martini, with blue-cheese-stuffed olives, not dirty, and his, a scotch, McAllen 18.

They started with oysters. A trio played jazz standards, "Cry Me a River," "Round Midnight," and some she recognized but couldn't remember their titles. They ordered a shared steak and asparagus. His detached demeanor had dissolved, replaced with a warmth that felt stable, even a little fierce, like loyalty perhaps. He lifted the thick crystal rocks glass and tipped the amber liquor to his lips, lips that she very much wanted to kiss. When he placed the glass on the bar, he covered her hand with his. He looked into her eyes, and the sweet thrill came back, and his usual slight smile returned.

He said, "What's your favorite movie?"

"Hmm…It's not my favorite movie ever, but I really

liked *Who Is Jackson Pollock*. It's a documentary about a lady who thinks she bought an original Pollock at a thrift shop, and she sets about trying to verify it." She added, "Let me guess; your favorite movie is *Heat*."

He laughed. "That obvious, huh?"

"I know it's hardly a chick-flick, but I love that movie," she said, chuckling. "It's got everything: love affair, heartbreak, the most massive shootout ever in the history of movies…"

Stade nodded agreement. "What was your best vacation ever?"

"Oh…that's easy. Puerto Vallarta. My aunt took me to this place overlooking the Pacific. Stunning. Waves crashing through the night, tropical everything. I'd go back there in a heartbeat." She smiled at the memory. "You?"

He said, "Maybe a time I spent in Costa Rica, but I like the sound of yours."

The waiter interrupted, and after a second leisurely drink and small talk, he drove her back to the building. She unlatched the car door but didn't push it open. "I'm pretty freaked out about the Lads being back. It'd be great if the case could be solved, find the killer. Or if it's the Lads, get them locked up."

"It would, but then I'd have no excuse to come see you."

He reached across, slipping his hand under her hair, cupping her jawline, sending a torrent of goosebumps down her neck and torso. His hand was warm, she was willing, and he leaned in to kiss her tentatively, then more assertively. She reciprocated.

He slowly moved back, watching her, and said, "Well."

"Well."

Stade said, "I've wanted to kiss you since the first time I saw you."

"Are you sure it wasn't because I came bearing pizza?"

He smiled. "I'm sure. Do you want me to walk you to your apartment, seeing as how the nasty Lads are back?"

She smiled and sighed. "Thank you for the offer. As much as I like the idea of a bodyguard, I think I'll be safe. Plus, it's pretty weird…with the party going on there's no privacy. It's like having chaperones."

"Call me if the Lads act up."

She nodded, stepped out of the car, and at the door she waved. He watched until she stepped into the elevator.

Upstairs, the Lads were still entertaining a rowdy crowd. She made it into the apartment without incident, put on Fran's sound-eliminating headphones and turned on the TV. Between reliving Stade's devastating kiss and considering his gentlemanliness, she binge-watched a series of shows about people working on a chartered yacht.

Finally, she switched to the news, which featured shootings, road rage, and car accidents. The next item showed an abbreviated clip of Fairfield and photos of the Lads. She removed the headphones to head to the bathroom and noticed the noise from the Lads' apartment had dropped. Given that it wasn't quite midnight yet, the party had ended unusually early, and their current sounds matched Fran's TV, which meant they were also watching the news. Their conversation was loud enough over their TV that she could almost make out their words. Placing her ear against the peephole in the wall, she tuned them in.

Shawn said, "Fookin' Fairfield. Old codger, but he's got boatloads of cash, yeah? He's out to git us, in't he?"

Declan said irritably, "Oy mate. Them detectives ahn't half daft now, in't they? Got their noses up our arses now, don't they? We're good for now, but that bloke Stade will be back, I can tell. We'll just tell 'im to sod off, roight?"

Shawn said, "Bugger 'em, mate. I don't give a shite about 'em swingin' dicks. Reckon they got nuthin on us or we'd still be in the pokey."

Declan laughed, paused, and said a few indecipherable words. Shawn said, "Shut yer gob, you stewpid eejit."

"There's no one here but us, mate!" Declan said indignantly, "Untwist yer knickers."

"Yeah, yeah. How much cash we got left, mate?" Shawn asked. "Hand me that joint, mate."

"Ah got it lit perty good, roight?" They both chuckled. "Round twenty-G's, I reckon," Declan said, laughing.

Shawn laughed again. "Just hope it don't mess wiff our hair conditioner."

Marilyn shook her head. What were they talking about? Sometimes she was amazed they were all speaking English.

"Fairfield. His daurter, that Darby. Bloody hell. Stewpid as a box of hammers."

"Yeah, and batshit barmy, that one." He paused. "Oy mate, we're out of jail. That's what's good. That guy in my cell, a fookin' prat. Nonstop whinging. Well, I'm knackered. Gonna get some kip. G'night, mate." Footsteps went to one of their bedrooms.

Marilyn replaced the sticky note on the peephole and checked that the doors to the hall and the balcony were locked. She turned off the TV, crawled into bed, and amid thoughts of Stade, her desperate circumstances, apartment and job hunting, and more Stade, she fell into a restless sleep.

Chapter Fourteen:

The Debacle

A primitive cry pierced Marilyn's sleep. Her eyes snapped open, and she was instantly out of bed. Tiny hairs on the back of her neck bristled. The darkness was dense, velvety. Faint sobbing, and then two thumps reached her.

She heard movement in the Lads' apartment. Slowly, quietly, she edged around the bed. Then crept from the bedroom into the hall, peeled away the Post-it, and looked through the peephole, which, with the camera removed, was almost an inch across. The much larger spyhole on the Lads' side allowed a fairly wide view. The Lads' floorplan was the mirror image of Fran's. Directly ahead was their hallway and bathroom, to the left their living room, and to the right a bedroom door. Low-wattage lights were glowing and there was the flickering blue of a TV or computer.

A man came into view and moved closer. He was a

side of beef in a hoodie and baseball cap, probably a weightlifting enthusiast, but not the monster who had accosted her earlier. A second man appeared. This one was tall with a slight frame and stooped posture. He also wore a hoodie and ball cap. She couldn't see their shadowed faces.

The fit guy opened the door to Shawn's bedroom. He held up the type of flashlight cops use as a billy club, illuminating Shawn, who had scrambled into her sightline, and stood at the foot of his bed. He mouthed *please, please*, probably whispering, given the silence. The thin man raised a handgun with a silencer.

She clamped a hand over her mouth to stifle a gasp or scream. Time slowed. The man squeezed the trigger. Red mist and brain matter were suspended in the air. Shawn fell back on the bed, arms wide.

Marilyn, in shock, still covered her mouth. Her stomach was clenched, her hands shook. Adrenaline, sometimes a curse, sometimes a gift. The earlier noises must have been the men shooting Declan.

The men came her way, and the flashlight swung in her direction. She turned and flattened her back to the wall beside the peephole and held her breath. The man with the gun whispered, "Did you hear something?" They went silent, listening. "Look. Here's the fucking hole *the Lads* got arrested for," he said with disgust. "They did it to video the chicks next door. In the fucking bathroom. Degenerate assholes."

Look who's talking, Marilyn thought.

Footsteps came close. The killers' flashlight made a laser beam through the hole. Marilyn gritted her eyes shut. The man with the gun said, "What can you see?"

"Nothing. Just the hall and bathroom." he said, right next to her ear.

"What a pair of lowlifes, these two."

When she was certain the shooters had moved away, she looked through the peephole. They went through the Lads' apartment, opening closets and cabinets, searching for something. So, a shakedown, a drug deal gone bad, maybe a gambling debt, or a straight-up robbery.

Their footfalls left the apartment and moved quickly past her door. Hugging the wall, she tiptoed to the bedroom window. She moved the curtain an inch and watched them approach a dark Jeep. The first four digits on its plates were PITA, as in flatbread, or the acronym for *pain in the ass*, easy to remember.

The fit guy suddenly turned, and despite his face being in shadow, there was a glint in his eyes as they locked with hers. She moved away. Could he identify her if he saw her again? Only a narrow sliver of her face had been visible, plus it was dark. But more to the point, he knew someone had seen them. Tire noise indicated their departure, and taillights vanished a block away. What to do?

She dialed Stade and got voicemail. She didn't leave a message.

Zabi said, *Didn't the Lads just say they stashed twenty grand somewhere?*

"Hell yeah, Zabi. And wasn't I thinking how broke I am?" She pulled on navy shorts, a black tank top, and Fran's slippers for her mission, which was twofold. If they required an ambulance, she'd call 911, but if a hearse was appropriate, she'd find their stash. No love lost here. She poked her head into the hallway and then raced into the Lads' apartment.

The stink was an assault; earthy-iron blood, stale cigarette and marijuana smoke, and spilled alcohol. She flicked on her phone's flashlight and went to Declan on the sofa. He lay with vacant glassy eyes. A star-shaped bullet hole with singed edges was at the center of his forehead. His nose was crushed and blood covered his mouth, chin, and neck. She turned his head slightly. A large portion of the back of his head was blown out. No need to check his pulse.

For a moment she let her feelings distill and her eyes

adjust to the semi darkness. The Lads' obnoxious behavior, the possibility they were serial killers, and that they most likely had done something to Fran, were reasons enough to fend off sadness, but the horror of their murders would likely haunt her forever.

She went to the bedroom. Shawn's condition matched Declan's. The clusters of flies that usually buzzed at their windowpanes—so many you'd think the Lads lived near a cattle ranch—had found him and were already busy. She backed away from the corpse and went to the kitchen.

According to movies, the freezer is the ideal hiding place for guns, drugs, and money, but she was rewarded with only a half-gallon of Ben and Jerry's vanilla and a bottle of vodka. She put the vodka on the countertop among dirty plates, pizza crusts, and half-empty glasses. Several roaches scurried away.

She propped up her phone so the flashlight lit the kitchen countertop, then threw care and orderliness to the wind as she swept jars of salsa, jam, peanut butter crashing from the cabinets, grabbed boxes, ripped them open, poured, flung, emptied their contents—cereal and crackers, Doritos, and Cheetos, tortilla chips and noodles. Broken glass and chips crunched underfoot.

Where the fuck was their money? Maybe the bad guys took the stash. After all, the peephole hadn't allowed her to see their entire search; however, crossing the parking lot to their car they'd been emptyhanded. Just a few more minutes. The building's other tenants were conspicuous by their absence. With good reason, they were afraid. Adrenaline was flooding her system, making her hands shake and perspiration form on her forehead and upper lip.

The toilet tank and vanity were empty. In Shawn's room, trying not to look at his corpse, she dumped the contents of his dresser drawers on the bed around him, then moved her arm like a wand under his mattress but found only a folding knife and several bunched, stiff tissues. Ugh. She pulled down some flyspecked posters and looked behind framed pictures, searching for a wall hideaway.

She repeated the procedure in Declan's bedroom without luck. Back in the living room, Rigby's life-drawing of Marilyn was on the coffee table. Rigby had written *the lovely Marilyn Connor* across the picture and signed her name. She scanned the room. The Lads' conversation came back to her. Shawn had said, "…got it lit…" Then "…our hair conditioner."

She'd assumed he was referring to lighting the joint, but maybe instead of 'lit' he'd said, "…*hid*" and instead of "hair conditioner" he'd said, "*air conditioner*". She dragged a kitchen chair under the air-return in the ceiling, stood on it, and turned the wingnuts holding the louvered panel. It fell open, and she dropped the dirt and hair clogged filter on the floor.

In the duct was a shoebox amid copious rodent droppings. Pulling the box out caused an avalanche of shit, and she ducked away but couldn't fully avoid the rain of pellets. She stepped down from the chair and shook the crap from her hair. Inside the box were stacks of well-worn, used fifties and hundreds, held together with rubber bands, no bank wrappers, or dye-packs. Perfect.

She picked up the TV remote and clicked the off button, but instead of going black, the screen changed images, and she was looking at herself. Now what? One of the Lads' laptops was on their kitchen table and when she moved it, the view on the TV changed. The laptop was videotaping and sending the image to the television. Between the peephole and the video-cam the Lads were obviously voyeurs. "Come to mama," she whispered. When she closed the laptop, the TV went black.

Shawn's laptop was on his bedroom dresser, videotaping his bed. As she closed his laptop, a gleam on the floor caught her eye. She nudged the fringe of a scuzzy throw rug next to the bed and uncovered a large, heavy gold ring.

The sound of a car disturbed the quiet. She pocketed

the ring, snatched up the Lads' laptops, the vodka, and the box of money, and rushed back to Fran's apartment, securing the deadbolt and the chain lock. She checked the parking lot through a slim gap in the curtains. The same Jeep was parked with one occupant in the passenger seat, the driver running, headed into the building.

Unlike the killers' first quiet foray, this time his steps in the hall were a loud gallop. He entered the Lads' apartment, slammed their door, and turned on lights. Marilyn moved to the peephole and held her breath, watching him as he stood scanning the space. He exhaled, and shouted, "Fuck, fuck, fuck, fuck!" pissed that the place was tossed. She tiptoed into the kitchen and took a can of wasp spray from under the kitchen sink—poison that could hit an intruder thirty feet away. She backed into the bedroom and silently closed the door.

Who was he? Not the giant drunk, but possibly the other man, the one who talked the big drunk into leaving. Over time so many people had invaded the Lads' apartment and knew about their drug dealing; it could be anyone. But this was weird. Why did he come back after they killed two people? Had something spooked them the first time? Or was he still hunting for the Lads' drug money? More significantly, did the killer assume whoever had tossed the Lads' apartment was someone nearby? Someone in an adjoining apartment? Someone he had locked eyes with at Fran's window?

Fear like she'd never experienced gripped her. The scenario would parallel a hundred movies—the door splintering, swinging open, a large hand over her mouth. The business end of a gun bruising her temple; the man demanding the money. There was nowhere to hide and if she tried to leave the building, he would hear her running down the hall and the stairs, chase her down and kill her. She wanted to look through the peephole again, but she was paralyzed with terror. Her heart was pounding, and her hands had grown damp. Could he hear her breathing?

Next door, the thumps and bangs were systematic, room by room objects were being thrown around. Marilyn's hands trembled and she fumbled the wasp spray and nearly dropped it. She imagined the clatter of the can on the floor, him stopping, coming her way. After what they did to the Lads, it was likely, even if she gave them the money, he'd rape, torture, shoot her—the flashlight coming at her, the crunch as it connected with her skull like biting celery. She told her imagination to shut the fuck up and placed the wasp canister carefully on the bed, within reach.

The murderer's search was taking an eternity. She grimaced thinking of robbing of two dead men. It wasn't something she'd ever thought would be in the cards for her. What did this theft make her? Smart? Callous? No better than the looters roaming the city after the storm? How to justify this crime of opportunity? As the law of the jungle, as necessity, as survival? She wasn't sure what it said about her, although Zabi had often referred to Marilyn as resilient, adaptable. Or could this be genetic or learned behavior, culled from her grifting mom, who traded sex for other pleasures, necessities, and comforts—everything a transaction?

After about ten minutes, the killer left, running down the hall and stairs. She watched the Jeep drive away, but the threat was too close. Now she was certain they weren't done and they'd be back for her. The smart move might be to put the money and the ring back where she'd found them, but that might lead to all sorts of unintended consequences. Besides, she wanted the money, needed it. She transferred the cash from the box to a tote bag.

Time for logic. She tiptoed into the Lads' apartment where, listening intently for the murderers' return, she used the TV's remote to delete the television's video memory. She balanced the television on a skateboard and rolled it to the cluttered trash-chute room, where she picked up a broken office chair and swung the wheels at the screen, making a substantial crack.

Back in Fran's apartment fight or flight kicked in, and she chose flight. Satisfied that since she was not on a lease and Fran's dad paid the rent and utilities there was nothing to identify her, she shoved clothes she'd arranged earlier, the gold ring in its baggie, the tote bag of money, the vodka, and the Lads' laptops into Fran's rolling suitcase. With her hair tucked under a baseball cap, she left, leaving the key on the kitchen counter.

If the killers came back, they would probably stop in the front parking lot near the exterior stairs they climbed before, so she humped her suitcase down the interior emergency-exit stairs to a fire door at the back of the building. Plenty of tenants used this door, and she'd never heard the alarm sound, but maybe it was on a timer to operate overnight. Holding her breath, eyes shut, she backed up against the door's latch-bar and pushed.

Chapter Fifteen:

The Getaway

The security door opened without sounding an alarm. Marilyn exhaled, and bumped Fran's rolling suitcase over the threshold into the rear parking lot. The sultry air was cloying. She moved away from the building into shadows and looked back. Weak light shone in a few windows. In one a figure appeared to be pacing. She strode across the pavement and through a weedy perimeter to a long laneway riddled with potholes and lined on both sides with garages. One dim motion-activated fixture came on. Aware that cell phone calls to 911 were untraceable, she dialed and informed the operator of the dead bodies, the address, and the car make and model with the tag digits of *PITA*. She declined the operator's request for her name and number and hung up.

Emerging from the lane onto a side street, she walked close to dark shrubbery that separated lawns and the sidewalk. She googled extended-stay cheap motels on her phone. The closest was about two miles away. She called and amazingly, at this ungodly hour, a woman answered, "Tout Suites. All suites all the time!"

Marilyn said, "Hi. I'm so glad you answered at this time of the morning."

"No problem," the woman said warmly with an Asian inflection, "you'd be surprised how many people arrive on business at four in the morning. What can I do for you?"

"Well, I just had a major fight with my boyfriend, and I'm afraid of him. When he went out for a cigarette, I threw some stuff in my bag and took off."

"Honey, I can relate." The woman clucked. "You're not the first, and you won't be the last. You need a room?"

"You read my mind." A car approached. She spun toward the sound and ducked into some shadows. A sedan, the wrong shape for the boxy Jeep, drove by without slowing. Jittery, she picked up her pace.

"You're in luck. We've got one suite. I was about to turn on the vacancy sign. We didn't flood in the hurricane, and we've been packed until now. Anyhow, it's a nice efficiency with a queen bed and a kitchenette. "

"I'd like to pay cash. Is that okay? Don't want to leave a credit card trail."

"Smart girl. No problem, but I'll need a week's deposit."

"Great. I'll be there pretty soon."

Back streets were deserted but the Jeep could appear at any moment, and despite her dark clothing, headlights could highlight her pale limbs. In windows, yards, and driveways, light and shadow morphed into fearsome forms. A cat jumped onto a fence startling her. Movement in the underbrush, armadillos or possums, started her heart pounding and she hiked more briskly, flinching at every sound or motion. First, she'd been afraid of the Lads for killing the women, and now she feared another pair of killers. How many murderers could one gal run into?

A few blocks into her hike, Marilyn was perspiring and parched. Her clothes were damp and strands of hair that escaped the baseball cap plastered her skin. Sweat burned her eyes, her feet were swollen with blisters forming. The going was slow as the suitcase's wheels caught on debris or cracks in the sidewalk, its handle repeatedly slipping from her sweaty fingers. She was losing strength. She called Rigby and reported to her voicemail that the Lads were dead, and that she was gone.

A headache was forming. Zabi said, *Bet you'd kill for a car right now.*

"Amen, Zabi."

And then, as the sun broke over the horizon and bathed the squat houses and industrial buildings in a gold glaze, she turned a corner and the hotel's black-and-white sign, with *Tout Suites* in script surrounded by a decorative border, an attempt at a French flavor, appeared above the long narrow building. Invigorated, she picked up her pace, finally pulling open the door to a blast of frigid air.

She paid with the Lads' cash. At the end of the hall, she entered her accommodations, which spanned one end of the rectangular building. The unit was a linear layout of kitchenette, living room, bathroom, and bedroom. Miniblinds above the kitchen sink opened to a view of the parking lot, which thank God, was missing last night's Jeep. The furniture was woodgrain veneer, appliances were miniature and worn, and the bed had a magenta-and-teal duvet which had presumably been chosen to disguise any stains. She removed and heaped it in the closet.

The bathroom separated the living area from the bedroom. A sofa and coffee table faced a sliding door. She opened the yellowed vertical blinds which revealed a courtyard with a small pool and groups of banana and palm trees along a high fence. The pool needed replastering, the fence needed painting, and the pebbled concrete slabs underfoot needed power washing. Maybe she could score a job here. There were times when Marilyn was happy for her humble beginnings, like now, when this tired motel was as welcome as any penthouse suite.

She checked for evidence of bedbugs behind pictures, in the mattress seams, between sheets, the headboard and wall, and found none. She slipped the do-not-disturb hangtag on the doorknob and locked the deadbolt and chain-lock. The flimsy lock on the sliding door concerned her, and she found a broom tucked beside the fridge, unscrewed its handle, and placed the dowel in the sliding door's track. While her security measures were to thwart the killers' entry, she also took the tote bag of cash into the bathroom for safekeeping from motel staff armed with a master key and a coat-hanger to slip the chain-lock. She stripped and showered away her dried sweat. Then, sitting on the side of the tub she soaked her swollen and blistered feet in cold water.

Her exploding overlapping thoughts were like popcorn popping, until unexpectedly, a force within took over and started her tears streaming. Tears for the violence, for the fear, for the lives of dead women, two dead men, and she wept until her wretchedness and adrenaline were washed away.

In panties and T-shirt, she sat on a towel on the sofa and gazed out at the courtyard. What was her plan? How dangerous were the killers? She almost giggled at her thought. Obviously, the answer was *very*. She collapsed on the bed and lay still, exhausted, thankful for the few hours of sleep she had managed before the Lads were murdered.

The main worry was whether those murderers could track and find her, and for a moment she faltered, convinced she should skip town. Then she reversed her thinking. Screw that. The murderers were two-bit hoods, punks, who wanted to score whatever cash and drugs the Lads had lying around. It wasn't as if they were sophisticated hitmen. They couldn't know there was a 911 call and even if they did, they wouldn't have the knowhow to find her. They weren't cops so they couldn't get security camera footage from local businesses. They were strangers to her, and she to them. They were unaware she'd swiped the Lads' drug money. Even if the killer that was in good shape had seen her in the window, it was Fran's apartment, not hers. Plus, she hadn't seen their faces clearly, couldn't identify them. Maybe running had been premature, and she didn't need to hide. Oh well, she had to leave the apartment anyway. In any case, a new phone was probably a good idea.

The only weak link was probably Rigby, who might guess her whereabouts because this was the closest motel to the apartment building. However, even though Marilyn didn't know Rigby's character well, and they certainly weren't close, she hoped Rigby wouldn't give her up. All in all, the coast was reasonably clear. And a strange calm settled as she became confident the men hadn't followed her, couldn't chase her down.

She reached across the adjacent pillow to the nightstand and took a folder that extolled the Tout Suites' features. There was what they referred to as a dining room; a space off the lobby stocked with breakfast fodder and snacks, and a small gift shop. She got up and pulled on Fran's floral-printed capris, a white T-shirt, and flip-flops.

Zabi's voice said, *Leaving your money in the room is asking to be robbed.*

"I know," she said aloud. She looked in cabinets and the closet but found no safe. If the motel staff were crooked, they would search her room while she was at breakfast. They would probably be a team; the check-in lady and a maintenance guy or maid. The money was portable in her tote bag, but she didn't want to lug around the Lads' laptops, so she shoved them between the mattress and box spring. But she still wanted to know whether the staff were thieves. She needed to trap them in the act, not boobytrap the place; this was intel-gathering.

Marilyn rummaged in her purse for a quarter, closed the sliding closet door as she held the quarter between the door's edge and the jamb, leaving the door ajar the width of the coin. Next, she tore two small corners from the hotel brochure and closed them in the lowest dresser drawer's overlapping edge. Then she ran a length of white dental floss across the top of the white fridge and its door and a couple of inches down the front. She stacked some ceramic cereal bowls on the floss on top of the refrigerator.

The Asian woman at the front desk said good morning through a big smile as Marilyn headed to the dining area and she smiled back. From the buffet counter Marilyn observed the woman take out her phone and turn her back.

There was a basket of muffins, butter, orange juice, and coffee—not exactly a feast, but she couldn't have been more grateful if it were eggs benedict, caviar, and mimosas. Three male guests were at separate tables, two in business attire, the third in vacation wear. They all glanced up, and vacation-guy nodded her way. She gave him a small smile, and the other two returned to studying their phones. Vacation-guy was either absentmindedly looking in her direction, stalking her, or ogling. He seemed somewhat intense, but she assumed that after the events of last night she was on high alert and paranoid, and rightly so, and she relaxed. Last night. It was just last evening that she and Stade had kissed. It seemed unbelievable that he'd picked her up to go to dinner just twelve hours ago. She loaded a tray with muffins, butter, plastic cups of coffee, and juice. She ate slowly and deliberately, knowing her aversion to food wasn't real. It was shock and stress. Finished, she refilled her coffee and orange juice to take to her room.

As Marilyn strolled past the front desk, the Asian woman again dialed her phone. Marilyn picked up her pace and as she turned into her hallway, the maid came bustling toward her. In her room, the sliding closet door was completely shut, as anyone who was snooping and trying to be thorough and neat would leave it. The tiny paper scraps had been released by the drawer, the dental floss was still trapped under the bowl, but the other end had fallen inside the door when it had been opened and closed. She was pleased to find the laptops still in place.

She couldn't give the maid the benefit of the doubt that she'd made up the room and disturbed her security measures in the process, because damp towels were still in the bathroom, and the duvet was still in a heap in the closet. While there was pride in foreseeing the danger, she was also pissed off.

She added vodka to the orange juice. That's right, self-medicating, day-drinking, but screw it. Carrying the tote bag and drinks she opened the sliding door and stepped outside. Two middle-aged female sunbathers; one in sunglasses, reading, the other bouncing sun onto her face with a reflector, occupied a pair of chaises. The women glanced her way. Marilyn waved, and they waved back, then went back to their sun-baking and reading.

Marilyn sat at a plastic table in the shade. She considered calling Stade to tell him all about her wildly insane night. However, she felt so wrung out, exhausted, and afraid, she was worried she might say something wrong.

Zabi said, *Stade's nice…and sexy…but we're talking about a double homicide here. And he is still a cop.*

Marilyn nodded to herself. Stade was probably at the Lads' murder scene, since after all, he was a homicide detective. Stade investigating the Lads' killings presented problems. There would most likely be consequences for taking their money and the ring. The Lads weren't going to wake up, so talking to Stade would have to wait until she was ready.

A text came from Earl. Their date was in two days. Damn. She texted him, saying something had come up and she couldn't make it. A reply came, *No probs.*

While she sipped coffee and surfed the internet on her phone, Vacation-guy emerged from a room three doors down. He was wearing shorts, no shirt. Marilyn had to admit his physique was pretty much ideal and her libido had a nudge in his direction. He spread a towel on a chaise and commenced swimming laps. The ladies watched him intently and whispered, then looked over at Marilyn. The one with the reflector waved it like a fan, her expression simulating a raised temperature. They both looked at Marilyn, smiling and giggling like schoolgirls. Marilyn smiled back. He finished his laps and stretched out, reading a tablet, swiping to turn pages.

Back inside, she checked the locks, put the broom handle in the sliding door's channel, silenced her phone, and went to sleep. When she woke from her nap an hour later, it took a moment to get her bearings. She needed to figure out her next moves. She inhaled and exhaled deeply several times to settle her ping-ponging thoughts. Then she divided her immediate future into two categories—survival and remaining incognito.

Zabi said, *It'll be keeping track of it all that will be difficult and dangerous.*

"Indeed. I can't write anything down, so it'll all be in my head." It was tempting to destroy her phone, to eliminate being tracked, but she needed to see who contacted her. She turned off her phone's GPS feature and other locator apps. When she made calls, if necessary, she would block her number. Online, she ordered groceries for delivery.

She called Rigby, got voicemail, and left a message that she was fine, and she'd keep in touch. Checking her recent calls revealed that Stade had called twice. She debated calling him, but to preempt him calling in the cavalry to find her, she dialed him, and to her relief got voicemail. She left the same generic message that she'd left for Rigby.

Marilyn scooted onto the bed and sat cross-legged, upended the tote bag, and counted the Lads' cash. There was a cool twenty-seven thousand, seven grand more than the Lads had thought, which prompted a brief happy dance around the room. The money was nice, but it wouldn't tide her over forever. She needed a job.

She put the money thoughts aside and set up the Lads' laptops, but oh the irony, the batteries were as dead as their owners. After plugging them in, there was nothing to do but think or watch television. Tired of her hamster wheel of thoughts, she tuned in the news and caught a two-minute news clip about the Lads' murders that showed the apartment building with several police cars in front, their lights revolving. The reporter breathlessly focused on the Lads' connection to Darby Fairfield but went on to assert that no charges were brought against them for her murder. The news anchor added that the Lads were known drug dealers.

Zabi said, *Sounds like they have no leads yet.*

"Yep, the killers are still out there and they're probably looking for me."

Her room phone rang, and the front desk announced her groceries had arrived.

Chapter Sixteen:

In the Wind

Two days passed without incident. Marilyn checked the parking lot regularly for the Jeep. Her fridge was stocked, and she had her favorite shady spot on the patio. She carried the tote bag containing the money and the ring wherever she went in the motel. The room was shabby without any chic, but clean, and it offered a well-worn familiarity, so that when she woke with a start during the night, she knew where she was.

In the lobby, she browsed the "library" of previous guests' cast-off paperbacks. Carl Hiaasen's *Skinny Dip* caught her eye and she plucked it from the shelf. Vacation-guy came and began examining the books. He smiled at her, and she reciprocated but was antsy that he might be following her.

He asked, "What've you got there?"

She held the book up. "Just one of my favorite authors

of all time."

"Please let me read it when you're finished. All that's left are romance novels." He feigned sadness.

"Ah, a worthy collection of the bodice-ripping genre." They smiled and she left for her room where she propped up pillows and stretched out on the bed to read. Vacation-guy was good looking and fit. Aside from swimming, that morning he had worked out with free-weights by the pool. One thing she was sure of, her libido was hungry and anxious and required feeding and release…soon. Her thoughts made her smile. Evidently her shock was wearing off, and her old self was recovering.

She called Rigby and this time she answered. "Hey, Rigby. Been any developments in the Lads' killings?"

"Nope. Nothing. The cops are still coming around, including that hunky detective, Stade. I tell ya, he could park his boots under my bed any damn time." She exhaled hugely in the way smokers do. "He asked about you."

"Really? What did he ask?"

"He wanted to know where you are, why you took off," Rigby said. "I didn't tell him dick-all—because hell, I don't have answers. But sittin' here thinkin' about this the last few days, here's what I don't get, Marilyn. Why *did* you take off?"

"Are you kidding? A bunch of reasons."

Zabi's voice warned, *This is bogus. Don't tell Rigby about the Lads' stash or the gold ring. Something is fishy.*

"Christ, Rigby, I was scared shitless. Earlier, some giant, weapons-grade asshole, a friend of the Lads, wanted to rough me up and threatened to rape me. He blamed me for their arrest. Then, just hours later the Lads were dead, and I saw the killers cross the parking lot when they left."

"Who were they?"

"No idea. I didn't see their faces. They had on ball caps and hoodies, and it was dark. I was worried the killers had seen me at the parties and knew I was staying next door. Plus, one of the killers came back and searched the place."

Rigby paused, and her lighter flicked. "How do you know?"

"I heard him going room to room."

"Searched the place for what?"

"How would I know? I would assume for cash or drugs. All I can tell you is that I don't ever want to run into those evil bastards again in my life."

"No kidding," Rigby said.

"Anyway, I've been kind of paralyzed. But I need to get my ass in gear."

"You at a motel?"

Marilyn's BS antennae popped up. "Nope," she lied. "My bank account is running on fumes. A friend from wa-a-ay back, high-school, is letting me crash at her place for a while. Anyway, gotta run." They signed off.

Rigby's questions could have been innocuous, or perhaps the killers had come back and passed themselves off as cops, or friends of Fran or Darby, or looking for information to supposedly help the victims' families. Maybe someone offered Rigby some cash, or she was playing Nancy Drew, trying to crack the case and collect Fairfield's reward. God knows Rigby was always broke— selling her art for a pittance on Etsy, buying her clothes at yard sales, bumming cigarettes and food—and a jarring thought occurred, that in some ways she and Rigby were alike. Maybe the only real difference was age.

Marilyn's gloom had seemed permanent, but something had shifted and cracked open, and optimism had begun to infiltrate, evaporating her despondency, making room for normalcy, even happiness, to fill the spaces.

Zabi said, *Hit the drugstore and help the recovery along with some B-vitamin gummies.*

Marilyn smiled. "Good advice, Zabi. Good advice."

She picked up her book but was distracted by the glint of the gold ring on the dresser, which had caught a sunbeam. She went close and peered at it from all angles, then lifted the baggie and held the ring angled to the light. There was a small dark mark and inscribed on the inside was *Baxter Ellington Fairfield III.*

"Fucking hell..." Marilyn whispered. On true crime shows it was common knowledge that killers keep souvenirs from their victims. The ring was too big for Darby Fairfield's slender fingers, but she could have worn it on a chain. The only logical conclusion was that the Lads took it when they drugged and killed her. Marilyn had previously harbored some doubts about the Lads' involvement in the murder of Darby Fairfield and the other women, but now she was firmly convinced of their guilt.

The ring. Now what? Return it to Mr. Fairfield. He'd want it back. Fairfield on the news had been so angry with the police and the DA. Marilyn opened her laptop and typed in *Darby Fairfield homicide.* The news clip of Fairfield came up. Looking dapper, he stepped before the microphones and began attacking the DA and the police for releasing the Lads.

Behind Fairfield was a bodyguard. The guy was a side-of-beef in a suit. The thought shook her. She'd recently had that same thought about someone, but where? Was it the steroid monster who had threatened her? No, it was the muscular intruder, the killer at the Lads' apartment. He was *a side-of-beef in a hoodie.* In the video, Fairfield's third finger of his right hand glinted in the sun. She paused the video, took a screen shot, and enlarged it until the ring was identifiable. The news clip was filmed the day the Lads came home, only hours before they were murdered.

Fear-bumps tickled her arms as fragmented thoughts formed a coherent picture. Suddenly her previous theories—that the killers were two-bit thugs out to rob the Lads, and that the Lads had taken the ring from Darby as a souvenir—were wiped away. Now, she knew Old Man Fairfield and his brawny bodyguard were the killers. Fairfield was the shooter, avenging his daughter.

On the news clip, Fairfield looked thin and drawn, no doubt due to worry over his missing daughter. Marilyn had been on the misery-diet herself over Fran. The Lads didn't take the ring from Darby. It had slipped from Fairfield's newly skinny finger during the killings, and the bodyguard had returned to the Lads' apartment to find it. Fairfield didn't give two shits about the Lads' money, but the ring was like leaving a calling card. If the cops had found it at the scene would the police assume, as she had, that it was a memento the Lads had taken from Darby? Maybe not. Fairfield must be frantic. His ring alone might not be enough to implicate Fairfield, but if the dark-colored Jeep with PITA in the license plate was one of Fairfield's cars, he'd be in deep trouble.

If the bodyguard was Fairfield's *fixer*, he was to be feared. Fixers are connected. They have ways to worm into all sorts of places and extract information, and fixers break kneecaps. He had looked right at her. Now she was sure he'd seen her and knew it was the apartment next to the Lads. Plus, if he could get his hands on the 911 call, they'd find that it was a female caller, and know how much info she had given. It was suddenly incredibly important that no one know she called 911.

Instead of returning the ring to Fairfield, maybe it should go to the police. She picked up her phone to call Stade but changed her mind and tossed it on the bed. Until now she'd thought that she and Stade would connect when she finally felt safe, but that might never be possible.

She resumed watching TV as a show that detailed real crimes started. The announcer intoned, "How did it happen? How, in a leafy suburb outside a big city, was a young mom kidnapped from her front yard? And more puzzling, how did no one see it happen?"

"Well, that's easy," Marilyn said to the screen. "In suburban America no one goes outside unless they're in a car."

She resumed the crime show. The intro music

subsided, the announcer reappeared, and said, "The disappearance of Belinda Morse is a cold case and a mystery. However, the actions of law enforcement turned out to be more mysterious." The show went on to implicate Belinda Morse's husband and his brother, a police officer. Her husband and his brother-the-cop hired a career criminal to kidnap and murder the woman because she had filed for divorce. Apparently, several officers were aware of the plan and didn't intervene. The show ended, and in the next episode, another murder by a police officer was described.

"Shit," Marilyn said aloud. She googled Fairfield and found the obvious, namely that he had tons of money; however, he also had mucho connections, not just socially but with the police. Videos and photos showed Fairfield cutting ribbons at new police headquarters, shaking hands with the chief, holding oversized donation checks for various branches of the police force, and at the annual policemen's ball.

No way was she taking the ring and her account of that night to law enforcement, Stade, or Fairfield. The ring was security.

Zabi whispered, *I bet they are hunting for you right now.*

"My thoughts exactly." Fairfield would have the means to find her, unlike a couple of two-bit punks. If he tracked her down or threatened her, the ring could keep her alive. Could she find a failsafe, some way that someone would release her evidence if anything happened to her? But what, how, and who? A flash drive with a detailed account of the killings? Given to whom? Who would she knowingly put in danger?

Her phone burbled and the caller-ID read, Stade. "Hello, Detective."

"I assume you know the Lads were killed." He sounded clipped, strained.

"Yes. I'm well aware, and I've left Fran's apartment."

"I know. My recent-calls list shows that you phoned me around the time of the murders."

"Yup. But I got voicemail and it was late, so I didn't leave a message." Her excuse was so lame, even to her, that she rolled her eyes. She took a beat to assess how much to tell him. Would mentioning Fairfield's ring, her 911 call, the Lads' cash, and what she witnessed, bring on an avalanche of unintended consequences, unexpected complications? Probably. Keeping quiet seemed a better strategy.

Zabi said, *Lying by omission is not exactly a great way to start a relationship.*

"What relationship, Zabi?" She had a sudden strong urge to distance herself from Stade and drummed up some bogus internal rage by fixating on how the police had treated the murdered women as disposable, garbage.

Stade interrupted her thoughts. "Marilyn, the crime scene was a mess when Garcia and I arrived. Did you hear or see anything?"

"I knew there was violence."

"Why did you leave? Where are you?"

"I was scared…okay? Look Stade, I can't help you. Please don't call me." Jesus, he was pushy. There was a stagnant pause, and she sensed his confusion, but all she said was, "Bye, Stade." As she took the phone from her ear to hang up, she heard him say, "Wait."

She opened one of the Lads' laptops and hit the power switch, then hesitated, unsure she wanted to see the carnage reenacted. Maybe she didn't need to check what had been filmed. She just needed to wipe the hard drive clean—there was online software to do that—and ditch the laptops in a dumpster someplace. She rejected that idea. Every time she turned around, it seemed there was another surprise, and she needed to see if the cameras had captured anything additional of interest. Besides, if the homicides were captured on video, they could act as insurance as well, like Fairfield's ring.

What would their password be, maybe zen-zen, or Transcendalia? It would have been smart to have changed the passwords the night of the murders, while the computers were up and running. Oh well, under duress, one can't think of everything. She hit the power, and to her surprise, with no password required, it went straight to the screen saver of a naked cartoon woman with balloon-like boobs, which were sprinkled with app icons. Marilyn clicked on the video icon, and a menu popped up. Scrolling down, she hit *Last 18 Hours*.

An image of people celebrating the Lads' release from prison filled the screen. Their apartment was packed with drinking, smoking, vaping, coke-snorting, and dancing rabble-rousers. The guests shouted to be heard over the pounding music. She scanned the crowd and recognized the huge musclebound guy who had blamed her for the Lads' arrest. Notably absent were Earl, Rigby, and Jon.

Marilyn advanced until the time read midnight when she'd noticed it had gone quiet next door. On the laptop's screen, Shawn came from the back of the apartment, got a beer, and he and Declan had their conversation about where he had hidden their stash. Then Shawn headed down the hall to his bedroom as Declan stretched out on the sofa. For a few moments, he halfheartedly masturbated, lost interest, and fell asleep. She advanced the video in five-minute increments. At 2:15, two hooded figures came in treading lightly. The muscle came first, holding his Maglite and a handgun together at chest height, sweeping the light across the room. Cameras are usually placed high and the killers' baseball caps would have obscured their faces, but the laptop had been on the kitchen table, and in the light from the TV, Fairfield and his bodyguard, Palmer, were recognizable.

Fairfield and Palmer moved close to Declan on the sofa. The old man took a handgun with a silencer from the kangaroo pouch of his hoodie, leaned toward Palmer, and whispered, "Wake him up. I want him to see this coming," and with an audible crack, Palmer struck Declan across the nose with his Maglite. Declan's scream was the primal sound she'd heard that night. Blood gushed from his crushed nose.

Fairfield lifted his gun, two-handed. There was a muffled thump as he shot Declan between his eyes. There was another thump as he shot him in the chest. Fairfield and Palmer moved to the hall where they were out of camera range, but where Marilyn had watched them from the peephole. She heard Shawn faintly pleading, then the thumps of shots fired. She assumed the video of Shawn's killing would be on his laptop. Fairfield and Palmer came back into range, opened a few kitchen cabinets and closets, and left the apartment.

Three minutes later, Marilyn entered, looking anxious, jumpy. She quickly checked Declan for signs of life, then disappeared down the hall to Shawn's bedroom. She came back and began tearing the kitchen apart, dumping drawers and the contents of cabinets. She ripped posters and art from the walls and pulled clothes from the closets. Finally, she stopped, hands on hips, breathing heavily. She grabbed a chair, climbed up, opened the air return, and pulled out the shoebox of money. The rain of rat shit was visible, and she shook out her hair. Then she stood very still. Appearing alarmed, she ran back to Shawn's room and came back with his laptop, scooped up the vodka, the box of money, and the second laptop, and she left.

Only a minute passed before Fairfield's fixer noisily arrived. He scanned the place, said *Fuck!* several times, shoved Declan off the sofa and patted him down, then went room by room, closet by closet, kicking at clothes littering the floor. He looked behind doors, under furniture and toe-kicks on cabinets, obviously searching for the ring.

She booted up Shawn's laptop and watched Fairfield shoot him, then she fast forwarded to her finding the ring and pocketing it, and finally dashing out with his laptop. She powered off and shut the laptop, congratulating herself on her presence of mind to take them and dump the Lads' TV. Things had just changed again. She was in possession of the most important damning evidence, namely the videos, plus Fairfield's ring, and she wasn't going to turn them over to anyone. She was breaking the law, withholding evidence. This definitely put the kibosh on any relationship with Stade.

Online she found the nearest Pack N Ship where she could rent a locker. She transferred four thousand dollars to her purse for expenses. Then, carrying the tote bag containing the money, the ring, and the Lads' laptops, she summoned a car.

At the store, the driver waited while she rented the locker and stashed the goods; then he waited again at Walmart where she bought a thin gold chain. She threaded the locker key onto the chain and slipped it over her head.

Back at the motel, she undressed, and slept naked for an hour, waking to a knock at her door. Through the peephole she recognized Vacation-guy. His shirt's slogan read, *Is your name WIFI, because I'm feeling a connection.*"

"Hang on," she said, and slipped into her kimono, cinched its sash, and ran her hands through her hair. She kept the chain-lock on and opened the door.

"Hey, just wondering if you could use some company, maybe want to go to dinner? My name is Ron, by the way."

"Marilyn. Nice to meet you. Well, how could I possibly turn down a guy who wears a T-shirt with the worst pick-up line ever."

"Exactly," he said, smiling. "Mexican okay?"

"Yes, Mexican is great."

"Mind if I come in?"

"I'm not dressed for company…I was asleep."

"Oh crap," he said apologetically. "Sorry."

"It's okay. I don't like to sleep too long during the day. It makes me disoriented."

He nodded. "There's a pretty good Tex-Mex place a

few blocks from here."

She wasn't confident about getting into his or anyone's car, and while she was quite certain now that he wasn't one of the killers, she didn't have a vehicle of her own as an excuse to meet at the restaurant. "Are you okay with ordering in?" she asked. "We could eat in the courtyard."

He appeared confused. "Really? You don't want to get out of here?"

"No. I'm hoping to check out tomorrow. And between the flood and some other weird stuff that's happened, well…let's just say I have my reasons."

"All right. How about we meet at six in the courtyard and order online. I'll order the food and supply the margaritas."

"Sounds perfect."

Propped by pillows on the bed, she considered her upcoming date and had a frisson of excited amusement. She hadn't seen any random women entering or leaving his room and there was the absence of a gold band. While Marilyn didn't have to be madly in love to have sex, she also wasn't without standards. Sometimes sex was maintenance for that section of her being that needed waking up or shutting down depending on the intensity of animal attraction, her deprivation, loneliness, or other relevant factors. Stade was now officially at arm's length. Ron was a candidate if the evening went well.

Chapter Seventeen:

Revelation

Marilyn showered, shaved legs and pits, applied makeup for the first time since she left Fran's, and dressed in Fran's short black cotton skirt and red camisole. In the courtyard's shady section, Ron had set up a table he'd borrowed from the breakfast buffet, with a bedsheet as a tablecloth, a rose in a bud vase, and two plastic margarita party glasses with green cactus-like stems. The smile it drew from her was spontaneous and genuine. They looked at each other a moment and she said, "Wow. I'm impressed."

"Welcome to Chez Ron. The finest eatery relatively near the Gulf Coast." He took a pitcher from an ice bucket and poured them both margaritas. "Only the best for us," he declared, and they chuckled, clunked glasses, and sipped.

She perused the menu on his tablet, and they placed their order of fajitas for two. "So. What brings you to the sumptuous Tout Suites?" he asked.

"Oo-la-la. The usual; the lush grounds, the fan dancers, incredible cuisine, and the diamonds they put under my pillow every night." She smiled sardonically.

"Don't forget the solid-gold toilet."

"Exactly. Basically, the flood left me homeless. I crashed at a friend's for a while but for several reasons I had to move on."

"Reasons such as?"

"To preserve my dignity, mainly. I'm too old for college-style living. How about you? Why this place?" At that moment, the restaurant texted that the delivery had arrived at the motel. She said, "Let's split the bill."

"Call me old-fashioned, but this is on me and the massive insurance settlement I'm about to get for my flooded house."

"You make it sound like you won the lottery."

"Far from it, but I can certainly afford dinner." He went to fetch the food from the front desk.

Ron returned and they unwrapped what appeared to be enough food for a family of six. "Well, good thing our suites have refrigerators. You'll be able to live off this for a week." They chuckled. She speared two slices of fajita beef and laid them on a tortilla, added guacamole, onions, shredded cheese, and Pico de Gallo, rolled it up, and bit into it. "Oh Jesus, that first bite kills me every time." She tipped her head back in a faux swoon.

He raised his eyebrows at her orgasmic response and said, "I'll have what she's having." He winked and grinned.

"So, you got interrupted by food delivery…"

"Yes. My house flooded. It was closer to Galveston, so as you can imagine, it's a write-off."

Are you working?"

"I'm self-employed, and the boss told me to take some time off." He chuckled.

"Why this motel, though? There are plenty of other

places that are nicer, even if they don't have gold toilets."

"Pretty much every hotel south of here flooded, especially this style where they were built on a slab at ground level. On the day of the storm this was the only place with an empty room. Trust me, if the Hilton was available, I'd be there. But hey, this is actually more than adequate. Counting my blessings."

She nodded. "Me too. So, was your house destroyed?"

"Pretty much. Actually, it was for sale and finally under contract, then came the flood. Guess I'll see what the insurance will pay." He sipped his margarita. "Were you nervous when you had to escape your place?"

"Well, yes and no. I had a destination, so I was confident I'd be okay, but still. If I had to spend some nights in a shelter, well, anything can happen."

"No kidding. I've been following the serial killer murders that the police are investigating. Terrible." He sipped again.

"I'll say." Marilyn wasn't in the mood to discuss Fran and searched for another subject.

Before she had a chance to steer him to another topic, he absentmindedly loaded a tortilla and continued. "They reported on the news that some homeless guy claimed he injected the women with heroine and had sex with the bodies." He looked up and realized Marilyn had frozen mid-chew. "Oh shit! I'm sorry! What a horrible thing to bring up."

"Yeah…how about them Astros?" she said, forcing a smile.

After a pause, he reciprocated. "Are you really leaving tomorrow?"

"It depends. I haven't found an apartment yet."

"Tell me about it. Scarce as hen's teeth."

"…Tits on a bull."

"…Rocking-horse manure."

"…fur coats in hell." She gave him some side-eye. "That's all I've got."

"Well, I hate to throw shade…" He returned her skeptical gaze. "…but if you don't find a place, maybe you'll be here longer, which would suit me fine."

"Aw, aren't you sweet."

When the pitcher of margaritas was empty but for lime slices, the dinner wreckage disposed of, they occupied two chaises and watched the sky dim and a full moon rise. Finally, Marilyn said she had apartment hunting to do in the morning and needed sleep. He walked her the twenty steps to her room, drew her to him and kissed her gently, then urgently. She was becoming caught up in his excitement and arousal but decided to put the brakes on. She slowly broke from his embrace. "I don't need to stay here for us to see each other, you know."

He grinned, shoved his hands in his pockets, and ambled away, turning once to look at her.

Morning broke already roasting as Marilyn sat on the motel's patio sipping iced coffee and surfing apartment rentals. Ron emerged and commenced swimming laps. She continued her apartment search until he surfaced and toweled off. He ambled over, and smelling of chlorine, bent to give her a kiss on the cheek. "Any luck in the apartment quest?"

"Not really. As expected, the pickin's are slim."

"Well, it would be great to do a rerun of our Tex-Mex dinner soon, if you're still trapped here," he offered.

"Yes, I'd like that." He headed to his room, and she resumed searching. Marilyn had been poor so long her frugal ways were ingrained, and she had a self-imposed budget. She skipped the Realtors' listings and went to Findit.com, a website more in tune with her rental price.

A one-bedroom, one-bathroom apartment on Yupon Street, in her preferred Montrose neighborhood, popped up. She clicked on the contact info button and dialed. It went to voicemail. Shit. No doubt already rented. Her phone rang.

A female voice said, "You called about the apartment?"

Marilyn introduced herself, and the woman said she could come to look at it at noon. The Lads' cash would cover her deposit and at least six months' rent, which would give her time to find work. She finally had a financial cushion. Not that she'd won the lottery, and the money came with strings attached, but she said a silent thank you for this break that would relieve some of her cash-related anxiety of late.

Marilyn hailed a car with the destination of the Menil Gallery, arriving ninety minutes early for her apartment appointment. The Menil was a favorite spot to immerse herself in its world-renowned private collection of modern art.

After absorbing enough of Rauschenberg's fierce energy to last a while, she walked several small blocks. There were the rhythmic sounds of hammers, shouts, and chatter by trades in English and Spanish. Their trucks lined the streets. Owners and workers emerged from buildings and houses, still emptying some structures, carrying buckets, and pushing wheelbarrows, dumping musty heaps of debris. The piles blocked driveways and sidewalks and encroached on the road. The city was still recovering and rebuilding.

She found the brick 1930s single-story duplex on a street almost untouched by gentrification. The door was answered by an overweight older woman with a bright smile and a ruddy complexion. She introduced herself as Allie. Allie confided the apartment was available because the previous tenant had returned to her abusive boyfriend.

Marilyn said, "Any chance she'll suddenly come to her senses, dump her boyfriend, and want the place back?"

Allie laughed, shook her head, and stepped aside to let her enter. "Not a chance I'd take her back. Too much drama."

Marilyn toured the vacant apartment.

"How soon can I move in?"

"Anytime is cool," Allie said. Allie was an old-school landlord who sized up her tenants and went with her gut, unconcerned with a background/credit/job check. Perfect, since being unemployed would disqualify her.

"No time like the present." Marilyn signed the lease, handed over her deposit in cash, and took her receipt.

Allie smiled. "Great. Here's the key. I had the locks changed in case the previous tenant's boyfriend comes around."

As Allie gathered her things, Marilyn stood in the small foyer and took in her new space. Sure, the windowsills showed some rot, the air conditioner was an old window-shaker, and a slight eggy smell emanated from the gas stove, but it was spacious and airy with ten-foot ceilings, original hardwood floors, and tall windows that opened and were fitted with screens. And a major plus was a walkout to a fenced yard with a huge live-oak tree. The place wasn't the Waldorf, but to her eyes, it was perfect, a godsend.

She made phone calls to take over the utility bills, then went for a walk, window shopping along Westheimer, and entered Common Bond, a place she'd normally walk quickly past, since restaurants like it—all clean lines and hip wait staff in cool black aprons—tended to be expensive. She took a table by the window—all the better for people-watching—and ordered Drowned Eggs, a plate of two soft-yolk eggs, stewed chipotle tomatoes, fresh cactus, and baguette. It felt good to have some cash.

Two young women, a brunette and a blonde, occupied a nearby table. They were photographing their food and each other with their phones. Blonde looked over at Marilyn. "Would you mind taking our picture?" She held out her phone.

"Sure thing." Marilyn obliged and the women posed in the ubiquitous selfie pose with their chests and butts pushed out, lips pouted.

"Can I take a pic of your food?" Blonde asked.

As Blonde was snapping photos, Brunette squealed, "OMG!"

Blonde rushed to see, they paused a moment, then in stereo, "OMG!"

Marilyn asked, "Something good?"

Blonde said, "That Fairfield thing. It's unbelievable."

Blood left Marilyn's head. "What Fairfield thing?"

"Hell yeah," Brunette squeaked. "There they are! There they are!" And she looked up round-eyed at Marilyn and said, "Come look!"

Marilyn moved to their table in time to see footage on her phone of Fairfield's bodyguard being led into the courthouse in handcuffs. Wearing a hoodie, he had looked chunky, but now, in a dark suit and handcuffed, he was a mobster—craggy-faced, black hair pomaded, crisply parted and combed, a thick, sturdy body like a pit bull—like you could punch him ten times and he wouldn't flinch. He smiled into the camera, displaying perfect white veneers. Marilyn said, "Talk about a bad boy."

Next, Fairfield came into camera range, without handcuffs, also being led into the courthouse and accompanied by another man. His expression was somber. Marilyn said, "Who's the guy with Fairfield?"

Blonde replied, "He's Fairfield's lawyer. Everyone calls him by his last name, Gwynne. He's my dad's lawyer too."

"Why is Fairfield in the news?" Marilyn asked tentatively.

Brunette said in a sing-song voice, "Remember the guys who killed Fairfield's daughter and some other girls, but they got off? The cops are saying that Fairfield and his bodyguard went to those murderer-guys' apartment and shot them to death." She made an exaggerated face of shock and surprise.

Marilyn said, "Really? Wow."

"He did the world a favor if you ask me," Blonde

offered.

"Yeah. It was revenge for his daughter. If I got murdered by those dudes, my dad woulda done the same thing."

"When were they arrested?" Marilyn asked.

"Like, just an hour ago. My dad phoned and told me, 'cause he does lots of biz with Fairfield and the lawyer, Gwynne."

Evidently, in the media's and these women's minds, the shootings were justifiable homicides. Marilyn suddenly regretted calling 911. If she had just taken the Lads' loot and left the ring behind, they wouldn't have been arrested. Damn.

Zabi's voice said, *Oh well, shoulda, coulda, woulda. No way you could have known, and no sense beating yourself up now.*

Marilyn silently agreed. The cops caught Fairfield quickly considering her vague description, so unless someone else called emergency, there must have been some connection to the car. Mainly she had wanted the bodies to be found and two bloodthirsty thugs off the street. The media was spinning a Dexter-ish, Robin Hood tale. She returned to her meal and gave herself a little shake. At least Fairfield was under scrutiny, which should prevent him from being obvious about finding or killing her.

Marilyn paid her check, and she and the girls left. At the motel a sticky note with Ron's phone number was on her door. She packed up her belongings, checked out, hailed a car, and emptied her locker.

At her apartment, she surfed rental furniture and ordered a package deal of three rooms, holding the salesperson to delivery in an hour, as the TV ads promised. With her furniture installed, she hit a home goods store for pillows, towels, sheets, cleaning supplies, window coverings, and kitchenware, and on the way home stopped at the local corner store for a bottle of wine and snacks.

Sleeping on her new bed was heaven, and she woke to sunlight, stretched, stepped outdoors into the continued hot weather, and sat on a plastic chair left by a previous tenant. The yard was a jumble of tropical plants and unruly shrubs, many with bent and broken branches from the flooding and neglect, some yellowed and others crisp and brown from drought, disease, or bugs, all in need of some pruning. Just over a month since the storm and a significant fire-ant nest was mounded at the live-oak's base, the resilient little assholes.

She strolled to the food mart. In the tools section, she found yard bags, fire ant killer, pruning shears, and a leaf rake. When the friendly, vaguely Middle-Eastern store clerk asked if she was new to the area, her hypervigilance kicked in. She immediately considered the store's surveillance cameras and gave a vague answer of visiting friends.

She pruned, raked, and cleared. The productivity took her mind off the threat of Fairfield and boosted her mood. Raking the yard unearthed sprinkler heads. She found the control box, and turned it on. Black cylinders pushed valiantly through the composted debris that covered them, sputtering and gasping, and finally spurted a continuous hissing spray.

The watering took her back in time, to the backyard of a bungalow, on a side-street, in the suburb where she and Zabi lived, a garden of sun-warmed tomatoes, herbs, and berries that she watered with a hose and a sprinkler.

For a time, she watched the water and inhaled the scent of wet leaves and loam.

PART THREE:
Six Months After

Chapter Eighteen:

The Holiday Season

Marilyn returned home from a modeling session, noting that many flooded houses had been demolished making the streets look like they had missing teeth. She rummaged in her purse for her keys and her hand came out with keys and the sticky note with Ron's phone number. It was six months since the hurricane, and over four months since she had checked out of the motel.

The holiday season had arrived, and Houston was celebrating, happy for a positive event to end a difficult year. Garlands of evergreen boughs with pinecones and baubles were strung along streets, and trees were wrapped in twinkling lights. The weather was cooperating with a cool front—she couldn't really call it a cold front with temperatures in the low fifties—but throughout the city festive sweaters and winter coats had been liberated from mothballs and were on display.

Marilyn had made it through Thanksgiving and Christmas the way legions of others without family do, by largely ignored the holiday season. She had considered getting a few of the Art Guild's artists together for eggnog but decided against revealing her address, although she bought some eggnog with rum added to encourage the Christmas spirit.

She put the sticky note on the kitchen counter. Ron was likeable. She'd enjoyed their impromptu outdoor dinner. He'd struck her as a bit of a charmer, but what the hell, she could do with some charming company. With her months-long resolve to keep Stade firmly in her past, she dialed and got Ron's voicemail which instructed, "This is Ron. You know what to do."

"This is WIFI." She laughed. "AKA Marilyn. If you still feel a *connection*, call me back." Leaving her number scared her. Marilyn worried constantly about Fairfield and his bodyguard tracking her down. The anxiety was wearing on her to the point that she considered contacting Fairfield's lawyer to make a deal, sign a contract not to snitch. But she wasn't naive enough to think a piece of paper or a promise would keep her safe. To Fairfield, she would always be a liability. She stayed home, only venturing out for groceries or a restaurant meal and her modeling gigs, and those forays were fraught with paranoia. To fill the hours at home, she drew, painted, cooked, watched movies and TV series, gardened, and read.

She cooked a curry of chicken tikka masala with Basmati rice and ate it in front of the TV, binge-watching a series about the trials and tribulations of a successful woman who owned an advertising agency, whose husband was a stay-at-home dad—*Mad Men*, updated. A text arrived from Earl: *Hey Marilyn, hope you're still up for a date. Can we reschedule?*

She replied: *Sounds good.*

He was calling it a date, but she'd insist on going

Dutch and write it off as friends getting to know each other a bit better. There was no word from Ron, and she wasn't averse to dinner with a relatively known quantity like Earl. They scheduled a time.

She slipped into bed, pulling her puffy duvet up to her ears. Every night, before drifting off, thoughts of Fairfield and his violence brushed up against her safety and wellbeing, and she wondered if tonight would be her last.

On the appointed day, a text arrived from Earl: *Hey Marilyn, hope you're still up for our date tonight.*

There was that word, *date*, again. Marilyn had some minor misgivings about agreeing to go out with Earl. She mentally enumerated his negative points. While he was what most girls would call *cute*, he seemed immature in his manner of speech and his somewhat slovenly personal presentation. Also, he didn't have a real job or career, which smacked of instability—not that she was gainfully employed, but her circumstances were different, what with killers most likely hunting her down and all that. Oh well, she figured it would be nice to go out.

She replied: *Sure thing. See you there.*

What to wear? The items she'd scooped from Fran's closet were starting to feel macabre. Marilyn stopped by her favorite discount store and spent an hour rifling the endless racks, settling on a floral-print blouse, black jeans, shorty-boots, and gold jewelry. She added a few T-shirts, jeans, a little black dress, and a pea-jacket.

At Empire Grille, at the appointed time, Earl was seated with an open bottle of Malbec, two glasses at the ready, and a single rose in a bud vase. For Earl, he was dressed up in a black T-shirt, a gray sport coat, and black dockers. Wow—and oh crap—it was a real date. Sitting opposite each other, she sized him up. His facial scruff was a fad she'd grown tired of, but that was an easy fix. His features were nicely proportioned and symmetrical. He was good looking, but there was also a bland innocence to his looks. She hadn't focused on him as a potential mate before, possibly a result of her self-imposed artist-model segregation. Her heightened and conflicted libido in Detective Stade's presence came back to her. Maybe Earl or Ron would be a safer outlet for sex, a friends-with-benefits arrangement. Except Ron hadn't called her back.

"Well. Here we are." Earl said, a bit nervously.

"Indeed," she said. "So, the whole official first date thing."

He laughed and said, "You start."

"I'll start in the present. For work, the modeling is all I've got right now. Are you still fixing stuff up and selling it on eBay?"

"I am. I might be the only person in Houston who is bringing stuff in instead of throwing stuff out." He added with a hillbilly inflection, "There's gold in them thar piles of junk."

"What sort of junk?"

"I know, right? Lamps, small appliances, electronics, just not upholstered stuff or absorbent things, because water equals mold, as you know. Anyway, I consider it restoration, recycling."

"One man's trash is another—"

"Man's treasure. Exactly."

She paused a moment and sipped her wine. The waiter came by, and they both ordered seafood pasta. "Can you make a living with the resto-recycling?"

"Not exactly, but…" He looked around then lowered his voice. "I also do some phishing."

"Oh, I didn't know you have a boat. Do you catch redfish and snapper, or do you mean sport-fishing, taking people out on charters?"

"P. h. i. s. h," he spelled out in a near whisper, "I phish on the internet, and catch fat cat-phish in my internet and eat their cash."

Stunned at his confession, her mouth became a small,

surprised o, and she took a second to close it. "Wow. That just happened."

"I know, right?" he said. "The restoration-eBay stuff and the old van are just a cover."

She didn't think it was possible after everything that had happened, but things were becoming even more bizarre. Why divulge his illegal activities to her, other than he was proud of himself and for some reason trusted her? She contemplated grabbing her purse and walking out, but what the heck, she might as well see what he had to say. After all, she was the girl who swiped the Lads' cash as they lay dead in the same room. She wasn't exactly squeaky clean herself. "Well. I didn't see that coming. How does the phishing work?"

The pasta arrived, and Earl paused. They both ate a few forkfuls. Then he said, "The hacking is strictly to make money, not mayhem. I'm not a nerd, and I don't subscribe to geek rules. I've designed my own methods."

"Really? Your own methods?" Marilyn asked.

"I know, right? Really. It's like this. Your typical hacker is an antisocial, lazy, pimply, underachieving, undernourished, fat, dungeon-dwelling hobbit. Those nerds think that staring at their monitor in their boyhood bedroom is some kind of birthright. I, on the other hand, live independently in a beach house. I have standards in my work."

"That's very cool," she said noncommittally. His criminal enterprise and an aspiration to be better than a "lazy, dungeon-dwelling hobbit" struck Marilyn as an exceptionally low hurdle.

"I know, right? Plus, unlike the indiscriminate assholes who throw out blanket phishing nets hoping to snag a mark, I do my homework. I use a scalpel, not a machete."

She hadn't noticed his verbal tic before. Saying, *I know, right?* made him seem even younger, an adolescent. Funny what can be a huge turnoff. She said, "This is interesting. Alarming and scary, but interesting."

"I know, right?"

She gritted her teeth, then relaxed and smiled, putting down her silverware and taking a large gulp of wine. "Earl, I have a question. Why do you trust me with this information? After all, the cops are all over me right now asking about the Lads and…everything."

Unexpectedly, he reached across the table and took her hand. "Marilyn, of course I trust you. You're amazing. You're everything I've ever wanted in a woman: beautiful, smart, hard-working, nice—"

"How old are you, Earl?"

"Thirty-two. And well, I've had a massive crush on you from the moment I laid eyes on you. You've got this fantastic cool edge to you, but it's so much more than that."

She placed her free hand over his. "Earl, you're a great guy…but this is a lot to take in."

"Please just hear me out." He inhaled deeply. "When you asked to come and stay at my place, I lied when I said I already had a couch surfer. I lied because nobody can be in my house, or they'd find out what I do. But I finally realized you can be trusted, and I'm in love with you. And the way I live, it's lonely."

"Jesus, Earl, you need to let me catch my breath."

"Anyway," he said, "it crossed my mind that this is good timing. With your apartment complex wiped out, you're between jobs. I could teach you the ropes. We could be partners. With you as a partner, we could expand, rake in big bucks."

She took another gulp of wine. "Wow. Just, holy fucking wow. I need some time to think about all the layers. You're talking about a relationship, a partnership, that spans every facet of our lives."

"I know, right? It will be fantastic. Of course, you should take a day or two."

She gasped. "A day or two! I need a week, maybe a

month. This is a big decision. And I barely know you."

"I know, and that's my fault, right?" He gave her his best big puppy-dog eyes. "I've always had to be so private, but I want you to know me now—the real me."

They clinked their glasses, finished the meal with a shared slice of carrot cake, and he paid the tab. At his van, she took the initiative and kissed his cheek. He offered to drive her home. Sure, give out her address to a scammer. She insisted on walking.

Back home she donned a sweater and jacket, sat on her patio. A cold front had moved in, and her breath made vaporous plumes. She tallied a mental list of Earl's proposal's pros and cons. The biggest pro was the cash. Also, with her paranoia of the killers, it was advantageous that the money would be untraceable. The scam's cons were everything else: its illegality, her guilty conscience, and the forced relationship with Earl. She'd be living an extension of her current life, except instead of Fairfield and his goons she'd be afraid of the law—or maybe she'd still fear Fairfield and getting busted for hacking would be just another layer.

Her phone signaled a text. Earl wrote, *I hope you'll say yes!* Followed by a heart emoji.

She replied, *I'll get back to you on that.* She added a happy face.

Her phone rang again. She checked that it wasn't Earl and answered. Ron said, "Hi, WIFI, I'm still feeling a connection."

"Ha. That makes two of us."

"Can we get together? Maybe have lunch or dinner?"

"Absolutely," she said. "Are you still at the Taj Mahal?"

"Yes, I am. I just can't tear myself away from the twenty-four-carat-gold toilet. Are you available during the week?"

Noon, two days later, Marilyn was seated at a Vietnamese restaurant near her apartment when Ron entered. He had movie-star good looks with chiseled, balanced features. The women in the restaurant turned their heads, tracking him like sunflowers turn to the sun. At the motel when they'd met, she'd judged his looks as just *good*, but certainly not stellar. Why hadn't she seen that earlier? No doubt her paranoia at the time, of getting close, had clouded her judgement of his appearance. He was hot. The top two buttons on his solid blue shirt were open and his sleeves were turned back over the cuffs of a black pullover. She stood, and they kissed cheeks. His scent was pleasant, a mix of woodsy and herbal. His dark hair looked freshly cut, and he was clean-shaven with a slight five-o'clock shadow. So much about him—his health, wit, looks, and his maturity made him desirable. A waiter approached, and they both ordered cilantro chicken.

He asked, "You found an apartment?"

"I did, just a block from here."

He didn't bother hiding his grin. "Sounds handy." They both chuckled.

"Down, boy. What about you?"

"Still waiting for the insurance to come through. Then I'll find another house...on higher ground." The food arrived.

"What line of work are you in?" She cut a piece of chicken breast.

"Consultation mainly, advising on the production potential for oil-drilling sites. You?"

"Currently unemployed. I was managing an apartment complex and I lived onsite. The entire complex is a write-off. So, everything got eliminated—job, car, possessions, living quarters."

"Are you going to stay in Houston?"

"Yes." She nodded. "You?"

"Not sure. The city's gotten expensive."

"Amen," she said. "I guess with your skills you can

work anywhere in the world."

"Pretty much. But at some point, the fossil fuel industry will be eclipsed by other forms, mainly solar and wind. Although maybe not in my lifetime."

"I've often wondered why, given the sunniness of Texas, there isn't a lot more solar."

"Probably because we're set up for oil, and we haven't run out yet."

"Right." She nodded. "Human nature. No incentive so far."

The waiter came by with the bill and collected dishes. Marilyn reached for her purse, but Ron said, "No you don't. It's on me."

"Thank you."

He stood and placed his credit card on the bill and said, "Restroom. Excuse me. Don't go shopping with that." He chuckled.

In his absence she turned his credit card around and read his name. Ron Rockwell. It took a moment for the name to register. She was suddenly lightheaded and leaned on the table. Was this the boyfriend Fran met online? He didn't say he was a geologist, but since he's a consultant on oil drilling sites the chances were good. Surely there couldn't be two Rockwells who were geologists. Could he be the one who killed Fran…and the other women? Was he the last person to see Fran alive? Marilyn had been so certain of the Lads' guilt. Could Rockwell be staying at the shabby motel for the same reason she was—because it was a good anonymous place to hide?

He came back to the table. "Can I walk you home?"

"I just had a callback about a job I applied for," she lied. "They want me to come in for another interview in half an hour, so I've got to run."

"That's good news. You're on the short list. Hey, it's New Year's Eve this Saturday. Would you like to get together? I'd be happy to kiss you at midnight." He grinned.

"Aw, damn. That sounds like fun, but I've got plans." She pouted sadly.

As they headed out the door, he placed his hand on the small of her back, then kept it there as they stepped outside into pleasantly cool, dry air. Christmassy garlands were swagged between streetlights. She asked, "Where are you parked?"

"Behind the restaurant."

"Well, thank you for lunch. If I get this job, it'll be on me next time." They paused a moment, then he kissed her gently, lightly, and not wanting to spook him, she reciprocated. "I'm this way," she said, indicating the opposite direction of her apartment. He watched after her, then turned and walked to his vehicle. Marilyn kept walking purposefully and turned onto a side street. She dialed Stade. "Hey, Stade, it's Marilyn."

"It's nice to hear your voice. I hope this is a social call."

"Not really. You're the first person I think of when I have a possible clue in a murder." She chuckled.

"Good to hear. Fill me in."

"Fran said she met a guy online and they were dating. She wasn't very forthcoming, but she told me that he was a geologist, and his name was Rockwell."

"Great name for a rocks guy."

"Exactly. Which is why I remembered it." She took the sticky note from her bag. "In some kind of weird serendipity, I happened to meet him. Here's his cell." She dictated the number. "I don't get a bad vibe from him, but she left the building with someone and maybe it was him."

"I thought you were convinced the Lads were responsible," he said.

"Maybe your skepticism has me on the fence. Now I'm wondering if it was him."

"Are you suggesting he's a serial killer or that he killed Fran? If you're thinking he's the serial killer, how do you think Rockwell was connected to all of them?"

"Sheesh, you expect a lot. I just now figured out who he is and haven't had time to think it through. However—let's see—he met her on the dating site CoupleUp.com. If he's the killer, maybe he met all of them on the dating site. What also bothered me is that he acted as if he didn't know who I am, but I think he knows. Fran had photos of me on her social media pages. It's like maybe he's stalkerish. Can your detectively skills get into Fran's laptop to find her emails to Rockwell? Also, when you sign up on a dating site, you have to give them a ton of information. So, if you can get that info…When I realized his connection to Fran, I got the heebie-jeebies and took off…"

"I'll look into it…" After a pause he said, "Marilyn, I'd like to see you again, soon."

"I'm afraid I'm not very good company. With everything that's happened, I'm currently on a dating hiatus." She winced. Keeping her distance was necessary, but still painful.

"Okay, got it," he said. "If you decide to end your dating pause, and you'd like to get together, please let me know."

"Thank you. I will."

Over the next five days, Marilyn roamed every museum in Houston, the Menil Collection, the Museum of Fine Arts Houston, Museum of Modern Art, the Twombly, the Lawndale, and every commercial gallery in the city, zoning out and considering Earl's proposition. Could she do it? Could she heartlessly scam people out of their money?

That was the thing. It wasn't just their money he was stealing. He was robbing them of their savings for the literal rainy day they'd just experienced with the hurricane, or for some other personal disaster. He was destroying their ability to ever get ahead.

In her life, except for the Lads' cash, she had worked for everything she had. She'd started working part time at sixteen. She'd always lived within her means, been careful and frugal. She'd been in the shoes of the people Earl was ripping off. Her hard-won savings had been stolen in a legit-looking investment fund that had turned out to be a Ponzi scheme. And there had been plenty of times she'd nearly clicked on a link in a bogus email designed to look like it came from a legit source such as her bank, a shipping company, or a pay-online site. It was just her gut, some sort of intuition that had stopped her. How she hated the scammers and their intrusion.

Between her childhood, her ex, and the hurricane, she'd been homeless three times. She'd known poverty. Sure, money didn't buy love, but it changed things. Money was control, confidence, security, optimism, a future. It was healthcare, food, indulgences, transportation, and shelter.

Earl had chosen her. Why? Did he smell her rudderless, junkie-mother's past on her? Or did he genuinely like her and feel a strong attraction as he claimed? Were they two of a kind? She'd felt minimal remorse taking the Lads' money and justified it as karma for their bad acts.

Back home, she counted her cash and found there was not much more than two or three months' rent and expenses left. Then what? She was self-sufficient, but tired. Just once, she wanted someone to fall back on.

She spent the rest of the evening and the following day online, researching phishing scams, related software, and catfishing. She came away fairly well acquainted with trojans, spyware, back door malware, and how catfishing works.

Should she, or shouldn't she?

Chapter Nineteen:

Indicted

Marilyn woke to shadows on the off-white walls of raggedy bird-of-paradise and banana trees that were frost-bitten a few nights ago. Thoughts of Earl and his internet scamming invaded, and she considered the plusses and minuses of partnering with him until she couldn't stand her indecision, and she showered and checked the news. Fairfield and his bodyguard, Ray Palmer, were to appear in court in the afternoon. An intense need to size them up took hold.

She headed to the food mart and bought a coffee, a granola bar, and five flash drives. The air was crisp. Zabi said, *It's no-AC season*, and Marilyn smiled. In her apartment, she downloaded the incriminating videos from the Lads' laptops to the thumb drives. Makeup-and-jewelry-free she pulled her hair back in a clasp and donned beige pants, a matching sweater, and a gray jacket—all the better to disappear in a crowd—and she headed out.

Marilyn stopped at a nearby bank, rented a safe deposit box, and stashed the thumb drives, Fairfield's ring, and the laptops. At the Franklin Street court building she made her way through the scanners and into the elevator with lawyerly, expensively tailored types, blue collar workers in their Sunday best, clothes that only got dusted off for weddings, funerals, and court, gang members sporting teardrop tattoos on their faces, and downtrodden women carrying their baby-daddies' burdens wrapped in hand-me-down blankets—all summoned to explain themselves for the offense they'd committed. On the seventh floor, she joined a crowd of hopefuls that shuffled into a courtroom lined in dark varnished wood. Marilyn was the last to enter as the bailiff closed the door after her, a tourniquet cutting off the stream of spectators. She squeezed onto a bench near the back.

Fairfield and Palmer and their lawyers were at one table, the prosecution at another. The judge entered, and after some formalities, the district attorney stood and introduced herself as DA Goldi Stein. Murmurs spread through the courtroom. Although Marilyn put Goldi's age at early-to-mid thirties, she looked too young to be a DA, and her outfit—with a knee-skimming kilt, white cotton blouse with a Peter-Pan collar, and white pumps—was more befitting a grade-school field trip than addressing the possible death sentences for two men. Alternatively, perhaps her getup was a strategy to have the judge and old-guard lawyers like Gwynne underestimate her, so she could blow them away with her smarts.

DA Goldi outlined Fairfield's motive as revenge for the killing of his daughter and his anger at the Lads' release. Then she played the 911 call. Marilyn sighed with relief to hear an unrecognizable voice overlaid by cell phone garble and static. The stress, heat, and humidity had made her sound breathless and labored.

Goldi dissected the anonymous 911 caller's

description of the two white men who matched Fairfield's and Palmer's builds, and the type of car they were driving with PITA in the license plate. Goldi explained that the vehicle was a dealership loaner, lent to a customer whose car was in for service. The car-borrower knew Palmer-the-fixer's cousin, and the cousin loaned the Jeep to Palmer. Had Palmer's cousin confessed to arranging the loan of the Jeep or was DA Goldi speculating? DA Goldi paused to allow her deductions to sink in, then continued, saying that the late hour indicated stealth.

She showed a grainy video from a local gas station with the car driving past, although the driver's and passenger's images were hopelessly vague. DA Goldi sat down again and appeared to take notes. She definitely had nerves of granite trying to indict the likes of Fairfield and Palmer on circumstantial evidence. DA Goldilocks would be much better off if she found and presented some DNA or other forensic evidence. She certainly had no smoking gun—that belonged to Marilyn in the form of video and, to a lesser degree, Fairfield's ring.

Fairfield's lawyer, Gwynne, stood. Marilyn recognized him from news reports on other high-profile cases. News coverage had spoken highly of his proficiency, as both an outstanding lawyer and as a skilled investigator. His prowess as an investigator was Marilyn's main concern. After observing the tactics and behavior of lawyers who'd handled her friends' divorces, Marilyn had long considered all lawyers to be crooks and assholes.

Gwynne's face was handsomely angular, even Patrician, and starting to soften, with a slight double chin, eye bags, and jowls. However, those features weren't unattractive and fit his image as a seasoned lawyer. The rest was a bit too flawless—teeth overly white, trimmed hair with a little distinguished gray at the temples, very expensive bespoke-tailored suit—sophisticated and slick.

He was poised as he addressed the judge, and he glanced at the DA when he spoke. "Judge, my *worthy colleague's* case is ludicrously circumstantial." His emphasis on "worthy colleague" dripped sarcasm, and it was noticeable that he didn't use the usual adjective, *esteemed* colleague. Surprisingly, Goldi blushed and took the bait, self-consciously shrugging into a short, fitted, navy jacket that had been draped on the back of her chair. Many in the gallery were smirking. Goldi's gaze turned to Gwynne, observing him, perhaps hoping for a slip-up.

Gwynne said, "Judge, these charges are without cause, and ridiculous. There are no witnesses, no weapons, no forensics, and no DNA evidence." Smart of him to focus on what was missing. He continued, "The men who Mr. Fairfield and Mr. Palmer are accused of killing were drug dealers and scam artists who had many enemies. While Mr. Fairfield detested them, and may I add—with good reason—that doesn't make him or Mr. Palmer killers."

He paused and smirked. "And then there's the car. The so-called connection to the vehicle is absurd. So, a cousin knew a customer of a car dealership, who had a friend, who borrowed a car…" He trailed off, lifting his shoulders and hands palms up, and smiled. Chuckles spread through the spectators. Gwynne said disparagingly, "Where does it end with this car? Did anyone else drive that car, ever? Are there fingerprints or DNA to indicate my clients were ever in the car?" His mocking turned DA Goldilocks pink. Gwynne concluded, "The prosecution's case is circumstantial, highly flimsy, and flawed."

While DA Goldi's evidence was tenuous, Gwynne's attempt to discredit the car's connection to Fairfield was weak. Goldi rebutted that they would soon have fingerprint and DNA analysis from the lab, and she reminded the judge that the labs had been backed up since the hurricane. She pointed out that Fairfield's motive was strong, he'd publicly come close to threatening the Lads, and with his money and connections he was a flight risk.

The lawyers' arguments took Marilyn back to the night the Lads were murdered. After what they had done to

Shawn and Declan, she hoped Fairfield and his fixer would be locked up, or at least be under house arrest, rendering them unable to do their own legwork to find and eliminate her, although they could hire people, and there was Gwynne to be reckoned with.

Marilyn refocused. Gwynne argued that Fairfield would surrender his passport, and DA Goldi pointed out that with Fairfield's vast sums of money, he could easily circumvent airport security, hop a private jet out of town, and be gone. Gwynne parried that Fairfield had many ties to the community and began listing his various charities.

Marilyn made a mental list of how Fairfield and Palmer had screwed up. There was the traceable car, the videos on the laptops, and the ring engraved with Fairfield's name left behind. It was odd that Fairfield wasn't wearing gloves. Or maybe he removed the ring before donning gloves, and somehow he dropped it. Another mistake was Palmer bashing Declan's face with his Maglite, causing the cry that woke Marilyn, made her a witness, and started all the cascading events to come. If they had been quiet and not woken her, Palmer would have retrieved the ring, and they would have gotten away with the killings altogether.

Those mistakes were sloppy for a professional knee-capper like Palmer. Perhaps he underestimated the distraction Fairfield's presence would create. If Palmer had worked alone, he would have parked further away, farther than old-man Fairfield could walk. He would have been emotionally detached and wouldn't have woken the Lads, just killed them in their sleep. Fairfield's ring wouldn't have been dropped, and he might have checked for surveillance.

One man can be incognito or look like he belongs, or take off running, climb a fence, hide in a shadow, grab someone in a chokehold, shoot someone, which was a far cry from two men in lockstep with one in his eighties. Fairfield was the shooter. It was personal, in-your-face revenge. He wasn't satisfied to chill at his country club while Palmer took care of the Lads, ditched the weapon and car, and brought him proof in the form of photos and maybe mementos.

The judge ruled house arrest for Fairfield and Palmer with several million in bail for each. The spectators and press scattered, and Marilyn waited outside the courthouse, watching. When Fairfield's driver showed up in his Rolls, they were mobbed by paparazzi. Fairfield menacingly waved his walking stick at a cameraman and growled, "Get the fuck out of my way."

Marilyn walked out of the courthouse into the brisk weather, turned a corner, and called for a car. At home, she placed the safe deposit box key in an envelope and taped it to the underside of the kitchen silverware drawer. Then, struck by fatigue, she collapsed on the sofa and fell asleep for half an hour.

When she woke, she was in the mood for self-maintenance and went grocery shopping. Back home, she put away the food purchases and spent two hours cleaning the apartment.

After a dinner of salmon, rice, and salad, she took a long bath and tried to picture what Fairfield's, Palmer's, and Gwynne's strategies would be now. They were obviously predatory, and it only made sense they would be trying to ID the 911 caller, and when she was identified, they'd have ways to track her down and be coming for her. She couldn't visualize any other strategies, and more importantly, she couldn't be sure what they'd do to her when they found her.

Like all kidnap movies, it would be stupid to kill her, the hostage, before getting the evidence, so they'd probably torture her until she gave up the goods. Beyond that, she had nothing. She gave up thinking, toweled off, and watched a documentary about a cold-case rape and murder solved by two women. Finally tired enough to sleep, she went to bed and fell into a solid slumber.

Two days passed. Marilyn called the Drawn to Perfection Gallery, a small art co-op nearby which had a newly formed figure-drawing group. As luck would have it, their model for that afternoon's session had canceled. She accepted the modeling job and got ready.

The life-drawing was held in a private room at the back, hidden from patrons in the main gallery. The model's platform was against the back wall surrounded by a half circle of artists. The room and the attendance were small compared to the Art Guild. Earl and Rigby were among the artists. The pose was three hours with breaks every half hour. At the first break, Marilyn and Rigby went through the back door into the parking lot.

Rigby lit up, blowing smoke out of the corner of her mouth away from Marilyn, who crossed her arms and focused on some small weeds growing through the gravel. She asked, "Any news at the building?"

Rigby inhaled and shook her head. "No, but Detective Stade's been around. Asked about you again."

Marilyn looked up. "What did you tell him?"

"Nothing. Just that you moved away. Because you split, I think he suspects you were the 911 caller, or you saw something, and he wants to talk to you."

"Did he say that?"

"No. Just reading between the lines."

"Right. Maybe I'll give Stade a call," she lied.

"Fairfield and Palmer were indicted this morning." Rigby took a deep drag on her cigarette. "I like Fairfield's lawyer, Gwynne. He good-looking…and rich."

"Yeah. I watched it online." Marilyn said, nodding. "I agree he's handsome. He's also a shark from what I've read."

"His wife's a big-time art collector. Also, a big-time dominatrix."

Marilyn stifled a gasp. "Really, Rigby? Are you

sure?"

"It's true. She has a huge following online."

Marilyn shook her head, Rigby snuffed out her cigarette, and they went inside. The artists went to their easels and waited as Marilyn stepped up onto the platform. The door to the gallery opened, framing a man's silhouette. When the door closed, she recognized Stade. Well, well, speak of the devil. She turned away from him, opened the kimono and slipped it off her shoulders, catching it at her elbows. She turned obliquely toward him, shoulders and breasts exposed. A small smile played on her lips. Pivoting away, she slipped the kimono off and resumed the pose, seated on a chair. When she glanced his way again, he was gone.

Marilyn finished her pose, changed, shrugged into her pea coat, and left the gallery. A short distance along, a sedan idled at the curb. Two stubby antennae identified it as an unmarked police car. Stade. For a moment she contemplated dashing in the opposite direction, but he stepped from the vehicle and stood waiting, watching, hands in the pockets of a long, black overcoat.

Chapter Twenty:

Stade

Marilyn met Stade's eyes. Other than her phone call about Rockwell, it had been months since they last spoke, and longer since their dinner date, which still stung her with something like heartbreak, given it was so promising, and then the Lads were killed that night—the night everything changed. He still had that distant demeanor about him, and she wondered if he maintained it even in bed. The thought brought on an unexpected wave of lust. Was it his standoffishness that was so compelling? He was physically imposing, and she could imagine what the act would be like, his weight, scent, his voice, his energy, complemented by her own until he reached that point of no return, those moments of utter helplessness.

He said, "Marilyn, it's okay, I won't bite. Come talk to me."

She frowned. "I told you I can't help you and I asked

you not to call."

"I'm here on police business. It's important."

She sighed. "All right."

In the vehicle he turned to her. "Here's a question, Marilyn. Why do you do it, the modeling? Aside from the extra cash."

"This is police business?"

"I can't get away with anything, can I?"

"That's right." Marilyn tipped her head slightly, considering his question. "Why do you think I do the modeling, and why do you ask. And for that matter why do you care?"

"Oh, I care. I definitely care, and I'm not looking to judge."

"I'm aware that plenty of people view modelling naked for a bunch of artists as a strange, even an amoral, occupation."

He smiled. "I assume some prudish jerks think so."

"If I look at you strictly as law enforcement," she said, "I have to point out that it's not sex work. It's unlike other professions that require getting naked for cash, such as stripping, porn, prostitution, or webcam sex."

While Marilyn assumed there were other clean, sober, and sane life-study models, the gig tended to attract the desperate. Other models at the Art Guild included a morbidly obese woman whose fat hung like a bread-dough apron over her thighs, and at least two junkies, all needle-tracks, atrophied muscle, and sunken eyes. There was a man who had a wasting disease, and a woman Marilyn thought of as *granny*, who was probably eighty, with her saggy-everything and scraggly gray bush. Granny was perhaps the most mainstream of the bunch.

"Got it," Stade said, looking through the windshield. He turned to her. "So, why? Why do you do it?"

"Why do you want to know? Do you disapprove?"

"No. Just curious, I guess."

His question brought to mind all of her mother's

transactional sex she'd witnessed. She knew that not everything is about money. She inhaled deeply and exhaled. "For me, modeling is kind of altruistic. Maybe it's my silly, tiny attempt at immortality, along with the romantic idea of being someone's muse, their inspiration. I consider having my image captured forever on paper or canvas to be a privilege. Consider Vermeer's *Girl with a Pearl Earring*, or da Vinci's *Mona Lisa*. Without Mona's smile, without the intrigue surrounding Vermeer's girl's age, her station in life, and the question of her identity, the artist wouldn't have the painting." Marilyn smiled. "Of course, Vermeer and da Vinci were revered, the rock stars of their time, unlike the artists who are drawing and painting me."

"You're beautiful, Marilyn."

His compliment seemed awkward. Flattery? Uncalled for? She looked at him skeptically. "I like being on both sides of the easel. Maybe I'm weird, but between modeling and drawing, I have no preference. I studied art in college, and I believe I've got talent and ability. But like virtually every art student, I never landed the career that confirms it." She shot him a stern look. "And by the way, Detective, if you ever show up again where I'm modeling, you'd better have paper and pencils."

"Yes ma'am," he said with mock seriousness. He changed the subject. "Did you have a good Christmas and New Year?"

"Quiet. You?"

"Same."

Through the passenger window a man dumped shovelfuls of mold-covered smashed stucco, wood, and sheetrock then turned back. "It's been over six months since the hurricane, and this is still going on."

He followed her gaze. "Given the catastrophe, six months isn't long."

She nodded, "So, your detectively instinct brought you here?"

He smiled a little. That thin smile was like a crack in his self-imposed barrier, probably designed to put his suspects at ease. He shifted in his seat to turn toward her. "Yep, when I first met you, Rigby said you did *nekkid modeling.* And I've been checking the schedules of places with artists' models, and voila, here I am. So, why are you hiding?"

"Why do you think I'm hiding?"

His eyes were deep brown, with that spot of hazel, that calico bit, like a mote. His gaze was steady and seemed to say, *I know your gambit. Answering a question with a question, but I'll play along.*

"Let's see," he said. "No known address."

"FYI, Officer, half of Houston is displaced with no permanent address right now. Besides, I couldn't stay in Fran's apartment because her dad sublet it." She looked out the side window again at the worker dragging more wreckage from the house. "Plus, a double murder next door makes a girl want to get out of Dodge."

His thin smile spread and softened. "Did you make the 911 call when the Lads were killed? For the DA to have the car's partial license, make, and model the caller must have been observing from the building."

Marilyn turned to him. Zabi whispered, *The call can't be traced. Deny. Deny. Deny. Hang tough.*

"Lots of people live in that building. It wasn't me," she said with finality. She wasn't sure why she wanted to be secretive about calling 911, but on this, caution was her default. Besides, lying was justified. This was survival. Cops were allowed to play fast and loose with the truth to get information, so quid pro quo, Detective.

"Then, tell me. Why are you hiding?"

She stared through the windshield. Starlings had invaded, as they did every year, lining wires and crowding trees. She said, "Look at all the birds. I love the murmurations."

"Murmur, what?" he sounded annoyed at her

avoidance.

She ignored his tone and explained. "Yes. That's what it's called when the birds suddenly take off together as a black cloud and make patterns."

"I could get out and clap my hands," he offered, "make it happen."

She smiled but sat still, pretending to wait for the birds' murmuration, buying time, analyzing what might be going on with Fairfield and how to play this. Fairfield might have told his lawyer about the missing ring, but with the ring being so incriminating, they certainly wouldn't have told the cops. And nobody but Marilyn knew about the Lads' videos.

Deciding on part truth, part fiction, she said, "I'm just being careful. Look, Fairfield and Palmer might well be the killers. Your DA Goldilocks…" They both smiled.

"She's Goldilocks all right, but she's super smart."

Marilyn continued, "Goldi had enough to indict them, so they're probably guilty. If so, they're probably worried as shit and wouldn't hesitate to kill anyone they think is a threat. If they decide I might have seen something it won't matter if I did, or I didn't." She shook her head.

He nodded and said, "We can put surveillance on your place. Keep you safe."

"Yeah, great idea," she said sarcastically. "Then the whole cop shop and DA Goldilocks will know my address. Plus, my identity will be exculpatory evidence that Goldi will have to give to Fairfield's lawyer, Gwynne." She rolled her eyes. "No risk there."

He ran his hand over the top of the steering wheel. "You're asking me to withhold evidence."

There it was…exactly what she feared. If he knew she'd called 911 and that she had Fairfield's ring and videos of the murders, he wouldn't be able to bring himself to help her hide them. And now she was contemplating some out-and-out illegal activity with Earl and his internet hacking and phishing. She needed to get rid of Stade, and said, "What evidence? I was next door and heard the commotion. That's not evidence." She began opening the car door. "But like I said, I didn't see anything, and I didn't call 911. I don't have more information, okay? That's it, end of story."

"Fairfield does have a long reach," he admitted. "Okay, no surveillance, and I'll keep you under wraps."

"My turn to ask a question." She held the door slightly open. "Did you get hold of Ron Rockwell?"

"No. He's not answering his phone or returning my calls. I went to the motel where he was staying, but he's checked out."

"Wow. Is that suspicious behavior?"

"Maybe. If you hear from him again, please let me know."

"No problem. So, why are you really here?"

"I wanted to see you and make sure you're okay. Also, I'm still investigating the missing women. We still have three Jane Does, and I'm trying to identify them. I was hoping you could help."

"Well…I'd help, but there are no drugged-up, drunken parties at the Lads' place anymore, and that equals no *scene*. Plus, I don't live there or have any reason to hang out there. But Stade, can't you ID the Jane Does through DNA?"

"We tried, but they're not in the system."

Marilyn had blamed him for the lack of investigation of the women but realized now she'd done so to be mad at him and justify keeping her distance. The police were human and had made mistakes. It wasn't his fault. Besides, he was the one who had reopened the investigation, and he was doing his best to find the truth.

She longed to kiss him, but she'd be sending mixed signals. If she involved him and he was caught helping her withhold evidence, it would compromise his career. She had to ride this one out solo. "How many women are we talking about now? You had the five that you had identified…"

"Five identified and three more unidentified."

"All overdosed, all came to life-drawing, and all knew the Lads?" She lifted an eyebrow.

"It's not that simple," he said. "Two didn't come to life-drawing. However, those two belonged to the same book club, and one didn't belong to life-drawing or the book club, but she belonged to a garden club. And now that we're into it, we know these killings go back several years, and there may be more victims."

"Like Patty who used to come to life-drawing. Wow, so now you are trying to find a common denominator, right? Someone—a man—who, at one time or another, associated with all of the groups. Sounds like a lot of work." She thought a moment. "The upside is that a lot of those clubs are almost all women. The men are in the minority and tend to stand out."

"It is a lot of work, tracking down and questioning all the members. Sure, the men deserve extra attention, but we need to interview all the women, too. Questioning the men is obvious but often people on the periphery have observations or evidence that shouldn't be overlooked."

"Or some of his victims might have been random. Maybe he saw some of them somewhere repeatedly, at the grocery store, the coffee shop, the bank, anywhere." She gave him a resigned smile. He placed his hand over hers. "Promise you'll protect my identity?"

"Promise. Thanks for talking to me."

She turned her hand over and squeezed his and stepped out of the car. As she closed the door the birds lifted en masse, the sound of their beating wings and squawking reduced to silence as they soared higher, swooping, gliding, and folding as one entity into swirling patterns. She wished there were accompanying classical music, or opera. Stade stepped from his car to watch. The murmuration lasted a few minutes, and the birds descended to take up their places in trees and along wires, cackling.

Stade smiled, shook his head at the wonder of it all, got into his car, and drove away.

Stade had found her, which meant Gwynne, or an investigator hired by Fairfield, would no doubt be on her doorstep soon. Aunt Zabi said, *Oh well, if Gwynne shows up, it might be good to get it over with.*

"Hear, hear, Zabi," she whispered. "As long as there are no weapons involved."

Chapter Twenty-One:

Gwynne

At Rudz, she ordered the Tuesday rib-eye special and wine and sat reading advice columnists on her phone to deflect male attention, but that didn't deter a couple of aggressive men hitting on her. Not that she minded too terribly as long ago she had decided that however misguided, it would be less annoying if she viewed it as a form of flattery.

Between the men and their pick-up lines, thoughts about partnering with Earl came and went. Again, she weighed the pros and cons. Her desperate financial straits and her need to evade Fairfield and Palmer, whether she had the stomach for scamming, and the illegality; how long until he—and by extension, she—would get busted?

Tired of thinking, Marilyn paid and left the bar to walk the two short blocks home. The street was deserted. She turned onto a side street paved with cobblestones, one of the city's few. The sidewalk was broken and heaved, a hallmark of Houston's soupy underpinning, known as gumbo soil, definitely not bedrock. Shrubs cast deep shadows, potential hiding places for weirdos and muggers. She chose to walk down the deserted road's center, but even in the open, the streetlights were spaced too far apart for safety, and she clicked on her cell phone's flashlight. The air was cool and still.

She stepped aside to let a car pass. As she rounded the corner onto her street, there was the staccato of footsteps behind her. Staticky fear gripped her, and she turned, but the road was empty. Maybe it was an echo of her own footfalls. Her apartment came into sight, and when she reached her porch, relief flooded her. As the key turned in the lock, she was startled by a man who said, "Miss! Miss, you dropped your wallet."

Under the porch light, the guy was redneckish, chewing gum, wearing a loose threadbare Hawaiian shirt, and a ball cap. His glasses were big and black-rimmed, and his hair hung loosely around his collar, a mullet. "Oh," she said, flustered, still wary. He held the wallet out as if it were a bit of steak enticing a starving dog. The wallet— with its scuffed and faded pink and black zebra print and matching pom-pom dangling from the zipper's tab—was hers. But she was cautious. There was something off about him.

"Here." He wiggled the wallet impatiently.

She reached out. "Thanks. Where did I leave—"

He swiftly grasped her outstretched arm and spun her to him. Her back against his front, he pinned her arms with one hand, the other covered her mouth and pulled her head back. There was the smell of mint gum and expensive aftershave, which along with his tailored pants and polished loafers, didn't fit his persona.

Her feet cleared the floor, and they were suddenly inside the apartment. His breath was warm against her ear as he whispered, "Any noise and I'll hurt you. I just want to talk a minute. Everything that happens now depends on whether you keep your cool." He loosened his grip slightly. "Nod if you understand. Do not speak."

She gasped air and nodded. Maintaining a grip on her right arm, the stranger pushed her onto a wooden dining chair. He produced zip-ties from his back pocket, pulled her arms behind her, secured her wrists to the chair, and stuffed a facecloth in her mouth. He stepped away and observed her, and she returned his gaze.

He removed the joke-store thick glasses, and the ball cap with the straggly mullet attached. Gwynne. He closed her laptop and checked under it, tipped up her lamps and ornaments, took books from her bookshelf, and riffled the pages. In the kitchen, cabinets opened and closed, and dishes clattered.

He returned and tilted her chair onto its back legs and dragged her into the short hall that linked the bedroom, bathroom, and living room. He shook the contents of her purse on the bed—loose change, nasal spray, notebook, Tic-Tacs, tampons—found her cell phone, slipped out the SIM card, snapped it in half, and pocketed it. In Marilyn's bedside table, he found her birth certificate, passport, and social security card and examined them. He peered inside her jewelry box, then underneath.

Finally, he stood before Marilyn, with his forefinger to his lips. He was good-looking, groomed, and fit, in his late forties or early fifties. She nodded in agreement. Gwynne removed the gag, produced a pocketknife, and cut the ties. He stood her up and twisted her right arm behind her back and bent her wrist. The hold seemed simple, innocent, but whenever he tugged even slightly on her hand, the pain was excruciating. They left her apartment looking like an affectionate couple walking together. In his big black Mercedes, he locked the doors. She asked, "What do you want?" Cool and collected.

"I'm Joseph Gwynne. Everyone calls me Gwynne. I'm the attorney for Mr. Fairfiel—"

"I know who you are. In fact, I was starting to wonder what was taking you so long to show up."

He gave a surprised chuckle. "So, you want to bargain, is that it?"

"That depends. What exactly do you want?"

"I'd prefer you not insult my intelligence," he said. "You know what I want."

She prevaricated. "What were you looking for in my apartment?"

"Devices. Recorders, commonly known as bugs."

"No one has been here since I moved in, so I doubt my place has been bugged. And I didn't appreciate you killing my phone. Now I'll have to get a new one."

Gwynne shrugged. "Sorry about the phone. I'll get you a replacement. But I was doing my due diligence."

"Make it the latest iPhone with the same phone number."

He smiled. "All right. Look, I'm aware Stade has been sniffing around, and cops tend to be competitive. They can get so caught up in a case they trip over their own dicks. If Stade wanted to snoop nothing would stop him. In my jaded opinion, all cops are shady, and if I can find you, others can, too."

"In my jaded opinion, all lawyers are shady, too."

"Touché." He grinned and paused chewing a moment. "Here's what I know. You've been in Houston since you came from Detroit as a kid to live with your aunt. She died a while ago, cancer. You've got no pets, no boyfriend, no job, no car. How am I doing so far?"

"That's pretty much it." She shrugged. "How did you find me?"

He turned in his seat to face her and said, "I went to the Lads' apartment building. There was a skinny, old cat-lady there, smokes a lot."

Marilyn chuckled. "Rigby. Did she hit on you?"

He nodded, eyebrows raised at the memory. "Rigby knew who I was from watching the news, and she invited me into her apartment. My god, what a dump." He grimaced. "She told me about you, how you escaped the hurricane and stayed in Fran's apartment. She thinks you might have seen the shooters. Then I asked her to call you, find out where you were, but she refused."

"Huh. Good old Rigby. But how did you find my address?"

"My office got crime-scene photos, and on the Lads' table was a piece of art. A figure drawing."

Marilyn inhaled sharply. "Rigby's drawing that she left behind with my name on it."

"Exactly. I asked Rigby about it, and she confirmed that you were the subject of that drawing." He shifted in his seat to face her. "So, Rigby's painting gave me your name, but there was no traceable paper trail on you, indicating you were lying low. But I figured I'd see where you might model for the artists."

"Really?"

"Really." He paused a moment then continued, "At the Art Guild, there was a display of life-drawings that had been done on the premises. Unlike the drawing Rigby left in the Lads' apartment, which to me was just a big mess of paint, some sketches were very realistic, and they helped fill me in on what you look like. After that, I just showed up wherever a life-drawing group was meeting. I saw you go into the gallery called Drawn to Perfection. Then who comes out of the gallery but Stade. Did he come into the drawing group, see you nude?"

She gave him her best disdainful gaze. He chuckled and said, "I'll take that as a yes. I watched you talk to Stade in his cop car. The starlings' murmuration was amazing, wasn't it? Then I followed you home."

She looked over at him, then half-smiled cheerlessly and shook her head. She had expected him to find her, but though it wasn't a surprise, it was still unsettling. Tracking their prey is what men like Gwynne and Stade train for and live for. Both Stade and Gwynne had unapologetic, unabashed predatory natures that contrasted with their sophisticated looks and manners. The James Bond effect.

Earl was predatory too but in a hands-off, once-removed way. Earl was a sneaky user, a taker. In any case, there was a small libidinous tug in Gwynne's direction. *Men!* "Yes, the birds were amazing." She was glad she hadn't kissed Stade.

Aunt Zabi's voice said, *Darlin' you need a booty call. Scratch this itch and get it out of your system.* Marilyn tamped down a smile.

"What happened the night of the killings?" he asked, studying her.

Her mind was racing, deciding what to reveal or conceal. She decided to leave out her dinner with Stade, and shrugged, "The Lads partied, celebrating getting out of jail and beating the murder charges." She looked into the distance and shivered, as if she were back in that moment, in Fran's apartment. "A scream woke me around one."

"Who screamed?"

"It was Declan. Fairfield and Palmer killed both Declan and Shawn."

"You saw Fairfield and Palmer?"

"Well, I saw two men through the peephole the Lads were originally arrested for. But I didn't know they were Fairfield and Palmer until I put two and two together later. When they left, I went next door. I found Fairfield's ring. I noticed later that his name's engraved on it, there's blood, and probably gunshot residue too."

"So, where is Fairfield's ring?"

She squinted. "No fucking way. That's my insurance. I've set it up so that if anything happens to me, it'll go straight to DA Goldilocks with a letter explaining exactly how and when I found it," she lied.

"DA Goldilocks. I like that." He grinned. "So, you have the ring. Good. It's time to play *Let's Make a Deal.* Are you with me, Marilyn?"

"I'm listening."

He said, "I'm pleased you aren't losing your shit. Here's the plan. First, we need a witness. That's going to be you. You will testify the Lads were in the process of beating and raping you, about to kill you like the others, and Palmer and Fairfield—who had come to talk to the Lads about Fairfield's daughter—saved you by shooting them."

"Whoa." She frowned. "So, supposedly Fairfield came to *talk* to the Lads, armed to the teeth? That doesn't sound right."

"Palmer will cop to the killings. He's always armed. It's part of his job." Gwynne looked in his rearview and side mirrors then became quiet and still as a pedestrian walked their dog past the car.

"How am I going to pull this off? I took some acting classes once and did a few commercials, but I'm not an actress."

"You will pull it off, Marilyn. A big part of it will be your look; demure and vulnerable. If you can cry, all the better." He shifted in his seat, and added, "Right now, I probably can't get Fairfield off. And I need a not guilty on this case. The pay will be generous."

"How generous?"

"I can probably get you half a million."

"I don't know. I have a feeling there would be all sorts of unintended consequences. I have to think about—"

He put both hands up, palms out. "Don't say yes or no yet. This is a two-part scenario."

"What's part two?"

"We'll blackmail Fairfield for several million and tell him we have evidence of him killing the Lads, but it needs to be set up so it can't be tied to either of us, so we need a patsy."

"Are you aware that Stade isn't one hundred percent convinced that the Lads are the serial killers? If he finds out someone else did it, how would that impact your scheme?"

"He won't. Anyway, back to our patsy. Know anyone?"

"Maybe." She smiled. "And don't forget my new phone. I want it tomorrow morning."

Chapter Twenty-Two:

The Partner

Marilyn woke early, just after five, and sat on her sofa drinking coffee, thinking about Gwynne's scheme. The pluses: money, lots of money. Also, it was a one-off, unlike Earl's phishing, which would be endless. Plus, the money would be from one source, namely old Money-Bags-Fairfield, and he had buckets of it, so unlike Earl's phishing, she wouldn't be stealing from people who couldn't afford to lose their savings.

Plus, she needed the money because the Lads' cash would soon run out, and because she was on the lam, she couldn't hold a normal job. Working with Gwynne would solve a whole load of problems. However, what if Ron Rockwell, not the Lads, was the killer of Fran, Darby Fairfield, and the others, and Stade could prove it, or if Rockwell confessed? That would make Fairfield guilty of killing two innocent men, and it would blow up the scheme. Oh well, nothing ventured and all that…

Being part of Gwynne's witness and blackmail schemes made her valuable to Fairfield and Gwynne until the trial. After the trial would be a whole other story. Whether she partnered with Gwynne's plan or not, she would always be a liability to Fairfield and on the run, forever. So why not be on the run with millions, rather than broke? Fairfield's ring also gave her some insurance, as did the videos, which so far where her secret.

At seven, there was a knock on her door. Through a window she observed a delivery man hop into his truck and drive off. A small package was on the porch. She programmed her new phone, then sighed and texted Earl, *I'm in. We need to talk.*

He replied, *Awesome!!!!! Come for breakfast?*

She replied, *No. Lunch, at your place, noon.*

Great!!! Looking forward to it. He replied with his address.

Google's street view showed Earl's house as a nondescript, weathered, wooden box on stilts. It was in an area of waterfront properties, halfway between Houston and Galveston about twenty miles from her. Her cab was going to cost some bucks. Oh well, she needed to get to know Earl better.

At eleven, dressed in jeans, T-shirt, and windbreaker, she bought take-out shrimp salads at Café Express and hailed a ride to Earl's. The day was clear and mild. His house was in a row of cottages on pylons. Its blank front faced Todville Road and the back overlooked Trinity Bay, an immense expanse of water connected to the Gulf of Mexico. There were no houses across the narrow two-lane road, just marshy wetlands. Earl's place was as bland and dilapidated as it had looked on Google's street view. His van was parked under the house on a concrete pad that ended at a bulkhead of jagged rocks lined with reeds and water that stretched to the horizon. She inhaled the salt air and climbed the switchback stairs past fifteen-foot pylons.

The stair treads were warped with rusty, sprung nail heads protruding.

Earl was waiting at the top. He wrapped her up in his arms and kissed her enthusiastically, then smiling, released her. The house was as dilapidated as the stairs. Algae coated the weathered wood siding and the deck, which was narrow, unlike every other waterfront house with their rambling party decks. Earl's bistro table and two chairs barely fit into the space next to a small hibachi on a stand. She was drawn to the water view, but when she leaned against the rail, it moved. "Whoa!" she said, jumping back, then testing it with a push and a pull. "That gave me serious vertigo. It's wobbly."

"It's the salt water, corrodes and rots everything. Don't worry. It's still okay for a year or two."

She gazed at the celadon-green water dotted with sailboats and a ponderous tanker on the horizon. "I brought food." They sat at the tiny table and stared at each other a while, smiling. Marilyn read his grin as infatuation while hers played more toward awkwardness. She said, "Um…Not to be rude, but do you have something to drink with this?"

"Sorry!" He snapped his fingers, jumped up, and entered the house through its sliding glass door. In his absence, she inspected the house's exterior and considered whether the place was salvageable. A coat of paint could work wonders, but the railing, deck boards, and stairs needed replacing, and why was the deck so small? Earl reappeared with a bottle of white wine and two mismatched glasses. He used his T-shirt to wipe out the glasses and poured, still staring at her. She smiled and couldn't help laughing, and he joined in.

She said, "Are you renting this house?"

"No. I bought it a few years ago. It was originally a fishing shack, but I like it."

"I was just thinking that this deck is unusually small, but I guess it wasn't built as a permanent residence."

"Nope. Just built for some guys, beer, and fishing gear."

"And the other kind of fishing." They chuckled, and sat quietly awhile, eating. Finally, Marilyn said, "At first, I couldn't understand why you had approached the subject of your phishing the way you did, but then I put myself in your position, and I realized you can't do the dating thing with all it entails, falling in love and everything, and then suddenly drop the bomb that you're a, um…"

"A crook?"

"Yeah, a crook." She grinned. "It would be like the Roadrunner's Acme anvil falling on poor Wile E. Coyote." They both smiled.

They finished eating, picked up the lunch debris, and Earl ushered her inside. Most waterfront homes sported décor of blue and white, beachy shabby chic, but Earl's style was a huge letdown. The place was piled high with a hoard of nautical salvage—driftwood, porthole windows, grates, and piles of rope and nets. She made her way along narrow spaces between stacked buckets and crates full of beach glass, cleats, glass floats, and shells, as well as myriad unfamiliar boat fixtures. In some areas the piles reached shoulder height. Much of his collection had value, if it were in a shop to be sold as curios and rehabbed as decorations, not in a private residence.

A pathway led to the kitchen, which was mainly usable, although the breakfast bar was piled with more stuff, including ships' wheels, and reproduction figureheads of double-D-bosomed mermaids. The living room had a path to a cleared sofa. There was also a bathroom and two bedrooms on the side of the house facing the street. Adding to the cringeworthy effect was a visible layer of dust, like dryer lint, that coated his hoard, and a stink of murky water, mold, and decay. Earl was a first-degree hoarder. It was only a matter of time before the floor rotted through and his hoard fell onto his van.

On the way to his house, she'd indulged in some

romantic speculation of beachfront living, but now she'd rather have a root canal than spend time in this house.

He led her through to a back room. "This is my office." Surprisingly, the room was orderly and spotless. A thick sheet of glass ran the full length of two walls and held four computers, all running, plus a filing cabinet built specifically for CDs and flash drives.

"How about I show you the ropes a little?" He pulled up an office chair for her, then moved his mouse, and a file appeared. He clicked on it, and it opened to show several documents that looked like bank statements. He said, "This is our new best friend, Marsha Brun. Marsha is a good case in point to demonstrate how I go about setting my hook and reeling in my phish. Unlike the usual scammers on planet Geek, I do legwork and research. First, I meet the mark—I like to refer to them as marks, so they are like checkers or chess pieces to me."

"Ah. You dehumanize them, make them pieces in a game."

"Exactly. I meet them in person at a social event and acquire their email address and business card. Then I find out their home address, and I look up the family-home's appraised value in the tax rolls. I also stalk them, follow them to work, assess their office, car, their nanny, cleaning staff, yard maintenance, and whether the children are chauffeured to expensive private schools. Plus, I observe their recreational squandering on stuff like vacations, memberships to private clubs and gyms, personal trainers, spa days for the missus, how much they spend on their drive-through coffee, and where they shop."

Marilyn was wide-eyed. "Okay, I'm a bit shocked. I figured it was all done on the computer."

"Oh, believe me, most scammers, that's all they do, and it's what I did at first, but it can take ages for someone to take the bait and click on your Trojan, and then you find out they're in debt up to their titties, and you're screwed. Anyway, I enjoy all the research, but out of everything gathered, the crucial piece of intel is where the mark banks. If they have a street mailbox, it is a fairly fast process to watch the mailbox for a statement, open and scan the contents with the app on my phone, write a little anonymous note on the envelope to the effect of, *Sorry, neighbor, your mail came to my house. I opened it before noticing it wasn't for me!* If they don't have a mailbox or if all their statements and bill paying is online, it can take longer, requiring subterfuge in the form of bullshit phone calls."

They talked the afternoon away, finally doing the real first-date protocol of where they came from; him, born and raised in Chicago, moved to Houston three years ago when his family started to suspect he was a thief. She filled him in on some highlights of her Detroit upbringing. "My mom was a woman of substance. Actually, she was a woman of substance abuse, ahead of her time, a heroin user," she said with a grim smile.

Earl ordered dinner from the local Vietnamese takeout. They discussed the art group, the Lads, Fran, and Rigby, and soon the sun started to set, a spectacular watermelon pink on the horizon that blended from purple to turquoise with a crescent moon rising. A few people were fishing from the nearby pier, silhouetted by the blushing sky. Earl said, "I'm in the mood to float, bob along on whatever wave comes my way. How about we go out for some live music at T-Bone Tom's, and you can stay the night." He wiggled his eyebrows and hopped up to retrieve another bottle of wine.

Marilyn shook her head. "Listen, let's take it slow, okay, Earl?" Her eyes implored him. Meanwhile she thought, *No way I'd sleep in that house. And sorry Earl, but you're not my type.* Instead, she said, "What we're talking about, well, it's forever, and it needs to be a hundred percent solid. I want us to feel our way to the right level before we are intimate. So…I'm going to hail a car and go home."

"Are you okay?" he asked with concern.

"Absolutely!" she said brightly, and they hugged and kissed.

Zabi whispered, *This guy is a jerk. Can you really manage him, his expectations, his ego, his personality defects?*

"Yes. I have to. I don't see a way out, Zabi."

Chapter Twenty-Three:

Big Phish

Two days later, late in the afternoon, Marilyn was in an Uber headed back to Earl's house. The weather was unseasonably hot for February, and she was wearing taupe linen shorts and a sleeveless T-shirt that read *Too Nice for New York, Too Naughty for LA*. She was deep in thought when her phone startled her, and she answered. The man's voice said, "Hey, Marilyn, what would you say to a happy hour drink. I could meet you at Hugo's patio in twenty minutes."

She quickly checked for caller ID, but it was blocked. "Who is this?" she asked.

He chuckled. "It's Ron."

"Oh hi, Ron." Rockwell. She quickly assessed what would be the best strategy to lead him into Stade's orbit. "Hey, Ron. Good to hear from you. Would you mind holding a minute?"

"No problem."

She dialed Stade and he picked up. She related the phone call. "Any chance you can intercept him?"

"Sure can," Stade said.

"Please let me know how it goes," she said.

She went back to Rockwell's call and said, "Sounds good, Ron. I'll see you at Hugo's in half an hour."

"Look forward to it," he said, and they hung up, leaving his fate to Stade.

At Earl's place, she climbed to the deck, and he greeted her. "Your shirt speaks the truth," he said. "The only option is Houston. Can you believe it's been more than six months since the hurricane?"

"Oh, yes, I can believe it. There are constant reminders, like the blue tarps on roofs everywhere," Marilyn said. They sat on Earl's deck, watching the water, drinking beer.

"The city is slowly recovering."

"Amen."

"Glad to have you back," he said.

She inhaled deeply. "You know, it's times like this when I miss Fran the most, sitting and enjoying the view, the pleasures of life. Everything good she's missing. Fuck."

"Yeah. It sucks. I really liked her a lot."

"Stade is still investigating the murders," she said, crossing her legs "He wants more connections and forensic evidence. He doesn't seem convinced that the Lads were the serial killers."

"I'm totally convinced the Lads were the killers. He should give up, quit wasting his time."

"Yes. I think you should set him straight Earl. Tell him how to do his job," she said with a laugh. "So, I saw you have a FSBO sign on your house." She pronounced it *fizbo*. "Are you moving?"

"Nope, not moving."

"The sign wasn't there the other day."

"You're right, it wasn't. The house is listed on a *For Sale by Owner* website, but I only put out the sign when I have a supposed *showing*."

"I don't understand." She frowned.

"It's to attract well-off people, so I can get their info. I don't put the sign up all the time because I want to select who comes to see it, and I don't want calls from endless tire-kickers who call because they saw the sign."

"Oh my god. That's genius. Diabolical genius, but genius nonetheless."

"A couple is coming by in an hour. You'll see." He leaned over and kissed her.

Marilyn asked, "Do we need to do something? In those house-flipping shows, they bake cookies and stuff." Not that even a five-star gourmet meal would distract a buyer from his pigsty.

He chuckled. "Nope. I guess if this were a farmhouse, we would, but not for this place."

A Mercedes pulled in and parked under the house. A slim, fit, and expensively dressed middle-aged couple climbed the steps.

The woman wore a white designer shirt and dark jeans. She said, "Do you think we'd have to install an elevator? This is a lot of steps to carry groceries."

The man was in gray Dockers and a navy golf shirt. "Good exercise, darlin'," he said. "Some serious repairs needed here."

The woman shushed him. They appeared at the top of the stairs looking flustered, no doubt wondering if they'd heard his comment. Hands were shaken all around, and they introduced themselves as Molly and Vern Rowan from Fort Worth. As expected, the couple gravitated to the deck's rail and gazed out over the water. The gulf matched the cloudless blue sky, a rarity as the water was usually green with a brown tint. A tanker moved almost indiscernibly on the line where water met sky, its green and rust softened by distance and haze. When the railing moved as they leaned on it, they stepped back in alarm.

The man said, "Are you selling this place as a fixer-upper?"

Earl said, "Not exactly. I love it, and would rather not sell, but there's some family business that'll take me out of the area for up to a year, so I have to let it go."

"Oh," Molly said. "Not an illness, I hope?"

Marilyn said, "Unfortunately, yes. His mom has a rare cancer of the stomach lining, and there have been complications and side effects with her medications."

The couple nodded in unison, and Earl changed the subject. "I hear it's dry up there in Fort Worth. People are talking about Dallas running out of water in about two years."

Vern said, "Yes. We have a drought right now. As a friend of mine said, it's about as wet as cracker juice." Everyone laughed.

Earl said, "Or Gandhi's sandals." They dutifully laughed again. Earl asked, "Can I get you a beverage?"

"Oh, no, thank you," Molly said.

Vern immediately said, "Thanks. I'd kill for a beer."

Molly composed an expression that indicated she was sorry for her husband's boorish behavior. "Really, we're fine, that would be imposing."

Earl laughed. "It's okay. Please come in." They followed him into the house, their expressions instantly crestfallen as they took in the hoard and dirt. Vern immediately declined the beer.

He said slowly, "This isn't exactly what we're looking for."

Earl led them through the living area. "Don't worry. I'll get all this stuff out of here once it's under contract."

"It's for our retirement. Vern can retire next year," Molly said.

"Neither of you looks old enough to retire," Earl flattered.

"Oh, go on…" Molly said. The compliment had its effect. They both smiled and studied each other. "Our kids are grown and have their own lives now. We just aren't ready to sit around all day doing Sudoku or whatever old people do."

"Or bridge or Yahtzee," Vern added.

"Mahjong." Earl said, contributing his two cents to the conversation, and they all laughed again.

The couple took a quick look through the house and Vern said, "That's quite a bank of computers."

Earl said, "I'm in IT. I've got a couple of apps patented. My big client right now is NASA. I'm under contract."

Wide-eyed, Molly said, "Goodness, you're so talented. I barely know how to send an email." She laughed too strenuously at her ineptitude.

Zabi whispered, *Oh brother, the I'm-just-a-stupid-little-girl tactic.*

Their awkward politeness couldn't overcome their disgust and desire to make a hasty retreat. As they edged toward the door, Earl went to his kitchen, opened a drawer, and took out a fake business card which read "Earl Madison, IT specialist, NASA" with the NASA logo and a dummy email address. Vern reciprocated, pulling a silver card case from his pocket. Earl said, "This is your work email. If you give me your personal email, I'll send you some pictures of the house."

Vern said, "No, that won't be necessary—"

Ever overly polite, Molly cut him off. "I'll give you mine," and she wrote her email address on the card's back. Marilyn wanted to grab the pen from Molly's hand and smack the conditioned people-pleasing out of her.

Back outside, the couple thanked Earl for the showing and made their way downstairs to their car. When they disappeared along the road, Earl said, "I invented a new drink. I don't know whether to call it *Smashed on the Rocks*, or *Blood on the Rocks*." He went inside and arrived with two tumblers filled to overflowing with ice cubes and a clear liquid. Crimson syrup was drizzled over the cubes.

"Yikes." She sipped. "Yum, it's good, and potent. A couple of these and I'd be smashed all right. Phew. Tough call about the name. Smashed suggests a shipwreck, but blood suggests a killer has been busy."

He laughed. "I like your assessment."

"Okay," she said. "Tell me how this phishing works."

"Well, obviously, since Vern and Molly are in Dallas, I won't be able to tail the couple and learn about them, so I'll snap some shots of the house and the view, download them, and embed a trojan. I'll wait a week or two to be sure they're at their home computer to send them. When Molly opens the attachment, the invisible trojan will overtake her home computer. From there, we can gain their passwords and scoop their retirement savings. I love computer illiterates like her." He rubbed his hands together.

"Holy shit," Marilyn said. "That's so, I don't know, clever." She looked over at Earl and his innocent good looks. He was like the trojan, or a different fable—a wolf in sheep's clothing.

"Didn't you hate them?" he asked.

"Um, no. Why would I hate them?"

"The guy was a total asshole. Guys like him all have boss complexes. They're used to giving orders, probably fantasized about being a general in an army," he said acidly. "And the wife was a total controlling bitch. All her crap, trying to find out why we're moving." It was the first time he'd exhibited this venom. "Yeah," he said. "Fucking rich snobs. It's going to be fun ripping them off. I love the idea of working with you. You're my soulmate."

Oh brother, a soulmate? More likely a cellmate. Marilyn was quiet a while. She had spent days weighing Earl's phishing scams against Gwynne's blackmail scheme and she'd concluded she wouldn't endlessly hack and steal from innocent people. His attitude toward Vern and Molly had just confirmed her decision, but she and Gwynne needed a patsy, and Earl fit the bill. He was the only person either of them knew who was both smart and crooked enough. She said, "There's something I want to discuss with you."

Chapter Twenty-Four:

Ransom

Marilyn paused a moment and said softly, "I've been hired to do something. It's a huge secret. It's highly illegal."

Earl turned to her, alert. "Yes?"

"I have incriminating evidence against Fairfield and his bodyguard." She checked Earl's reaction. He was intent, eyes bugging out. He opened his mouth to speak but stopped when she raised a forefinger. She went on, "Fairfield dropped his ring at the Lads' murders, and I found it. The ring is engraved with his name. I also watched through the peephole in Fran's apartment, and I saw Fairfield shoot Shawn."

"Holy crap."

"Yes, it was awful." She cleared her throat and sipped her drink. "Anyway, the lawyer, Gwynne, who is representing Fairfield and Palmer, tracked me down and said he wants to call me as a witness at Fairfield's trial."

"Why call you as a witness? You saw Fairfield kill Shawn, so it seems counterproductive for Fairfield."

"Well, here's the thing. There's evidence—mainly to do with the car they used—putting them at the crime scene so they need a reason to justify their presence. Gwynne wants me to testify that the Lads were raping me, so Palmer shot them."

"Holy fuck!"

"Yeah, and Fairfield will pay me five hundred grand for the gig."

Earl's eyes were saucers. "That's a nice chunk of change."

She nodded. "I told him I'll do it, and I'll hand over Fairfield's ring when I testify." She swigged her drink. "I like his plan because I was scared shitless that they'd find me and just kill me like they did to the Lads, but I told Gwynne that if anything happened to me, I've set things up so the evidence would be sent to the authorities. Maybe he believed me, maybe not, but it's my insurance, at least until the trial." She turned in her seat to face him. "What do you think?"

"I think it's amazing!" he exclaimed. "And I think you'll be great as a witness. I'd like to help you with any strategy and the details of what supposedly happened, make sure everything lines up so there's no screw-ups. Okay?"

"Sure. But there's something else. Gwynne wants to blackmail Fairfield. He thinks we could score ten million, maybe more, but we need one more player. I told him I know someone who might help."

"Are you referring to me?"

"Of course."

"Wow. I love the idea, but how would it work?"

"You, my friend, would be the anonymous blackmailer who has proof they killed the Lads. Gwynne acts as the go-between who relays info to Fairfield. Gwynne is working on getting some incriminating evidence together."

"What kind of evidence?"

"I'm not sure."

Earl looked perplexed. "Why would I need actual evidence? I just know. Let Fairfield worry how I found out." He chuckled.

"No. Put yourself in their shoes. They have already been indicted, so anyone in Houston could say 'I know you're guilty,' but without proof they won't pay a ransom. Why would they when they'll have my testimony to get them a not-guilty verdict?"

"That makes total sense. Your witness gig will be crucial for the blackmail to work."

"It's dangerous. But the ten million makes it worthwhile."

"I know, right? We can do this." He paused. "You've thought of everything. Tell me we're a go. I like it."

"Yes, we're a go. I'll let Gwynne know." She thought for a minute. "Do you think the Lads might be innocent? Do you think someone else killed Fran, Darby, and the other women?"

"Naw. They did it for sure. Everything pointed to them."

"God, I miss Fran so much."

Earl begged her to stay the night, but Marilyn reiterated her desire to take things slow. She hailed a car and kissed Earl goodbye.

The next day brought unseasonable warmth and sun considering it was still winter. She dressed in jean shorts, sandals, and a satiny blue camisole, her bright coral bra straps exposed. Midday, Marilyn walked from her apartment to Houston's urban recreational area, Hermann Park. In summer, the park was lush and dense, but now despite the heat, it seemed defeated by winter. About half the trees had dropped most of their leaves and stood skeleton-like against the sky, and a brief freeze a week ago had knocked down swaths of vulnerable tropical plants.

She headed to the section with statuary and stonework lining a man-made stream. Of the enormous acreage, its Parisian vibe made this one of her favorite areas. Gwynne was seated on a shaded bench. He was wearing an expensive gray suit. Cufflinks flashed in his French cuffs.

Gwynne and Marilyn had settled on some rules: they would have monthly meetings in the park and phone calls only on dedicated, secret burner phones Gwynne had supplied, and even then, only for important news. She knew Gwynne would have scouted the area for cameras. She scanned the nearly empty grounds. The only visitors were nannies with their charges at the kiddie playground.

He stood, shrugged out of his jacket, and draped it on the back of the bench. Then he hugged her, running a hand over her back. He was chewing gum. "Are you wired?"

"No."

"Armed?" He felt around her waist, inside her waistband, and ran his fingers up under the camisole and the band of her bra.

As his hands moved under her arms and edged close to her breasts, she grabbed his wrists. "Are you flirting with me, counselor?"

He grinned. "Would you like me to?"

"Actually, this seems more like foreplay."

He smiled as he opened her purse and peered inside. Satisfied, he sat down, patted the seat, and she sat next to him. Gwynne opened a small, insulated carrier. He handed her a bottle of Perrier and a plastic clamshell containing a sandwich.

She smiled and said, "Perfect weather for a picnic. How civilized."

He used a napkin to remove his gum and asked, "Still in?"

"Of course, I'm still in." Examining the sandwich, she asked, "What's in this?"

"Roast beast on baguette." He smiled. "You're not vegetarian, are you?"

"Roast *beast*, huh? Nope, not vegetarian." She chuckled and said, "I saw a sign outside a burger joint once that said, 'Vegetarians—if you care so much for the animals, stop eating their food.'"

He grinned and nodded. They both took a bite, and she said, "Mmm, good sandwich. I like the arugula with the roast beef."

"I did some research and found that you were a dancer."

"Yes. Ballet lessons, a hundred years ago."

"I'm impressed. I can just picture you in a tutu and those pink shiny pointe shoes with the ribbons." He took another bite, chewed, and swallowed. "I always wanted a ballerina to walk on my naked body in those shoes."

She said, "Might give new meaning to *The Nutcracker*." They both laughed. "Well, my dance days were over long ago. I had an injury. I took the acting lessons after that." She winked. "But I might be able to accommodate your ballerina role play."

"You still have the ballet shoes?"

"No, but I can get some."

He smiled. "I'm going to hold you to that." After another bite of his sandwich, he asked, "Are you brushing up on your acting skills?"

"I'm confident I can pull off the witness gig. In fact, I'll be Oscar-worthy."

He grimaced. "I hope you realize that overacting is as bad as freezing. You'll have to be vulnerable and very authentic, measured, believable."

"I will be. So, you called this meeting, Gwynne. What's up?"

"I have something to show you, and I need our friend Earl to do something tonight."

"He's totally on board. In fact, I'd say he's enthusiastic."

"By the way, I did a thorough background check on him." Gwynne sipped his water. "He's squeaky clean in the eyes of the law and has no family ties. Obviously, he can't be connected in any way to either of us."

"I emphasized to him that he and I can't know each other." She took a sip of bubbly water.

"Poor Earl, his dreams of bedding you, dashed." Gwynne smirked.

"Sucks to be Earl," she said lightly, and returned his smirk. First the ballet shoes and now this. He certainly liked sexual innuendo. "What have you got to show me?"

"A video of Fairfield that was shot in my boardroom. Fairfield and Palmer—two bad actors—talking about their bad acts. Fairfield is a unique client because he knows if he doesn't come clean, he'll tie my hands when I'm putting together his defense." He cued the video on his tablet, attached earbuds, and handed it to her.

She put the buds in her ears and tapped the play arrow.

On the screen, Palmer and Fairfield are sitting in the boardroom of the lawyers' offices, waiting for the attorneys. Fairfield says, "Gwynne told me there's a new development in our case—" He is interrupted by a young woman entering through huge, black-tinted glass doors. She is grinning like a toothpaste ad, introduces herself as Roxanne, apologizes for the lawyers being late, then leaves the room.

"Wonder if her teeth get dry," Fairfield says gruffly. "These days every female in every law office looks like her, pretty, and boringly predictable. Fucking clones. Where do they find these law-girls?"

Palmer smiles and nods. Roxanne enters again, still grinning, carrying a tray with a carafe, bone-china cups, a plate of pastry, and linen napkins. She puts the tray on the table next to pads of lined paper, speakerphones that look like three-legged robot-insects, and pens printed with the law firm's name Gwynne, Bass, Simpson & Sharpe. Off to the side, there is a video camera on a tripod.

Roxanne gives Palmer a coy flirtatious look. He ignores her, and she turns away, miffed, a young woman used to things going her way. She stands near the door and waits, hands folded in front of her, still smiling. Palmer points to the camera and asks her, "Is that camera filming?"

She strides quickly to the camera. "Yes."

Fairfield says, "Shut it off."

Roxanne peers at the camera from different angles and pushes a button. "There. It's turned off now," she says confidently.

Fairfield says, "You can go now, sweetheart."

Marilyn stopped the video. "If she turned it off, why did it continue recording?"

"Good point. She only thought it was turned off. It captured some good stuff. Keep going," he said, smiling.

On the screen Roxanne's smile dims. "Ah…" She hesitates. "Mr. Gwynne told me to stay."

Fairfield openly ogles her. "Gwynne isn't in charge, sweetheart. I am. So, get the fuck lost." Roxanne's smile collapses, and she yanks the door open and dashes out. Fairfield says, "I know her father. Rich girl, new to the real world."

Palmer chuckles. "She better buckle up. It's gonna be a bumpy ride."

"Indeed." Fairfield laughs. "Bet she's weeping in the ladies' room as we speak."

Gwynne enters and shakes hands. They get comfortable and distribute coffee and food. Gwynne clears his throat. "The trial will be within the next ten months."

Marilyn removes the earbuds and stares pointedly at Gwynne. "Ten months seems pretty far off."

"Not really. Some cases take several years to come to trial." She put the earbuds back in and hit the play arrow.

On the screen, Fairfield nods and waits a beat. "What effect does that have?"

Gwynne shrugs. "It's okay. We always like more time to separate the jury from the news stories that came before. I'd say it's a pretty standard timeline. Putting us a year and a half after the murders. It also means the prosecution has to stop dicking around and get their exculpatory evidence to us. You're going to be tried together."

Fairfield asks, "Is getting tried together good or bad?"

"Both," Gwynne says. "The bad part is, how much you each participated in the murders doesn't matter, because you're both culpable under the law. The good part is that the jury will sentence you separately. They can choose to be more lenient on one if they want."

Fairfield jumps up and slams his palms on the table with the agility of someone half his age. Gwynne and Palmer are calm with indulgent, slight smiles as Fairfield growls, "Sentencing? I won't do time for it. You got that, Gwynne?"

"Absolutely, and I've been working tirelessly to make that happen, sir."

"There will be no sentencing! There will be *acquittals*!" Fairfield adds, "You hear me, Gwynne? If you want to keep Fairfield Oil and every company I ever referred to this firm as clients, you'll make it happen."

"Yes sir," Gwynne answers assertively. "On that note, I'd like you to give me an account of what happened that night. To work effectively on your defense, I need to understand your motivation and everything that happened."

Fairfield says, "Bullshit. I don't need to run through anything. Find a way to prove our innocence—whatever it takes—evidence, or a technicality."

Gwynne asks, "Did they attack you, anything that would make it self-defense?"

Fairfield glowers at Gwynne and says, "I'm happy those two evil cockroaches are dead, but we weren't there. Got it?"

Gwynne doodles a moment and looks up "There's too much evidence placing you at the scene to get you off, but I have a proposition." Fairfield sits straighter, interested, and Gwynne says, "I wasn't sure about this, but I think it's our ace in the hole. A woman came forward. She has your ring, Fairfield. The cops never got hold of it."

Palmer asks, "The one who lived next to the Lads' apartment?"

"Yes, but she lived there only for a short time after the hurricane," Gwynne says.

Chapter Twenty-Five:

The Incentive

Marilyn continued watching the video on Gwynne's tablet.

Fairfield, ecstatic that Gwynne has located his ring, slaps his palm on the table again, and shouts, "Hallelujah! Now we're talking!"

"It gets even better," Gwynne says, grinning. "For a fee, she's willing to testify that she was being raped, and you saved her by killing the assholes."

Fairfield looks up quickly and laughs heartily. "Now we're getting somewhere," he says through his toothy grin.

Gwynne says, "Indeed, we are."

"How much does she want?"

Gwynne looks thoughtful. "A million."

"No problem." Fairfield smiles happily. "Now, where's my ring? I feel naked without it."

"She's keeping it until the trial. Insurance."

Marilyn hit pause, gasped, and removed the earbuds. "A million?" She turned to Gwynne. "Wait a minute, are you taking a cut?"

"No. My fees will be double that. It's all yours. I went with the million because Fairfield's a cheap bastard who will grind down any price, and I wanted to have some wiggle room to bargain." Gwynne laughed. "With your cut of the ransom, you'll be set. You know you'll have to be in the wind after this, right?"

"Oh, I am well aware I'll have to leave Houston permanently," she said emphatically. She inserted the earbuds and resumed the video.

On the screen Fairfield says, "Make it happen, and don't fuck it up." He rubs his hands together.

"How did you find this *witness*?" Palmer asks. "I sent our guys out, and they came back with nothing."

"I have my ways." Gwynne smiles. Outdone, Palmer scowls.

Marilyn laughed and pressed pause. She removed one earbud and said, "Palmer messed up once again. First, multiple screw-ups with the killings, then he couldn't fix it, either. Lucky they've got you on the case, Gwynne."

Gwynne raised his eyebrows. "In his defense, it's pretty hard to get things done when you're under house arrest. Never. Ever. Underestimate Palmer. The guy is a ninja pit bull with no conscience."

"A ninja pit bull. Hmm, I'll keep that in mind. But he's still screwed up a lot of stuff." Marilyn popped the earbud back in and tapped the play arrow.

In the video, the ever-smiling Roxanne arrives again. She pours water into glasses. Fairfield flicks his hand at her to leave. She looks at Fairfield with a perplexed frown until Gwynne shrugs and dismisses her.

Fairfield says angrily, "She gives me a look like that again, you'll be firing her."

Gwynne appears pissed. "She's okay. I would've let her stay."

Fairfield says heatedly, "Look, Gwynne, I'm a believer in the old saying, *two people can keep a secret if one of them is dead.* So, get this straight. Be careful and keep the witness angle quiet even from the other lawyers and staff. Everything is on the line. If your little dick-sucking doxy, or anyone else, gets wind of our witness, there will be more bodies."

Marilyn flicked her gaze onto Gwynne and hit pause again. "In public he comes off as a gruff-yet-lovable grandpa, but he's a pig in private."

"A ruthless piggy."

"Is Fairfield correct? Are you screwing that intern or assistant, whatever she is, or was Fairfield just being crude?" Gwynne was like the older, sophisticated, rich men on the sugar daddy websites. She could see how a young woman like Roxanne would find him secure, protective, and attractive.

"Heavens no. That would be sexual harassment." He winked.

"Well, that was ambiguous," she said, and winked back. She started the video again and watched Fairfield attack, his color high, spittle spraying, "You need to get your heads out of your asses and get this perfect. You've got one chance. Your actress better be real good. If she blows it, heads will roll."

Marilyn closed her eyes momentarily in dread and considered, given Fairfield's inclination to default to violence, whether she was making a huge mistake taking on the witness gig. Everything depended on her performance. Even the blackmail, the real money, was an offshoot of her testimony because without it Fairfield would be found guilty and jailed, and he'd have no reason to pay a ransom. She restructured her inner scaffolding, her confidence, sat straighter, and brushed her negative thoughts away.

"Tell me about this girl, our witness," Fairfield says on the tablet.

"I've met her and talked to her. She'll be believable," Gwynne says confidently.

Fairfield says, "I want to meet her before the trial."

"That's tricky," Gwynne replies.

"The story won't fly if I've never seen her, heard her, talked to her, beforehand."

"All right," Gwynne says. "I'll figure something out."

"Well," Marilyn said grimly. "This should be interesting." She closed her sandwich container and placed it in her bag. "That was a fascinating video. I like how you introduced the witness idea. But you didn't tell Fairfield about the blackmail. And I'm not sure why you called this meeting since we need to keep our relationship secret."

"I, or I should say we, have a problem." Gwynne reached over and placed his hand on her thigh. She looked at it pointedly and he ignored her reaction. She caught the scent of Gwynne's gorgeous, pricey aftershave. He said, "We need evidence to hold over Fairfield for the blackmail."

"Isn't it enough to have Earl say he was staying with a friend at the building and saw Fairfield and Palmer coming or going, and recognized them?"

Gwynne thought a moment and said, "No. It doesn't definitively tie them to the killings."

"And if Earl says he knows about the fake witness *and* saw them?"

"That would muddy the waters for your testimony. Fairfield will smell a rat for sure. When I finally realized the camera had recorded the meeting, I hoped Fairfield had confessed on video in which case I'd have Earl steal the camera. Fairfield came close but didn't spell out what he did."

"Yeah. Fairfield's pretty sharp. Bummer."

He swept Marilyn's thick dark hair behind her ear, an affectionate gesture, and ran his fingertips down her cheek and along her jawline. He said, "I haven't been able to come up with any evidence incriminating enough to use as leverage against Fairfield for blackmail. So, we both need to put on our thinking caps."

"Okay. Here's a thought. Can you convince Fairfield that he did confess, and you have it on video?"

Gwynne laughed. "Not a chance. He'd want to see it."

They both stood and he hugged her again. His embrace felt stable and all-encompassing, and he smelled wonderful. After a moment, he released her.

As she left the park her phone rang, and she answered. Stade said, "After your call about Ron Rockwell, I intercepted him at Hugo's. It was crowded so I made an appointment to question him at the station. He came in this morning and I interrogated him. His real name is Ronald Roquel."

"Can you spell that?"

Stade spelled the name, and explained, "He says it with a French accent, rolling his r's and all that and it comes off as Rockwell. He's not a geologist. He's a grifter, takes advantage of lonely women who are on the dating site, usually older women, but I'd say he's an all-around player. Turns out your intuition was right. He went out with Fran three or four times, and he knew who you were. You both ended up in that motel by coincidence and he says he liked you and was curious what your story was, so it's hard to say if he was stalking you. He has alibis for when Fran and Darby went missing. Namely, he was doing what you were doing, escaping the flood. I'll check the people he supplied as alibis, but I think he's innocent."

"Hmm…bet he's pissed at me standing him up, and turning him in." She laughed. "Did he know any of the other murdered women, maybe meet them on the dating site?"

"Doesn't look like it, but we're going through each of them. He was a prolific dater. I'll let you know if there are any breakthroughs."

Forty-eight hours after her meeting with Gwynne, the heatwave had broken and resumed seasonal chilly temperatures and rain. In the parking lot of Earl's neighborhood Walmart, she climbed into the passenger seat of his van as she collapsed her umbrella. He grabbed her and kissed her. "Stop that! It'll draw attention." She pushed him away. "Christ, it's cold."

"Yep. Sure feels like winter…Marilyn—"

She cut him off. "There's something I need you to do."

His eyebrows knotted. "What is it?"

She removed a thumb drive from her bag. "This is evidence, and it's our leverage for the blackmail. I downloaded it from one of the Lads' laptops."

"Whoa. What's on this?"

"The Lads' laptops were on and recording when they were killed. Right after they were shot, I went into their apartment and grabbed them. This has a half hour or so of video of the killers. I don't have the software to do it, so, as our resident computer whiz, I want you to extract a twenty-second GIF—here, I marked the times on its case." She pressed the thumb drive into his hand. "We need to give Fairfield a taste of the shit that will rain on his parade if he doesn't cough up the ransom. The story for Gwynne to tell Fairfield is that you stayed with someone in the building that night and grabbed the Lads' laptops after the killings."

"Wow. I didn't know you had this stuff."

"No one knows. I was keeping it a secret, as insurance."

"You're something else…But only twenty seconds?"

"Yes. Just enough to get their attention. The twenty seconds that I marked shows both Fairfield and Palmer's faces and Fairfield shooting Shawn."

"Holy fuck. That's fucking awesome."

"Yes. Yes, it is. Put it on an endless loop so it runs

over and over. Then you need to send the GIF to Gwynne on an ultra-secure, self-destructing server. Don't download the whole thing anywhere because if you get hacked, if this gets leaked, our plan will be toast. And after you send the GIF to Gwynne destroy the thumb drive and the GIF.

"Will do. But holy fucking wow," Earl said. "This blackmail is awesome. No hostage, no violence, no gunfire, just a little GIF of our friend, Fairfield."

"Well, no violence yet. Let's keep it that way. Our roles are perfect," she said. "Gwynne is ideal as the go-between. He meets with Fairfield often, and Fairfield trusts him, plus he can act as a buffer, providing separation for you and me from Fairfield and shielding us from whatever violence the bodyguards or their other minions might inflict on us."

"Awesome. Good points." He turned to her. "I've been thinking. Since it'll be split three ways the ask has to be high, like at least fifteen million."

"Don't worry about Gwynne demanding enough ransom. I think he's greedier than the two of us put together."

"What about that cop, Stade? Is he still hanging around?" Earl was talkative, chatting excitedly, his blue eyes wide and innocent. For a con man, Earl's innocent looks were probably his greatest asset.

"The last time I talked to Stade, he seemed to agree with me when I said the Lads were the serial killers. He's only asked about Fairfield a couple of times. Just basic questions."

"Good," Earl said. "So, when will I get to see your apartment? I miss you every day." He seemed genuinely forlorn.

"Earl." She stifled the urge to roll her eyes. "Fairfield is probably watching my place, so, *never*. We need to keep a low profile. We can't have any contact until after the trial, and we need to plan how to disappear. It would be really bad if Fairfield's people identify you as the extortionist, saw us talking, and put two and two together. If that happens, we're as good as dead."

"How do you keep in touch with Gwynne?"

"We both have dedicated burner phones, not used for anything else but to call or text each other."

"That's awesome. After I send the GIF to Gwynne, I'll get a dedicated phone for him as well. And we should too."

"Okay, but we can't have any more face-to-face meetings." She tried to appear disappointed, but it was a fortuitous turn of events that took the pressure off her regarding Earl's expectations of intimacy.

"Are you still modeling? I can at least see you there."

"Earl." She exhaled in exasperation. "Yes, I'm still modeling. But you shouldn't attend my sessions. Gwynne found me partly because Rigby couldn't keep her trap shut. He's super-sharp, and Fairfield's people are too. You going to be able to handle that? After all, once it's over, we'll have millions in our hands, and we'll be together as much as we want."

"Sure. Of course," Earl said sadly. "It's going to be awesome."

Marilyn left Earl's van. At home she sat for half an hour, turning her phone over in her hands Before she finally called Gwynne. "I assume you haven't come up with any blackmail-worthy evidence for our friend Fairfield," she said. More a statement than a question.

"No, I haven't. You?"

"Watch your email. I've directed a little present your way."

Shortly after she hung up Earl called and said, "I sent the GIF to Gwynne in an email via a secure routing system. In the email I said that I have the Lads' laptops. By the way, where are the Lads' laptops?"

"None a yer beeswax," she said laughing. "Bye Earl." As she hung up, she heard him say, "Marilyn…"

The thought of Earl sending the GIF gave her

butterflies. With his supposed ridiculous love for her he was pathetic. Add the stress, fear, anxiety, pressure, and secrecy of the blackmail, he could crater and rat her and Gwynne out to the police. She'd be guilty of withholding evidence and other illegal stuff to do with the false witness conspiracy and lying to a sexy detective.

Zabi said, *Ha. Anything involving sexy detectives should be illegal.*

Would witness protection be an alternative? She could stop this craziness now. Come clean with Stade and get shipped off with a new identity to an alt-right, hellish, tiny town in a flyover state. If she wanted to vanish, she could do it herself without Stade's help, but either way she'd be looking over her shoulder constantly for Fairfield's goons. Ugh.

Was there a different way to handle this? Maybe she should demand ten or twenty million for her testimony, split it with Gwynne, and tell Earl the blackmail was a no-go. No. It would be too complex. She would need to coordinate the exchange of cash with Gwynne, and she didn't trust him. Earl was a safer bet. It wouldn't be as if Fairfield was paying a bill, and he'd send her money by PayPal, or a check in the mail. The exchange would have to happen while she was still holding something over Fairfield and testifying.

She tried to imagine how the switch might go down. Zabi asked, *Would it be like a drug-deal scene in a movie?*

She imagined the scene, in a flat open place. Fairfield and Palmer would drive up in a big black car. Both she and Palmer would get out of their vehicles carrying their firearms and walk to within ten feet of each other. Palmer would open an oversized briefcase full of cash to show her the money, then he'd close it. She would place the bag of evidence on the ground. They would circle each other. She'd grab the briefcase, get into her car, and drive away.

Except, she knew better. Palmer would shoot her before she got back into her vehicle. She needed Earl to facilitate the exchange while she was in court, on the stand. He seemed to genuinely care for her, and while she suspected it was delusion or a lie, if true, did that translate to trustworthiness?

Chapter Twenty-Six:

Sketchy Characters

In Hermann Park, the Japanese Garden was drenched in tranquility. It had rained in the night, and the early morning air was crisp. In the sun, droplets glistened on foliage. Marilyn, in a long black skirt, denim jacket, and short boots, walked along a winding path edged with a variety of Asian plants. She sat on a stone bench surrounded by Japanese maples and cherry trees. Gwynne arrived and sat beside her. A bubbling water-feature covered their conversation.

"Great weather, isn't it? There's nothing like winter in Houston," Gwynne said.

"Except for the five consecutive days of rain last week with near freezing temperatures. But at least you don't have to shovel it." She shrugged and smiled. "Have they set a date for trial?"

"No. It can take years to get to trial, but I'm guessing

it will be in about three to six months."

"Yeah?" She glanced at him. He nodded and handed her his tablet and she put an earbud in her right ear. "What's this?"

"Fairfield's reaction to the GIF Earl sent me." He raised his eyebrows.

She smiled and touched the play arrow on a video. On the screen, Fairfield, Palmer, and Gwynne are in Gwynne's boardroom again. Gwynne says, "There's another thing. A slight problem."

Fairfield looks up, intense. "What kind of problem?"

"I got this yesterday." Gwynne hands his tablet to Fairfield and touches the screen, activating the GIF.

After watching a few seconds Fairfield shouts, "What the fuck!" His face is an unhealthy purplish-red. "Where the fuck did this come from? Who sent it?"

Palmer scowls. "How the hell did someone get this?"

"The guy who sent it to me says he was in the building that night, heard the commotion and went to the Lads' place after they were dead. He took their laptops and there's full video of the killings on them. Apparently both laptops were taping."

"Jesus fucking Christ on a crumpet!" Fairfield says angrily.

Palmer looks ashen. "Yeah, when I went back to find the ring the place had been tossed."

"The blackmailer—I don't have his identity of course—sent me this via an untraceable, self-destructing email."

"Not a chance we give in to blackmail," Fairfield says emphatically. "We'll find and kill this fucker."

Gwynne says, "He wants twenty million. If I tell him to get lost, he'll more than rat you out. He'll post it on the internet. He says there's a lot more footage. This is just a taste."

Palmer, taking back control, says, "We need to keep this going. It's the only way to figure out who he is and eliminate him. Tell him we need to see the full video."

"I'll tell him, but we're completely at his mercy," Gwynne says glumly.

Fairfield nods. "I still don't fucking like it. I understand the girl wanting to be paid for being a witness because she'll be scared and want to disappear after the trial. But blackmail is bullshit. Once you pay, they keep wanting more. They never go away."

"I'll get rid of him. I'll fucking find a way," Palmer says.

"With all due respect, sir," Gwynne says smoothly, "even though it's a lot of cash, if it's the difference between prison and freedom, it might be worth just paying it and moving on. And Palmer has a point about keeping this asshole in our sights, so I encourage you to agree to the blackmailer's terms."

"Palmer and I will discuss it." Fairfield grunts, sips coffee, places a cinnamon bun on a linen napkin, and he and Palmer leave the boardroom.

Marilyn removed the earbuds and held out his tablet. He took it and placed his hand in hers. Gwynne said, "Thanks for sharing the video. It's very effective and much better than me trying to squeeze a video-taped confession out of Fairfield. By the way, where are the laptops?"

She gave him some side-eye and a smirk. "In a safe place. They're keeping Fairfield's ring company." She traced a finger over the back of his hand that was still holding hers. "You raised the blackmail amount from ten to twenty mil?"

"Yes. But keep in mind, it's possible the ransom won't get paid. They might only be agreeing in order to keep Earl close and quiet so that at the right moment, they can annihilate him. Just be happy it's not us in his place."

"If that's a strong possibility, my witness fee should be much higher," she said, frowning. "Also, I'm pretty much broke. I need an advance on the witness money."

"How much?"

"Fifty percent."

"I'll see what I can do."

"Seeing *what you can do* isn't good enough, Gwynne. I need the advance, five hundred grand, not only because I'm broke, but to prove Fairfield is serious. Presumably, as a witness you will want me to be a surprise and don't want the DA to find me, which means I'm a ghost. I can't have a job, and I have to pay for everything in cash."

"Okay."

"Fifty percent, Gwynne," she said sternly. "If I don't get the advance I'll have to pull out, vanish, and take Fairfield's ring and videos with me as insurance."

"Okay. I said okay. You are such a tough girl," he said mockingly, smiling. Gwynne took out a Post-it with a name and number on it. "Another thing. Before you make your getaway, go see this guy. He'll make you a new identity—passport, social security, driver's license, the works. Change your hair and makeup first."

"Okay. I'll get a blonde or red wig." She flipped her hair.

They stood and he turned toward her. "You okay?" he asked.

"Sure, why?"

"You've had so much loss and trauma." He swept his fingers through her hair, taking hold of it at the nape of her neck. His face was inches from hers and heat passed between them.

His simple statement of caring brought an ache to her throat and tears filled her eyes. There wasn't the sexual electricity she got from Stade nor the affectionate puppy love of Earl's infatuation. This was different, solid, grown-up, settled. He moved in to kiss her, but the reality of his marriage and being in public intruded, and she bit his bottom lip hard enough to be a threat. Then she let go, and said, "Don't worry, no blood."

He stepped away and touched his lip. "I didn't think you were into the rough stuff."

"I am into it. And so are you."

"I am?" He raised his eyebrows.

"Someone told me your wife's well known for her sexual proclivities. She's considered highly talented in certain circles."

He laughed. "Would you like to try your technique on me some time?"

"Definitely. Before the trial." She wasn't sure why she'd agreed, except to keep all options open.

They stood assessing each other for a time, then parted, trailing their hands across each other's fingers before strolling in opposite directions. Neither looked back.

She was back at her apartment when the Earl-phone rang.

He said, "Just checking in."

"Okay. On my end, things are moving along smoothly. Gwynne is very happy about your GIF. It sounds like Fairfield is cooperating with the blackmail."

"Cool," Earl said. They hung up.

She made a grilled cheese sandwich for lunch and considered her options. Her nerves were still bristling about her meeting with Gwynne.

Gwynne had tapped into her vulnerability. He had only said a few words about her loss, and she'd been brought to tears. Maybe because part of being a good defense lawyer was that he mined his clients' defenselessness. But it wasn't as if Gwynne had come to her without any information about her. He said Rigby had filled him in on how Marilyn had lost everything in the hurricane, that Fran was her bestie, and that Marilyn was scared of the Lads' killers. He was a skilled manipulator tapping into a known reservoir of feelings.

The idea of meeting Fairfield gave her goosebumps. It

would be a dress rehearsal for the trial. Picturing the pitfalls gave her stage fright. Then there was the blackmail. Given Fairfield's and Palmer's propensity for violence, extortion would certainly bring out their worst. Not for the first time she considered whether she could say no to the blackmail and just be their perjuring witness. In a smaller, cheaper town than Houston, the million dollars for the witness gig would support her for quite a while, as well as buy a paid-off house or condo. She could get a job and live within her means, keep her head down. She ate the last of the sandwich, rinsed her plate, and headed out for a brisk walk to clear her head.

Two days passed without word from any of the players, which created dread at what might be brewing, especially since Gwynne was late delivering her five-hundred-thousand-dollar advance. Then at noon there was an unexpected knock on her door. She hid in the archway of the dining room and peered along the hallway to the pebbly glass of the door. Stade. Instantly irritated, she opened the door and stepped onto the porch. "First Gwynne, now you. I'm not even going to ask how you found my address. Wait—did Gwynne give you my address?"

"Nice to see you too," he said facetiously, ignoring her question.

"Stade, look, I made it clear that I've got nothing for your investigation."

"No. Gwynne didn't give me your address. By the way, I've known him for a long time."

"Really? How long have you known Gwynne?" She wasn't entirely surprised by Stade showing up, considering Gwynne had found her apartment. But as attractive as he was, she couldn't have him in her life. What a great couple they would be, the cop and the felon. She needed to get rid of him and tried to think of something that would repel him permanently.

Zabi whispered, *Maybe have sex and in the middle of it, ask the four words all men dread, namely, "Is it in yet?"*

Marilyn clamped her lips into a thin line to strangle a chuckle.

Stade continued, "We move in some of the same social circles. Plus, with him being a criminal-defense lawyer, he tends to represent the criminals I arrest who have deep pockets. I run into him in court."

"Are you here about Fairfield? Gwynne is all about Fairfield," she said.

"Mind if we go inside?"

Marilyn pursed her lips. Going indoors meant privacy and access to the bedroom. She would have to be careful. "What is this visit about, Detective? Is it police work, or personal?"

Disappointment clouded his expression. She recognized this frown as subtle manipulation—the sulk. She was being difficult, and she should try to please. "Here's an idea," she said. "Let's go to your house to chat."

His laugh at her audacity was spontaneous, and he shook his head. "I'm not sure I see your point."

"You don't? I haven't tracked you down, stalked you, invaded your workplace and personal space. I don't know where you live, Stade, but you, and Gwynne, and whoever else connected to Fairfield, have done those things to me, and you guys always excuse it as *dedication* to your *job* or your *investigation.*"

"Got it. I'm sorry." He appeared genuinely surprised. "I've never looked at it that way. I guess for us in law enforcement, the job becomes all-important, overshadowing all else. We trample on people's boundaries and rights unintentionally because of our tunnel vision." He exhaled. "And yes, I am here concerning the investigation of more missing women…And I'd be happy to give you my home address and show you my house, anytime. Just say the word."

"Fine," she said, and despite her frown, opened the door to the small foyer and narrow hall. In the confined space Stade smelled wonderful, fresh like the starch of his shirts mixed with something herbal, perhaps his soap, and something unique that drew her in. Those darn pheromones. She counteracted by stepping away and they went into the living room.

He looked around, assessing her surroundings, apparently looking for something to compliment, as he commented, "I like the—"

She cut him off, "Don't bother. It's all rented, and the apartment is temporary." She indicated the sofa, "Have a seat."

He sat on one half of the loveseat, no doubt expecting her to sit next to him, but she chose a chair with the coffee table between them, and asked, "What do you want to know?"

"There are three more murdered women. Cold cases. They've been identified but we're looking for connections."

"Are these different from the three you asked me about last time?"

"Yes. These go back several years, and according to their families, they had jewelry they wore constantly, and it was missing when their bodies were found. We've been checking the usual pawn shops and thrift stores to get a description of the seller, but we're coming up empty. For this one..." He placed a photo of a high school cheerleader on the coffee table and slid it across to her. "She had a thing for hearts," he said. "Her parents gave her a ring with a heart-shaped setting for her sixteenth birthday. This photo is old. Lately she had lots of heart tattoos."

"I don't know her," Marilyn said.

This one..." He slid a photo of a young woman in a business suit across the coffee table, "wore an ankle bracelet with topaz and ruby stones."

"Sorry. I've never met her, either."

Stade produced a photo of another young woman on a beach wearing a bikini. He said, "She had a diamond stud in her belly button that she never removed. You can see it in that photo."

"I'm pretty sure I haven't met or even seen them. They might have been at the Lads' parties, but like I said before, you should talk to Rigby since she went to the Lads' parties a lot more than I ever did, especially that long ago."

He said, "Assuming the Lads killed them seems like a narrow net to cast. As a case it's too circumstantial for me. I'd feel better if we had found the missing jewelry in the Lads' apartment."

"Sorry I can't help, but I'll take a look at social media again," she said. "But if I find out anything about them, what does that mean? After all, the Lads have already been executed."

"The Lads haven't been proven guilty yet. The killer may still be at large." He added, "It would help the victims' families to know what happened, and I just want to get to the bottom of it."

"You're a good detective, Detective Stade."

"Can I offer some detectively advice?" He frowned.

"Sure."

"Actually, it's just friendly advice. Don't get mixed up in any of Gwynne's schemes."

"Why? Did Gwynne say he has a scheme for me to get mixed up in, or is this your detectively instinct at work again?"

"Just…Gwynne is one helluva sketchy character. Speaking of sketchy characters, are you still modeling for all sorts of sketchy characters to sketch you?"

"Haha. Sketchy characters, huh? Good one, Detective. Yes, I'm still modeling. You going to come and draw me?" She smiled, and stood up. "Anything else?"

He stood as well. "Yes. I really want to see you again. Can I take you to dinner?"

"Thanks for the offer but…it's complicated."

"You've met someone."

She gazed at him with an ambivalent expression. It worked and he said, "Ah, okay there's someone else in the picture—got it. Not Gwynne, I hope. Sorry, none of my business." He held his hands up, palms out, then dropped them.

As she let Stade out and watched him cross the road to his car, the dedicated-Gwynne phone rang. He said, "I have your advance. Where do you want it delivered?"

She checked the time, one o'clock. "Chase bank…" She gave him the location.

"Fairfield's driver will be there in twenty minutes," he said.

She walked around the corner to the bank where a man in a dark suit left his shiny black SUV and handed her a cardboard box. She took it to her safe deposit box and opened the top. Gazing at the hundred-dollar bills she thought, *Now I'm really in deep.*

PART FOUR:
One Year After

Chapter Twenty-Seven:

The Meetup

It was a Sunday afternoon when Gwynne phoned and said, "Fairfield wants to meet you this week."

"I was hoping he'd forgotten," Marilyn said with a half-smile.

"No such luck," Gwynne said with a laugh. "I'll set something up for Tuesday evening. It'll be somewhere private. Fairfield will send a car."

"No, no, no. You need to drive me to the location. I won't be alone with Fairfield's guys. I don't trust them." He agreed, and they hung up. For the next two days Marilyn practiced her performance.

Midafternoon Tuesday, in the hour before Gwynne's arrival, she swept her hair back, wound it in a chignon at the nape of her neck, and dressed in a white shirt with a black knee-length skirt, black stockings, gold stud earrings, and short boots.

A year since the hurricane, since Fran's disappearance and murder, since the meetings with Stade to solve the serial killings. There was still not a day that Marilyn didn't mourn Fran, that she didn't think about the other murdered women, including Darby Fairfield. Now she would come face to face with Darby's father. One more step leading up to the trial.

She and Gwynne had met infrequently over the last months. Gwynne had emphasized maintaining clarity and sticking to their plans. He'd also pointed out that while the trial seemed far off, it would suddenly be upon them. Fairfield still vacillated about the blackmail and Palmer still swore he would find the perpetrator and kill him.

A text announced that Gwynne was out front. Marilyn was quite certain that someone from Fairfield's staff would follow Gwynne to her house, and she had rigged her apartment to catch the invader. There was lightweight clear fishing line tacked across the kitchen doorway, and all doors were left in an unlatched but nearly shut position, appearing to be closed. And as she left, she sprinkled a fine dusting of talcum powder just inside the front door on the off-white tile.

Outside, it was typical Houston weather for July: hot and spitting rain. She popped her umbrella and trotted to Gwynne's Mercedes. After half an hour, they pulled into a long secondary driveway to a porte-cochère at the back door of a country club. They were greeted by a square-jawed security guard in black, with an earpiece, who walked them along a hallway that put them in an anteroom that resembled an oak-paneled library. Gwynne closed and locked the door.

Fairfield sat in a maroon leather wingback chair, and Palmer stood nearby. "Come here, dear," Fairfield said.

Time to kiss the ring.

Awkwardness crept in as if she was approaching

royalty but ignorant of protocol, that she should bow, or curtsy, or something. Zabi whispered, *Be yourself; you're the best person for the job.*

She walked up to the old man and shook his hand. It was peculiar to see Fairfield and his fixer in person, the way it must feel to see a screen idol perhaps. They were both at once larger and smaller than she'd expected. Larger because there was no doubting their power and wealth, and the compelling memory of them and their violence. Smaller because on TV they had two-foot-tall faces, but here they were just regular-sized men.

"Did you make the 911 call when the Lads were shot?" Fairfield narrowed his eyes.

If she admitted she was the 911 caller, it would blow up the story of Fairfield and Palmer rescuing her. A rescued victim doesn't call emergency and turn in her rescuers. It was a detail she had overlooked until now, a detail that would unravel all of their plans. She quickly searched her memory. Had she told anyone she was the caller? Earl? No. Stade? No. Rigby? No. Not even Gwynne. Everyone had asked, and she had stubbornly, repeatedly denied it. Now it seemed she'd had a subliminal and shrewd impulse. "No sir. I did not call 911."

Fairfield nodded and Gwynne said, "Tell Mr. Fairfield and Mr. Palmer what you recall from that night when the Lads were shot."

Marilyn stepped back several feet and shifted from one foot to the other. She dropped her arms, which had been crossed. Her delivery was flat, her eyes downcast, in the way she'd read trauma victims usually presented from the pain of reliving the experience. She started hesitantly. "It happened after the hurricane. I was staying at my friend Fran's apartment. Next door to the Lads. Fran's body had been found near Darby Fairfield's body." Mentioning Fran's death flooded her with pain, anger, frustration, hate.

Marilyn paused to let her childhood memory take hold. She only needed a moment. The episode came in like a wave, the smells, the setting, the sounds complete, as if in one gulp.

And she was once again in The Crying House, shivering. Marilyn said, "I can't feel my toes."

Her mom reassured her that after the next "client" they would have enough money for a motel. She and her mother trudged past rooms. Peeking around the doorframes she made out shadowy forms.

Mom whispered, "Let's go upstairs."

Finally at the end of a long hallway on the third floor, they found an empty room.

There was the large hole in the ceiling where the attic fire had burned through, and this charred room was where two men had died. The floor was littered with ash, and the room stank of an acrid combination of smoke, water damage, and the leftover effluent of wretched humanity.

The plywood on one window had been kicked out allowing an eerie light to angle in. Marilyn sensed a foreboding presence but busied herself rummaging through trash—mainly empty Amazon boxes from deliveries stolen from porches, plastic, and paper of all sorts.

Her mother cautioned, "Mar, be careful not to get stuck by needles and watch out for bugs."

Marilyn said, "Whatever." She intended to lay on some cardboard in the closet, ignore the sucking and lapping sounds, and wait for the sex to finish. But suddenly he was there. He must have already been in the room. But where? Probably behind the open door. The man was a regular, but he'd never seen Marilyn because while she had watched him many times, she had been hiding during the sex. She had nicknamed him Giant for his bald pate, his robust build, and large frame. He was unlike the skinny junkies her mother usually serviced, and who paid her in drugs. Giant had money and wore proper clothes: a plaid-wool winter jacket with leather trim, a wool scarf and toque, jeans, and construction boots.

At the sight of Marilyn, he tensed. Ropey tendons popped out in his neck and a pulsing vein throbbed in his temple. Marilyn froze. There was something boiling under the surface now.

He growled, "Well, well. Lookit what we got here." He grabbed Marilyn by her wrist.

"Don't hurt her," Marilyn's mom said.

He turned to her mom. "Git on yer knees," he demanded, and opened his zipper.

Mom said hesitantly, "Let her go, and I'll do whatever you want."

"Fuck you, bitch. Git on yer knees."

Marilyn heard herself whimpering. There was a loud slap and her mother spun. He let go of Marilyn and caught her mom off balance, his massive hands seizing her neck. Her feet cleared the floor, and he shook her like she was boneless. Marilyn put her head down and charged him, hitting behind his knees, which collapsed. Startled, he dropped her mom, and she crumpled, passed out, and lay gasping in the filth and ash.

Giant's arm snaked out and his big-knuckled fingers plowed into the depths of Marilyn's tangled nest of hair. He turned and delivered kick after vicious kick to her mom's torso. The final kick sent her partway across the room. Marilyn made herself dead weight to slow him, but in two steps he was at her mom's side and kicked her head. Marilyn pulled ferociously away, her hair ripped from her scalp, sounding in her head like Velcro peeling apart.

Her mom screamed, "Run, baby, run!"

But Marilyn went after him, scratching, biting, punching. He grasped her hair again and locked his elbow to hold her away. Marilyn sank her teeth into the meat below his thumb. Giant howled and punched her face, but still he didn't let go. Tears sprang to her eyes. He forced Marilyn to the floor and held her down with a hand on her chest.

While she had just relived one of the most painful and crucial times of her life, she had only been silent a moment. She looked up at Fairfield, held his gaze, and continued, "The Lads had been arrested, but they somehow got out of jail. They were back in their apartment. The Lads were partying. They were very loud. When they'd first been released, a rumor started that I was the one who got them arrested. I was accosted by some of the Lads' friends who threatened me and pushed me around."

She paused briefly, then looked up directly at Fairfield, holding his gaze, her expression stricken.

Fairfield said, "Go on."

"I worked that day and had drinks with some friends, and I deliberately didn't get back to the apartment until nearly midnight because I didn't want to run into the Lads or their partyers. I was planning to move out as soon as possible, within days. I had started packing my stuff. When I got to the building, one of the Lads, Declan, was in the hallway with a big guy who had threatened me before. As soon as I saw them there, I turned and took off, but they caught me near the stairs. The big one took my upper body and covered my mouth with his hand, and the other took my legs. They were dirty, and they stank like sweat, alcohol, and something rotten." She wrinkled her nose.

She paused again. Her voice thick, she said, "They carried me inside the Lads' apartment and the second Lad, Shawn, came and the big guy kind of moved away and was watching. They started pulling and ripping my clothes off, and I guess it started to get real because the big guy left. Maybe he got scared. They kept hitting and punching me, loosening my teeth, bruising me as they shouted cunt, whore, bitch. I tried to fight, so they gagged and blindfolded me and tied my hands, and they both took hold of my legs."

She closed her eyes, eyelids fluttering, back in the cold, filthy, Crying House, and thinking of Fran. And

Marilyn was there with her mom, and she was also somehow with Fran who was being tortured, and she was helpless to stop it. Marilyn's tears flowed. She sobbed, and Gwynne handed her a tissue.

She said, "Declan was raping me while Shawn removed the gag and forced his penis deep into my throat, and I was suffocating. They thought that was funny. They said they were going to kill me like they'd killed Darby. They said it over and over. They joked about how they'd beaten her and Fran and injected them. I was terrified."

She dropped her face into the palms of her hands. "Shawn began strangling me, and Declan started anally raping me." Marilyn knew Fran had fought. The news had reported her fingernails had been ripped, there were defensive bruises, and she knew Fran had begged for her life, and she heard her pleas as if Fran were standing right there. "All I could think of was that this was the end, that in a few minutes, I'd be dead, like Fran and Darby." Marilyn dropped to her knees, sobbing, watching her tears fall.

In that moment, she returned again to the Crying House. The terror, the fear of that time so long ago returned, channeled through every nerve and fiber. Back then, Marilyn had resigned herself to whatever hell Giant was about to inflict upon her. The Crying House had enfolded and held her in sadness and grief

From the corner of her eye Marilyn saw her mother lifeless on the floor. And in adrenaline-fueled high focus, she saw two-day stubble, saliva that bubbled on Giant's upper lip as he drew it back in a snarl. Yellowed teeth, a wolf now with hackles raised. Beef-jerky skin glazed with a sheen of tangy nervous sweat that dripped off his chin. She smelled cigarettes and bad breath. And running through the otherworldly, slow-motion scene was the soundtrack of her screams, cries, and begging as he began to lower himself onto her.

Then came a muffled crunch. Then another. Then

another. Body-temperature liquid dribbled on her face and Giant abruptly slackened. His face sagged, his hands went limp, her legs and arms were released. He shuddered and fell on her.

With jagged breaths, Marilyn wriggled, scrambling out from under him, and when she looked up, Auntie Zabi was there a bloody aluminum baseball bat in her hands. Marilyn crept close to the man to pull her clothes from under him. The back of his head was like a stomped melon. The wounds poured crimson. Blood spatter was arced across the floor and up a wall.

Outside, the weather had changed. The wind had died, and big wet flakes of packing snow drifted down.

"Looks like God had a pillow fight," Aunt Zabi said almost absentmindedly. "God gets the feathers for his pillows from angels' wings." She dropped the baseball bat in the yard, they rushed into Auntie Zabi's car, and drove slippery streets to the hospital.

Marilyn caught her breath, looked up at Fairfield, and said, "Then everything changed. You came. You saved me. Suddenly, I was free. I peeled off the blindfold and saw you both. There was fighting, and I saw Declan pull a knife from the kitchen, and Shawn ran towards the back of the apartment, where he kept a gun. I heard a scream, then thumping sounds of a weapon with a silencer, and I left. I ran. If you hadn't come, they would have killed me."

Gwynne stepped over to Marilyn, took her hand and helped her up. Fairfield smiled broadly, satisfied, then flicked his hand in her direction, dismissing her. A man gave Marilyn her purse and ushered her and Gwynne through the back door to his car.

Chapter Twenty-Eight:

Invasive

After meeting Fairfield, the rain had stopped but roads and sidewalks were still wet. Marilyn had Gwynne drop her on the next block, and she walked home. The lock was scratched, a sign it had been picked. She pushed the door wide to inspect the entry. There were prints in the talc from a man's hard-soled, rain-dampened shoes. The fishing line across the kitchen doorway hung from one door jamb, and the unlatched doors had been closed.

Marilyn tipped her head back and groaned. The reenactment of the Lads' killings had been more emotionally challenging than expected. She had missed Fran, been sad, angry, helpless, and irritated, but she'd never pictured the scene of torture, rape, and Fran's terror in graphic detail. Reliving her mother's and her own attack by the man she called Giant had transferred her anger onto the Lads. It was now a rage and hate so intense and fierce it might swallow her whole, make her weak by sapping her focus and energy. Her wrath needed to be harnessed and put to work for her benefit. Whether it be Gwynne, Earl, Stade, Fairfield, Palmer, or for that matter even the Lads, all were aggravating men imposing expectations and demands. However, no matter how stressed, upset, beat up, or tired, she couldn't let her guard down.

Who had picked the lock and let themselves in? It had to be one of Fairfield's goons looking for the ring. This invasion of her physical space made it clear that no one would protect her, that she was merely a pawn, and she was certain that if they got the ring back, they would eliminate her. There were plenty of other women they could hire who could stand in as the supposed witness.

When they didn't find Fairfield's ring, they'd probably installed cameras and bugs in the hope she'd lead them to it by rushing to check it was still in its hiding place.

Obviously, this fake witness scheme wasn't a partnership. She needed to run the show and take control. She admonished herself. Up until now, she hadn't been coasting exactly, but she'd adapted to the men's agendas and demands. That was over. She was now at the steering wheel of this battleship.

She told her fatigue to take a hike and began a thorough search of the apartment. There was a small hole in the living room wall. The peephole the Lads had drilled between the apartments came to mind. While it seemed too small to be a camera, she filled it with white toothpaste anyway and repeated the process for every other nail hole she could find. Then, repeating Gwynne's moves the night she met him, she turned over every ornament, her laptop, throw rugs, and the dish for keys at the front door. She ran her hands around the doorframes, checked behind the headboard, framed art, sofa cushions, fridge, microwave, and stove, and looked inside the thermostat—and bingo, then bingo again—in a panel of the AC unit. Two coin-like bugs. She debated keeping them in place to make use of them, feed Gwynne or Fairfield false information if she wished, but decided against it. What Fairfield needed was a stronger interest in keeping her alive. She picked up Gwynne's dedicated phone and called him.

"Hi, Marilyn," he said.

"Hey, Gwynne, a heads-up. If, for some reason, Fairfield isn't listening in on this conversation, you can tell him I found two of his wiretap devices in my apartment, one in the thermostat and one in the AC unit. I'm aware one of Fairfield's underlings broke into my apartment and planted them when I was meeting him. And as an aside, the intruder was sloppy."

"Mar—"

"Shut the fuck up, Gwynne, I'm not finished." She wondered a moment whether the fact that Gwynne's wife was a dominatrix inspired her tough side to show itself. "Here's what you, Fairfield, and his goon squad need to know. Fairfield's ring has actual blood on it, the Lads' blood."

"Maril—"

"No. Don't talk. I want to be their witness, but Fairfield and Palmer better not fuck with me. Also, given how untrustworthy Fairfield is, I want the balance of my million tomorrow." She hung up before he could respond.

She took the eavesdropping devices outside, left them on the patio table, and said, "Hey boys, if you're listening, nobody here but us crickets."

Her Gwynne-phone rang. He said, "Fairfield says there's one more bug. It's stuck behind your kitchen's undercabinet light fixture, and there's a camera in the smoke alarm. And he said he'll get the rest of the money to you tomorrow."

"Good." She hung up.

After removing and placing the third listening device and the camera outdoors with the others, she stretched out on the sofa. Her anger slowly abated. Gwynne came to mind. He was slippery, glib, cunning, and a charmer, and smart enough to dial into anyone's wavelength, all the while not overdoing his act. Gwynne needed a firm hand. All those more-than-friendly touches, hugs, hints of sex, and joking didn't have her fooled. Gwynne was married and his only feelings for her were for a roll in the hay and as an accomplice to the blackmail…to get what he wanted.

Then there was Earl with his pronouncements of love. Earl was to her what she was to Gwynne, a means to an end and a write-off, just useful for the moment. And Stade…well, if she was a problem for him before, now she was toxic, fatal.

Yup, Zabi said, *you're bad news for Stade, the only viable guy around.*

"Don't I know it, Zabi."

Meanwhile, aside from the men swirling around her life, whatever happened with her fake witness gig, she would get the balance of her million in cash tomorrow and then make her own plans. She lounged in a bubble bath for a while, then slipped between cool sheets and drifted into a haphazard sleep populated by faceless men who pushed and pulled her, who hid, revealed themselves, then hid again.

Chapter Twenty-Nine:

Jon

Morning brought a call from the Art Guild, with a request to fill in for a model who had canceled. Marilyn called Earl. "Were you planning to go to life-drawing today?"

"Of course."

"I'm modeling, so you can't," she explained. "You need to stay away."

He sighed, "Okay."

At the Art Guild, Jon and Rigby were at easels. Rigby was in high-waisted mom-jeans, a vintage Rolling Stone's T-shirt, a man's plaid sport coat, and bright red Mary Janes. Marilyn gave them a small acknowledging wave. After the warmup gesture drawings, she set herself up for the long pose, sitting on an armless wooden chair with knees together, her feet apart, and her hands clasped in her lap. She turned her head and watched Rigby splash bright acrylic paint.

At the break, she left the studio. As she passed the door to the coffee shop, one of the male artists stepped out, and she nearly collided with him, jostling his coffee and pastry.

They both laughed. "I'm Jared." They shook hands. "You are my favorite model," he said.

"Thank you."

Jared was one of the older men who came to open-studio. He was nice looking in an older-guy, silver-fox way; still fit, gray hair, a friendly and handsome lived-in face. He said, "If I may be so bold, may I buy you a coffee or lunch sometime soon?"

"Ohhh," she said regretfully, "I don't date Art Guild artists. But thank you for asking."

He tipped his head to the side and said, "I asked the director if dating you would be overstepping Art Guild rules, and she said *no*."

Hmm, this one was persistent. Marilyn stepped back. "I'm sure you're a good guy, but I like to keep some distance between myself and the artists. That's one of my personal guidelines, nothing to do with Art Guild rules. Besides that, there are two types of men I don't date, one *plays* in a band, the other *wears* a band, a gold one. And you, my friend, are the latter."

Jared looked at his left hand as if the wedding ring had just magically appeared. "Well, my wife and I, we're separated."

Marilyn smiled and huffed, then said, "Of course you are. Break time is over. Gotta go." She started back to the lab.

Behind her, Jared said, "It's just coffee. No big deal."

In the studio, she took her place on the model's stand. A minute later, Jared entered. She resumed her pose, glad to be staring at Rigby flinging turquoise, chartreuse, and fuchsia paint.

After the session, Marilyn got dressed, and paused near Rigby, who was sitting in the Art Guild's small courtyard, lighting a cigarette. Rigby snickered. "Poor Jared, can't get into your pants. He told me he was going to ask you out."

"These guys. They get confused about the nudity." Marilyn grimaced. "Yes, Jared, wearing his wedding band for all to see and acting like all he wants is coffee. Ugh. I need a T-shirt that says, *Hey, train-wreck, this ain't your station!*"

"Of course, he wants coffee—if coffee means, y'know, pussy." Rigby snorted.

Rigby patted the seat next to her, and Marilyn removed her large shoulder bag, placed it on the table, and sat. Marilyn gazed across the parking lot. "Anything new at your building?"

"They've finally cleaned up and rented out the Lads' apartment. That's about it. No parties anymore." Rigby shook her head. "What's happening with you?"

"Detective Stade came to my apartment and asked if I knew of any connections between the Lads and three other missing women. Whenever I see anything about missing or murdered women I'm right back into Fran's murder, wondering who did it, how it happened, if she suffered. It's horrible."

"You'd think Stade would stop the investigation at this point and spare us dredging up bad shit over and over." Rigby blew smoke from her nostrils like a dragon. "After all, the Lads were the killers, and they're dead."

"True. I said the same thing. But Stade says in order to find the ones who are still missing, the police need to know how they are connected, who they knew in common. Also, that he's still looking for connections between the ones that have been found. Stade is looking for some jewelry mementos that the killer, or killers, took from the women. The police looked for the jewelry in the Lads' apartment but didn't find them."

"So awful," Rigby sighed. "We could have been next."

"The killings were brutal," Marilyn said.

"I still wonder about Patty. She disappeared and hasn't been found, but I wonder if she knew the Lads. It doesn't seem to fit. She wasn't the partying type." Rigby dropped her cigarette butt and ground it out with her shoe.

"She's been missing more than two years. Maybe it's unconnected to the recent killings, which were all within six months and left at the homeless camp."

Jon came and loitered nearby, edging into their space. "Hellooo, ladies."

"Hey." Rigby blew smoke in his direction, and he pretended to be choking to death, falling to the ground. When he stopped, he sat on the other side of Rigby, wiggled his eyebrows, and asked, "Say, do you two dames wanna come see my bachelor pad? It's sexy, and just around the corner."

"Sounds dangerous." Rigby blew more smoke.

Marilyn asked, "When did you move in?"

"Almost on the hurricane's anniversary. I can hardly believe it was a year ago," Jon said.

"Sure, c'mon Marilyn. Let's go see Jon's place."

His apartment was similar in layout to Marilyn's, but that's where the resemblance ended. Compared to Jon's Bat Cave, Marilyn's apartment could have been an HGTV staged home. His living and dining room walls and floors were lacquered black, and the ceilings were silver with strings of LED rope lights hanging like vines. His soft furnishings were burgundy velvet.

"Whoa!" Rigby laughed. "I think you outdid me."

"What would you like to drink?" Jon was already taking wine glasses from a cabinet.

"No can do," Rigby said. "I've got a doctor's appointment where some twelve-year-old doctor will tell me to quit smoking…again." She rolled her eyes.

"Great place," Marilyn said as she moved to view one of Jon's highly realistic life studies that hung on the living room wall. Disturbingly, the model wore bondage gear—

handcuffs, a ball-gag, and a blindfold, and Marilyn got an uneasy clench in her diaphragm. The background was blurry making it drop away. Something about the setting and the woman seemed familiar, but Marilyn wasn't sure where she'd seen her before. "A friend of yours?"

"Not exactly. That drawing sells a ton of prints on the Masterpieces.com print-on-demand website."

"Is that one of the pieces you had in the plastic canister when we were rescued from the flood?"

Before Jon could answer, Rigby said, "Wow. It's so realistic I almost feel like if I touched her, she'd be warm."

"Bathroom?" Marilyn requested.

"Down the hall, second door on the right."

Marilyn stopped at the first door which was ajar, and pushed it open. The black plastic canister he'd brought with him in the hurricane was on Jon's drafting table next to a pile of drawings. On top was a drawing of another woman in bondage. It took a moment to register that the trussed, gagged, and blindfolded woman had heart tattoos, and was the missing woman Stade had asked Marilyn about. She took a photo with her phone, used the bathroom, and returned to the living room.

"Hey, Jon, I forgot I've got some stuff to do too, so I can't stay," Marilyn said. They said goodbye and started for the Art Guild's parking lot, leaving Jon frowning, standing at the door of his strange living space. Outside, the heat sank into their skin.

Rigby smirked. "I wonder what his landlord thinks of all that black shiny lacquer."

"That could be the least of his problems. Look what was on his drafting table. It's the missing girl with the pink and red heart tattoos—Stade told me about her."

Rigby grabbed Marilyn's phone and spread her fingers across the screen, enlarging the photo. "Holy mother of pearl! She's all tied up. Jon's the serial killer?"

"I'll let Stade know. Let's keep this quiet for now and give Stade a chance to take care of it."

"I always thought he was weird." Rigby opened the door of her car.

Marilyn shuddered. "He used to hang around my office, flirting. He likes to joke a lot, but he's pushy."

"To draw those drawings…Did he have her there, tied up like that? Shit." Rigby got into her car.

Marilyn left the parking lot and spotted Earl in his van waiting at the curb. She kept walking, ignoring him, turned a corner, and continued until she was certain she was out of view of the Art Guild. Earl pulled up next to her, and she swiftly hopped in, ducked down, and hissed, "What the fuck are you doing here?"

He said, "Sorry, babe, I'm so crazy about you, and I wanted to tell you what happened. Forgive me? Please?"

"Fuck no, I don't forgive you." She shouted. "You're going to get us fucking killed! We're not supposed to know each other! If we get caught together, we're dead!"

He drove to a parking lot nearby, where he tried to pull her to him. She shoved him away forcefully. He paused a moment. "Okay. Okay. Don't be mad."

"If you pull anything like this again, you'll be out. If Fairfield finds out who you are, and worse, that we're in cahoots with Gwynne, he'll kill all of us. Get a fucking clue, dude."

"Marilyn, please don't be mad. I'll be good."

"Asshole! If I can't trust you, I'll get rid of you in a heartbeat. I mean it." She was suddenly exhausted and concerned. How could she control these egocentric men?

Earl looked chagrined. "We're here, let's talk for a while."

"No. Fuck this. You're going to ruin everything." She opened the van's door, climbed down, slammed the door behind her, and headed home.

Zabi said, *Keeps things interesting, doesn't it?*

"I wonder what he wanted to talk about, Zabi." Marilyn managed a wry smile, then laughed.

She called Stade, got voicemail, and hung up without

leaving a message. Now what? Was calling Stade about Jon's drawings premature? If Jon was the real serial killer, then Fairfield and Palmer were guilty of killing two innocent men. Fuck.

Chapter Thirty:

The Zoo

The day after being ambushed by Earl in his van, Marilyn had a midafternoon meeting with Gwynne at the zoo in Hermann Park. Dressed in a tropical-print camisole, white jeans, and red canvas-and-rope espadrilles, she took the safe-deposit box key from its hiding place under the silverware drawer, went to the bank, removed the baggie containing Fairfield's ring from the safe-deposit box, slipped it into her pocket, and left for her meeting with Gwynne at Hermann Park. He was waiting in a hidden, shady alcove in the snake exhibit. The heat had driven people into air-conditioned spaces, and the zoo was nearly deserted. Gwynne was in a bespoke lightweight midnight-blue suit, white shirt, blue silk tie, and sunglasses.

As she approached, Zabi said, *So, how would you characterize him?*

"He's Mr. Slick, Zabi."

Gwynne was reptilian, but he was good at morphing it into a dashing, moneyed, businessman's air—the thong-moistening stuff on which romance novels of the worldly-man-seduces-innocent-virgin stories are based. *Fifty Shades of Gwynne.*

She pressed the video app on her phone to record their conversation but kept it in her bag. He gave her a hug and kissed her cheek, then stepped back.

He said in a low voice, "Fairfield didn't appreciate your phone call after you met him. He doesn't respond well to threats."

Ah, now comes the shaming. "Y'know what, Gwynne? Fuck Fairfield." She stared at him a moment. "His happiness or ruffled feathers are not my concern. Besides, listen to yourself. I called *your* phone, and the only reason he heard the call was because he had wired my apartment."

"Good point." Gwynne conceded, then smiled, and looked away.

She raised her eyebrows. "Besides, you should be pissed too. I sometimes talk with Earl, and Fairfield's wiretapping shenanigans could blow our cover."

"Shit. I didn't think of that." His face flushed.

"I have a question. The blackmail is twenty mil. What's my cut?"

"You and Earl can split ten mil. The rest is mine."

"Hahaha." She pretend-laughed. "No way. The blackmail hinges on me, the *witness*. Without me, there's nothing. Earl, you, and I each get a third. Do you know how and when the money will be collected?"

"Not yet," he said. "But I have some great news, Marilyn. The trial is in ten days."

"Wow." Her head pulled back in surprise, like whiplash. "That's good news. Sudden. But good news." She noticed he had skipped over the ransom's delivery.

Young voices approached. Gwynne and Marilyn turned toward the nearest terrarium where a snake that evidently wasn't very hungry was lounging and eyeing a live mouse. In the glass's reflection, she watched two preteen boys enter the display area. Their mom hung back at the entrance as the kids headed for the python, the biggest and showiest reptile. They whispered and giggled, and then scampered away.

"Maybe the zoo wasn't a good idea," she whispered. "We're overdressed and don't really fit in here."

"The zoo isn't just moms and kids. Lots of people come here. We're good."

As the boys' voices moved away, Gwynne took a pack of gum from his inside jacket pocket and offered it to her. She shook her head no, and he broke a piece from the wrapper and popped it into his mouth. They made eye contact. He stopped chewing a moment, smiled, and touched her upper arm. She watched his hand trail along her inner elbow past her wrist and fit into her palm.

His touch was suggestive, and released a twinge of sexy, and she looked away to a glass-terrarium where a snake raised its head, unfurling from a heap of dead leaves. Christ, she was overdue for some slap-and-tickle. Even the snake had an erection-like quality to it. She turned her attention to him and sensed agitation. Something was seething beneath his calm facade.

She asked, "You okay?"

"Just got some divorce drama happening."

"Sorry to hear that."

"We weren't a good match. It's been coming for years. I'm out of the house, and staying at the ZaZa Hotel, up the street." He smiled and raised his eyebrows. "Perhaps after our meeting?"

Why not throw caution to the wind and head to the posh hotel, just a block away? No emotional attachment, just a passionate afternoon with room-service strawberries, champagne, and tangled sheets would be just the thing for their mutual stress relief. However, a warning bell clanged, telling her that sex would interfere with her objectivity, that she couldn't trust him or his motives, and things could get complicated if not downright deadly.

"Sorry about your split. I had a friend who married an attorney. She said the best thing about marrying a lawyer was the divorce was free."

He chuckled. "And the worst thing was probably the iron-clad prenup that son-of-a-bitch had drawn up."

"Touché." She smiled. "No doubt. But if I may be so bold…why are you splitting?"

"The usual."

"Which is?"

"Things like cheating, arguing, incompatibility, falling-out-of-love." He squeezed his lips into a grim smile. "Vanessa's very particular. The day before I left, I made her an omelet. She said she wanted her eggs scrambled, threw the plate at me, and she came at me with a butcher knife."

"Bitchin' in the kitchen, huh?" Marilyn smiled. "You cook omelets?" His story rang false. "People can be so fussy about their damned eggs. Or was it all part of your wife's sadomasochistic routine?"

"Among other things." He laughed.

"Such as?" She summoned an encouraging smile.

"Well." He hesitated. "I prefer your age range in women."

"Ouch. Poor wife."

"Indeed," he said.

"So, Gwynne, your share of cash from our deal will be your undeclared and unshared bachelor fund?"

"'Undeclared and unshared.' I like that. I'll use that in my next high-profile divorce case. The media love those sound bites."

"It's my gift to you," she said and dipped in a small curtsy. "Divorce cases? I don't think of you as a divorce lawyer."

"I'm not usually. I defend people who are accused of a crime—anything from shoplifting to murder. Over the years as I won more cases, my rates rose, and my clientele became the wealthy. I've also brought in a lot of corporate accounts to the firm just because I schmooze a lot in those circles, but they're handled by the corporate specialists. Divorces too, and when friends get divorced, I've been known to step in and help. A lot of the work comes from my circle of friends. In my opinion, ninety percent of legal hiring happens through one's social construct."

"So…" She removed her hand from his. "You called this meeting. What's up?"

"Fairfield's being a hard-ass about the twenty-million-dollar blackmail and your witness pay. I'd say Palmer is embarrassed at how he botched the killings, so now he's convinced Fairfield he can eliminate the blackmailer and get the incriminating laptops. No videos mean no blackmail."

"Palmer needs a basic computer lesson," she said, "to teach him videos can be copied—and distributed—in many different ways."

"I agree. He also believes there's another defense, one where he wouldn't need you as a witness, in which case he'd off you too, find the money they've paid you and get it back. Plus, Palmer has assured Fairfield that you don't really have his ring."

"That's crazy. If I hadn't found the ring, how would I even know he'd lost it?" She laughed and rolled her eyes.

"They're clutching at straws."

Marilyn shook her head and said, "They've already killed two guys, and now they want more bloodshed? I'd say Fairfield puts the dick in ridiculous. He'll risk everything for twenty-plus million. That money is a pittance to a multi-billionaire like him."

Gwynne removed his sunglasses and squinted into the distance. "Palmer's point is not only to save the money, but to eliminate ongoing threats from you and the blackmailer."

"This is scary shit. I'll warn Earl to be careful."

A snake slithered and twined around a branch and flicked its tongue. Marilyn said to the snake, "Welcome to our club of rich rats and poor snakes."

Gwynne said, "Snakes eat rats, you know."

"That's right. This snake holds the cards, so rich-rat-Fairfield better keep me happy. I brought something that should convince him I'm not bluffing." She took the baggie containing Fairfield's ring from her pocket. Gwynne reached for it, and she slapped his hand away. Holding it up next to her face, she said, "Take my picture to show Fairfield."

He took a photo with his phone. "That's blood on the ring," he said as he zoomed in, then slipped his phone into his breast pocket.

Marilyn's phone rang. Caller ID indicated her bank. She looked at it quizzically and answered, and a woman asked, "Is this Marilyn Connor?'

"Yes, this is Marilyn."

"Ms. Connor, your sister is here requesting access to your safe deposit box." Marilyn scowled at Gwynne, and he made a questioning face.

"Wow. I don't have a sister. Can you snap a photo of her?"

"I just texted her picture to you. She has a key, but it looks like a copy, not the original, and she has a note, supposedly signed by you, giving her permission to access the box."

"Please don't give her access. Thank you so much for calling me."

"You are most welcome. Oh, she just left. Well, have a great day."

Marilyn tapped and enlarged the photo of a plump nondescript woman in a cotton tentlike dress. She wore a straw hat and sunglasses. "Who is this, Gwynne?"

He squinted at the picture and said, "No idea. Why? What just happened?"

"This bitch knows where I bank, probably because

Fairfield's driver met me at the bank with the witness payment, so it made sense I bank there. She also had a copy of my safety deposit key. This reeks of Fairfield and Palmer trying to find Fairfield's ring."

"Holy shit." Gwynne seemed genuinely surprised.

"Whoever copied my key was probably the guy who wired my apartment while I was meeting Fairfield."

Gwynne nodded. "He probably used one of those clay molds."

"I've just about had it with these fuckers. Keep in mind, Gwynne, that the nasty little GIF Earl sent you of Fairfield pulling the trigger, came from me, not some random blackmailer."

"That GIF took me by surprise. Why didn't you tell me you had the Lads' laptops and their videos?"

"Pretty much for this exact reason. The more desperate Palmer and Fairfield are the worse it is for me. Something else you should keep in mind…think of how Fairfield would react if he thought for a second that you were the mastermind behind the blackmail."

"Ah, a threat." Gwynne raised his hands in a pose of surrender. "Well, well. The knives come out. Look, I'm sure Palmer is behind all this crap, and that he also convinced Fairfield that you'll run off with the payment, and you won't show up for the trial. Fairfield's just worried."

"Fairfield should be worried. I'm going to see if face recognition software can ID this woman. I bet she's got a white-collar record—forgery, embezzlement, along those lines. At least now the bank will be on the lookout for anything unusual. Let Fairfield and Palmer know I'm onto them. Tell him I called you and I'm pissed, and because of their malarky I've changed banks. And remind him if he kills me, he won't have his star witness—and by the way, keep in mind that you won't have any ransom. For that reason, you need to get out in front of this situation."

"I will," he said.

"And where is the balance of my million? I'm not going to put up with any delays."

"Go to my car with me. A private car will meet us and take you home. You'll find your cash in a case on the floor behind the driver." He started walking toward the car park.

Marilyn didn't move. "Gwynne," she said, and he stopped and turned. "That's just stupid. I'm not getting in Fairfield's car. I can't be seen with anyone connected to him, or you, or we could blow this. Our deal will unravel if someone notices. Contact the driver and tell him you'll be removing the bag, and you'll bring it to me. No monkey business. And speaking of monkeys, that's where you'll find me, at the monkey house."

He texted someone and put his phone away. "Come on, Marilyn. This heatwave is like a sauna. It's too fucking hot to be running all over hell's half acre. Walk with me." He took off his jacket and hooked it over his shoulder.

"Nope. See you at the monkey house. Five minutes." She laughed.

As Marilyn walked to the monkey house, her phone rang and she answered to Jon. "Hey, Jon, how are you?"

"Well...Listen, that drawing in my living room that you were asking about?"

His mention of the drawing brought back the same disturbing feelings. "Yes. I looked you up online and couldn't find any of your artwork."

"Rigby called me, and she was freaking out. She went on and on about how I fucking killed some women. She's out of her fucking mind, man. I didn't draw that girl, it's Earl's art. She said you also thought it was me killing those women."

"Oh. When you said it sold lots of copies on online galleries, I thought it was your work." She inhaled sharply and rolled her eyes. Damn it. So much for keeping their suspicions quiet. Rigby could get herself killed running her mouth. "You explained to Rigby that it wasn't your drawing, right?"

"Of course. I just hope she believes me. Earl told me that Masterpieces.com sold lots of copies. It's his drawing."

"Sorry. I believe you. Your drawing styles are very similar, and we assumed it was yours, because it was in your apartment."

"No probs, Marilyn. Just don't be going around saying I'm a murderer." They said goodbye. Now the bondage drawings were Earl's. Things were getting weirder all the time. Did this mean Earl was a serial killer? She was glad she hadn't reported her suspicions about Jon to Stade, yet. Her bullshit-detector, which was getting quite a workout these days, had popped up. Was Jon lying? Obviously, he wouldn't admit to being a killer. She needed to think through the ramifications of Jon versus Earl. It was noticeable that with the Lads dead there had been no more killings. Then she called Rigby and left a message saying she believed Jon. She wasn't sure she did believe him, but Rigby needed to calm down.

At the monkey house, the apes began their deafening chittering and shrieking, then subsided. Across the lawn, a black Dodge Charger rolled up to Gwynne—for once not an SUV—although the Charger was an intimidating muscle car, making it a good substitute for the oversized toasters. Gwynne had loosened his tie against the heat and rolled back his shirt sleeves. The idea of his air-conditioned hotel room and some chilled wine was highly inviting, but she decided the timing was off, way off. The driver handed a medium-sized duffel bag to Gwynne and drove away. Gwynne walked to Marilyn, handed her the bag, briefly pulled her to him and held her, then let go. She called for a ride.

Marilyn stopped at a wig shop, tried on many styles, while laughing at most of them. She chose a light-brown chin-length wig with short bangs. The saleswoman demonstrated the use of a liner to contain her hair and how to put on the wig. She googled a theatrical store and bought clear-lens glasses with heavy red rims. Then she went to the address Gwynne had written on the Post-it, a nondescript small bungalow in the city's northwest corner.

She rang the doorbell and a man who bore a resemblance to Ichabod Crane opened the door. After she donned her new wig and glasses and made her makeup more dramatic with smokier eyes and crimson lips, he ushered her into a back room outfitted with computers, cameras, printers, and scanners. She handed him her old passport, social security card, and driver's license.

Once Ichabod had taken some pictures, she waited in the living room, which was furnished with overstuffed, large, brown chairs, brown wall-to-wall carpet, and a massive TV. On her phone she typed in Masterpieces.com and entered Earl's name in the search bar. Nothing came up. Whether they were Earl's or Jon's drawings, it only made sense that they had removed them now that the missing women were all over the news.

Zabi said, *Can anyone be trusted?*

I guess not, except for maybe, Stade.

Ichabod-the-forger appeared and handed her several authentic-looking pieces of identification. Now her first and middle name was Mary Lynne, still very similar to Marilyn, but he had changed her last name to Montgomery. He said, "Most people have a very hard time changing their first name."

She looked through the items and said, "Wow. These are great. Can I have my old passport and stuff back?"

"Those *are* your old ones. They've just been altered. I have to use the real thing because of all the watermarks and stuff embedded in the paper. You'll also find that you have a pretty decent credit score and no police record. You were previously a secretary for a firm that manages owner-rental vacation properties, and now you do a variety of jobs for a temp agency."

"I'm so mundane."

"Good to be anonymous."

She nodded, paid him his fee, and left, again summoning a car to the bank, where she removed everything from the safe deposit box and handed in the key. The old Marilyn was as good as dead. Her previous online persona was still floating in the ether, but there was no cyber breadcrumb trail for Fairfield, or anyone else, to find. She walked a block to a competing bank and opened an account as Mary Lynne Montgomery, received a debit card and credit card, rented a safe deposit box into which she placed the money and the evidence, and signed up for online banking.

Back at her apartment, she toyed with the idea of calling Gwynne to meet at his hotel room, but her dedicated-Earl phone rang. He said, "I want to see you."

"No. It's too risky. Gwynne told me that Fairfield and Palmer are hell bent on finding and killing you, so now more than ever we have to be super discreet."

"Okay, okay," he replied despondently.

"But Earl, here's some amazing news. The trial starts in ten days."

"I saw you with Gwynne," he said, ignoring her comment.

What the hell? She inhaled sharply. "Where?"

Thirty-One:

Ethan

Earl said, "I saw Gwynne leave his office and followed him. He went to Hermann Park and met you at the zoo." There was a plaintiveness in his voice that hadn't been there before. "You guys looked pretty cozy, holding hands and all."

Refusing to justify his accusation with an explanation, she said assertively, "Are you stalking me and Gwynne?" Invisible tentacles had suddenly invaded her space, swarming. A certainty struck her, that he had invaded her computer and email, followed her, seen her comings and goings with Stade and Gwynne. Had he eavesdropped or planted a bug or a tracking device in a jacket pocket or her handbag. Of course, he had.

Fear swamped Marilyn. She had misjudged him, trusted him. Why? Perhaps his constant love-bombing and transparency about his thieving had made him seem believable. Did he trust her? During the time that she and Gwynne thought they were using Earl, was he using them?

Maybe the woman at the bank trying to access her safe deposit box was sent by Earl, not Fairfield.

Earl barked laughter. "No! I'm not stalking you. You don't seem to realize what you mean to me." He exhaled. "I want to marry you. I don't want to go one minute without your beauty and intelligence. I feel as though we've known each other forever. We can do so much together."

Wincing, thrilled that they weren't face-to-face, she said, "Earl, I care very much for you. This separation is temporary. Also, you need to realize that I have to play along with Gwynne. He's a player and he's coming on to me, so I want him to think I'm interested. Trust me. There's nothing going on."

He said, "Promise me we'll be together."

"I promise." Part of her wanted to warm to Earl. His scamming nature was a turn-off, but maybe he could go legit after this. They wouldn't need money, and they were both interested in art. They could open a gallery...or something. She tuned in again to his plangent tones to hear the end of a sentence that had been garbled. "What did you say?"

"My son, Awesome-Ethan."

"You have a son?" She tried to calm her voice and sound neutral. Having a son meant the kid had a mother, a mom with custody, and visitations. A kid meant schools, friends, family, and most of all complications. There went any fantasy of a relationship with Earl.

"We'll be the perfect family, as soon as that bitch Sandy is out of the way."

"Sandy? Hold on, Earl. Start at the beginning."

"I have a five-year-old son. I call him Awesome-Ethan. His mom is Sandy. It was a one-off, like a one-night stand, and even though I love the little guy, Sandy is a bitch. For a long time, I've been thinking of how to get custody of Ethan, but I kept putting it off. Lately, she's been talking about getting a DNA test and making me pay support. The way I see it, I didn't know about the pregnancy, and she decided to keep the kid so I shouldn't be on the hook."

"Does Sandy have a job?"

"Yeah, she's a bartender at Juan-derful, that Mexican restaurant on the highway."

"Holy crap, Earl, I'm speechless. Why didn't you tell me about your son and his mom before?"

"It only occurred to me the other day that you, me, and Ethan would be a perfect family. Until now, I always thought of him as outside my life. The only obstacle now is Sandy, but you and me as a couple, we'd be perfect for the little guy."

"Wow. Just wow, Earl."

"I know, right?" He exclaimed. "You're the only one I can talk to about everything, the only one who understands. Marilyn, you're my soulmate."

"Uhhh, well, this certainly is big news. So, you'd have to fight her in court, and I hate to say this, but there are roadblocks. First, we're leaving soon. Also, they tend to favor the mother, especially in a case where she's been his only parent for years. I think you'll lose, and you'll have to pay support if the DNA indicates you're the father."

"Ethan's definitely my kid. He looks just like me. For sure going to court would be a hassle. Maybe there would be a way to avoid the whole court situation."

"How Earl?"

"Maybe Sandy should fall into a pond full of gators, or she could maybe have a drug overdose. Overdoses are popular at the moment."

Marilyn held back a gulp. "You're kidding, right?"

"Of course, I'm kidding, although I wouldn't mind hurting her a bit." He paused a moment. "Can I tell you my real plan?"

"Please do."

"I have a friend with a ranch about twenty miles outside Houston, kind of in the middle of nowhere. I'll take her there, cuffed and blindfolded. He'll keep her until you, me, and Ethan are gone. My friend will enjoy it. He likes messing with the ladies."

Marilyn winced. The drawings in Jon's apartment came to mind. Did Earl lure and deliver women to his friend's ranch and stick around to draw them? Could things get any more hideous? "Wait a minute. Is your friend the serial killer?"

"I'm not sure," he said innocently. "Maybe."

She needed to somehow ignore this new wrinkle and concentrate on how to save Sandy and her child. "And when do you plan to do this? Like I said, it's only ten days to the trial."

"I'm thinking I'll do it in a few days. Then when we have the money, we'll get the hell out of here with Ethan."

"Yeah. Uh, that sounds like a solid plan," she said, deadpan.

Excited, Earl said, "I knew you'd get it. You'll love Ethan. The kid's awesome." They said goodbye and hung up.

So…Awesome-Ethan and his soon-to-be-abducted mom. Marilyn dialed Gwynne on his dedicated phone and he immediately jumped to sexual conclusions, and said, "Are you on your way to my hotel? I'm—"

She cut him off. "Earl has a kid! A five-year-old son! You said you investigated him, and he was clean with no family ties!"

"I did. There are no legal family ties. It's possible he was never declared as the father on the birth documents."

"Shit." She groaned. "You're probably right. He said he didn't know about the pregnancy, and he doesn't pay child support. But here's the thing, he's planning to do something weird to the kid's mother, kidnap the child, and run when we get our payoff."

"Shit. That's awful."

"What should we do, Gwynne?"

"Nothing." He laughed. "Nothing that might botch the

trial or your testimony. Personally, I won't get involved in Earl's family drama. Let's just get the trial over with, and we'll figure it out from there."

"Gwynne—"

"Forget about Earl and his kid. I've got another call. Gotta go." He hung up. Marilyn was speechless.

After sitting awhile, absorbing Earl's news and his plan to alleviate his problems, Marilyn dumped out her handbag and searched every pocket, finally finding a tiny tracker in the lining. "Shit!" she exclaimed and flushed it down the toilet. When did Earl do this? How had she not been aware? Had he sneaked into her apartment? She headed to Best Buy and had one of their maintenance staff check her phone for tracking and hacking software and found it to be clean. Back home, she went through her apartment thoroughly but found no other bugs. All these fucking guys were invasive as hell.

Marilyn googled the restaurant where Earl's baby-mama worked. The website photos showed the dining area and bar replete with sombreros, piñatas, Mexican tile, and chairs painted red, chrome yellow, and blue. In a photo of the staff, they were outfitted in Mexican guayabera shirts and black jeans. Sandy wore a name tag, and grinned as she held a basket of tortilla chips.

Marilyn blocked her number and called. A young woman answered enthusiastically, "Have a Juan-derful day at Juan-derful's!"

Oh brother. "Hi, may I please speak to Sandy?"

She was transferred to Sandy, introduced herself and said, "Can you talk a minute?"

"Yeah, I guess. We're not busy," she said, sounding profoundly disinterested. Marilyn could almost hear her shrug.

"It's about Earl, Sandy. He's planning to kidnap Ethan."

Sandy inhaled sharply, suddenly attentive, and alarmed. "What? That doesn't make sense. He doesn't want to commit himself to my son, all he wants is to keep the status quo, where I do all the work, and he doesn't even pay child support."

Marilyn figured that in Earl's misogynistic brain, Marilyn would be Ethan's primary caregiver if his fantasy-family materialized. She said, "He confided in me. What he's planning is bad. I want to help, but you have to promise me you won't tell him we spoke. We need to meet and talk, but it has to be someplace he wouldn't suspect. Lately I've been suspecting he's following me. He's devious. He may have hacked your phone, so we shouldn't call each other after this."

Sandy paused, then said, "I go part-time to school, interior design. Tomorrow we are doing a tour of the Interior Design Center building. Meet me there at noon. I have half an hour for lunch."

After Marilyn hung up, a text came from Rigby: *There's an art opening this evening at the Art Guild. Meet at 7?*

While it was best to lay low, the Art Guild felt like home. Surely, it would be harmless to mix and mingle a bit; after all, it would just be a small-time amateur artist feeling like they got a big break—their own solo show. Marilyn replied: *Okay*.

Marilyn, weary of Ubering, rented a midsized, nondescript car, and drove to the Art Guild. She went to the front gallery, where there was always a wall of life-drawings by the group's members. Some had captured her likeness with just a few lines, others with careful shading. Fran, Earl, Jon, and Rigby's art were all represented. Jon and Earl's drawings hung side by side, both high realism, their color choices and styles practically identical. Zabi whispered, *Separated at birth?*

Marilyn recalled the art at Jon's apartment. Was he lying, claiming it was Earl's work? Both images she'd seen at his place had women in restraints, their discomfort obvious, but she hadn't seen any disturbing drawings at Earl's house. She again thought of calling Stade, but Jon had been so upset when Rigby accused him, it felt premature to suspect Jon or Earl, or both, without more evidence. Besides, now Earl had added his weird out-of-town friend to the mix, and she still thought the Lads were the murderers given their connections with all the women. She sighed.

Chatter and laughter emanated from the second gallery. The space was packed with attendees amid a wonderland of brightly colored oversized papier-mâché candies, bringing to mind piñatas, hanging from the ceiling and walls and littering the floor. On offer, in addition to the usual wine and cheese, were candies in old-style gumball machines that didn't require nickels or quarters, just a twist of the handle.

After touring the papier-mâché sweets, Marilyn observed the crowd. It was well-attended and included regulars from the society pages. The show's attendees were more sophisticated than she'd expected, and the artist must have some pull to get these high-rollers to attend. Present were several women well known for their philanthropy, a famous doctor, and a pod of lawyers and their wives, people who generally moved in very tight, private, and moneyed circles.

A familiar-looking, thin woman, almost albino-white, her distended lips slathered in scarlet lipstick, approached Marilyn. The wraith wore a skin-tight, floor-length aubergine dress shaped by seams and ruching. Elbow-length purple gloves, vertiginous heels, and a hat that appeared to be constructed of sea urchin spines completed the outfit. She said, "Hello, I'm Vanessa Gwynne. You are a life-study model, correct?"

Marilyn swallowed a gasp. Gwynne's wife, whom she had only seen on the internet. "Yes, I am, but you should model for us in that dress. It's amazing," Marilyn said, openly examining her getup head to toe.

"I purchased a drawing of you," the woman said. "It's representational, and so realistic, I recognized you."

Rigby sidled up and said, "That must be either Jon's or Earl's. They do high realism. By the way, I'd kill for your outfit." Vanessa looked Rigby up and down, smiled ambiguously, and drifted away.

Marilyn said, "Y'know, Rigby, if you let Vampirella bite your neck, I bet she'd give you that dress."

"I said I'd kill for it. I didn't say I'd die for it." She smirked.

Across the room, Gwynne's wife stood motionless, resembling a very large eggplant. Gwynne, looking more casual than usual but still pulled together in a black T-shirt, gray sport coat, and tobacco-colored pants, approached the eggplant and led her from the gallery. Marilyn was quite certain he hadn't noticed her. However, something wasn't adding up, unless it was a rich-person thing, to still be seen out together socially during a hostile divorce.

Rigby said, "That's that lawyer, Gwynne, the one representing Baxter Fairfield."

Marilyn said, "I know him…" and instantly wanted to shove the words back down her throat.

"What? How do you know him?"

"I mean I know him from the news about Fairfield's trial coming up." Her face had flushed at her near slip-up, a blunt reminder to keep her wits about her.

"Let's go see which drawing she bought," Rigby said.

They headed to the other gallery and found a green sticker. Marilyn said, "This must be the one. You called it, Rigby. She bought Jon's drawing. He'll be happy."

"I still think Jon might be the serial killer. I don't care if he tried to blame Earl," Rigby said. She stepped aside to look at other drawings. "Earl seems totally nice and innocent, while Jon is always doing weird stuff and acting like an asshole. Besides, look at his apartment. It's like a dungeon with all that black paint and shit."

“I don’t know. I still think it was the Lads.”

“Well, Marilyn, I think we shouldn’t be around either Jon or Earl.”

“Amen, Rigby.”

Chapter Thirty-Two:

Sandy

As Marilyn drove to the Interior Design Center building, she debated how much to tell Sandy and settled on as little as possible. Walking to the front doors, she surveyed the parking lot and half expected to see Earl ducking behind shrubs or trucks.

Inside were shops displaying high-end products, furniture, carpet, accessories, kitchen cabinets, antiques, everything to outfit a home in collections sold solely to the design trade. Clients of designers and architects could depend on exclusivity, that no one else in their social circle would own the same items.

Designers-in-training were wrapping up a lecture on how to buy for their future wealthy clients, learning about designer-discounts, budgets, bookkeeping, and collecting payments. As the teacher wrapped up her lecture, Marilyn recognized Sandy from the restaurant's website. She waved to Sandy and she broke away from the group. Marilyn asked, "Is there a cafeteria here?"

"Yes, but even better, the lobster-roll truck is here, and I'm starving."

When they had their lobster-lunch in hand, Marilyn said, "Let's eat inside. It's too hot, and I'm worried Earl might be following one of us." They took a table away from the crowd of design students. Marilyn said, "Earl is involved in a major shady deal, and he said that before he collects his cash, he's going to harm you and take Ethan."

Sandy went noticeably pale. She chewed a chunk of lobster roll and said, "So I need to call the police."

"No. It's complicated. Do you know who Baxter Fairfield is?"

Sandy nodded. "Of course. The rich guy. His daughter, Darby, was murdered and they arrested him for killing the killers."

Marilyn swallowed a bite of lobster. "Earl is involved in a scam with Fairfield, and Fairfield is very connected with the police."

"So now the cops are corrupt? Why should I believe you?" Sandy frowned. "I don't even know you."

"True, you don't. But I'm here telling you this to protect you. I'm no psychiatrist, but I'm certain Earl is mentally unstable."

"I agree, but I think you're also some sort of nutcase." Sandy started quickly packing up her leftover lunch.

"Are you aware Earl is a thief and a con man? He hacks people's computers, gets their bank info, and steals their money. Plus, he's obviously a hoarder."

"I always suspected Earl was a crook, a hacker, but he never admitted it." Sandy stood. "He always maintained he was a dumpster diver who fixes stuff up and sells it online. He even drives that creepy van. I teased him that scary clowns have vans like that."

Marilyn chuckled. "The John Wayne Gacy van. You need to take me seriously."

Walking away, Sandy said over her shoulder, "Lady, I don't want anything to do with you and your weird delusions."

Marilyn shouldered her purse and followed. "Please listen. He's planning to dump you at some ranch outside Houston and snatch Ethan. You need to believe me."

Sandy stopped and turned. "Why are you involved in this?"

Marilyn shrugged. "An opportunity came up, and I took it. In hindsight, I shouldn't have, but I'm on the periphery, in a different context. Sorry to be vague, but the less you know, the better. Anyway, if you call the police, they'll question Earl and let him go because we have no proof of any wrongdoing, and that will make him more pissed and determined to pay you, and me, back.

"This makes no sense. I've got stuff to do." Sandy started walking again and Marilyn followed.

"Please don't let him know I contacted you."

Sandy huffed and tossed a sneer over her shoulder. "No problem. I never call him. I can't stand that dickhead, and besides, he never takes my calls. He only shows up when he wants to see Ethan."

"Your decision," Marilyn said. She took out a scrap of paper and wrote her phone number on it and dropped it in Sandy's bag. "If anything happens, please call me. Just so you know. He will carry out his plan soon, before Fairfield's trial starts in a week. I just want to keep you and Ethan safe until the trial, then you should be okay."

Sandy gave an exasperated sigh and walked briskly back into the building. Marilyn sighed as she watched Sandy leave, then drove back to her apartment. She was finishing her leftover lobster roll when Earl called on his dedicated line.

"Hello, beautiful."

"Hi, handsome."

"Have you recovered from my news that I have a son?"

"Yes, I'm fine, and looking forward to meeting him. So," Marilyn said smoothly. "What if you just take the boy and leave the mother behind?"

"No. I want to scare her to the point she'll never look for him. My buddy will put the fear of God in her." He laughed.

Marilyn shivered. Lately it seemed trying to keep her various personas straight—fake witness, blackmailer, Gwynne's flirt, Earl's girlfriend, Fairfield's nemesis/savior—turned everything she said or did into a lie. Some days she was a multiple personality case and losing touch with reality. "I don't know if you were joking that your friend may be the serial killer, or not, but consider this, Earl, if Sandy turns up dead after there have been no victims for over a year, it will mean the murderer is still at large. The media would love it and spin it that Fairfield and Palmer killed the wrong guys, so they aren't heroes, they're murderers; therefore, no blackmail or buckets of cash for us."

"Haha. I didn't think of that. Don't worry. My friend isn't the serial killer. Honest."

"When are you planning to do this?"

"Tomorrow."

The moment she hung up, Marilyn called Juan-derful and asked for Sandy. Marilyn said, "I'm really sorry about this, but it truly is serious shit. Earl said he's going to take care of you and take Ethan tomorrow."

Sandy said, "Okay. If he wants to see Ethan, I'll tell him no, and if he insists, I'll go out somewhere, so we're not home when he gets there."

"It would be better if you had somewhere safe to stay until the trial."

"Well, I don't. And I've gotta get back to work. Quit calling here. It's like you're stalking me or harassing me." Sandy hung up, leaving Marilyn with a dead phone at her ear.

There had been rain in the night which had broken the scorcher. The weather app predicted rising temperatures throughout the day. She was dressed in white capris and a turquoise tank top and sipping coffee in her backyard when her phone rang. Without preamble, Sandy said, "On my drive to class, I dropped Ethan at the sitter's house, and I thought I saw Earl's van, so I decided to stop at Walmart to see if he was actually following me. I'm worried he might already have Ethan."

"No," Marilyn advised. "He wouldn't want the responsibility of looking after Ethan. He'll dispatch you, then get the boy."

Sandy breathed a relieved sigh. "Anyway, Earl called me. He knew where I was. He told me what I was wearing and what aisle I was in. I nearly dropped my phone." Her voice sounded clogged, probably from crying and she said, "It was fucking creepy. He said I shouldn't be spending money because what I earned was for Ethan."

"If he's hacked or cloned your phone, he can see the number you called."

"I thought the same thing," Sandy said, "so I bought a burner phone. I asked how he knew where I was and what I was wearing, and he said he was right outside the store. He said he knows where Ethan is, but of course, I already knew that. I called Ethan's sitter and told her if he shows up before I get there to call the police."

Marilyn jotted down the store's location and said, "I'm on my way. Here's the thing. He's counting on you looking the same when you leave as when you arrived, and he's waiting for you to come out to grab you. We need to mix it up. You've got pale skin and dark hair, so first get some dark foundation, then get a muumuu or something oversized that doesn't show your figure. Add a blonde wig and a funky hat to the mix. And also get some makeup wipes to get yourself back to normal after. Oh, and grab one of those doorbells with a camera. Pay for them and go into the restroom to change up your look. Send me a selfie when you're done."

"Got it," Sandy said.

"What type of car do you drive?"

"A red Kia."

Twenty minutes later, Marilyn pulled into the Walmart parking lot wearing her new brown wig. Sandy wasn't the only one ducking Earl. The selfie of Sandy arrived with her Irish complexion now dark Hispanic or mixed-race. She was unrecognizable, with a white-haired pageboy wig, sequin-spangled cowboy hat, and a wide-load muumuu with what had to be pillows underneath.

Marilyn laughed and texted back, *Fantastic! You look like someone on those Walmartian websites.* Marilyn spotted Earl's van near Sandy's red Kia. Earl was slouched in his seat, staring in the direction of Sandy's car.

Her phone rang and Sandy said, "I'm still scared to leave the store."

"I know. I don't blame you. But you can do this. He might have gotten your location from your phone, but I think probably weeks, or even months ago, Earl planted a tracker on you, probably in your handbag or wallet. Take your driver's license, money, just important stuff out of your wallet, and drop everything else in the trash. Next, leave by a door you didn't come in. And we're going to leave your car where it is. He's fixated on it."

"Okay. I came in through the grocery door, and I'll leave through the garden center."

Marilyn said, "I'd like to get close, but it's blocked by delivery trucks. I have to park in the regular lot to blend in. Guess you'll have to hide in plain sight." She drove toward the garden center. "I'm parked five spaces past Earl's truck and two aisles over from him. On the plus side, he doesn't know this rental car I'm driving. It's a dark blue Ford something-or-other. You'll find me."

Sandy emerged waddling and studying her phone as absentminded people do. Earl noticed her and shook his head. Marilyn held her breath, hoping Sandy would keep her cool and go slow. Earl returned his gaze to Sandy's car as she calmly and slowly lumbered along, staying in character for the full white-knuckle stroll.

Chapter Thirty-Three:

Safe House

When Sandy slid into the passenger's seat, Marilyn drove away and said, "I'm impressed. You completely pulled that off."

Sandy smiled. "I admit, I surprised myself, but all I can think about is that I need to get Ethan," she said, catching her breath. "As soon as Earl realizes he's been hoodwinked, he'll go ballistic and try to kidnap him."

"Give me directions," Marilyn said.

Sandy obliged, and they both removed their wigs. Sandy shook out a makeup remover wipe and began rubbing her face. She said anxiously, "I can't believe this is happening. I don't have any place to go. And I'm broke. Between my rent and school, daycare and food, and everything else, I'm tapped out. I'm on overdraft at the bank, and my credit card is maxed out at three grand. Thank god my apartment didn't flood, or I'd be in a shelter."

"I can relate," Marilyn said. "But I've got some

money." She took an envelope from her bag and handed it to Sandy. "There's ten thousand in there. We're going to put you in a hotel suite. Tell your instructor and your job you've got a family emergency, and you'll be back in a few weeks. I'll move your car later."

Sandy's mouth dropped open in surprise and relief, and tears flooded her eyes. She reached over and squeezed Marilyn's hand.

They picked up Ethan, who instantly fell asleep in the back seat. Marilyn said, "Oh, to be a sleepy child."

"I'll say. Ethan goes a million miles an hour, then crashes."

At the downtown Hilton, Marilyn parked in the five-level garage. "Earl likes stalking people," Marilyn said, "so even if he figures out where you are, being in a busy downtown hotel will make it difficult for him with their security and cameras. It's better than being in the burbs where they have huge flat parking lots that he could sit in and easily pick you out. This is only until Fairfield's trial, then things can go back to normal."

"I'm sorry I doubted you, Marilyn. I don't want to think what would have happened if I didn't know."

Marilyn checked into the hotel using her recently acquired identity and credit card. In her suite, Sandy deposited the slumbering child on the king-sized bed. Marilyn followed Sandy's gaze. The place had a calm hushed feeling, with thick carpet, heavy drapes, wainscoting and crown molding, solid dark-wood furniture with upholstery in cottony blends, and white cloud-like bedding.

Sandy opened floor-to-ceiling drapes to French doors and beyond them an atrium with a jewel-like pool surrounded by flagstone, tropical greenery, and blooming hibiscus. "Ugh, gross. I can't stay here. It's too crummy…if crummy means amazing." She laughed.

Marilyn snickered and came to the window. "You had me going there for a second."

"Sorry. Sarcasm is my go-to deflection."

"Me too. So about Earl…Earl's an expert hacker, and he has obviously hacked you, which means he can see every keystroke you make on your computer, and he has all your passwords and so forth," Marilyn said. "Call your bank and close your account and open a new account with a new password." She handed Sandy her tablet. "Use this and the hotel WI-FI. I'll use my phone to wire some cash into your bank so you can pay off your credit card online and cancel it."

"Wow. You've thought of everything."

"I hope so. You also need to log onto your social media accounts and ghost him. Cancel all your shopping accounts and get a new generic email address that doesn't have your name in it. For the time being, pay cash for everything, no exceptions."

"Ghosting him is going to make him crazy."

"Probably, which means you need to keep Ethan out of school and daycare. If you talk to friends or family, block your number, and don't give anyone your location. I know it sounds extreme, and I get how weird it is because I've been living a lot like this for a year now."

"Got it," Sandy said. "I won't go back to my place at all."

"Absolutely. I'll go there now, and I'll be quick. Ethan will feel more secure here with some of his favorite toys, his clothes, and things, and you need some stuff too; clothes and whatnot."

"I can't believe this is happening. It's like a movie, witness protection."

"Yes." Marilyn inhaled and sighed. "It's not forever. Hey, do you have a way to break into Earl's house?"

Sandy snorted. "The weird thing about Earl is that while he's all ego he can't remember anything worth a shit and loses stuff all the time, so he makes notes in his phone." Sandy nodded. "When he parks, he leaves his car keys on a tire, and he hides his house key somewhere under his house. Unfortunately, I never saw where. He even sets timers for all kinds of things."

Marilyn took Sandy's keys and drove to her apartment, located near the restaurant where she worked. The unit was fresh-smelling and tidy. Clean folded laundry was in a pile on the kitchen table, and Ethan's toys were picked up. Marilyn phoned Sandy and FaceTimed as she packed clothes in two suitcases and put Ethan's favorite toys in a garbage bag.

"Almost done," Marilyn said. "I'll see you soon." She attached and programmed the doorbell, bundled Sandy's and Ethan's belongings into her car, and delivered them to Sandy's suite. Marilyn returned to her apartment and was cooking a chicken breast and asparagus when Earl's dedicated phone rang. He said, "What a fucking day. Sandy is acting crazy, and Fairfield's being a dick."

"What happened?"

"First, that bitch Sandy pulled a fast one."

"That's unfortunate. What did she do?"

"I was tailing her, and she ducked into a Walmart and never came out. I sat watching her car all day."

Marilyn nearly laughed as she pictured Earl waiting hour upon hour, frustration growing. "That sucks."

"Yeah. I finally went inside, and she wasn't there, which is weird because her car was still in the lot when I finally left. Tomorrow, I have to track her down and get rid of her once and for all." He huffed in exasperation.

"That is very strange. Maybe her car had a problem, and she took an Uber."

"Maybe. And fucking Fairfield…I sent instructions for the ransom's delivery, but according to Gwynne, Fairfield's still arguing. I wish I had direct access to Fairfield. I don't trust Gwynne."

Finally. The discussion she had been waiting for. "What were your instructions for the drop?"

"I told Gwynne I want the money in bitcoin, delivered to my cryptocurrency account on the first morning of the trial."

"Really, bitcoin?"

"Yeah, cryptocurrency. It's efficient, but Gwynne said Fairfield won't deal in bitcoin."

"Earl, don't forget the guy is older than dirt. He's probably not computer literate and doesn't understand the concept. Hell, I don't understand the concept. Besides, bitcoin's value is volatile."

"So, then I told Gwynne, okay, he can wire the cash into an offshore account. But he was all 'No, no, no, Fairfield won't wire it.' It's gotta be old school, cash."

"What's the matter with cash?" she asked.

"It's so cumbersome."

"Still manageable, though."

"On top of that, Gwynne says Fairfield's got a new defense, and he's going to find me and fucking kill me. I told Gwynne I didn't appreciate being messed with, and he and Fairfield better watch their backs."

"This makes no sense. If they had a new defense Gwynne wouldn't be negotiating the payment. And they certainly wouldn't warn you they're coming after you. They'd be sneaky. It sounds like posturing." What the hell was going on? Death threats? Did Fairfield really have a new defense? For an instant, she hoped he did. She already had her witness pay and she wouldn't have to testify. All the scheming would vanish. If Gwynne confirmed that there was another defense, she'd be out of Houston with the money and the evidence so fast…The thought was like lifting a foul, suffocating blanket, and breathing sweet-smelling fresh air.

Marilyn said, "Relax, Earl. I'll find out what's going on."

"Yeah," he said. "The trial is only days away and this thing is about to fall apart."

She called Gwynne. "What the hell is happening? I just had a phone call with our blackmailer."

"It really fries Fairfield's ass to give in to blackmail,"

Gwynne said. "Palmer has been scrambling trying to find the blackmailer's identity, eliminate him, and get the incriminating laptops with the videos."

"That's understandable, but the way it was presented to Earl was that Fairfield had found an actual defense, like it was a done deal."

"No. Earl misunderstood. Palmer has the idea that since the laptops were scooped immediately after the killings, before the police got to the murder scene, it's someone living in the building. He has a team investigating all the building's residents. Obviously, he's way off base."

The awful blanket settled over her again. Marilyn said, "Okay. But at what point will Palmer realize he needs to quit his search?"

"Don't worry. When it's obvious he's run out of time, he'll quit," Gwynne said. "Earl first asked for the payment in bitcoin, then he wanted it wired to an offshore account. I promise you, if Fairfield wires to an offshore account or pays in bitcoin, Earl and the money will vanish."

"Probably. By the way…" Marilyn thought a moment. "Now that we know it'll be cash, have you figured out how the cash should be transported and divvied up? Time's a-wasting. It's less than a week until the trial."

"Not entirely, but I'm working on it. I'm thinking using a storage locker might be a solution."

"A storage locker?" she asked in disbelief. "How would that work?" A storage locker seemed like a good place to be cornered and shot by Fairfield's men.

"It would be a matter of exchanging codes to enter the facility and access the locker."

"But you'd have no security. We'd all be sitting ducks."

"I'll work out the security, no problem."

"Gwynne, you need to keep me in the loop."

"I'll do my best. Would you care to join me for dinner tonight, here at the hotel?"

"By tonight, you mean, now?"

"Sure. Room service. My room has a great view of the park. And you could bring your ballet shoes."

"Well, that's tempting, but I've got plans." They said goodbye and hung up.

She dialed Earl and explained Gwynne's phone call. "Obviously Gwynne didn't explain adequately what's going on. If the old guy wants to do cash, let's do cash."

"It's so dumb. A million in hundreds weighs twenty pounds, so the twenty-mil ransom will be four hundred pounds. So bulky and heavy."

She sighed, "Two million per carton. Ten forty-pound boxes isn't that bad. And at least we'll know we have the money."

"I'm tired." She held back a yawn. "I'm going to watch some TV and go to bed now."

"Okay. Good night, sweetheart. I love you a ton."

Marilyn drove to the Walmart where Sandy's Kia was parked. She checked under the car for GPS devices, found one in the wheel well, and placed it on the base of a light standard. She drove to Sandy's hotel, parked, and called a ride back to her own car.

Back at her apartment, Marilyn's thoughts raced, banishing sleep. Were both Earl and Gwynne scheming to double-cross everyone else? If that was the case, she needed to have a separate, successful plan that would eclipse both of their plans. But what?

Chapter Thirty-Four:

The Dilemma

Marilyn considered heading to bed, but she was wide awake and sprawled on her sofa despite the clock reading nearly midnight. Worry—about serial killers, the witness gig, Ethan and Sandy, the blackmail, and what Gwynne and Earl were plotting behind the scenes—was keeping the sandman away. Earl was a wild card, intelligent, malevolent, and slippery as an eel. Like every psychologist, novelist, cop, and homicide detective, she wondered what happened to people like Earl to make him so cold-hearted. Was it a childhood issue, maybe a parenting problem, was he lazy, always looking for an easy way to score, an easy way out? Obviously, he was insane, at least a narcissist, and maybe a psychopath.

Finally, she sighed and turned on the late news, which featured a reporter standing in the homeless camp with police personnel. The footage must have been shot earlier given it was daylight. Her stomach did a little flip at the sight of Stade. Damn, he looked good. The setting was bleak with crime-scene tape strung between posts and highway noise in the background. Had another woman been killed? If there'd been another murder, she and Gwynne had a big problem.

The reporter turned to the camera and said, "We are here with Houston PD, at the location of a killing field, where the bodies of at least eight women were dumped over the last couple of years. The police are again combing the area for evidence and interviewing the homeless here to shine a light on the women's killings, including Darby Fairfield's murder, whose body was found not far away after Hurricane Harold. The deaths had appeared to be drug overdoses, but police are now framing them as the work of a serial killer. If you have any information about these victims, please call the police."

Phew, it wasn't a new murder. She exhaled. A powerful impulse shook her, and without examining the urge or its possible consequences, Marilyn dialed Stade, and her call went to voicemail. She said, "I just saw you on the news. Um…if it turns out it wasn't the Lads, I hope you catch the bad guy."

She turned off the TV and her phone's ringer, undressed, pulled on a black satin chemise over her bikini panties, and went to bed. Sleep eluded her, and she lay in bed staring into the grainy darkness. Things with Earl had certainly taken a grim and horrific turn. Earl had changed. Partnering with him in a phishing expedition seemed positively innocent compared to kidnapping a woman and her child. Would it be possible to neutralize Earl, to somehow get him to back off his plans for Sandy, but still get the money? Or, now that Sandy and the little boy had been drawn into danger, was the blackmail even worth the risk?

Zabi whispered, *Good one. You've snagged a thieving narcissist who claims he's in love with you.*

"So true, Zabi. I sure know how to pick 'em." Earl's so-called *love* was a problem. So far, using the secrecy of the blackmail to avoid intimacy with him had worked. However, he was a wolf in sheep's clothing. While he came across as nice, in reality he was dangerous. He certainly wasn't going to be Mr. nice guy with a woman who deceived him emotionally. Then there was Fairfield with his stonewalling, and his dirty tricks of bugging her apartment and sending the woman to get into the safe deposit box. And probably most frustrating of the lot, Gwynne. Of all of them he was the best at being two faced. Didn't he realize she saw through him?

Gwynne's sadomasochistic fetish came to mind along with the drawing of the woman in bondage gear in Jon's strangely decorated apartment. How common was this fetish? It certainly wasn't kept under wraps anymore. Maybe the women's deaths had been a result of BDSM— in the ilk of Gwynne and his dominatrix wife—that accidentally went too far. Or the dead women got lured into sessions with someone whose agenda was to kill. She wasn't interested in the dark, dangerous world of sadists and masochists, but however abhorrent, she'd explore it if it led to Fran's killer.

Marilyn sat a while, then watched an episode of *American Greed* about a woman who ran a Ponzi scheme and scammed hundreds of people under the guise of investing their savings for huge returns.

Zabi said, *While Earl doesn't run a Ponzi scheme, it's the kind of con he might try.*

"As someone who has been scammed, I hate this stuff," Marilyn said to the screen and added, "Hey, lady, it's easier if you just witness a billionaire murdering some guys and blackmail him." She chuckled. She couldn't concentrate on the show with her roiling thoughts of all the players and bad actors—Earl, Fairfield, Palmer, Gwynne, and herself—and their intentions, and turned it off.

Zabi said, *There's a saying that whoever discovered*

water, it wasn't a fish.

"Yes," Marilyn said. "When you're in deep, you can't see the context. I need some objectivity."

Aunt Zabi agreed. *Remember life with your mom? You were in deep there too, and you basically had to be deprogrammed.*

"Definitely. Good on ya to see the forest despite all the damned trees in the way." Marilyn had always admired Zabi's ability to cut to the chase. Her priorities and character were unyieldingly distinct, the opposite of her mother's wobbly and blurred moral compass.

Whenever Marilyn felt defeated, she tended to revisit the Crying House and beyond, to a time when she and her mother were a small, tight unit. Despite the unsavory nature of her mother's manner of earning money, it became an ordinary, daily ritual. When her mom worked on a guy, Marilyn would hide and peek at the action. The men who noticed her either winked or scowled. She didn't have the names for the acts, but she understood what the hand could do, and what a mouth was for, and what guys liked to have done to their wangs, as she called them back then.

Until Zabi entered her life as a guiding force, she had expected to grow into a pretty sex doll like her mom, and trade sex for whatever she needed—company, drugs, shelter, food, booze, cash. She knew that when the moaning stopped, her mom smoked a cigarette, and if they were at a man's room or his house instead of a trap-house, when the guy snored, her mom would search his place for dope, money, or something to sell. Then whatever the time, day or night, they would leave.

Discussions with Zabi led to revelations of Marilyn's depraved and neglected upbringing. Soon a gentle Hispanic lady named Maria came every day to watch Marilyn after school. Marilyn loved Maria. Maria taught her some Spanish, and Marilyn taught Maria English.

Zabi also arranged weekly visits for Marilyn with a lady named Lena to talk about everything she remembered of life with her mom. Lena had anatomically-correct dolls, and she noticed Lena was happiest when Marilyn showed her what her mom did with wangs, and what the men did to her mom. That part, the mechanics of it, was easy and Marilyn liked making Lena happy. But the visits to Lena's office, the part of trying to explain emotions, such as the acceptance mixed with revulsion, the things that couldn't be fully explained, had been exhausting. But she had learned to articulate those things and it made her feel less lost. And now the lost sensation was on her again and she needed gravity, something, some explanation, to hold her down.

She said aloud, "I miss you, Zabi, and I miss Fran, and my displaced friends. Hell, I even miss the Lads, or maybe just their parties."

She flopped around, messing up the bedsheets without finding a comfortable position. Maybe she was just stressed and needed release. Her hand began to travel south, and she stopped herself. An orgasm wasn't going to solve her dilemmas. The trial was looming, and she needed to think everything through.

A thought was scratching at the far reaches of her consciousness trying to get out. Had her memories of her mother returned because her boundaries were blurred? Would a normal person, someone who had always been on a wholesome path, have gotten involved in Gwynne's perjury and extortion scam? Sometimes, it all made sense. Really? It made sense? Well, from an everything-got-washed-away-in-the-hurricane manner of speaking, yes.

If the hurricane was her justification, it was because the storm had upended everything, like a bomb that blew apart so many carefully constructed communities and existence, that corrupted trust and confidence in the present, and hope for the future. Despite having an apartment, she was a drifter, a wandering fugitive.

Marilyn could admit she had been desperate for money, and the witness money was important. But maybe she'd be fine without the ransom money. It had been Gwynne's idea, and Earl was just their patsy. Again, she considered what would happen if they called a halt to the blackmail, or if she simply quit and let Gwynne and Earl proceed. Her fee for being Fairfield's fake witness was enough for her, wasn't it? She would have to leave Houston, but she could find a less expensive place to live, buy a modest house, maybe in a medium-sized town, get a job. Her desperation to live comfortably without worry about money was possibly residue, like waxy buildup, or a stain from the upheaval caused by her childhood poverty. Through time immemorial, money has been known to blur, if not crush people's boundaries. The trial was coming up fast. Fairfield's threats were scary, and she was unable to stop this locomotive.

Still worried, but too tired to fight sleep, she drifted off.

She was dreaming of building a house, hammering a nail into wood, but as she surfaced, she realized someone knocking had blended with her dream. It came again and this time she was instantly awaken. The distinct rap of knuckles-on-door. Two o'clock. Palmer had no doubt figured out all the players and how they were connected, and he'd sent Fairfield's henchmen. Gwynne and Earl were already dead, and she was next. A jolt of adrenalin flooded her. Shaking with fear, she crept into the bathroom, which had the only window facing the back of the house. She unlocked it and yanked on its handles, but it was painted shut, and wouldn't budge. But wait, would Fairfield's guys knock? Yes, probably, just to see if anyone answered, a light came on, or curtains moved. Shit, she'd be visible going out any other windows or the side door to the yard.

She needed a weapon. How ridiculous that seemingly everyone in Houston owned a firearm except her. She tiptoed into the kitchen and pulled a butcher knife from the block. Tomorrow she'd buy a gun and go to a gun range, refresh her shooting skills. If she lived that long.

Crab-walking from the kitchen, her back tight to the wall, heart pounding, she inched to the dining room archway and peered down the hall. In the front door's rippled glass was the blurry form of a man. It wasn't Earl. This guy had a more confident posture, a more substantial build, and more businesslike clothing than Earl's T-shirts. Were there others? How many would Palmer send?

The man at the door said, "Marilyn. Are you there?" Then he added, "Marilyn, it's Stade. Open up."

She exhaled with relief, her head tipped back against the wall, eyes closed, and regrouped. Stade didn't know about any of the plots she was involved in, or her fears, and he couldn't realize the terror that knocking at her door would induce. "Hold on," she called out.

Stade said, "Marilyn, I tried to call you, but it went to voicemail."

Shit, she'd turned off her ringer to get some sleep. She put the knife away and debated opening the door. Oh, what the hell, she'd be leaving in a few days and never see him again.

Zabi whispered, *As they say, life is short—eat dessert first.*

She unlocked and swung the door open. Stade stepped over the threshold. Still wary of Earl stalking her, she quickly shoved the door closed and locked it. Stade closed the distance between them and pulled her close. She relaxed into his embrace, her arms around his neck. He lifted her off the floor as she hooked her legs around his waist, and they kissed as he carried her to the bedroom.

Stade tipped her diagonally across the bed and stood to undress, taking his time, opening one button after another, stepping out of Italian loafers. Then lifting her chemise over her head, kissing her neck, their anticipation, breathing, and heat accelerating. He ran his hands over her shoulders and torso, and she lightly gripped his biceps and gazed at the dip at the center of his clavicle and breastbone, the undulations and slight sheen of his tanned skin, the contrasting colors and texture of flesh, hair, the liquid shine of his eyes. He was watching her intently, that mote in his iris drawing her in.

And later, becalmed, his arms wrapped her up and held her to him. And for a time, she was exquisitely confident, protected, worry free. Breathing deeply, Marilyn lay a while, her head on his shoulder, inhaling him, before she said, "I needed that."

"Me too," Stade said. "From the first moment I saw you." He took her hand, and they lay quietly, then he asked, "Oh, where are my manners? Can I get you some tissues?"

"No. I like the wet spot."

He said, "Oh my God. You're perfect."

She laughed. "That's me all right, Miss Perfect. I'd feel more perfect if I had a glass of wine in my hand."

"Really? I can run to the corner. They're open all night."

"No, no, no." Marilyn laughed. "There's some el-cheapo chardonnay in the fridge, and you'll find my waiter-style corkscrew in the drawer. Help yourself to the scotch if you like."

He smiled, slowly sat up, pulled on his boxers, and left the room, returning with a glass of wine and a tumbler with a shot of scotch.

She sipped her wine and then placed the glass on the nightstand. For a while, they were comfortably quiet. She tuned her iPod to Michael Franks's *The Art of Tea*. "I love this old album. It's so romantic; light, jazzy, and so loving."

"What's really amazing is I own it too."

"Get the hell out!" She rolled onto her side, facing him. "We're bad. No condom."

"Are you thinking about birth control or STDs?"

"Just that everyone needs to be careful, y'know."

She sat up and sipped her wine, then straddled him, leaning forward, her hands beside his ears. She looked at him searchingly. A powerful urge to confide, to get Stade's take on Gwynne's entire plot, rushed through her. It was an almost physical need, wrapping itself around her mind and squeezing. She grasped the sheets in clenched fists to hold back, and thought, *He's a cop. He knows nothing. Keep him out of it.*

"What?" Stade looked at her quizzically.

"Has Gwynne said anything to you about me?" She turned and squinched her eyes shut at her stupidity of mentioning Gwynne. There was no reason to think Stade would even be talking to Gwynne. She rolled away and sat up, took another sip of wine, then lay down.

"No. But I don't need a crystal ball to know he's probably up to something. Gwynne is always walking a fine line. He has an expensive wife and a lavish life. It's also rumored he has a a gambling habit. All of which are probably unsustainable. Why?" He turned on his side to study her and pushed a strand of her hair aside.

She shrugged. "He tracked me down, kind of like you did. He's representing Fairfield and Palmer and wanted to know if I saw anything else the night the Lads were killed."

"If he's pressuring you to do something, or to *not* do something, that's known as witness tampering."

"No. No pressuring, and I had no info for him. There's nothing to tamper with. I'm tamper-proof." She shrugged. "Is your detectively instinct satisfied?"

"It is. You satisfy me."

"Likewise…By the way, you look good on TV, Detective. I'm assuming since you're still hunting the killer, you haven't found the dead women's jewelry."

"You assume correctly."

"Did Rigby tell you she'd seen those women wearing their jewelry at the Lads' parties?"

"She did."

"I appreciate that you don't want to rush to judgment, but if the Lads knew all of those ladies…"

"Call me crazy, but I would like to get more proof.

Anything forensic would do. While all the women visited either the Lads' apartment or the drawing group, it also works against us because it can explain away their DNA and so forth being on the premises."

"Hey, Detective, it just occurred to me that there haven't been any more killings reported since the Lads died."

"I noticed. You're a good case-builder."

"Thanks."

Stade's expression turned serious. He said, "About Gwynne. If you're even talking to him. Well…be careful. He's good at manipulating the truth."

"Right. What certain politicians have referred to as 'alternative facts.'" She looked at him wistfully. Talking about the murders of so many women, while important, was distant now. She and Stade were living in different universes.

Chapter Thirty-Five:

Art Delivery

Marilyn woke to the smell of coffee and the sound of the shower running. She sat up and donned her panties and slip from last night as Stade, wrapped in a towel, emerged from the bathroom trailing a plume of soap-scented steam. He said, "Go back to sleep. No need to get up yet."

She padded over to him, and they kissed lightly, another dimension separate and apart from the passion of last night. This guy. There were layers to him. "You made coffee. Careful, you may never be allowed to leave."

"How do you take yours?"

"Light. No sugar. Would you care for some eggs?"

"Please, that'd be good."

"How do you like them?" She took out a frying pan and turned on the gas burner as she removed eggs, butter, and bread from the fridge.

"I like them however you like yours."

"Bullshit." She laughed. "But scrambled it is." Gwynne had joked about his wife coming at him with a knife because he made an omelet. Could Stade be so easygoing, or had they just stepped into a rom-com?

After breakfast, and another lovemaking session, Stade held and kissed her, then left, leaving behind his scent on the sheets, the aftershocks of another orgasm, and the sense of safety from being in his arms. She showered and dressed and called the Art Guild. Andy answered, and Marilyn asked if they had an opening for her to model.

He said quickly, "No life-drawing today. We're changing the exhibit."

Marilyn said, "You sound a bit stressed."

Andy said, "Yeah, I'm currently going at a hundred what-the-fucks an hour."

"What can I do to help?"

"Probably nothing."

"C'mon, Andy, you know that stressed is desserts spelled backward. I'll bring you some Ben and Jerry's, and you should let me take on some of your tasks."

He laughed. "I like that. Okay, you asked for it. Take your pick. You can help the new artist hang their show, or document buyers who are coming to pick up their drawings. Or, deliver three drawings." He clucked his tongue. "River Oaks customers."

Marilyn smiled. "I'll take the River Oaks deliveries."

"Ha. You might be getting in deeper than you thought. Our esteemed director promised one of them we'd not only deliver the drawing, but we'd also hang it, too."

"No problem." Marilyn laughed. "I can handle it. Which one is it?"

"Vanessa Gwynne, on Hewlett."

"Sure thing, Andy. I'll be there in half an hour," she said.

Zabi said, *Gotta love serendipity.*

"No shit, Auntie."

In the front gallery, all the life-drawings were off the

walls and lined up on the floor. Andy was on a ladder filling nail holes in the drywall. He climbed down and took the pint of Cherry Garcia. "You're the best!"

Marilyn, brimming with glee, packed the drawings, along with a small hammer and picture hangers, and left. She wasn't sure why she wanted to get into Gwynne's house, but some internal warning bell had been telling her to find a way. She had considered pretending to be a reporter covering art collectors, but after meeting Vanessa Gwynne that wouldn't work.

Marilyn rang the bell, and an Hispanic maid in uniform answered and asked the standard questions in halting English to gain entry. As expected, Gwynne's house was huge, maybe six thousand square feet. Marilyn stepped inside the large marble-lined foyer, and the maid went to fetch "Miss Vanessa."

The foyer's closet had double doors, and Marilyn quietly opened them. It was divided neatly in half, his and hers. On his side, there were shiny pairs of men's black Cole Hahn loafers, sport coats, and windbreakers. As she closed the closet doors, through a side window, she spotted a Jaguar rolling out of the driveway.

The maid returned and said, "Miss Vanessa gone to appointment. She say hang painting in bedroom, bathroom, or closet because painting is rude."

Marilyn held back a snicker. No doubt Miss Vanessa had said the painting was of a *nude*. "Great," Marilyn said. "Can you show me the way?" This was getting better by the minute. She trailed the maid through the expansive, minimalist décor with sleek low furniture and walls of glass. A massive black-and-white abstract dominated the far twenty-foot-high wall. Marilyn said, "Mrs. Gwynne collects abstract art."

"Be more paintings at Dallas and California houses." Three residences and each with its own art collection. Stade was correct. The Gwynnes lived large. The bedroom was decorated in keeping with the rest of the house with a huge modern four-poster and streamlined furniture. The maid hadn't made the bed yet. She quickly tugged the covers, but not before Marilyn noticed that both sides had been slept in, and there was some bunched Kleenex. So much for Gwynne's supposed sex deprivation, unless Vanessa had a side-guy.

The maid then showed Marilyn to his-and-her bathrooms, each with adjoining huge closets and dressing-room combos complete with tall mirrors and sets of drawers—Gwynne's inner sanctum. There was also a "butler," a short stick-figure construction on which to hang clothes as he undressed. It was draped with Gwynne's suit from their last meeting at the zoo. Marilyn placed the hammer and picture hook on a dresser and went from one wall to another, holding up the framed drawing and looking thoughtful, until she'd covered every possible placement.

When she started the process over again, the maid lost patience and said she'd be in the kitchen. Marilyn went into Gwynne's bathroom and felt his toothbrush. It was still damp, and his razor sat in a small puddle in a soap dish. Why would Gwynne lie about separating from his wife? He had flirted and invited her to his hotel room, but surely, he wouldn't tell such a ridiculous lie to get into Marilyn's panties. If she had acquiesced, he would have needed to take a room at the ZaZa and make it look like a semi-permanent living situation. Married or single, men like Gwynne could easily find plenty of attractive women to sleep with. Something else was going on.

She started a quick search in his closet, unsure what she was looking for. A bank of drawers contained socks, underwear, and his watches and cufflinks. The jewelry, being portable and valuable, would have gone with him if they'd split. The tap-tap of the maid's shoes approached but passed by and she heard bustling in another nearby bedroom, then the footsteps headed down the stairs. Soon she would get kicked out. Sweat bloomed on her forehead.

A full-length mirror looked suspiciously thick. She

ran her hand down the side and discovered full-height piano hinge. Was this the door to their S-and-M dungeon? Pulling on the opposite edge detached the mirror from magnets and it swung open. The dungeon she'd anticipated didn't exist, at least not here. Instead, there was a shallow cabinet containing a safe. Well, well. Now what had she stumbled onto?

Tapping footsteps echoed in the hallway and Marilyn quickly closed the mirror. The maid entered and asked, "How long is gonna take?"

"Just a few minutes." Marilyn smiled. The maid harrumphed, turned on her heel, and left.

What was the safe's combination? Marilyn searched her memory for clues, perhaps something that Gwynne dropped in conversation, an address, a golf score, something personal and meaningful. Across the room, was a framed European-style license plate with six large numbers—162873. She recalled a photo she'd seen in her research, of Gwynne at the wheel of a Morgan, the hand-built British sports car. There would be time for just one attempt to open the safe. If it didn't work, she'd go.

Listening intently for the maid, her heart pounding, her hands damp and shaky, she turned the dial to 16, then back past zero to 28, and finally to 73. She pushed down on the lever, and the door swung open. Ha, apparently Earl wasn't the only one who couldn't remember stuff, although hanging the combination just ten feet from one's safe was pretty arrogant.

Inside were envelopes. The first held Gwynne's new identity with photos of him sporting darker hair and a convincingly realistic mustache. She took photos of his passport ID page, driver's license, and social security card. There were two Rolex watches and a small hard case that, when opened, contained the fake mustache. Then another envelope. More papers for a trip—one way to Monaco on a private jet. That his flight was printed on paper and not stored in his phone suggested that Gwynne was avoiding

Earl's ability to hack him even if he obtained a separate secret email address.

There was a notebook. Turning the top page revealed a memo that read *Banque Suisse*, along with some code numbers. Under that was a list of *life insurance*, *retirement*, *personal account*, and *line of credit*. Each had a figure written next to it and a password. She tallied the numbers, which added up to nearly eighteen million. Marilyn photographed the pages, locked the safe, hammered a nail in the wall, hung the drawing, and made her way out, calling out to the maid, who answered with a cheerful goodbye.

As she drove to the two remaining deliveries, she considered what Gwynne might be up to. She called Hotel ZaZa and asked for Gwynne's room and was put through. She hung up. So, he did have a room there, but why? This made no sense. Then, like mist clearing, his plan began to become clear. He'd lied that he'd separated from his wife, but he was planning to leave her. The accounts he'd listed were marital assets to steal from Vanessa and move to his offshore accounts. Plus, the covert offshore bank account, his disguised appearance, fake travel documents, and the private jet clearly indicated his intention to double-cross Marilyn and Earl. He was going to take off for Monaco with his wife's money and the blackmail money. All of it.

He was telling the truth about having a room at the hotel, but its purpose wasn't separation from his spouse; it was to stage his getaway, although he would boff Marilyn there if the opportunity presented itself. It was where he kept his get-out-of-Dodge clothes and electronics, and spent time away from his home and office, in private to arrange his secret travel itinerary, plan the blackmail, and move marital assets to the offshore bank.

There were loose ends, however. How was Gwynne planning to intercept the cash when Earl was supposed to be the go-between and pick it up? Also, how would Gwynne deposit hundred-dollar-bills to an offshore account? There were plenty of questions without answers, but one thing was certain, Gwynne was fiendish. He'd never intended for Earl or Marilyn to get their cut. Where was all that *honor amongst thieves* stuff she'd heard about? Even though she never intended to stay with Earl long term, she had always expected him to collect his share.

What to do? Confront Gwynne? Would he own up and get back on board with their original plan, or in desperation, would he double down and become even more devious? She settled on her usual tack. Outsmart the bastard. But how?

Marilyn called Sandy. "Everything okay?"

"Oh yeah, I'm not leaving—ever." Sandy laughed. "This place is sooo nice. Ethan is going to turn into a baby porpoise, he loves that pool so much."

"Well, at least this heatwave is good for something. Have you left the hotel at all?"

"Nope. Don't need to and don't want to. This is like a vacation. We watch TV, play in the pool, sleep, and order room service. I've been to the gift shop a few times, but I haven't had the nerve to go to the dining room. It's been room service since we got here."

"Good, Sandy. I think you deserve a vacation. And I'm so glad that you're going with the flow. Are you still okay for money?"

"Yes! Got tons of cash. But truth be told, Marilyn, I'm still definitely on edge for when Earl finds us gone and loses his ever-lovin' marbles."

"I agree. So, all the more reason to lay low. Sandy, I might need your help with some boxes in the next few days."

"Boxes?"

"They need to be driven to a specific location. Would you be up for that?"

"Sure. But only because, you know, you saved my

life." She laughed. "I guess I can. But what about Ethan?"

"I talked to the front desk. The hotel uses a highly reputable babysitting service. They even install a nanny-cam to keep an eye on the care the child is receiving in real time."

"Sounds good," Sandy said. "Whatever you need, I'm in. Just let me know when and where." They goodbye'd and hung up.

Marilyn's phone signaled a text from Earl: *Gwynne says Fairfield won't pay more than ten million. I'm sick of Gwynne and Fairfield dicking us around. Tomorrow, real early, go past Gwynne's and Fairfield's houses.*

She replied: *I'm sick of their bitching and complaining too. What's going on?*

Earl: *I have to go visit a friend of mine now. He lives out in the country toward Austin. I'm going to give those guys a big surprise.*

Marilyn: *Is this the guy you said would keep Sandy on ice for a while?*

Earl: *Nope. Different guy.*

Marilyn: *What are you going to do, Earl? It's only three days 'til the trial. Don't fuck things up.*

Earl: *You'll see. Don't worry, Marilyn, no firearms or dynamite will be involved. Promise. LOL. BTW, I hacked Gwynne's computer and got into his bank account. The guy is totally broke. It looks like his wife is the rich one. Her maiden name is Proctor. She's heir to a huge mining fortune. She gets several million a year from a trust fund, and when her parents die, she'll inherit a couple of billion.*

Marilyn: *Weird, considering he has a successful law practice.*

Earl: *He's a gambling addict, especially the ponies.*

Marilyn: *How did you find that out?*

Earl: *I have my ways. He has a box at the track. Also standing reservations at a casino in Lake Charles, Louisiana, and his Amex Black Card is only used in Vegas, and it's used a lot.*

Marilyn: *I'll go jogging early in River Oaks.* ☺

Well, well, Earl is really good at this hacking stuff. Interesting about Gwynne. He's a gambler running to Monaco, the equivalent of sticking his head in the lion's mouth. Sure, it's far away, but he might as well go to Vegas, given how quickly he'd probably lose his money.

What was Earl planning? It was puzzling that the GIF of the Lads' execution, and the photo Gwynne had taken of her with Fairfield's ring at the zoo, hadn't been sufficiently fearsome to scare Fairfield into complying. Although maybe Fairfield hadn't insisted on cutting the ransom by half to ten million. Maybe it was Gwynne trying to get more than his share, and he wanted to see how far he could push before Earl pushed back.

Chapter Thirty-Six:

Taxidermy

Up at five, Marilyn pulled on yoga gear, slipped into runners, and tucked her hair into a cap. She parked a block from Gwynne's swankienda just as the sun was starting to rise. It was already hot, and the weather forecast called for a scorcher. She left the car and walked in the shadows of trees.

Irrigation systems were finishing their rotations on several yards. The neighborhood reminded Marilyn of a Joni Mitchell song, "The Hissing of Summer Lawns," about wealth and isolation. Were sprinklers the symbols of wealth in that song? She couldn't remember. She'd read somewhere that Houston is sinking like Venice, from sucking the water out of the ground.

Zabi whispered, *Until we're so thirsty we're forced to drink our own piss, everyone will continue to dump precious drinking water on lawns to keep them green.*

Yep, just another concealed man-made catastrophe at the tipping point. She dodged another property's sprinklers that were chugging and blipping, watering half the roadway. Across the road, there was a rock, agave, and cactus garden—no sprinklers.

She rounded a corner in sight of Gwynne's front door. Lying across the porch was an alien brown shape. On closer scrutiny, it was a disemboweled deer carcass, its entrails spooled down the stone steps. A trail of blood pooled under the deer and led along the walkway. Fifty feet away, Marilyn could smell the nauseating death stink.

Gwynne's Mercedes was parked in the driveway. *Tell me again how you don't live here, Gwynne.* Even her thoughts were becoming sardonic. She eased her way along the deep shade of a high hedge and looked through the rolled-down windows into the back seat. Three dead skunks reeking of their spray and decay were strapped in, looking like freakish toddlers happy to be going for a drive. The skunks were poorly taxidermied with patchy fur and plastic eyes that didn't fit the sockets. One held a glass of scotch and a half-smoked cigar, the second had a judge's gavel, and the third sported a legal-looking document and twenty-dollar bills fanned out on its lap. She crept closer and saw one-word notes attached to each skunk with a spike. In combination, they spelled out, "Crooked lawyers pay."

Closer to the porch, she saw another note nailed to the deer. It said, "Cooperate or lose it all." Marilyn covered her nose. *Where the hell did Earl get three dead stuffed skunks and a dead deer?* He had mentioned meeting with someone near Austin. Whoever it was that supplied them, she was thrilled to be uninvolved. Maggots writhed over the deer's guts, eyes, and protruding tongue. The heat had risen, unleashing the stink of rotten carcass, and she fought the wrench to her stomach.

She trotted across the street and stepped through trimmed creeping jasmine, on the lookout for fire ants, black-widow and brown recluse spiders, and snakes. Déjà vu of working for The Verminator, although in River Oaks, the pests were most likely eliminated.

A few minutes later, the dark-wood front door was cracked, then opened wide, and Gwynne emerged in an open robe and boxers to pick up the *Chronicle*, which was lying in a plastic bag past the deer. He looked half asleep. Earl had unscrewed or disconnected the porch light, and Gwynne practically tripped over the carcass. Marilyn watched as, in the dark, Gwynne bent close to the deer's corpse, realization dawned, and he jumped away.

Gwynne suddenly ascertained that he had stepped into and dipped the hem of his terrycloth robe in the stinking viscera. He wiped his feet vigorously on the hemp doormat and wrenched at the bathrobe's sleeves, flailing, dancing a frustrated ferocious jig. Then, stripped of the soiled garment, he wadded it up and threw it into a rose bed. Marilyn quaked with silent laughter at the spectacle.

Gwynne's abdomen spasmed violently as he registered the smell. Given her own stomach's sensitivity, she looked away and covered her ears. However, she couldn't fully block out Gwynne's sounds as he threw himself against the stainless steel and glass railing that skirted the porch to puke into the gardenias and bird of paradise. Stifling laughter, Marilyn crept through front yards to her vehicle.

She had to hand it to Earl—nicely played. He got marks for originality, humor, and menace. The photo of her with Fairfield's ring, the GIF of Fairfield executing Shawn, and now this gruesome display, which was also a threat, ought to convince Fairfield to get with the program. Still chuckling, she drove out of Gwynne's wealthy section of River Oaks and into the megabucks portion of the area, a stunning collection of enormous mansions. Not even winning the Powerball lottery could buy one of these babies since they were handed down generation to generation. She wondered how astronomical their utilities and groundskeeping bills were, but obviously, if money was a concern, this life wasn't for you. She slowed as she approached Fairfield's high stone wall.

A beat-up pickup truck carrying tools and a ladder passed her, the driver's silhouette outlining a cowboy hat. Marilyn considered how demoralizing working in a neighborhood like River Oaks would be, always having your face rubbed in the wealth. Saying yes-ma'am and no-ma'am, yes-sir and no-sir a hundred times a day, trimming their shrubs, wiping their kids' noses, cooking their food, cleaning up after them, knowing full well that they could replace your sorry ass at a moment's notice.

Careful of surveillance cameras, guards, and dogs, she pulled over at Fairfield's gate and heard hysterical, staccato Spanish. Along the wide, curved stone driveway with its edging of English-garden-like flowering landscaping, Marilyn recognized the large suit-wearing guard as Palmer. He was arguing with a woman in a maid's uniform. She was a full foot shorter than him but refusing to back down, shaking her fist, and Palmer was gripping her other hand, which was clasping a cell phone. Behind them was another deer corpse, the coagulated bloody mess causing others nearby—two men with a large cart who were trying to remove the deer—and a few bystanders to pull up their T-shirts over their noses. Marilyn deciphered from the tableau that the maid wanted to call the cops, and Palmer was restraining her, knowing that the grisly scene held a private message that wasn't to be fucked with.

Palmer wasn't some off-duty rent-a-cop or low-intelligence bar bouncer who had been hit over the head too many times with barstools swung by drunks. The guy was a thug, but smart, smart enough to be cool, inquisitive, and measured. Palmer felt Marilyn's stare and casually turned to look as she drove away. Being part of his boss's murder plan bound Palmer to the old guy forever, and vice versa.

Marilyn bet the oilman looked upon Palmer as the son

he never had, plotting and planning together, the younger man helping him reach his goals, keeping him safe. The dude would probably inherit a fortune from the geezer, especially now that Fairfield's daughter was dead. When the geezer passed, Palmer was no doubt supposed to stay on, guarding Fairfield's grandson.

Marilyn phoned Earl. "Where did you get those gross critters?"

"They're courtesy of my good buddy Virgil, the taxidermist." He laughed.

"I'm glad I've never met this Virgil guy."

"Yeah. I know, right? Virgil's the type of redneck they wrote blue-collar comedy about. If he went to SeaWorld, he would take a fishing pole. He really does consider a six-pack and a bug zapper to be high-quality entertainment. And so on."

"Where did you meet someone like him?"

"I was picking up some stuff on a county road one day, and he pulled up in his truck, which was covered with animal pelts, and heads and horns, and feet and stuff. I call his vehicle *Fast and Furry-ous*. Anyway, we started talking. Sometimes I think Virgil is so awful because he has stuff switched around in his head. For instance, Virgil's taxidermy is inside his trailer, and his furniture is outside on his porch, along with a fridge, a Coleman stove, and tons of empty bean, beer, and soup cans. And of course, there's a whole lotta firearms."

"Jesus. Well, your display ought to have the desired effect. I watched Gwynne come out this morning and lose his breakfast."

"That's awesome," Earl said. "I couldn't risk sticking around, so I missed that highlight. Wonder if he'll ever be able to get the skunk smell out. One thing about Virgil's taxidermy is that it stinks, literally and figuratively. His place reeks of death, and his skill level is at the anchor-end of the learning curve." He sounded excited. "Basically, though, I'd say he's mental—about as confused as a mosquito in a mannequin factory."

Marilyn laughed. "Have you heard anything from Gwynne? It's only forty-eight hours 'til the trial. You guys don't even have a firm plan in place, do you?"

"Not yet. I checked fifteen minutes ago, and there were no texts or email."

She was tempted to call bullshit, but having Earl and Gwynne think she was an unsuspecting helper was smarter. "What are you doing today?"

"Running errands mainly, and I'm going to take care of that bitch Sandy. The next time I see you, I'll have Ethan."

"Not a moment too soon!" Marilyn exclaimed, and Earl laughed.

Then he said morosely, "My god, Marilyn. I just want this to be over and for us to be together."

"I know, sweetheart. So do I. It's countdown time." They said goodbye and hung up.

Marilyn had a moment of guilt. Earl's fantasy relationship with Marilyn and boatloads of cash from the blackmail scheme had hatched his scheme to eliminate Sandy and kidnap Ethan. With her planning, orchestrating, and tacit approval she was more than a little responsible. The only way to fix things was to keep Sandy and Ethan safe. She called Sandy and warned her that Earl was on the hunt. Sandy assured her she was staying in the hotel.

Next, Marilyn called Gwynne. "Jesus, Gwynne, what is going on? Have you planned the drop yet? Earl is super pissed."

Gwynne snorted. "Earl gave me and Fairfield a very nasty shock this morning and it convinced Fairfield to give up his cockamamie idea to cut the dollar amount or to find another defense."

She said, "Not a moment too soon. Please let Earl know. While I liked Earl's stunt, we can't have him flipping out like this again."

"I know. I'll talk to him."

Chapter Thirty-Seven:

The Snoop

She'd learned a lot about Gwynne from being in his home. The house had given up Gwynne's secrets in unexpected ways, and no doubt Earl's would do the same. Therefore, snooping in Earl's house seemed prudent, and no time like the present since he was going out to run errands—and kidnap Sandy. Sandy was just another item to cross off his to-do list.

On the drive to Earl's house, she tried to nail down the purpose of her mission but could only come up with sanitizing his hard drives and collecting phones or anything else which might link them. If Jon was being truthful and the bondage drawings were Earl's work, there should be more drawings in Earl's house. She hadn't seen any, but maybe they were hidden. The website, Masterpieces.com, didn't have work for sale by either Earl or Jon. She pictured the drawing in Jon's living room with its blurred background. Maybe the background was Earl's junk, loosely sketched.

Earl's van was parked under his house, and she drove three houses past it to sit and wait. When Earl emerged and drove away, Marilyn left her car. She walked on the pavement to avoid losing her footing on the road's soft shoulder, which would plunge her into the deep water-filled ditch alongside the road. Sandy's knowledge of where Earl kept his keys was fortuitous. Below his house was a wooden tool shed. Inside the shed was a jumble of rakes, shovels, a tarp, containers, and tools. A canister of weed killer had handprints in its dust, and under it was a key.

She dashed up the stairs onto the deck, unlocked the sliding door, and entered, making her way to Earl's office. His computers were running but asleep, and twiddling each mouse woke them. Ha. Earl was making her job easier than expected. He certainly wasn't Mr. Security.

Adrenaline kicked in, rattling her heart as if it were clattering against her ribs. Sweat trickled down her back and sides, which made her want to rush. She employed the technique Zabi had taught her when she was hurt as a child. Aunt Zabi would tell her to breathe deeply, like *smelling the roses and blowing out the candles*, calming through over-oxygenation.

To erase Earl's connections to her and Gwynne, she started by logging into his Google account, which required a password. He said he called Ethan *Awesome-Ethan*, which got her in. She clicked the Google icon, then clicked "My Google" on the menu, and it took her to a list of email contacts. She deleted them, then did the same thing on Yahoo and every other search engine that had email, eliminating each account.

Next, she clicked on an icon marked *Sullivan*. She scrolled through the contents; a video of a family in their Land Rover leaving their large suburban house, their children entering a private school, a maid photographed through a window, and interior pictures as Earl posed as a cable guy. There were *before* and *after* screenshots of their bank statements showing he had siphoned off nearly two hundred thousand, and a file of receipts for eBay purchases of diamonds and gold coins bought using their credit cards. Holy crap.

She clicked on more files, each labeled with a name: Pullman, McGregor, Anderson, Rowan, Vern and Molly, the people who had come to look at Earl's house. In Vern and Molly's file were banking and retirement savings records. Under her breath, she said, "People, this is why you need a realtor. An agent would have protected your privacy."

After running through more files and finding them all to be Earl's hacking victims, she saved all the files to a thumb drive. Maybe she could turn it over to Stade and if they found Earl's assets his victims could be reimbursed. She repeated the exercise on all of his computers. Then she took a flash drive from her bag, which contained software that, when turned loose, would eat everything stored on the hard drive. It would erase his scamming data, every document, his favorite websites, and photos.

Each computer would take several minutes to sanitize. While she waited, she started a search, lifting some portholes and buckets of odds and ends. A sudden creaking sound reached her. Was it on the outdoor stairs? Surely, he couldn't be back already. Another creak came, and another. Footsteps. Panic flooded her. She tiptoed, moving quickly and quietly through the pathway to a spot where she could crouch behind a pile of ropes and anchors.

The footfalls crested the stairs making a hollow sound on the deck. There were women's voices. Not Earl, after all, but who? She peeked around the pile of stuff. Two women dressed in the Sunday-going-to-meeting style of pesky, religious-pamphlet proselytizers stood looking over the water until one leaned against the railing. It moved under her weight, and she stepped back. The women turned, knocked on the door, and rudely cupped their hands to the glass to look inside. Finally, they gave up and left their publication on the table under Earl's bug-repellent candle. Marilyn exhaled as they creaked down the stairs.

She was unnerved, and wished she'd had the foresight to attach a GPS tracker to Earl's van. Still unsure what she was looking for, she entered the bedroom. It was also a storeroom for his nautical stuff, with narrow paths around the bed to a window, and between the bed and the dresser. She opened the drawers. Undershirts, briefs, and socks were in a tangle, and she rifled through them, but found nothing of interest. The bedside table had one locked drawer and a shelf below. Feeling under the drawer, she found and sprung the locking mechanism, something her mom had mastered when her johns fell asleep. Inside was a blizzard of lists written on the paper tape from an adding machine. On closer examination, she saw they were names, email addresses, and passwords.

There was also a revolver. Thanks, Earl. It had been at least three years since she'd held a gun. Her boyfriend at the time considered target practice at the shooting range to be stellar entertainment. Smoke and the deafening crack of gunfire had apparently been a turn-on for him. The weapon's shape and heft felt good in her hand. She swung the barrel out. It was loaded. She snapped the barrel closed and engaged the safety.

She circled the bed and sprung the lock on the other nightstand. The drawer was full of hundred-dollar bills in bunches bound by rubber bands. "Whoa," she whispered. She made her way through Earl's debris-maze into the kitchen, found a garbage bag, and bagged the lists, the money, the gun, and ammo.

She opened cabinets in the bathroom and kitchen but found nothing of interest. With the sanitizing software working on the last computer, from the bedroom's doorway she studied the construct of Earl's warren. The piles of paraphernalia would be impossible to search. His paths led to doorways and around the kitchen island. There was also an area that was draped in nautical flags. She pulled the flags aside and uncovered a barely noticeable narrow path which led to a low, wide cabinet buried in propellers and anchors. It was a flat file, with several shallow drawers commonly used for storing artwork or blueprints. She opened the top drawer. There was a large manila envelope, unsealed, and inside were several layers of paper, the same paper Earl used for figure drawing.

Given the woman-in-bondage print in Jon's living room that he attributed to Earl, maybe Earl indulged in drawing taboo subjects. She braced herself for whatever was about to be revealed, pulled the paper from the envelope, and set it on a low pile of portholes. On the top sheet was the life-drawing of the young woman with the heart tattoos, hogtied. This was the original drawing and more detailed, with a cloth stuffed in her mouth and a blindfold, unlike the print at Jon's apartment.

If she ignored the subject matter, the drawing was a beautiful rendering in watercolor, delicately shaded with pastel and colored pencil, a masterpiece, the figure perfectly proportioned and appearing nearly three dimensional. Earl had captured the subject's vulnerability, her pretty and delicate features, her pink, purple, and red tattoos. In the hands of a lesser artist, the tattoos would have appeared flat, drawn as an afterthought, but he had incorporated them into her skin, highlighted and shadowed where her flesh undulated, distorted where she strained or flexed. Her distress was obvious in her pleading eyes, contorted mouth, the tracks of her tears, but not in a maudlin or saccharine way, not sympathetic toward the woman, more clinical than anything else. However, his exquisite depiction of her captivity in such a detached manner would probably heighten any viewer's recognition of, and empathy for her suffering.

Marilyn hesitated and inhaled, steadying herself for what was next, and lifted the sheet of paper. The next drawing showed the same woman on plastic on Earl's bed with a leather belt as a tourniquet on her upper arm and a syringe in her vein. In this drawing, however, there were torture marks—blood, ligature abrasions, burns, bruises, injuries that would never heal. She placed the image on the floor and took a photo of it with her phone.

The next image showed Darby Fairfield with a daisy-adorned comb in her long hair. "Fuck," she said under her breath. "It wasn't the Lads, or Jon, or Rockwell, or Earl's friend with the ranch. Earl is the serial killer." There were several drawings of Darby alive and in death. He had also done studies of her bruised and abraded body parts.

Zabi said, *Darby and Fran were found together. Is Fran part of his collection?*

"God, I hope not, Zabi, and these drawings could just as easily be of me. I've been alone with Earl." All these poor women. She shot more photos of the Darby drawings. The next rendering was the original art of the print that Jon had on his wall, but this girl wore a showy ankle bracelet. "Here you go, Stade," she whispered. "Here's some missing jewelry."

Marilyn's phone sounded a ringtone of harps and showed video from the doorbell at Sandy's apartment. Earl was on the porch. He waited a few moments then hammered on her door and rang the bell several more times. He shouted through the door then dialed his phone and cursed, kicked the building's siding, and exasperated, turned in a circle. Repeating his actions prompted a bull-shouldered male neighbor to open his door. The man stepped out wearing boxer shorts and a tank top, and said, "Dude, you hammer on her door one more time, you'll be down the stairs and on the parking lot, and not necessarily standing."

Earl said, "Where's Sandy?"

"Why? Are you a cop? Oh wait, I know who you are. You're Ethan's dad. The fuckin' deadbeat. Take a hike, dude."

"I have a right to see my son."

"Bullshit. One more word…" He moved toward Earl.

Earl didn't reply. He quickly left her porch, stumbling on the stairs, and got in his van. Marilyn couldn't help but grin.

If Earl left Sandy's place and came directly home, he would arrive in twenty-five minutes. She went through more drawings—the blonde, Brittany, and the woman with the belly button piercing—and took more photos. Then it was time to get moving.

Chapter Thirty-Eight:

Denial

Marilyn checked the time. Seven minutes until Earl would probably arrive. She'd prefer to be more thorough, but realistically, to search his house properly would take days. She carefully replaced the drawings and went room to room to check she hadn't forgotten anything. Slinging the bag of money and her purse over her shoulder, she left, replaced his key, and ran to the car. As she drove away, Earl's van appeared in her rearview, and he turned into his parking space.

Driving on I-45, Marilyn told her phone to call Sandy, who picked up, giggling. "Hi. Sorry to be out of breath, but this little piranha has been chasing me in the pool."

Ethan's irrepressible laughter in the background gave Marilyn a chuckle, and she said, "I'm on my way over. I'll be there soon."

"Cool." They hung up.

As she drove, she considered Earl's drawings. Were they the definitive proof Stade wanted? It seemed incredible that so much had pointed to the Lads as the killers when it was Earl, the innocent good guy. Stade could wait. She needed to think this through.

In the hotel parking garage, Marilyn opened the trash bag and transferred Earl's loot to a tote. At Sandy's suite, Sandy gestured Marilyn to the bedroom door. Ethan was sleeping, his small form making the bed look gigantic. Her pride and love for Ethan touched Marilyn. They tiptoed to the living room, and Sandy said, "I don't know how I'm going to thank you or repay you for, first of all, saving my life, but also putting us here. It's such a lovely place."

"It's great that you're both happy. Right now, it's super-important that you don't leave the hotel because Earl just found out that you're not at home." She filled Sandy in on what she'd seen of Earl at her door, and his run in with her burly neighbor.

Sandy giggled. "It's about time Earl met George. He handles security at my job, and he is my guardian angel."

"Earl looked pretty meek." Marilyn joined Sandy in giggling.

"We're definitely safe here. Even if Earl figures out we're hiding, he would expect us to be staying at a crappy motel, not this amazing place."

Sandy's humility and the new knowledge of Earl as potentially the serial murderer, the devastation and tragedy caused by him, made tears threaten. She decided against telling Sandy of her grim findings and leaned forward and hugged her. "You and Ethan deserve to be protected, deserve to be comfortable without threats and difficulties from the likes of Earl."

Sandy's eyes filled. "You're an incredible person."

"Nope. Just a girl trying to get by, a lot like you. By the way, the help that I need with some boxes, that'll happen tomorrow morning before Fairfield's trial starts. It's one of those things that we'll have to play by ear. I'll call tomorrow early, but I've already lined up the sitter. She'll be here at six-thirty. Hope that's okay."

"Absolutely!"

"There's something else. I've ordered a standard, official looking, work outfit, the type of uniform that maintenance staff wear. It will be delivered to the front desk today. I'd like you to wear it tomorrow morning."

Sandy said, "No problem."

They exchanged a hug, and Marilyn handed Sandy the tote bag and said, "Courtesy of Earl's house. Call it overdue child support."

Sandy opened the bag and looked awestruck. "I don't know what to say…except, again, thank you. Thank you so much." She grabbed hold of Marilyn in a bear hug.

Marilyn laughed, "You are so welcome. Give lots of hugs and kisses to that little piranha." And she let herself out.

Marilyn sat in her car. Was Earl the serial killer? If so, he had probably enticed the women with the same line he used on her, made them feel like a partner in a business deal. Was the blackmail money worth letting Earl go free—even if it meant no justice for Fran, for all the women? She took out her phone and sat, turning it over in her hand. If she called Stade now there would be cops swarming Earl's place in minutes. They would tear the place apart and find every possible shred of evidence.

She needed to talk this through. She called Gwynne as she drove up the coiled ramp at his office parking garage to the top, open-air, empty level. "Hey, whatever you're doing, drop it and meet me in your parking garage. We need to talk."

He came from the building, looking as sharp as ever, and angled into the passenger seat. Gwynne smelled expensive, as always. He took her hand and said, "What's up? You're agitated, wanting to meet face to face, with the trial starting in under twenty-four hours. Risky."

"I'm seriously freaked out. I found evidence that Earl is the serial killer."

Surprised, Gwynne looked down and his mouth dropped open, pressing his chin into a bulge against his collar and the knot of his tie. After a minute, he resumed his lawyerly persona. "What evidence?"

"Look." She pulled out her phone and said, "He drew this."

"That's a drawing? It looks like a photo."

"He has talent. But add this to the equation; because I do figure drawings, and I've watched him at the Art Guild, I know that a drawing that detailed would have taken a whole day, and the subject would have been tied up like that for the entire time." She watched for a reaction, but he showed none, and she added, "So, I'm scared shitless of him, and we need to abandon all our plans—the witness, blackmail, all of it."

"If he's the killer, sure it's horrible, and I feel for the women and their families. But they're dead, and we can't fix that, so, *no*," Gwynne said affirmatively. "No. We're not abandoning the plan."

"Gwynne, he's a fucking serial killer, for god's sake! He needs to be locked up. He'll kill again. Plus, it means Fairfield and Palmer killed two innocent people."

"What a clusterfuck." Gwynne thought a moment. "Look at it this way…His drawings aren't incriminating. If I were Earl's defense lawyer, I'd say the drawings were his fantasies. After all, they're drawings, not photos. If he had drawn monsters torturing elf-women, no matter how realistically he depicted them, they wouldn't be real. His vivid imagination and his talent don't make the pictures reality. I think that having known the women, he's been fascinated by their murders, and he released some pent-up anger or grief by drawing them."

"You've got to be shitting me right now." She paused briefly. "Are you in total fucking denial?"

"No. It definitely sounds like a bad scene, but until there's forensic evidence to connect this guy to the women, if he were my client, I'd have no problem getting him a not-guilty in court."

"So only DNA, fibers, photos, and so on would convince you? Well, Gwynne, think of this as a circumstantial case…"

Gwynne shook his head. "Didn't the cops have DNA tested from the bodies, and it came back to a homeless guy?"

"I can't believe you aren't keeping up with this story. It's been all over the news that the DNA was from a homeless nutjob who got off on having sex with unresponsive women, meaning it was deposited after the bodies were dumped." She paused a second. "But fuck the forensics. Let's get real here. This isn't about going to court, or trial, or you as his lawyer, it's about knowing there's a guy who's a serial killer and having him on the loose, and if I testify for Fairfield and Palmer, two more murderers will be free."

He chewed a moment, thinking, and said, "So you're convinced he's the killer?"

"It all fits. Keeping trophies is standard serial killer protocol so they can relive the murder, and to me, the drawings are to re-experience the crime. Those drawings…They are so sensitive, so immediate, so accurately portrayed, that the women are perfectly recognizable. I don't see how anyone could imagine and draw like that without either photos or a live model. Each of those drawings took many hours. He sat there, examining the women and drawing them, enjoying their torture. It's like sadism on steroids. You're so sure you'd be able to raise reasonable doubt in a jury, but you need to stop thinking like a defense lawyer and consider our current situation. Our so-called *patsy* is a serial rapist, torturer, and murderer."

"I'm not an artist, so I wouldn't know about any of

that, but I'll take your word for it."

She ignored his thick-headed response. "Even without the drawings, it all fits…" Gwynne had turned his head to watch a bird hopping along the barricade edging the lot…Avoidance? She gave his shoulder a little shove, and he turned to her. She said, "Earl went to all the parties and the life-drawing group and knew all the women. He was always such a nice looking, sweet guy, offering rides to stranded or inebriated girls. He came off as completely helpful and not at all dangerous."

"The Ted Bundy phenomenon. The good-looking, charming, homicidal maniac."

She shifted in her seat and looked at him full on. "He murdered Darby, and he probably murdered my best friend, Fran, a smart, hardworking, beautiful, incredible woman with her whole future ahead of her. He stole her life. She won't get to experience her career, her wedding, children, love, and all her accomplishments…" The list could have gone on and on, but the last thing she wanted to do was cry in front of Gwynne.

"He gave them rides? That's classic. Once you're in someone's car, you've lost all control."

"His van…my god. He might have killed them in that scary-clown white van of his. He drove me home in his fucking van. Recently he talked so easily of his plans to kidnap the mother of his son and have her held by some guy in the middle of nowhere. It was shocking. I should call Stade and tell him, get this murderer locked up and out of society."

"No. We're going to stay the course and get the money," Gwynne said, sharply. "Then you can tell Stade your suspicions. Personally, I think you don't have enough for a case. Look, I know a thing or two about fetishes." He looked at her meaningfully. "There's a whole world of stuff that gets people off. Drawing girls in bondage hardly tops the list of deviant behavior."

"This stinks."

"You need to let this go. If you had reliable forensics, I'd agree he's the killer, but even so, I'd move ahead with our plan. Bottom line, you don't have enough evidence. He's not the killer. End of story." Gwynne turned and gave her a hard stare. He said disdainfully, "Having a crisis of conscience?"

"Fuck, yes! You can try to bully or shame me, but how about this—you're in denial."

"There's nothing to be gained by putting Fairfield in prison," Gwynne said, "He's old and decrepit and might die of natural causes any minute anyway. It's not going to do anything to help the dead women or their families. Might as well let them all think of Fairfield as a hero."

"Consider this, Gwynne. Earl is lying low, letting the Lads take the blame for now, but at some point, he'll kill again, and one day, he'll get caught. When that happens, we'll get caught too. I'll be guilty of perjury and obstruction. You'll get witness tampering and maybe a murder charge since you knew Fairfield killed the Lads and you helped cover it up, and Fairfield and Palmer will get murder-one."

Gwynne shrugged. "After this they won't find me. I'll be gone. And so will you."

The papers she'd seen in Gwynne's personal safe came to mind. He was going to Monaco, but she suddenly realized that Monaco was only the first leg of his disappearing act, Monaco was a bucket-list wish to be James Bond for a day or two. Then he would shove off to a third world country where he could live out his life as a rich bigshot.

"In the meantime, just make sure you aren't alone with this weirdo."

"How is the cash drop going to happen tomorrow? I need details, dammit."

"Hang tight, okay? I'll call you when I know how it'll happen."

"You are certainly leaving the planning 'til the last

minute, aren't you? Why?"

He looked out the passenger window and then turned back, serious now, "Keeping it on the down-low is only smart. The worst scenario would be if word gets leaked, and we end up with a shootout."

She wanted to say, *Or another scenario is you don't want to divulge plans because you are going to rip off me, Earl, and Fairfield.* Instead, she said sternly, "Don't underestimate me, Gwynne."

"Oh honey, believe me, I don't." Gwynne chewed his gum a moment, and said, "Gotta hand it to Earl, the dead animals were a stroke of genius. My god, the stink. He certainly made his point. And along with you having the ring, and the GIF of Fairfield shooting—well, Fairfield is completely on board now."

"Or Fairfield has realized Palmer never found an alternative, and he's out of time."

"Maybe," he said, and casually placed a hand on her thigh. He shifted toward her for a kiss, and she let him. If he was looking for an indication of her trust, she was happy to give it, and Zabi said, *Let him think his sex appeal has addled your brain.*

He left the car, dropping his gum into a garbage can at the elevator door and breaking out a new piece as he went. Obviously, Gwynne was one self-serving double-crossing, unreliable, greedy jerk. He acknowledged the danger Earl posed, but with his imaginary courtroom scenarios he seemed oblivious to anything but getting the money. However, the meeting had given her clarity, and reinforced that she was on her own.

She sat awhile considering her options. What would Gwynne and Earl not expect? How do you outwit a crook, someone who thinks outside the box constantly? Someone who is always plotting and planning how to duck and dive around the status quo and the rules. Gwynne's arguments as a defense lawyer for Earl were interesting. He made Earl's drawings seem like a silly blip, even ridiculous. As

Stade had said, 'he's good at manipulating the truth.' When Gwynne spoke in court, he had the floor. Opposing counsel could object, but they couldn't yell out, *that's ridiculous!* Or *Liar!* Part of Gwynne's credibility was his reputation and his previous successes—that he'd never lost a case at trial. People believe a winner.

Marilyn drove to TJ Maxx and bought a carry-on suitcase. She crossed the parking lot to her bank, and emptied the safe deposit box, loading Fairfield's ring, her fake-witness million, the flash-drives, and the Lads' laptops into the carry-on. Then she canceled the safe deposit box, handed in her key, and locked the bag in the trunk of her rental car.

She stopped at Dance Galaxy on the way to her apartment. It had been a long time since she'd shopped the racks of pink tights and black leotards, and the nostalgia hit her hard. While Marilyn browsed, the saleswoman found a used pair of pointe shoes in good condition, in her size, broken in, and with ribbons already sewn on, one of the many pairs routinely traded in by girls cured of their dance fantasies by the grueling practicing and excruciating pain of ballet en pointe. She added a spool of wide, pink, satin ribbon to her order. With a quick stop at Cindy's, the local sex and lingerie shop, for appropriate attire, Marilyn headed home.

At her apartment the Earl-phone had texts that read, *Call me!* and *I've been ripped off!* She dialed him. "What's going on?"

He said angrily, "Where were you? I've been trying to call you."

"Earl, I went shopping! I need the perfect outfit for my court appearance. I didn't take your dedicated phone with me. Now, tell me. What happened?"

"Fucking Gwynne and Fairfield! I got home from running around looking for that bitch Sandy, and they've been in my place and wiped my hard drives. Plus, they took my cash. It's a disaster. A huge disaster."

"No," she said gently, "it's not. Tomorrow we'll be wealthy, and you won't need any of that computer stuff or the cash they took. It's fine, Earl. Besides, it might be for the best. No one will be able to trace us when we leave."

"Adding to this fucking mess, Sandy is gone, and she's taken Ethan."

"Right now, your priority should be how you're going to pick up the cash tomorrow morning. I want to know every detail—where, when, and the timing of the plan—before it happens. Would you mind if I came by later? We can go over the plan."

He exhaled again. "Of course, you can come over. I want to see you, but I might be watching Sandy's place tonight."

"Oh, okay."

After ending the call, she decided on some research, and watched S-and-M videos on YouTube of women in black leather get-ups and extreme stiletto-heeled boots, disciplining their submissives. There were dog collars, leashes, whips and paddles, leg spreading devices, handcuffs, ball-gags, and other gadgets she couldn't decipher. After an hour of the strange roleplay of those with a taste for dominance, she was filled with a sensation like ennui laced with degradation. She'd had enough. Ugh.

Zabi said, *It takes all kinds.*

"Hear, hear Zabi. Not judging. It's just not my thing."

Marilyn closed her laptop and lay down for a nap, slept an hour, and woke to her timer. She took a quick shower and packed a suitcase with her most important and basic belongings, some additional casual clothes and sandals, plus the clothes for her court appearance—Fran's sky-blue pantsuit, a pink silk blouse, high-heeled pumps, plain gold hoop earrings—and the wig and glasses for her escape. She wouldn't be coming back.

Chapter Thirty-Nine:

En Pointe

The evening air was sultry and soft, heavy with the scent of blooming magnolias and impending rain. Marilyn rolled her getaway-suitcase to her car and put it in her trunk. She checked neighboring windows and the empty street before transferring the million dollars from the carry-on bag to her suitcase and taking the flash drives and Fairfield's ring into her apartment.

Her phone chimed with harps. Earl was ringing Sandy's doorbell. Marilyn chuckled at his nervousness, as he checked repeatedly whether Sandy's neighbor, George, had come out of his apartment. Finally giving up, he got into his van. After a while she checked the doorbell video and he was still there watching for Sandy's return, probably throughout the night. Poor Earl.

Typing between bites of her dinner of a chicken salad sandwich, she composed two letters, inserted them into envelopes, and placed them in her tote bag. She cut the roll of ribbon into four three-yard lengths, rolled them up, and added them and the ballet shoes to her tote. She dressed in the lingerie she had purchased, a short A-line skirt and a buttoned sleeveless blouse. Time to go.

The sun was setting as she pulled up in front of Gwynne's house. Someone was watching TV in a room off the living room. Marilyn sealed the envelope and wrote *Vanessa* across the front. She trotted up the wide walkway and rang the doorbell. A female silhouette rose and walked past the living room doorway. The intercom asked, "Who is it?"

"It's Marilyn Connor. I have an important letter for Vanessa Gwynne. I can leave it here on the threshold if you wish. But Vanessa needs to read the letter tonight."

"All right. You can leave it there."

Marilyn returned to her car and watched as Vanessa's slim form in silk pajamas, opened the door and retrieved the envelope. The letter warned Vanessa Gwynne of her husband's plans. Included were the safe's combination and pictures of papers, his fake passport, flight info, their assets, and his offshore account.

Zabi whispered, *Knowledge really is power.*

Marilyn whispered, "Even more powerful than dressing in black vinyl and leather, brandishing a whip, and walking your submissive around on all fours with a dog leash. Good luck to her. She knows herself, and I wish her nothing but the best." They waved to each other, and as Vanessa turned to enter the house, she began opening the envelope.

Marilyn called Gwynne and asked, "Hey, have you heard from Earl? I can't reach him."

"Nope. Nothing from Earl."

"What do you think is going on, Gwynne?"

"I'm pretty sure he's going to try to double-cross us. I just haven't figured out how yet."

"Yep," she said. "A lot of that going around these

days. An epidemic, I'd say."

He laughed softly. "I'd never rip you off, Marilyn. Earl will rob you blind but I won't."

She shook her head. Ah yes, pit her and Earl against each other. The old divide-and-conquer, a strategy even toddlers can master and use on their parents. "How do you see the exchange working?"

"It's simple. I told Earl to rent a storage locker. He said he already had one and he'd rent another one. He'll give me the location and the lock's combination before nine tomorrow morning, and Fairfield's guy will put the cash in the locker. During your testimony tomorrow Earl will take his and your share from the locker and you'll meet up with him later. And I'll get mine from the locker whenever I get out of court tomorrow.

"Okay," she said innocently, hiding her anger at his lying and insulting her intelligence. She accepted that Earl rented a storage locker. Given Earl's hoarded house, he probably had several lockers. Hoarders are generally delusional about the volume of their stuff. Everything else Gwynne said were lies. First, he claimed he thought Earl would try a double-cross, then, he supposedly trusted Earl to take only his share. She shook her head. "Am I still invited to come see you tonight?"

"We've got a big day tomorrow," he said hesitantly.

"Don't I know it, but I have a special treat for you."

"Well, in that case…" He chuckled. "Sure. Come on over. Room twelve-two-two."

Zabi said, *How fitting, twelve-tutu.*

"As long as I don't end up getting shot…a twenty-two in the tutu." She drove out of River Oaks.

At the ZaZa Hotel, she valet parked and walked past their fleet of Cadillac SUVs with longhorns attached to the grilles. She entered the lobby, which smelled of an indeterminate, beautiful floral and herbal scent, walked past their five-star restaurant, and took the elevator to the twelfth floor. She strolled the hushed, canned air of the hallway to Gwynne's room where she kicked off her sandals, dropped them in her bag, and put on the ballet shoes, wrapping and tying the ribbons around her ankles. Gwynne had turned the slide lock inward to keep the door from latching. She pushed open the door, stepped over the threshold, flipped the slide lock, and the door closed and locked behind her.

It had been more than fifteen years since she'd danced en pointe. Hopefully, it was second nature, muscle-memory. Marilyn reached into her bag and retrieved the lengths of ribbon. With a palm on the wall for balance, she pointed her right foot, elongating her instep, locked her knee, and rotated her leg outward from her hip.

The pose suddenly brought back the dance studio's atmosphere with its high ceiling, the barre, and mirrored walls, the sweat, the barked commands. She pushed forward, lifting onto the toe of her right shoe, and then added her left foot, distributing her weight. She stood a moment to balance and absorb the crushing pressure on the ligaments, muscles, and tendons of her toes and feet. Cramp-like stitches bit into her arches and a sharp pain traveled her spine.

Zabi said, *A little rusty, are we?*

No other way to get this done, Zabi, Marilyn reassured herself.

She carefully peeled her hand from the wall and channeled her former strict dance teacher's orders. Then the movement came back, and she was twirling into the luxurious suite, trailing the ribbons like streamers. Gwynne, wearing a hotel robe, came into view. He gasped, and grinning, backed away to watch. She performed a short routine she recalled that was all showy arabesques and pirouettes. With her feet, shins, calves, and thighs burning—overstretched and overly-flexed by the unnatural affectation of turned-out legs and feet peculiar to ballet— every movement was agony. Perhaps the torture of dance was perfect for a sadomasochistic adventure.

Three more twirls put her within his grasp, and he swept her from the air, wrapped her in an embrace, and they kissed. Under normal conditions his kiss would have been devastating, sweet yet aggressive, soft yet eager. But Marilyn didn't for a moment forget that Gwynne was the enemy. He tasted of scotch, not his usual mint gum, and he was a smidgeon legless, swaying, and unfocused, which was surprising, given the importance of waking tomorrow without a hangover, He was pliable, not drunk enough to fall. Good. She'd been worried he wouldn't go along with her gambit. Some impairment of his judgment ought to smooth the way. She trailed the ribbons across his back and circled his neck somewhat threateningly, then pulled them free.

She broke free of his grasp. Again, en pointe, Marilyn glided to a credenza where Gwynne had poured two glasses of wine. She took a sip and turned to face him, still on her toes, her back against the narrow table taking some weight off her feet.

He opened the robe's belt and let the sleeves slide down his arms. The robe fell from his naked body. He was buff, strong, although hopefully his imbibed state would level the playing field if he attacked her.

Taking his cue, leisurely, button by button, she undid her blouse, slipped it off one shoulder, then the other, exposing her new pink satin bustier that mounded her breasts like ice cream scoops. Part of this type of foreplay was its slow pace, edging, a kind of tension-building, torturous languor. She dropped the blouse onto the hardwood. Then she inched her skirt's zipper open and let it fall, revealing a matching pink-satin thong and lace-top stockings.

Gwynne had taken a seat on the sofa. She knelt on the cushion next to him and began sliding the ribbons across his chest and legs, circling his neck and face and down his torso approaching his semi-erect member.

Then, unexpectedly, in one sudden motion he was on

his feet and carrying her into the bedroom. "Put me down," she demanded, sternly, "Lie on the bed. On your back, spreadeagled." To her surprise, he obeyed, and as he arranged himself on the bed, she noted his suitcase was open on a luggage rack, fully packed, ready to run. A suit, shirt, and tie were layered on a hanger that hung on the doorknob, all set for the morning. She grabbed the necktie from his ensemble and climbed onto the bed, placing her feet on either side of his waist, then dropped, her knees pinning his elbows.

"What are you going to do?"

Close to his ear she said breathily, "This is about sensation, not about sight," and she wrapped the silk tie around his head as a blindfold. He didn't argue. Vanessa had trained her submissive well.

She slithered the silky ribbons along his chest and arms, followed by her fingers and an occasional slap. One by one, she grasped each of his wrists in both of her hands and twisted her hands in opposite directions, a stinging torture that kids used to call an Indian-burn. Hopefully the pain was desensitizing him. She removed a zip-tie strap hidden in her cleavage and attached it snugly around his wrist. Then she slipped a ribbon through the loop, knotted it, tied it to a bedpost, and repeated the exercise on his other wrist.

"Uh, Marilyn. This isn't feeling very sexy."

Shit. Since nothing in the BDSM videos was sexy to her, she was suddenly at a loss. Maybe adopting a bully's persona was the trick, though it was all she could do to curb her laughter. "Oh really?" she said gruffly. "Who the fuck asked you?" He made a small move to get up, and as a quick diversion, she stroked his thighs and edged toward his package, which had lost its stiffy. It worked. His temperature was rising—along with his impressive member—and she was tempted for an instant to hop aboard for a quickie. Then she shook the impulse away and said, "Don't you dare orgasm."

He sighed. "Don't stop."

"I'm in charge here, so like I said before, shut the fuck up." Holding back laughter was proving difficult, but she needed to keep it contained until she'd immobilized him. With just his hands tied he could still use his legs to flip her off the bed and then shimmy higher in the bed to untie the ribbon. She continued stroking and slapping him along his thighs and calves, until she had each ankle zip-tied and lashed to bedposts.

As she ran her hands over his chest and shoulders, the poor man trembled with anticipation. "Are you ready?"

"Oh my God. I'm so ready! Walk all over me. And then fuck me."

"Say please."

"Please, please, a thousand times, please."

"Hang tight." Again, she had to stifle giggles. Marilyn found socks in his suitcase and came back to the bed. She trailed her fingertips along his shins and thighs, his chest, and over his neck. She pried open his mouth by pressing on the sides of his jaw, the way you feed a pill to a dog. "Open," she commanded. He obeyed and she jammed the socks into his mouth. It wouldn't do for his shouts to bring security to his rescue. He gagged a little and then settled, waiting.

She untied and removed her dance shoes and bustier and placed them in her bag, then dressed in black sweats and a hoodie. She checked the tenacity of her knots on his wrists and ankles and doublechecked he couldn't reach the ribbons to chew through them, although she was aware that the ribbon's pretty pink sheen was deceptive. It was anything but fragile; tightly woven, its edges bound, it was a whole different animal than the ribbon on gifts. Even sharp teeth weren't likely to cut through it. He was making noises through the gag and pulling on the restraints. She called his burner phone dedicated to communicating with her, followed its ring to the nightstand, and dropped it into her bag along with his cellphone. After she rinsed and wiped down her wine glass, she left the suite with the do-not-disturb tag on the doorknob. At the front desk she informed the staff that Mr. Gwynne would be tied up all day tomorrow, and he didn't want to be disturbed for any reason until tomorrow night.

Next stop, Earl's house of horrors.

Driving, she thought about Gwynne's extremes. How odd that he accepted being her submissive. Maybe it was the scotch. Was he drunkenly caught up in his ballerina fantasy, or was he simply arrogant and underestimated her? Bingo. Yes, that was it—arrogance, narcissism, hubris—he wouldn't question that he was in full control, with Marilyn as his serf.

As much as he played the submissive, his personality was the opposite. Roleplaying a weakling must be a release for a guy so tightly wound in his everyday life—giving himself over to a dominatrix's will would release him from responsibility and decisions, probably much like his gambling habit—to not be in control and just allow whatever happened to happen. She texted, then phoned Earl. No answer. It was strange that he wasn't answering his phone.

Zabi said, *Going to visit a possible serial killer in the dead of night is nuttier than squirrel poop.*

"I know, Zabi, but I need to know how the cash will change hands. I want that money and right now I risk losing it. Also, while the ransom money is super important to me, Gwynne was right when he said I'm having a crisis of conscience. I need evidence to get justice for the raped, drugged, murdered women. Gwynne's dismissiveness of the drawings definitely got to me. I really, really want to find more evidence to nail the killer, whether the evidence is the jewelry Stade is looking for, or something else. Tomorrow I leave forever, so time is of the essence."

She took a deep breath and continued, "Besides, Earl hasn't hurt me so far, and he needs me alive to get his big score, so I think I'm safe, at least for now." He should be home, and most likely asleep if he's not out hunting for Sandy. If he were home, she would have to decide whether to make like a stealthy cat burglar or wake him up and act like she's okay with him being the serial killer and get him to confess.

Her thoughts returned to the ransom, which would be ten, forty-pound boxes of money. She only had a few hours to make a plan and execute it—how to handle the cash, where to take it, how to save or spend it. While she didn't doubt that Gwynne or Fairfield knew people who could cash out that money and move it around online, she didn't. She recalled some TV series—*Breaking Bad* and *Ozark*—about criminals overwhelmed with trying to launder their ill-gotten cash.

Gwynne's plan to send the money to an offshore account was obviously the best solution. But when Earl wanted Fairfield to pay in bitcoin or to wire the currency, Gwynne said Fairfield had refused, but now she was certain it wasn't Fairfield's insistence the money had to be in bills. It was Gwynne's. He wanted the reassurance of having all the money in his hands in a tangible form. But how would he collect it if he were in court with Marilyn on the stand? And how would he deposit all that paper money into his offshore account? Hopefully, deciphering Earl's plan, would help her determine what Gwynne had up his sleeve.

Zabi said, *You already know that Gwynne's world is different. Just because you can't arrange the movement of so much paper money, doesn't mean Gwynne can't. Who does he know?*

"Correct," she said aloud. "Gwynne's world is full of high rollers and criminals. The type of people who do each other 'favors' and call on them to reciprocate, when needed."

To get his hands on the money, he undoubtedly had a hitman poised to kill Earl and scoop the money at the exchange. The guy wouldn't be just any old, retired gumshoe-cop he knew from the courthouse. Those guys weren't in the hitman biz. More likely, it would be a former client of Gwynne's, a criminal Gwynne knew was guilty, but defended him and kept the robber, rapist, murderer, cartel kingpin, whatever he was, out of prison. He would also know finance people, money-moving middlemen—a white collar criminal he also got out of the slammer, a Ponzi-grifter, an embezzler, conman, or fraudster who knew his way around banking institutions and trust companies, who wouldn't ask questions—someone who regularly dealt with large sums and had the wherewithal to deposit the twenty-million into one, or several, institutions and then wire it into Gwynne's account.

Marilyn parked two properties away from Earl's house and jogged through light rain. Between the houses she could see the foreboding tar-like water swell and retreat at the bulkheads and piers. At Earl's house, his van was gone. So, he was out searching for Sandy. She retrieved the key from his tool shed.

Chapter Forty:

In Pursuit

Marilyn trotted up Earl's switchback stairs to the deck where she slipped on the rain-slick algae-covered boards. She grabbed onto the siding and regained her balance, edging her way toward the sliding door. In the house, his absence, and the danger of him showing up at any moment was unnerving, but far preferrable to creeping around, trying not to wake him.

One of Earl's burner phones was on top of his bedstand. One tap and it came to life, unlocked. People and their strange habits, Earl's lack of security measures was due to his poor memory, as Sandy had mentioned, but maybe it was something else. Someone had once told her that the easiest person to sell to is a salesman. Perhaps the easiest person to hack is a hacker. Was it a sense of superiority, infallibility? Gwynne in a different form.

This was his dedicated Gwynne phone, and she scrolled through recent texts between Earl and Gwynne. Evidently, wherever Earl was now, he didn't need to contact Gwynne. Or maybe he forgot to take it, an oversight. She read a thread dated a day ago: Earl texted Gwynne: *Put the money in Home Depot boxes, two million in each. 10 boxes. Each box will weigh 40 lbs. They'll be easy to lift.*

Gwynne: *No problem.*

Earl: *You, Fairfield, Palmer, and the witness will be at the courthouse at 9 a.m. If any of you aren't in court at the correct time, the video of Fairfield killing the Lads will go on the internet.*

Gwynne: *Ok.*

Earl: *Fairfield's driver needs to text me at 8:45 a.m. and I'll text him the storage locker's location for the drop-off. He must make the drop at exactly 9:15 a.m. If the drop isn't made exactly as directed, the evidence will go to the DA.*

Gwynne: *Got it.*

Not surprisingly, both Gwynne and Earl had lied, saying their plan wasn't in place. Were they serious about their storage locker plan? If so, it was extremely lazy thinking, since so much could go wrong. She knew Gwynne was plotting to screw everyone over and escape to Monaco, although the details of his double-cross were out of her reach, but what was Earl's strategy?

Earl's plan would be simple, and the simplest was that since Gwynne and Marilyn will both be in court when the money changes hands, Earl will take all the cash and run. Just one problem, Earl—Gwynne's goon will kill you when you show up to collect the money. She pictured a shootout in a hi-rise storage facility, the gun smoke, the deafening gunfire, the bullets ricocheting off metal locker doors, the shooters ducking around corners and creeping along the corridors of the mazelike structure.

Sandy said that Earl made lots of notes. She touched

the phone's *Notes* app, then chose one titled *Storage locker*. "It read, "Big Tex Storage, Westheimer location, fifth-floor #5145. Entry code, 6789. Lock combo: 12 34 56." Maybe this really was their plan after all. Weird. She copied the info into her phone. Time would tell what would happen next. Now to find concrete evidence that Earl was—or wasn't—the serial killer.

Despite Earl's drawings, Gwynne hadn't believed that Earl was the murderer. Maybe he was right because the news reports had noted that the serial killer was meticulous and organized. A profiler had reached this conclusion citing the killer's consistency in how he murdered the women, posed the bodies, and left them in the same location, with no identification, and none of his DNA. And at that moment, observing his hoarded house, she was also doubtful. Earl's house, and Earl for that matter, were anything but meticulous.

Besides, why would Earl kill the women? He had everything going for him, looks, intelligence, ability. It made no sense. But does any murder make sense? That's the whole thing, the thing that fascinates us, *the why*. It was time to stop questioning and start acting.

Marilyn accessed the doorbell video again. Earl's van was gone. She called Sandy but got no answer, and a sliver of dread pierced her. Was she overreacting? Maybe Sandy was in the shower, or her phone was turned off. But still, Marilyn was concerned.

She took the revolver from her tote bag and slipped it into the back of her waistband. Then, opening Earl's flat file, she pulled out the envelope and spread his drawings on the piles of his hoard. There were several of Darby posed in different places on his junk heaps and more drawings of different women, including the girl, Brittany, trussed and crying.

A noise like a wail reached her, and she froze. A drop of sweat trickled down her ribs. The sound came again, and she recognized it as a cat fight or maybe possums, probably under the house, given the rain.

The next drawing was of a girl she didn't recognize. She looked underage, in her early teens. Shit. Marilyn sped up, shuffling through the stack of drawings, ignoring the women's expressions of pain and terror. As she came to the last few her gut heaved. Fran. Alive and dead. Then laid out on his bed on plastic.

The last drawing was someone familiar. In the instant it took to recognize herself, her heart stopped, then thudded. In the drawing she was sitting on Earl's deck. Was this done as a *before* picture? Under it was an unfinished sketch of Marilyn lying on his bed, a syringe in her arm. She examined the beautifully detailed rendering of her. How had he drawn the sketches when she'd never posed for the drawings? There had to be photos for him to copy; otherwise, Gwynne was right that the drawings were simply Earl's musings. Were the drawings of a living person depicted as dead the exception that proved his innocence?

On the other hand, he had drawn Marilyn many times at the Art Guild. Maybe he had secretly photographed her while she was in a prone pose. In any case, she needed more evidence, not only for the law, but to contradict her own new doubts.

Marilyn surveyed the junk. Where would Earl hide his photos or video, or the women's jewelry?

Zabi whispered, *Don't overthink things. He's articulate and talks a good game but he's not the brightest bulb in the chandelier.*

"Right. With his shitty memory, he would put his souvenirs somewhere easy to find." She checked the flat file's drawers and found a few more sketches and paper in different colors. Then, reminiscent of tossing the Lads' apartment, she started her search in the kitchen, pulling jars and boxes out of cabinets and food from the freezer. In the bathroom she lifted the lid on the toilet tank, and searched the tub's plumbing-access compartment. In the bedroom she rifled through his drawers and swept her arm under the mattress. Her hand bumped something hard. Come to mama. She pulled out a small black box with a USB cable, a hard drive. She plugged it into his computer and sat in Earl's office chair.

A list of videos filled the screen. She clicked on the top one, listed as *Hurricane*. Earl's junk-fest living room filled the screen with his face in the center, talking. He had filmed himself as he walked through his house, then he hit the turnaround button on his phone and showed a portion of one of his salvage piles.

He said, "This is all about Darby. She was my big attention-getter. At first, I didn't recognize her at the Lads' party, but she introduced herself, making sure I caught that she was a *Fairfield*. I played dumb, made her get pouty and anxious—little princess throwing an unbecoming tantrum.

"I told her I wanted to draw her and brought her here. I hogtied her right over there on top of that pile of rope. At first, she thought it was a joke, but not for long. I waited to add the neck ligature because I needed time to do the drawing. She wasn't a strong girl, so she would have choked out before I finished. But I also took this video in case I ever wanted to do more sketches."

He again turned the camera to show Darby draped across another pile of his horde. Moving closer, he zoomed in on her face. Her eyes were glassy and there were wounds—bruises and cuts on her excruciatingly pale, vulnerable body. He said, "Rigor mortis is setting in. Time to get rid of her, but all the media attention about her being missing has been fun. I'll put her in Buffalo Bayou and let her float someplace. It'll look like the hurricane got her."

Marilyn's stomach had a squeeze of nausea, and she used an artist's trick of squinting her eyes, a technique to assess a piece of art, removing detail so its basic composition and contrast can be observed. She was looking through her eyelashes at a fuzzy, indistinct image.

Earl was still talking, and she tuned in. "Then, for

some reason, I don't know why, the craving came back faster than usual, and I ended up with the second bitch, Fran. Not that killing her wasn't satisfying. It was."

Chapter Forty-One:

Justified

And there it was. A confession. Absolute proof.

Marilyn splashed water on her face. Her hands were trembling, and she struggled to keep her heaving stomach under control. She went back to the office chair. On the monitor, Earl was still talking, sounding smug, an authority discussing his expertise.

His inflection had swagger, "But again, the flooding prevented me from leaving them in my favorite location for that crazy pervert homeless guy to mess with them, so that dampened—pun intended—some of my satisfaction." He laughed. "Then finally, the floodwater started to recede, and I just sat back and watched the circus."

Marilyn skipped the video forward several minutes and the scene changed to the back door of Fran's apartment building. Fran was standing under the corrugated metal awning, wearing a yellow raincoat with its hood down, her blonde hair in a ponytail, her backpack hooked on one shoulder. Earl had driven up close and she was looking through the passenger window of his van, smiling as unbeknown to her Earl filmed from the driver's seat.

"The Lads have changed their minds They don't want to go out in the rain." Fran said, then added with a laugh, "Couple of wusses."

Earl said, "Yeah, I know, right?"

Fran looked away a moment, then said, "And Marilyn is trying to get here, probably by boat. I want to be here when she arrives. So...I should just get back to studying, I guess."

Earl replied too softly for Fran to hear, and she flipped up her hood and stepped out into the rain. He repeated, "But they're saying this is a thousand-year storm. We'll never see this again in our lifetime. And it's so cool to see how some areas have flooded, and others are totally dry. Come on, we'll just go around the neighborhood and check it out. Trust me. I won't get us drowned."

"Well, when you put it that way, why not?" She swung the door open and climbed in.

Marilyn briefly closed her eyes. The shock of seeing Fran so animated, so alive, was jarring. He drove a short distance, maybe two blocks, and pulled into a driveway behind closed shops in a shopping center, between dumpsters and a flooded field. She made a move to open the door but, in a flash, he reached over and snapped a handcuff on her wrist. His phone fell and he lost recording for a short while.

Then Fran was fighting with Earl in the back of his van. She started screaming, and he shoved a rag into her mouth. Her backpack spilled its contents; her purse, a wrapped sandwich, bottled water, pen and paper, lipstick, comb, and her phone. There was the sound of their heavy breathing and rain pummeling the van's roof.

He grabbed and pinned her flailing arms and said, "Come on, bitch. I've been nice so far. I told you, I've got a treat for you." He reached into a shopping bag and took out a syringe. "Just gonna give you half. Calm you right down." And he injected something into her arm.

Marilyn recalled him telling her that when he left the Lads' party, he slept overnight at a friend's apartment in the building, and he drove on backstreets that hadn't flooded to get home. But that made no sense because the water at his house and on access roads would have taken almost a week to recede. Now she knew he stayed in the van—with Fran captive—for at least a couple of days though probably not in that location behind the shopping center. It would have been somewhere more secluded, but where? She got up and paced awhile, the realization of how nearby they had been bringing on sobbing. Why hadn't she seen through his lie? And all that time Darby was dead in his house.

On the screen Earl was talking. "The cops never got close to catching me," he said acidly. "They're fucking dopes. I left the last eight bitches at that homeless camp. Eight! And they didn't connect the dots. Each new body got only a tiny mention in the online news pages and just a few seconds on TV news. Plenty of serial killers go to great lengths to dispose of bodies so they will never be found, and I'm sure those guys would tell me to be happy, but the idea of them hunting me was fun. I figured being consistent with the location would get more publicity and help the cops figure out that it was one man's doing. But still, they didn't catch on. Darby Fairfield was the one that was supposed to get their attention. I had her here ready to go, and then the hurricane came. It was disappointing."

Marilyn's breathing was shallow and her shoulders and neck tight. She paused the video to catch her breath. Fran. She wanted to run and not stop until she was far enough away that she'd never have to see or think about Earl again, but she was seemingly paralyzed, and couldn't drag herself away.

He started talking again. "Before I started using the

homeless camp, I used to have a small fishing boat, and I did the Dexter thing. Cut them up and took them out to sea. Fed the fishies. Scattered them far and wide."

Marilyn turned to look at the open water, black, endless, and hostile. "Too bad that boat didn't spring a leak and take you down, asshole," she said under her breath. On the monitor he checked Fran's ropes and tightened a knot. Marilyn shivered as she thought of tying up Gwynne. Obviously, it was a different scenario. She hoped like hell he hadn't gotten loose, but there was no going back. She said a little prayer the ribbons were holding.

Earl's voice said, "Once I got to my house, we had tons of sex. Then I did some life-drawings. Funny, huh? They're called life-drawings, but mine are death drawings," He laughed. "I got the idea from that serial killer in New Mexico, David Parker Ray. He used to have a trailer he called his *toy box* where he kept his ladies, and he'd draw his prey."

Earl was deep in thought a minute, then he sounded wistful. "That guy Ray, he wasn't so good at life-drawing, though. He just did crude line drawings, but when you see those sketches, you know they were real people because he captured something, their unique features, and their life force, in the sketches."

Suddenly, she couldn't watch more of his bragging, his cruelty and delusion. She would leave a message for Stade on his voicemail and let law enforcement take care of Earl. Should she take the drawings Earl had done of her? And now that she knew Earl was the killer, what should she do about Fairfield and Palmer's murder of the Lads, her witness appearance, and the blackmail money? She gathered her things to leave and paused, looking at the mess she was leaving behind..

Her thoughts were interrupted by a swish and clunk. The sliding door. A reflection skittered across the monitor. Shit. The rain must have covered the sound of Earl's van. Now she'd be alone with the serial killer. There was nowhere to hide. Her heart pounded and her hands shook. She took several deep breaths and reminded herself that he didn't know what she had found. She could talk her way out of this if she kept her cool. "Earl, I'm here," she called out.

He replied, "Marilyn…"

She turned and found Earl, but shockingly, also Sandy, her hands zip-tied and her mouth duct-taped. Sandy was making indecipherable sounds. They were rain soaked, and Sandy was shaking, her eyes wide and red rimmed.

Marilyn regrouped, gathered her wits, and asked in a jaded tone, "What the fuck is this? Is this that bitch Sandy you've been talking about?"

"Yes, she's Sandy. But you know that."

"No—"

"Don't fucking lie to me, Marilyn." He roughly sat Sandy on a heap of rope. "Sandy's old phone has been 'out of service' since that day I followed her to Walmart. But her new phone showed you phoned her tonight."

Shit. Fear snaked down her spine. "True. I found her number in your contacts. You left your phone here." She pointed to his dedicated-Gwynne-phone on the kitchen counter. "I thought if she answered I might be able to locate her whereabouts for you." He looked skeptical, and despite her heart banging like it wanted to break out of her chest, she asked calmly, "How did you track her down?"

The question appealed to his self-congratulatory tendencies. "A couple years ago, I put a GPS tracker in her spare-tire compartment, in the trunk. Then I forgot about it."

Marilyn covered her eyes, rubbing them as if she were simply tired and not supremely pissed at herself for missing it in her search. When she moved Sandy's car to the hotel parking garage, she'd assumed the tracker in the car's wheel well was the only one. Fuck. God is, as they say, in the details. If only she had left the car at Walmart. The only likely consequence would have been Walmart towing the vehicle.

"But Earl, you've been saying for the last week that you couldn't find her."

He laughed. "I know, right? There I was watching the other tracker, and according to that one, the car was still at Walmart. Finally, I went there to check, and the car was gone." He shook his head. "Then I remembered the one that was in her trunk. I found the app, and low and behold, her car was at the Hilton downtown." He hustled Sandy into the bedroom and Marilyn sauntered, nonchalantly she hoped, to the door and watched him zip-tie her ankles.

"All I did was sit in the lobby until she went to the gift shop, and I followed her to her room. I said I was room-service, and she answered the door," he said smugly. "People are so programmed to avoid making a scene. She came with me, nice and compliant."

He emerged and closed the bedroom door. Marilyn could hear the muffled sounds of Sandy's thrashing and attempted screams. In his office, he kicked off his shoes and peeled off the wet pants as he said, "I'll have to dispose of her in the water. There's not enough time to take her anywhere."

"What about Ethan?"

"After I get rid of Sandy we'll go and get Ethan. He was fast asleep when we left, and I've got the hotel key."

He took a syringe from the pocket of his hoodie and placed it on his desk. Then he dropped his wet sweatpants and cast them aside. As he pulled his soggy top over his head Marilyn took the gun from her waistband, aimed, and pulled the trigger. There was a click, but the gun didn't fire. Earl found himself looking down the barrel of his revolver.

He said, "That's mine, isn't it? That piece of shit always jammed." Then, so quickly he was a blur, he swatted the weapon out of her hand. It flew across the room, hit the wall, and fired, shattering the glass supporting his computers and they cascaded to the floor. He glanced at the damage and Marilyn turned to run, but he grabbed hold of her hoodie. She bent forward and let him pull it off over her head. Free, she took off along a path leading to the kitchen.

Earl climbed over stacks of salvage and headed her off. Now, face to face, she realized he had the syringe in his hand. His hand snaked toward her, and she retreated, stumbling backward, avoiding the injection. She regained her balance and began shoving piles of cleats, propellers, rope, ship's wheels, and compasses onto the path, piles which he easily traversed. Desperate, leveraging all her strength, she attacked tall, heavy stacks of portholes, teak doors, and ships' wheels, sending pile after pile crashing to the floor.

He deftly navigated each obstacle-pile. His pursuit had slowed, not out of fatigue or fear, but for his enjoyment of the slow chase. She desperately looked for an escape. Only two were viable, the sliding door or the kitchen window.

She was becoming tired. Still backing away, she tripped over a bucket of hollow glass floats. Regaining her footing, she hefted and threw one. It connected with his cheekbone, and he yelped. Good. She kept throwing them as hard as possible, and he ducked from side to side as they shattered around him, fragments flying. He shouted as slivers pierced his calves and feet, his wounds dripping blood. Her shoes had become an advantage. She continued shoving objects—lanterns, small and large floats, compasses, and seashells—a crescendo of smashing and tinkling. Then, a break. A shard pierced his wrist, and he dropped the syringe, and when he bent to find it, she seized a lantern, took two steps, and swung, smashing it against his temple. He staggered, dazed, and Marilyn got moving.

Breathing heavily, she climbed over heaps of ropes, anchors, and lanterns in the living room, and over the adjoining, piled-high breakfast bar, and slid off it into the kitchen. She made her way along the path alongside the counter, clambering over heaps of objects.

Earl skirted the breakfast bar, his feet crunching on broken glass. He had seemingly become oblivious to being cut—determination eclipsing the pain—but he was making his way to her, and she grabbed a butcher knife from a wooden block.

In a flash, he climbed over the debris blocking his path and lunged, and as he closed the distance, she swung, arm fully extended. The knife connected and slashed across his chest and the meat of his forearm. The cut was deep and bloody.

"Bitch!" he screamed.

She glanced toward the sliding door; its glass being thrashed by driving rain. He noticed and said smugly, "You won't get past me, Marilyn."

If she could escape, she could call for help and hopefully save Sandy. The outdoor stairs' landing was halfway down, below the kitchen window, at least a six-foot drop. She scrambled onto the countertop, unlocked, and attempted to raise the window, but it didn't move. He laughed. "It's nailed shut, bitch."

She could break the glass but there were bars on the outside. Earl lunged, grabbed her ankle, and she kicked out, but he held firm. In one motion, she picked up the knife and turned. From her elevated position she brought it down, slicing into muscle on his shoulder. He grasped her arm and shook it, flinging the knife away.

He pulled on her ankle again, throwing her off balance. She fell to the floor in a partial crouch. Scuttling away, she regained her footing, but upon standing found herself face to face with him. His hands seized her neck. She jammed her chin down behind his thumbs, preventing a stranglehold. Then she grasped his forearms, and hopefully unexpectedly to him, stepped back. Her retreat forced him to bend his upper torso toward her, opening space between them, and she kneed his crotch. He gasped and released her throat to grab his genitals, and she clasped her hands and brought them down hard on the back of his head, slamming his face into the countertop. He howled, "Bitch!"

She rushed toward the sliding door but tripped over a pile of rope and fell, her right knee landing with a crunch on the edge of a cleat. She shrieked and grasped at a stack of portholes to right herself, toppling them, their heavy brass rims crashing, biting, and bruising her flesh. When she finally stood, the pain in her right knee was excruciating. She hobbled forward toward the door. In her periphery Earl had recovered from his hoofed nuts and smashed nose. Smeared with blood, coming at an angle, he scrambled over coils of rope and stacks of salvage, picking up speed.

Marilyn flung the sliding door wide. She was midstride over the doorsill into the downpour when Earl slammed into her back, clutching her in a bear hug. His momentum carried them, turning, sliding across the rain-slicked deck as if it were greased. They crashed into the railing, and with a sound like the crack of a baseball bat. The wood fractured, but incredibly, the splintered rail and spindles held.

Earl still gripped her, his back against the cracked, bowed railing. While their feet were still on the deck, they were leaning back over a fifteen-foot fall onto the rocky bulkhead. She looked over their shoulders at the drop, and vertigo flooded her.

Marilyn inched her hands up behind her, between them, her palms against his torso. When her hands were above waist level, she pushed hard, breaking his hold, and pitching herself face-down on the deck. The railing groaned and crackled under Earl's movement. Flat on her front she crab-walked sideways and lay with a foot hooked inside the doorsill to forestall sliding. Rain pelted them.

Earl placed his hands against the railing and shoved, falling onto his front, but in the process, he dislodged two balusters. He began sliding toward the edge, frantically grappling at the slick boards. Soon, his torso was on the deck and his legs dangled. The broken pickets hadn't made enough space for him to throw a knee up and work his way onto the deck. He took a moment to assess his situation. "Come on Marilyn, give me a hand." His voice was feeble. He was shocky and the knife wounds and blood loss had weakened him. He lifted a hand in her direction, then dropped it wearily.

"Earl. Tell me the plan for getting the ransom, and I'll help you."

"Fairfield's guy is going to leave it at my storage locker, and I'll pick it up," he sounded resigned.

Marilyn lifted her head and said, "Bullshit."

Earl looked up and locked eyes with her. "Bitch. You lied. You're not going to help me, are you?"

"I might have if you told me the truth." Inexplicably he laughed loudly, a shrill hyena sound. Still laughing, he slid slowly to the verge, scrabbling, his nails leaving pale tracks in the algae and rotting boards, until he hung by his fingers from the rough rotted edges.

Finally, Marilyn watched as his fingertips let go. The rain obscured the thud as he landed on the jagged rocks of the bulkhead. Pushing up on straightened arms, she watched his pale form slip face down off the rocks into the dark and brackish water.

Still catching her breath, she stared at Earl a few moments and said, "If only you could die more than once. If only you could be tortured and killed over and over for every woman you preyed upon."

She flipped over into a sitting position, and pulled herself into Earl's miserable house of horrors, out of the cascading rain, and added, "Wow. No doubts now, Gwynne, and holy shit, I don't feel the slightest bit bad."

She limped into Earl's bedroom and cut the ties on Sandy's wrists. Sandy, still shaking, removed the tape from her mouth as Marilyn cut the ties on her ankles. "Are you okay?" Marilyn asked.

"Sure. I'm light-headed, but it'll pass. Thank God you were here, or I'd be dead right now. What about you?"

"I crunched my knee but it's already feeling better. But I can tell you who's not in good shape…"

"Are you referring to Earl?"

"Yes. Earl went through the railing. He won't be bothering us anymore."

"Holy shit! That was a heck of a commotion you had going out there." Sandy stood and rubbed her arms and hands. "I just need to get back to Ethan."

"I know. We'll get moving in a bit. A word of caution. The deck is super slippery." They glanced at each other and smirked.

Gwynne's cell phone dinged, and Marilyn fished it from her bag. She briefly wondered how Gwynne was doing, restrained on the hotel's bed. A text to Gwynne said, *I just got to the target's house. Let me know when you want me to take care of him.*

So, her deductions about Gwynne's plan were accurate so far. This texter was Gwynne's killer. Marilyn replied to the text with a thumbs-up emoji. There was more than a little pleasure in impersonating Gwynne. Through the kitchen window, she looked down the dark, rainy two-lane street. A car sped by, and its headlights backlit Gwynne's goon at the wheel of an SUV, lights off, parked in the entrance to a driveway, several properties along in the opposite direction of her car. Judging by his text, the guy didn't have a definite plan, which made him unpredictable, a complication she didn't need.

Marilyn and Sandy donned clean, dry jogging pants and hoodies courtesy of Earl's wardrobe. They blow-dried their hair and stuffed wet clothes in a plastic grocery sack.

Marilyn said, "Okay. Let's deal with Gwynne's son-of-a-bitch." It was still dark as they left, clinging to the siding to avoid Earl's fate, but the rain had stopped, clouds had parted, and a full moon had turned the water's surface silver.

Chapter Forty-Two:

Reporting

Gwynne's assassin's job, to kill Earl, was accomplished. However, if the killer mistook her or Sandy for Earl as they left, he might shoot them, so she needed to lose him. She contemplated texting him and saying the hit was called off, but it rang false. Action was required.

The keys to Earl's van were on his front tire. Marilyn told Sandy to wait under Earl's house for her signal. She started the van and stomped on the gas. With tires squealing—all the better to wake up the hitman—she backed out onto the two-lane road as if she were about to turn hard and take off to Houston. Gwynne's guy whipped his Suburban into a tight U-turn and hit the gas as Marilyn slammed on the brakes and stopped, blocking both lanes.

Marilyn left the van running, and she and Sandy trotted along the road to her car. Gwynne's guy, at the last moment, realizing he would T-bone the van, slammed on the brakes, and swerved onto the soft gravelly shoulder. The boxy vehicle with its high center of gravity tipped onto its side and slid into the gaping ditch. In her rearview, she watched the man clamber from the SUV. As he struggled up the embankment the earth gave way, and he dropped into hip-deep water.

"Well, that went better than expected," Marilyn observed.

Sandy took out her phone, called 911, gave the address, and said matter-of-factly, "There's a dead guy in the water. The man who killed him is still outside the residence, and his SUV is in the ditch. He's armed." She and hung up.

Marilyn said, "He needn't worry. Gwynne will get him off. I'm sure he knows not to talk to the cops without his lawyer present." Soon sirens approached, and she dutifully pulled over to allow the emergency vehicles to pass.

A text came to Gwynne's phone, *Sorry Gwynne. There's been a fuck up. Earl left his house but for some reason he parked his van on the road, and when I went after him, I had a wreck.*

Marilyn laughed and sent a response from 'Gwynne'. *No problem. I'll take care of him.*

Marilyn drove until she was certain nobody was following them, then she pulled into a mall parking lot. "Let's get you back to Ethan." She called an Uber. "Try to get some sleep. Sorry about the GPS tracker. That was sloppy of me. I should have just left your car at Walmart."

"You are the least sloppy, most amazing person I've ever known…and we're still here and alive." Tears filled her eyes. "As for sleeping, I'll try."

When the Uber collected Sandy, Marilyn suddenly had no strong persona to project and she relaxed, which brought on shaking and trembling, teeth chattering in shock, not regret, not weakness. So many people dead, all the murdered and missing women, Fran, Darby, the Lads, but her responsibility ended with Earl. Did she hate that she had to fight for her life and kill Earl? Of course. It would have been great for the police to nab him and for him to face a jury, although there was a downside to that. She visualized him and his demeanor, how he would have gamed the system and played his lawyers, judge, and jury with his charm and innocent looks.

She sent a text to Stade telling him Earl was the serial killer, where to find his drawings and his body, and that the exterior hard drive on the computer held the evidence. Earl said he dumped his early victims in the gulf. Hopefully, Stade would find more incriminating photos and videos, and more drawings that would reveal the identities of all the victims. A side benefit of Earl's death was that it would keep Stade busy, and he wouldn't be in court for Fairfield's trial.

Between the lack of sleep, the physical exertion of the fight, and the psychological toll of her discoveries about the murders, she was emotionally drained and exhausted. She explored her knee injury and bruises from the falling portholes. There was pain, but only to the touch. Her shaking had slowed; the adrenaline subsided. She breathed deeply and checked the time—six o'clock. She needed to pull herself together. She said aloud, "Don't mess this up. No mistakes." She found the businesslike pant suit, blouse, and shoes in her suitcase and changed in the car.

She touched up her makeup in the rearview mirror and took a nap that was cut short when a text came to Gwynne's phone. It read: *I work for Fairfield, and I have the boxes. Where is the storage locker for the drop off?*

The stupid, suicidal, nonsensical, storage-locker plot again! She couldn't help laughing. How did this nutty idea pass muster with Earl and even Gwynne? Obviously, it couldn't be real; it was camouflage to throw anyone, including her, off the real plan. So, what was the real plan? Had Gwynne and Earl been acting together to cut her out? Maybe, but more likely they were shining each other on as they plotted their own double-cross behind each other's backs. She had been so trusting, had waited for Gwynne and Earl to reveal their strategy.

Zabi whispered, *So, whatever Gwynne and Earl had planned was written in stone, right?*

It was, but not anymore. Time to turn this whole plot on its head. What could go wrong? Maybe the boxes will be full of newspaper. Or maybe there was another plan to divert the boxes to a different last-minute destination. Gwynne's ego was so huge he'd probably never considered Fairfield a threat. Maybe Fairfield knew Gwynne was the real blackmailer and Fairfield was about to double-cross Gwynne, while Gwynne thought he was double-crossing Earl, and Earl thought he was double-crossing everyone. With both Earl and Gwynne out of commission she couldn't consult them, so the only option was to devise her own plan. But what? "Brace yourself boys, Marilyn is on the case," she whispered.

She replied to Fairfield's guy: *I need to make sure you haven't been followed. Go to the parking lot at the West Gray shopping center and park in the middle of the lot where there are no other cars.*

The reply came: *Okay. I'm in a black Cadillac Escalade.*

Of course, you are. Back in the day, bad guys impressed and intimidated with menacing cars, big black Cadillac and Lincoln land-yachts. Now they drove big black Cadillac and Lincoln SUVs—giant shiny toasters on wheels. Nothing had changed. She replied: *Wait there for further instructions.*

Zabi said, *Trust your gut, Marilyn. You can have money wired, too, you just need to do it differently.*

"You got it, Zabi. And hey, if Banque Suisse is good enough for Gwynne, it's good enough for me." She accessed the bank's website and tapped *Open an Account.* She entered her information and double-checked that the account was active.

Then there was her testimony. Obviously, with Earl being the serial killer, Fairfield and Palmer had killed two innocent men. Her fake testimony—her damsel in distress act—could still get them acquitted. And she had already been paid. She sighed.

Marilyn texted Sandy. *Is everything okay over there?*

Sandy: *Yes! Ethan slept through all the excitement. He would have told me if he woke up and I wasn't here.*

Marilyn: *Did your babysitter show up?*

Sandy: *The sitter is here. She's great!*

Marilyn: *Was the work uniform delivered?*

Sandy: *Yes. I'll wear it.*

Marilyn: *Hope it fits! I've got a vehicle, a twelve-year-old Ford Expedition, awaiting you at Rent-a-Wreck.*

Sandy: *Never heard of "Rent-a-Wreck" LOL. I'll find it. I'll leave in ten minutes. Where am I going?*

Marilyn: *I'll send instructions in a few minutes.*

Marilyn drove to the shopping center, where it was too early for retail customers. The only cluster of cars was at a restaurant that served breakfast. The Escalade squatted in the center of the mainly empty lot. She drove slowly near the parked cars, ascertained all were empty, and parked among the vehicles.

What would Gwynne do? He'd simply give orders and expect not to be questioned. She texted Fairfield's driver: *The blackmailer changed the plan. Wire fifteen million into this account.* She supplied transfer and bank account numbers. *Do it now.* She noticed she was holding her breath.

The driver wrote: *Gwynne, what the fuck is going on? Mr. Fairfield won't agree. Phone me.*

Shit. There was no way she could imitate Gwynne's voice. Marilyn texted: *No. No phone calls. Too easy to trace. Texts are bad enough.*

He responded: *Fairfield is going to pop a gourd. Gwynne, this is not cool!*

She needed to convince and motivate Fairfield and

Palmer, with something they couldn't debate. Something drastic. Marilyn thought a moment, then replied: *The blackmailer figured out who the witness is and took her hostage. He says if the money isn't in that account in ten minutes, he'll kill her. Then Fairfield and Palmer will be toast. And don't forget, the blackmailer has incriminating video of Fairfield.*

She sat, agitated, her skin prickling, drumming her fingers on the steering wheel. Sandy texted that she had the truck, and Marilyn sent her instructions on where to go next.

Sandy okayed, and Marilyn checked the time—eight o'clock. She refreshed the inbox of her email. Banque Suisse informed her that there was a deposit. She tapped the link, and her bank page came up with a balance of fifteen million. Holy crap, it was actually happening. Because Fairfield had her banking info and may have a method to retrieve the cash, she opened another account and moved the money into it, then closed the first account. But shit could still happen. The feds could seize the cash or Fairfield might have a trick up his sleeve. She had her million, but that wouldn't last forever. She needed liquid cash as well as the offshore money.

Heaving a stressed sigh, she hoped like hell she wasn't missing anything, some unforeseen tiny glitch that would unravel her hasty, thrown-together plan. Then Earl came to mind. Shit! She checked the major local news feeds. Nothing about Earl had made it to the media yes. She didn't want Fairfield to see news of his death in relation to the serial killings. She didn't know how Fairfield would react, but it was better if he wasn't aware.

She sent another text posing as Gwynne: *We're not done. And just to be completely clear, any screw-ups, shenanigans, or switcheroos, and the blackmailer will kill Fairfield's witness.*

The driver texted: *Got it. What next?*

Marilyn replied: *Drive to Allen Parkway west of 145,*

where all the joggers park. You'll see an old silver Expedition sitting with its lift-gate open. Put five boxes of cash in the back and close it.

Zabi whispered, *Now, this is more like it.*

Marilyn laughed. "Yes. I've got a hostage and a blackmailer, and they're both me." She followed the Escalade at a distance through morning rush hour traffic to Allen Parkway and turned into the parking lot for the multitudes of walkers and runners. She drove past the Expedition with its lift-gate up like many other vehicles whose owners were donning jogging wear and sports shoes. Sandy was a short distance along the walking trail pretending to be preoccupied with her phone. She was wearing the navy-blue work uniform normally used by maintenance or pest control.

The Escalade arrived and blocked the driveway, backing up traffic, and the driver, in a black suit, climbed out. Car horns sounded, and Fairfield's delivery boy gave them the finger. He loaded the five boxes and slammed the lift-gate. Sandy immediately hit the lock button, which made the Expedition beep twice, and startled Fairfield's driver, who looked around and put his hand inside his jacket, giving away the location of his holstered gun. He looked around again but gave up, got in the Escalade, and drove away.

Marilyn texted Sandy: *Great! Check under the truck for a GPS device. Please drive it to the Art Guild and hang out for a while. But be careful! Be aware of your surroundings. Watch for suspicious guys and vehicles, esp the guy who dropped off the boxes. When you drive to the Art Guild, make some random turns to check you're not being followed.*

Sandy: *Will do. No problem.*

Marilyn: *Thanks! I'll let you know what's next.*

Chapter Forty-Three:

Trial and Error

Marilyn entered the courthouse building and went through security to the cluster of people waiting for the four elevators. Once again, every segment of society was present.

As she left the elevator, she surveyed the crowded hallway. Fairfield and Palmer weren't present, probably already in the courtroom. Groups of lawyers in suits huddled with others, like a rookery of penguins. Marilyn took a seat on benches lining the hallway. A plump middle-aged woman in a pink dress handed Marilyn a folded piece of paper, and quickly walked away. Marilyn recognized her as the one who had tried to access her safe deposit box. She opened the note. It read: *When you testify, there will be armed men at every exit of the courthouse. If your testimony doesn't go as planned, you won't make it a step outside alive.* There was a photo of Marilyn entering the building looking quite spiffy in Fran's suit.

Marilyn walked briskly to the women's loo and loitered waiting for District Attorney Goldilocks. Women like DA Goldi, on this, the first day of the most important and televised case of her career, would surely stop in for a final tinkle and to check makeup and hair before court. When Goldi arrived wearing a short pink skirt and jacket, and pink, patent-leather, remarkably high stilettos, Marilyn feigned applying lipstick until the DA was ensconced in a stall, then went to the door and slipped an envelope under the gap.

Goldi sputtered and attempted to open the door, but Marilyn held it closed and said, "Girl, don't blow this. Be calm. Read my account. You only need to call me as your first witness and ask me one question, and I'll take care of the rest."

As a witness she wasn't allowed to view the proceedings, so Marilyn stayed seated in the hallway. DA Goldi walked past and entered the courtroom. Marilyn tuned into the news on her phone, where the newscaster was breathlessly reporting on Gwynne's absence and his stand-in lawyer—which brought a smile to her lips. The reporter said Fairfield's lawyer had given his opening statement of Fairfield and Palmer rescuing Marilyn from being raped and possibly killed, which had brought gasps from the spectators. DA Goldi's opening statement was a five-minute summation of Fairfield's desire to avenge his daughter's death. She then said, "I would like to call my first witness, Marilyn Connor."

As Marilyn entered the courtroom and was sworn in, Goldi's co-counsel appeared bewildered. Fairfield, Palmer, and their lawyer whispered to each other. Fairfield's alternate lawyer stood and addressed the judge. "Your Honor, something's not right, here. This witness isn't on the DA's witness list. She is our witness."

The judge appeared amused. "Counselor, you intended to call this witness, correct? If your answer is yes, sit down and let's proceed."

DA Goldi stepped up to the witness box and turned to face the packed gallery. She motioned to two uniformed police officers at the back of the courtroom, and they walked up the aisle and stood behind Fairfield and Palmer, who, with their lawyers, were looking around, panicking, or perhaps bewildered. Palmer attempted to stand, and the officer with hands on his shoulders jammed him roughly back in his seat.

"Now, Ms. Connor," Goldi said, as she crossed her arms, "please tell us about the events leading up to, and exactly what happened, on the night Declan Rogers and Shawn Dawson, also known as 'the Lads,' were murdered."

Marilyn inhaled. "It all started with Hurricane Harold…" She reconstructed what happened, of witnessing the murders and leaving the apartment out of fear of the killers, of calling 911, her fear of Fairfield's police connections. She laid out how Gwynne found her and his scheme to hire her as a fake witness, although she left out the blackmail scheme. She then related how she discovered Earl was the real serial killer through his drawings, which meant the Lads had been innocent and she wanted their killers to face the consequences of their actions.

Goldi asked, "Were you ever attacked by the Lads?"

"No."

"Did Mr. Fairfield and Mr. Palmer save you from an assault, a sexual assault?"

"No."

Marilyn saw a combination of shock, anger, and fear infuse the men's features. Goldi produced the manila envelope containing the flash drives, Fairfield's ring, and Marilyn's written account. DA Goldi announced that police were at the home of the serial killer and had found evidence he was Darby's murderer. She turned on the courtroom's TV, plugged in the flash-drive, and played footage of Shawn's murder by Fairfield's hand. Goldi dismissed Marilyn, then nodded at the officers and said, "Officers, please handcuff the gentlemen, mirandize them, collect their cell phones, and remove the prisoners."

Goldi handed Gwynne's keycard to the bailiff. "You can find Mr. Gwynne at the ZaZa Hotel. Here is his key."

Aunt Zabi said, *Sometimes the simplest way to solve a problem is the best...*

"Indeed, Zabi...*Occam's razor.*"

Marilyn left the courtroom, and in the hall, she texted Sandy: *Leave the Expedition at the Art Guild, call a ride, and meet me at the courthouse ASAP.*

Fifteen minutes later, Sandy came into the courthouse building, spotted Marilyn in the lobby, and followed her to the ladies' room. Marilyn said, "We're going to swap clothes, but Fairfield's thugs will be at every exit looking for me in that suit."

They quickly disrobed, and Marilyn turned the jacket inside out, then did the same with the pants, the white lining with black pinstripes transforming it from a business outfit to a casual summer-weight suit. Marilyn dressed in Sandy's workwear and tucked her hair under a baseball cap.

A woman entered the restroom and went into a stall. When she came out and washed up, Marilyn asked if she would trade her chartreuse T-shirt for the Neiman Marcus pink silk shirt. "That's a no-brainer," the woman said, "but why?" Marilyn said they were trying to dodge Sandy's violent ex-boyfriend, and the grinning woman happily switched shirts, and left the bathroom.

Marilyn checked the local news on her phone. The announcer said breathlessly, "In an unprecedented development today, new incriminating evidence has surfaced against Baxter Fairfield, his bodyguard, Samuel Palmer, and his lawyer, Joseph Gwynne. Mr. Fairfield and Mr. Palmer have been transported to jail without bail. Mr. Gwynne is under arrest." A video clip showed Gwynne, hastily dressed in an undershirt, suit pants, and sandals, his hair in disarray, being led in handcuffs from the ZaZa Hotel. She continued, "The first witness dropped several bombshells with an incriminating statement of facts, along with additional video and physical evidence. The police and the district attorney have declined to comment…"

Dressed and ready, Marilyn took a deep breath, and they left the restroom. The huge marble-lined foyer was teeming with media calling in their news stories, lawyers conversing urgently, and the public milling about and talking on cell phones. Marilyn said, "We need to get the hell out of here, and Fairfield's troops are gunning for us at every door."

One of Fairfield's unmistakable men-in-black stood at the street doors on the far side of the security conveyer belt. He was scanning the entrance, on high alert. One positive note was that he couldn't enter the building because he was packing heat. However, her thumping heart and churning stomach were reminders that Fairfield's henchmen were dedicated, angry as wasps, armed to the teeth, and ready to take her down. No one reneges on a deal with Fairfield.

Marilyn said, "I hate to do this, but…" She took out Earl's phone, steadied her shaking hands, and dialed 911.

The operator answered and Marilyn's voice quavered as she said in a near whisper, "I'm in the courthouse foyer, and a man at the security entrance to the courthouse told me he put a bomb somewhere in the building, and all he has to do is dial his phone, and it'll blow up every lawyer and judge! Hurry, please! He's in a black suit, and he's just standing there, but…Oh no! He's taking out his phone." She dropped Earl's phone into a garbage receptacle as alarms started to wail. Two burly security guards at the entrance launched themselves onto Fairfield's guy, dragging him into the foyer. As he slipped and fell on the shiny marble, his gun fell from his jacket and slid across the floor.

A woman screamed, "Gun!" and someone shouted,

"There's a bomb!" Pandemonium ensued. Throngs of people burst from doorways and poured down the stairs. There were cries and screams, grunts and groans and yelps of pain as bodies collided. Panic-stricken people pushed from behind.

"Let's go!" Marilyn shouted over the din. "Stay on your feet. Don't fall." Holding hands, they blended with the crowd, the crush carrying them through the doors into the street, finally breaking free, and running to Marilyn's car. Obeying the speed limit, she drove out of downtown into Montrose heading to the Art Guild.

"Well, this is an adventure I could have done without," Marilyn sighed.

"It's all so crazy." Sandy shook her head. "Earl's really dead. I can hardly believe it."

"Couldn't have wished it on a more deserving fucker. He was a bad dude, Sandy, worse than you can imagine. It's all going to come out, and you'll need to protect your privacy. Stay off social media and the phone." Marilyn looked over at her passenger, who was smiling and shaking her head in disbelief.

"Lordy," Sandy said. "It's been a wild ride."

Marilyn said, "Gwynne, Fairfield, and Palmer are all in prison and I have to go away, far away where Fairfield can't find me, but you're going to be fine. Truly." She turned into the Art Guild's parking lot. "Stay at the hotel a while longer, then you'll find your way."

Marilyn opened one of Fairfield's boxes to check the contents and was gratified to find bundles of used hundred-dollar bills. She put two boxes into her rental car and gave the keys to Sandy. "These are for you, Sandy."

Sandy nodded. "Is this what I think it is?"

"Yes. It's Earl's cut from the deal we were working on. And it's your future. Go straight to a bank and rent a safe deposit box. Put the money in it, then please return this car. I'm keeping the Rent a Wreck vehicle." Marilyn smiled, although tears threatened, and she hugged Sandy.

"Watch the news, and it'll all make sense. And good luck. I wish you and Ethan everything good in life."

She watched Sandy drive away and took the remaining boxes of loot into the gallery that was still showing the display of papier-mâché candies. Settling on the four oversized M&M's, one by one, she used a box-cutter to remove the bottom of the piece. Next, she opened the boxes and transferred the bundles of hundreds into the hollow forms, then very carefully glued them closed so that the cut lines were virtually invisible.

Marilyn left an envelope containing cash for double the price listed for the papier-mâché candies. She flattened the empty boxes and loaded the art-form confections into the Expedition and drove away.

Chapter Forty-Four:

And These Days...

These days Marilyn lives on this twenty-acre property south of Puerto Vallarta. It is lush with tropical gardens, fountains, flagstone patios, and a pool. Thirty stone steps lead down to the beach and the Pacific Ocean, ceaseless and moody, sometimes lapping, sometimes sighing, sometimes pounding. There are stunning sunrises and sunsets, torches that illuminate the pool at night. Tourists—singles and couples—come here seeking something romantic, or quiet, or an adventure. There is a sprawling mansion converted into eight luxury suites. As the owner of this deluxe casa, Marilyn talks to the guests and gives them brochures for local attractions.

When she first got to Mexico, she moved from hotel to hotel, resort to resort, and tired of being on the run. Tired of fear, anxiety, checking over her shoulder. This place suits her. There are always plenty of people around and she vets those who come to stay.

She observes them all. She must. Once, one of Fairfield's men came. Even before she searched his room, she could tell by his looks and demeanor: his overtly military posture and rigidity, his ceaselessly seeking eyes, his clipped manner of speaking. During a complimentary fishing excursion which he had happily accepted, Marilyn went through his room. She opened the hotel-safe with the master key. Inside was a tablet, which when hacked, revealed messages between him, Palmer, and Gwynne, and photos of Marilyn. She alerted the fishing boat captain of the situation, and as it transpired, the guest agreed to stay out for some night fishing. Unfortunately, he became excessively inebriated, lost his footing, and fell overboard in the dark, disappearing into the sea. Like so many tourists he had refused to wear a life vest. It's a fact—the combination of tropical sun and piña coladas can easily be lethal for a tourist. While the ocean looks tame, even gentle, the jellyfish and sharks don't ask permission and the sea has no conscience.

Marilyn lives separate from the main house, in a casita on the property—in reality, a spacious house—with lofty ceilings, tile in cool marble, a Mexican-modern sumptuous living area, two bedrooms, and a state-of-the-art kitchen. She uses one bedroom as an office and studio. The French doors to her suite are wide open, allowing birdsong and the dulcet breezes to drift through.

Walkways edged by palm trees and bird of paradise lead to the resort's dining area, kitchen, and an attractive bar with barkeeps knowledgeable in wine and how to mix margaritas and good American martinis, and two chefs who specialize in local seafood, but aren't above preparing a Tex-Mex-style taco. A young honeymooning couple are enjoying the pool, and their laughter brings a smile to Marilyn's lips. Room service is delivered on trays by staff dressed in black-and-white.

Her love life is still nonexistent, at least the love

portion of it. However, if she's in the mood, there are plenty of dalliances with recently separated or divorced men, temporary guests recharging their egos. Those rendezvous tend to be quick and satisfying, and then the men are gone, which has suited her until recently. Lately there's been a void, an emptiness within the everyday that the daily routine can't fill.

Marilyn has been on this cliffside for two years. Twice a month, a group of ex-pat American artists gather for figure drawing sessions in a studio she built on the grounds. Marilyn doesn't model for these sessions; she is at the easel these days. Sometimes when she studies her drawings, they have a Gauguinesque feeling; so many copper bodies and Inca-featured faces. But art—it is what it is; it is what you see. Or to paraphrase Patty, who has never been found and whose body Earl probably disposed of at sea—art is to Marilyn's life what music is to a song's lyrics.

Marilyn followed the news regarding Gwynne, Fairfield, Palmer…and Stade. Her fear didn't diminish when Fairfield and Palmer, drew first-degree murder convictions and were sentenced to life. Fairfield died in jail a year ago. However, that still left Palmer, who no doubt inherited a fortune from Fairfield. Gwynne got twenty years for his shenanigans, and Vanessa divorced him, taking pretty much everything they owned. It is clear Gwynne is plotting revenge with Palmer. Marilyn will not become complacent. Those men can reach far beyond their prison cells.

Stade sifted through all the evidence and cleared Earl's house of horrors one piece of marine salvage at a time, finally finding under floorboards, a stash of money, gold coins, expensive watches, and a fishing tackle box containing a much larger stash of jewelry than the three pieces Stade had shown Marilyn. Earl had been a prolific killer. The last tally, based on his drawings, videos, and mementos, was twenty-three victims. Stade, in an interview, said he believed there were more.

Marilyn often questions whether she could have saved Fran. If she and Jon hadn't let the other tenants board the escape boat first or if they hadn't stopped at the library for a while. If she had somehow gotten to Fran sooner.

When she runs out of those scenarios, she wonders whether she could have solved the murders without entering into the plots and the lives of Gwynne and Earl. She has unraveled the scenarios, the what-ifs of each scheme over and over, to see what might have happened if she'd followed a different thread, and each time she's run into a roadblock.

What if she'd found someone else to be the blackmail patsy instead of Earl; maybe Jon would have accepted the gig. Well, then she wouldn't have slowly woken to Earl's evil character because she wouldn't have gone to his house, wouldn't have knowledge of Sandy and Ethan, wouldn't have been in a position to know he was planning to harm Sandy.

What if she had simply told Gwynne she wanted a few million dollars for the ring and the laptops so she could vanish, and Fairfield had agreed? Again, she wouldn't have gotten to know Earl and his evil. What if she'd gone into witness protection?

What if she had searched farther afield and found Earl's van? But finding an anonymous white van would have had no connection to Fran or to Earl for Marilyn back then. It would have been meaningless at that time. What if…what if.

Zabi whispered, *Fuck the what ifs.*

"Right, Zabi. I played the hand I was dealt. I lost Fran, but achieved some justice, however much that may be cold comfort." She swipes away a tear. "I miss you like crazy, Fran."

Marilyn has inspected the rooms, consulted with the chefs, and is lounging on a chaise, reading in the shade of an umbrella near the pool. The sound of landscaping, of clippers, sweeping, and a mower reach her.

She lays her open book face down on the side table. At times like this, times of ease and contentment, she revisits her escape from Houston. She had mailed a note, the key, and three months' rent to her landlady with instructions for the return of the rental furniture. Then she drove the seven hundred miles to the Mexican border where she had crossed without incident and completed the two-thousand-mile journey across Mexico to Puerto Vallarta. She had been terrified of being picked off on the road by Fairfield's assassins or drug cartel members, but it didn't happen. Not yet.

It's lunchtime, and a waiter interrupts her reminiscence, delivering a glass of white wine and a mango and avocado salad. She eats at a bistro table on the patio adjacent to her French doors, then goes back to her chaise with her book. On page nineteen footsteps and the sound of rolling luggage approach and stop beside her. She looks over at suit pants that break exactly right on the instep of polished black leather loafers—a guest who just arrived and will soon change into sandals and shorts. She holds the book high to shade her eyes and lets her gaze travel up the dark trousers to a leather belt with silver buckle, a white dress shirt, a lightly tanned face with a stunning smile, and finally to his eyes—one with a calico-hazel mote.

She says, "Ah, your detectively instincts found me. Are you here for me?"

"Not in a way that involves handcuffs…unless you're into that sort of thing," he says and takes her hand. And they both lean in to kiss.

Acknowledgments

Thank you, Ike and Harvey. Without you guys passing through with your catastrophic high winds and flooding, I couldn't have written about a hurricane. But stop, already.

Thank you, life drawing, for the pencils, charcoal dust, watercolors and oils, the tempting blank sheets of paper, the very patient artists' models, and the sheer pleasure of drawing.

Thank you, Brantly, for your insightfulness, and for phoning as I was composing this page to tell me this joke… "Why shouldn't you write with a broken pencil? Because it's pointless."

To avoid leaving someone out, I'm not naming names—you know who you are! A huge thank you to my editors, beta readers, and proofreaders. Thank you for having the balls to X-out in a minute what took me months to write, and for not backing down. You make my words better, and I couldn't have done it without you.

Also, hugs and thanks to my sons, Max, Graham, and James, and my friends and family, for your encouragement and patience.

www.ingramcontent.com/pod-product-compliance
Lightning Source LLC
Chambersburg PA
CBHW060619100726
47907CB00006B/1682